Also by Marcelle Bernstein

THE NUNS
SADIE

The Russian Bride

Marcelle Bernstein

Simon and Schuster
New York

Published by Simon and Schuster
A Division of Simon & Schuster, Inc.
Simon & Schuster Building
Rockefeller Center
1230 Avenue of the Americas
New York, New York 10020
Originally published in Great Britain by Victor Gollancz Ltd., as SALKA
SIMON AND SCHUSTER and colophon are registered trademarks
of Simon & Schuster, Inc.

Designed by Deirdre C. Amthor
Manufactured in the United States of America

10 9 8 7 6 5 4 3 2 1

Library of Congress Cataloging in Publication Data
Bernstein, Marcelle.
    The Russian bride.

    I. Title.
PR6052.E6415R8   1986   823'.914   86-20282
ISBN: 0-671-63158-6

For Andrea

Chapter 1

Jonas and Dora Radin waited twelve years before their first and only child was born. Under medieval law Jonas could have had his wife declared barren, made out a bill of divorce and set her aside. But this he would not do. Dora knew it must be her fault, that she was being punished for a forgotten transgression, and spent much of her time seeking remedies, trying combinations of herbs and words and rituals to combat her sterility. In a town the size of Polotsk on the Dvina river everyone knew the other's business, and none better than the *shlimazel-nitses*, the sloppy housewives, who sat in their wooden homes chewing sunflower seeds and watching the scurry of neighbours as they marketed and bartered, squabbled and worshipped. When Dora was a young bride, hair newly hidden beneath the wig of the Orthodox, they had smiled at her anxiety. Then they had commiserated. Now in her late thirties, Dora had almost given up hope. Almost, but not quite. Every night she would recite the last prayer of the day: "Thou who makest the bands of sleep fall upon mine eyes and slumber upon mine eyelids" and then add her wordless, constant plea.

Jonas in his turn consulted the rabbi who had told him gravely that a man without children was a piece of wood which, though kindled, would not light. "Hope for a miracle," he told Jonas, "but don't depend on one." After more than ten years had passed Jonas feared there would be no miracle, but all the same, when a holy man with magical powers, a *tzaddik*, arrived in Polotsk and set up court in the Street of Ironworkers, he went to listen. He was impressed, and the next evening tucked some silver into his wristband before he set out. He spoke to the *tzaddik* and received some very practical advice. When he returned home he put his fingers to his lips and reverently touched the *mezuzah* upon his doorpost, then called Dora's name eagerly. That night she forgot the last prayer.

They hoped ardently for a daughter, since the birth of a girl is a good omen for further children, and from the early days of her pregnancy Dora kept under her pillow a long-bladed knife to ward off Shibta, the evil spirit who preyed upon the newly born. Not merely custom suggested this, but caution also.

For many years the Jews, almost four hundred thousand of them, had been allowed to live only in that portion of Russia which stretches from the Baltic to the Black Sea: the Pale of Settlement. All but a fifth lived in towns and townlets, and in many—Kovno, Brodno—they were more than half the population. Their poverty was abject and without any hope of cure. They were taxed, and taxed again: for schools and institutions, from the benefits of which they were expressly excluded, for every animal killed according to Jewish rites—and then again when the meat was sold. They were taxed if they worked in glass or copper, in iron or tallow. To be permitted to wear the ritual black cap they were taxed five silver roubles a year. And always there were new restrictions. Now they were forbidden to leave the place where they were born, then forced to give up their official names and be known by their ghetto denominations, the derisory diminutives like Joschko and Molko. They existed under the Russian yoke, these piano tuners, fish curers, land-surveyors, and told each other bitterly that "before the sun rises, the day may eat one's eyes out."

Sometimes the situation improved briefly, and for a short period they would be allowed a measure of freedom, permitted to travel on business, while some universities even opened to their sons. But always the pendulum swung back and the Jews felt again the ominous undertow of anti-Semitism. Thousands of them were forcibly expelled from Moscow; a wave of pogroms erupted across the Pale, many carried out by soldiers and condoned by the local authorities.

When Dora was in her eighth month, the combination of a bad harvest the previous year and an outbreak of animal disease brought hunger to the peasants in the *dorfs* around Polotsk. They were patient people, and they bore it until their children were starving. Then they looked for a scapegoat and—when a government agent suggested it—saw that their misfortunes were indeed the result of maledictions by the rich Jews of the town. "The drinking. The singing. Then the pogrom," went a Jewish saying born of years of harsh experience. The night the peasants worked themselves into a killing frenzy they were not so much drunk—they had not the money for that—as angry and bewildered, desperate to vent their hurt on something or someone.

Just before midnight Dora awoke, disturbed by a sound alien to the night hours, the smashing of glass. Her sleepy brain decided some neighbours were having an argument. She touched Jonas in the other bed and was almost asleep when the screaming began, high and frantic, a sound she had heard once when boys skinned a cat alive. Then she knew what it was, and the hairs pricked on her head as she listened. When Jonas went to the window and they saw the red glare in the sky, they looked at each other . "Like Konotop," whispered Jonas, his voice hoarse. "Like Kiev." Nearby towns where the inhabitants had descended on the Jewish quarter, set houses alight indiscriminately and then, as the panic-stricken families scrambled out, thrown them back into the flames.

Konotop. Kiev. Where the blood of babies was spilled in the streets before their parents' eyes. Jonas and Dora knew all this. Knew that if they ran, impeded by her heavy pregnancy, they would undoubtedly be caught. So they each took a weapon: he a poker, she the long-bladed knife from beneath her pillow, and they huddled together in darkness to wait out the night. They did not speak, lacking even sufficient words to pray for survival.

When it became light, and the satiated and spent peasants had dispersed, Jonas and Dora joined the tearful groups who tried hopelessly to shift through the charred timbers, the smashed cooking-pots, the filthy bedding in what had been their homes. No one spoke, only the smallest children whimpered. And when, the following afternoon, those of the Jewish community who dared followed the earthen jars containing what could be found of the slaughtered, there were none of the traditional cries of loss; no wails, no laments, only the stunned and haunted hush.

Many Jews began to plan their escape to America, the magic land. But Jonas and Dora decided they, like most of their friends and relatives, would remain in Polotsk. "When you have no choice," the rabbi had told the men as they stood in the cemetery, "don't be afraid." Slowly normalcy asserted itself. New houses were erected upon the blackened stumps of the old. Dora gave birth to a daughter. The Jews told themselves that the unspeakable event had been like the lancing of a boil to release poison: it would not happen again. Nor did it, for a time. Polotsk remained peaceful, though Jews elsewhere were hunted and harassed. But the town did see three more pogroms in ten years, saw heads split apart, limbs hacked off, pregnant women beaten, babies hurled from windows.

Then in 1895, when the Radin girl was seventeen years old, cholera came with the autumn and the cycle of hunger, fear and hate began again.

This time, Jonas and Dora bought one train ticket, gave what money they could to their daughter, and sent her away.

Chapter 2

Salka stood on the platform of Hamburg Central Station struggling to keep her balance among the streaming passengers. She clutched her shabby carpet-bag, her father's old suitcase with tin corners and a leather strap to reinforce the worn locks, and a basket which had held her food. All around her porters stacked piles of valises and leather travelling-cases, colourful hatboxes and portmanteaux. She watched a tall blond German sweep down the platform, starched shirt and stiff collar gleaming, to welcome a woman in a plumed hat descending from the ladies' coupé; an army man with impressive muttonchops and a chestful of medals was hurried away by an aide-de-camp; two children in sailor suits and hats were led by a governess towards their waiting parents and, to Salka's amazement, she saw them all shake hands with every formality.

She revolved slowly, wondering which of the hurrying figures could possibly be her father's cousin. She knew only his name and his blurred likeness from a photograph sent many years before, and she could see no one who even vaguely resembled it. Throughout the past five days she had been buoyed up by the nervous excitement and fear, the strangeness of her fellow travellers and the constant demands of the journey. Now it was almost over. She had reached her destination and there seemed to be no welcome for her. She ached with tiredness, and felt herself shivering although she knew it was not really cold. Everything was strange and foreign: the buzz and chatter of a language she could not understand, incomprehensible signs above her head, gaudy posters on billboards. Her eyes were smarting from lack of sleep, and she longed for a glass of tea.

Close behind her, she heard someone tentatively clear his throat preparatory to speech. Turning, she saw a fat man whose broad stomach was encased in a black frock-coat. Sharply creased trousers tapered to small feet in polished European Oxfords. He touched his derby with a white-gloved hand, and his chins shook as he spoke.

"I am looking for a young lady from Polotsk. Salka Radin?"

She nodded. "Then you are—my second cousin Jacob?"

His words reassured her, for he spoke Yiddish. Only she had somehow expected him to be like her father. She thought of Jonas as she had last seen him, tall and lean, with his beard and traditional sidelocks, his shirt open at the throat and his broad-brimmed silk hat. This man could not have been more different. He looked so much at his ease here, so—she searched for the unfamiliar word—so prosperous.

Jacob Radin beckoned to a porter in a blue cap who obligingly seized Salka's bags. But she held fast to the handles, bewildered by his attempt to take her only possessions, still intent on guarding them as she had for so many days. For a long minute the two of them tugged in different directions until Jacob Radin intervened and nodded reassurance to her, shepherding her towards the main concourse as she craned her neck to keep her luggage in view.

They joined a queue of travellers to whom a policeman was handing out metal tickets. The man before them said curtly *"Gepäckdroschke,"* received his ticket and hurried off, two porters pulling loaded trolleys in his wake. Salka's escort ordered *"Eine Taxameter-Droschke, bitte,"* and ushered her to the pavement. She saw a row of vehicles, open on both sides but without horses. A figure in a grey coat with silver buttons sat high in front, hands resting on a shiny disc, like a small wheel with a long shaft. Nervously Salka watched her possessions piled up at the back, then Jacob Radin turned to her, "So. Get in, please."

The driver leaned back to open the door for her and hesitantly she mounted the steps and seated herself. When her companion had joined her he slammed the door, and then a terrible noise began. Salka was so alarmed she gripped the seat with both hands. Then she saw that similar vehicles, also without horses, were hurtling past beyond the station entrance: it was evidently nothing strange. The cab lurched, its thin metal wheels catching and grating on the cobbles, but when they reached the street it began to run more smoothly, now at an astonishing pace, so that she had to hold on to her headscarf. She glanced at her second cousin. He did not attempt to speak above the din but nodded at her. He looked quite composed. "This must be commonplace for him," Salka thought, and felt calmer.

The cab chugged past a low cart loaded with bottles and tin cans and pulled by two goats; then a narrow wagon drawn by four horses on which perched rows of people, back to back. Salka could see them all clearly, for above them hung the illuminated globes of great lamps which lined the streets, making them so bright that people were apparently able to carry on walking, shopping and meeting as though it were day, seemingly oblivious to the din of the traffic beside them. Her eye was caught by the windows of a vast store, bigger than anything she had ever imagined, also brilliantly lit, in which wonderful fabrics cascaded from gilt pedestals to lie in folds of colour: lace and satin, something pale trimmed with swansdown, velvet like grey cloud, silver . . . fabrics she had never seen before in her life, so rich and rare it seemed impossible they should be worn by human beings.

11

Jacob Radin noted her absorption with amusement. For a time on the platform he feared he would not find her but he need not have worried: in her heavy dark clothes and that white headscarf, she was a real little Russian. And then there was the family likeness. He did not see her parents in her face, for he hardly remembered them, but she reminded him of Sossel, his paternal grandmother and Jonas's also, a fiery old woman with eyes to kindle stone. This great-granddaughter of hers had brought her vividly back to him for the first time in two decades. He sighed. The ties of blood bound them all.

Gradually, the streets through which they passed became quieter and Salka sank lower in her seat, lulled by the rhythmic chugging and rocking of the vehicle. She roused herself only when they stopped at last in a quiet square and had a fleeting impression of a colonnaded stone facade as Jacob Radin urged her into the flagged hallway. He led the way up to the first floor. Beside a door a porcelain plate announced the family name, and then there were corridors and inner rooms until finally they entered a drawing-room with a high-polished parquet floor laid with Turkey carpets.

A stout, plain-faced woman rose from a sofa with a wool-work back. Jacob's wife Magda kissed Salka formally on both cheeks and started to make polite conversation until she noticed the state the girl was in, saw the droop of her shoulders and the smudges of exhaustion beneath her eyes. Instead, she led the way to a bedroom furnished with simple cotton curtains, a chest of painted drawers, a wooden wardrobe. She left Salka to wash at the hand-basin, while looking longingly at the small bed with its oversized *federdecke*, a bag stuffed with down.

When Salka returned to the drawing-room a bright-coloured cloth had been placed om the table and a tureen of rich soup was brought out, accompanied by *Englisches brot*, quite new to her, of fine white flour made with butter and milk and baked in small cakes. Self-conscious at being watched while she ate, she started tentatively, but the food was so good and her hunger suddenly so great that she laid down the spoon and lifted the bowl to her lips: she did not see the wry glance that passed between her relatives.

A little later, lying at last beneath the down *federdecke*, she felt sleep evading her. Unaccustomed to the horsehair bolster and the two vast pillows, unused to sleeping in a room alone, she found the darkness and silence frightening. Gradually, despite herself, the warmth of the covers relaxed her tense muscles and uncurled her hands. She was so tired she could not remember the words of the last prayer of the day, so tired she could not keep her thoughts on Jonas and Dora, so tired that the bed unaccountably moved with the rocking motion of the train . . . .

She slept at last, but only briefly, her mind reeling with the impact of

12

all that had happened on the five-day journey from Polotsk. It seemed to her that she was still on that speeding train, jolted by the grating shiver of its passage, smelling smoke and sweat and coarse sausage. Outside the window she could see the yellow sky was darkening with the dusk her father called "the hour of the wolf", and she knew that Jonas would be in the wooden synagogue at Polotsk, sitting at the eastern wall. She started to cry, and just then the train stopped at Verzbolovo; only now the sun was hot on the carriage seats and bright awnings on the platform provided shade in which people ate at long, laden tables, drank pale wine and read newspapers.

Salka twisted in her sleep, fending off a nightmare in which a blue-uniformed official refused her a ticket at Eidtkunen. She murmured, "But my father said I must get it," and the official became another man, seated at a desk with long documents before him, asking her abrupt questions and pointing to a notice in German with Russian translations below in large letters: WARNING—CHOLERA.

She thought she was awake now, sweating under the down cover, remembering how he told her there was an epidemic in Russia, and all her belongings must be smoked as a precaution. She could smell in the room the sweet odour of something he sprinkled out of a bottle on to his handkerchief, which he held pressed to his face while he talked to her. Then he reached out and pressed it to her own face and she tried to evade it, but now it was someone else, it was Jacob's wife Magda, who touched the damp, sweetsmelling cloth to her cheek, and Salka heard her say, "It's all right, you shouted in your dream. Go back to sleep."

Obediently Salka sank back amongst the jostling images. The bed felt hard beneath her back, it had become a narrow wooden bench again and she was lucky to get a seat at all when so many sat on their luggage, or crouched with their backs against the sides of the carriage. The sweet smell still hung in the air, and she realised it came from a girl who was walking along the corridor, a peasant from her dress. She smiled at Salka, and held out the little bark baskets she was selling, of fruit and field flowers. Reluctantly, for she had no money to spare, Salka shook her head, and as she did so the girl's face became melancholy, and she resembled Rosje Feldman, only Rosje was dead, wasn't she?

Dead, like the birds. Their feathers billowed out of the ripped pillows in the waiting room, while the women frantically tried to reassemble their bedding-rolls after the cholera cleansing at Eidtkunen, the boundary with Germany. The feathers flew, and the silent children laughed and stretched out thin arms, their faces brightening. Salka could see them clearly now, for the elderly attendant had arrived, as he did every evening, slowly traversing the length of the train with a taper in a brass holder, lighting the oil lamps. But somehow the stooped man had become a girl no older than herself, soft brown hair elaborately braided round her head.

Salka hauled herself into consciousness and found the room around her full of light: the girl was still there, pulling back the curtains and humming. She must be one of Jacob's three daughters, Salka thought. Just then the girl turned and, seeing she was awake, smiled.

"Good evening. I'm Adele." She moved across to the bed. "Will you take *Kaffee*?"

Salka pushed herself up against the high pillows, puzzled. "Isn't it morning, then?"

Adele laughed. "But no. You've almost slept the clock around. It's nearly four. Here." She held out a large cup and Salka looked at it doubtfully, hesitantly sipped. It was wonderful, she thought, sweet and rich. While she drank Adele perched on the side of the bed, chattering in Yiddish.

"Papa says your father wishes you to learn German, but he doesn't think we should start until you are familiar with us. In a moment I will leave you to bathe, and Jette has ironed one of your dresses for you. When you are ready, we will be in Mama's room."

A knock on the door announced the arrival of Jette, a thin woman in list slippers, a cap and a loose jacket over her coloured apron. She acknowledged Salka with a cautious smile, then led the way into another, smaller room which contained the japanned tub and white towels on wooden stands. The tub was almost full of water and Jette gestured for Salka to test it. When she nodded the woman withdrew, and Salka locked the door.

She looked round the room with considerable interest. On a shelf beside the handbasin stood bottles and jars: she opened one or two and sniffed experimentally at lavender and rose-water, bergamot and lemon. She picked up the soap from the fluted dish: almond. The carpet under her bare feet was soft, the room warm with steam. She removed her nightdress and climbed carefully into the tub.

The last time she had washed had been in Berlin, and even in the warm water her skin crept at the recollection. Officials there had made a list of all travellers from Russia, and after the train had pulled away from the station with its wealth of gilt and marble, they had travelled for twenty slow minutes to an open field where the track had ended at a solitary house with an enclosed yard. Men in white coats had taken their bags and piled them into a disorderly heap. Full of consternation the travellers had protested, but their pleas for information were met by brusque German of which they could make out only one word: "Plague."

They were herded into the house, men and women separately, while the attendants shouted incomprehensible commands to which they added

14

in Russian, "Quick! Quick!" so that everyone was gripped by frantic hurry. A woman with white sleeves rolled over brawny arms shoved Salka in the small of the back. "In here, quick," and she was thrust into a side room damp with steam from the great black kettle boiling on a stove. All around her women were undressing and the woman said in bad Russian, "You, too."

Lying in the warm water, soaping her hair reflectively, Salka recalled how the attendant had rubbed her with a harsh-smelling substance while she gasped at the affront. Someone else had poured a shower of tepid water over her and handed her a rough towel. "Quick, find your clothes. You'll miss . . .'

She couldn't hear what it was she would miss, but in a panic she tried to find her clothes in the chaotic heap on the floor. They had been steamed, so that she couldn't force her arms into the sleeves. At the doorway a male attendant held out a box and demanded from everyone two marks for the bath, deaf to the wails of the women to whom it represented a day's food for the children.

Salka sighed and sat up. She had never before bathed in a tub with running water, and it took some time to work out how to empty it afterwards. Dressed, she rubbed her hair again and left it loose to dry. She tidied the bathroom and made her bed. Then she stood in the parquet-floored hall, uncertain what to do. A child giggled from a room across the hall, and she knocked on the door.

"*Komm herein sie im*." It was Magda's voice. Salka took a deep breath and entered what was evidently a bedroom, though she could see no sign of a bed. Magda and Adele were on a small sofa with embroidery in their hands, and two little girls of about ten and eight played on the rug with stockinette dolls.

At home in Polotsk, their house had two rooms and there were curtains at the windows and good wooden floors, and furniture which her father had made himself. They were warm and comfortable, and not everyone lived as well as they did, Salka knew. They had Dora's great beaten-pewter candlesticks for *Shabbes* and a few ornaments, like the two tall vases given to her parents on their wedding-day which bore their likenesses painted on to the china. But a room furnished with the elaboration of the one in which she now found herself was quite outside the Russian girl's experience.

For one thing, it was too warm. The fire was stoked so high that the children were protected from its heat by a screen inlaid with mother-of-pearl, and the china pug-dogs on either side of the blaze understandably displayed long red tongues. Above them, on the overmantel, spelter vases held coloured osprey feathers and several open fans. Nearby a round table covered with decorated cloth bore a lavish tea-service. Every chair

15

had patterned tidies: Turkish, Persian, Armenian. In one corner of the room a carved wooden screen was festooned with Arab scarves, brass table-lamps wore pleated silk shades heavily fringed and weighted with myriad glass beads. Even the cushions were ornamented.

In the midst of all these knick-knacks Magda sat square in her red dress with crocheted lace at the throat, holding upon her knee a long-haired grey cat: the only inhabitant of the room, Salka observed, who was not regarding her with interest. The two younger girls, prompted by their mother, scrambled to their feet and Adele introduced them. Bertha, the younger, with the same soft brown hair as her elder sister pulled back into a bow, giggled uncontrollably until admonished and then hid her face in her pinafore. Rosa, demure in a bertha collar, clasped her hands before her and bobbed a curtsey. Then, like the others, she too gazed expectantly at Salka.

"Tell me about your dear parents. How were they when you last saw them?" Magda's tone was kind, but Salka turned to her with a stricken expression: the parting was too raw in her mind for recounting, a jumble of searing emotions and noise. On the platform at Polotsk there had been a deafening cacophony as shouting peasant women juggled bundles and babies, men herded bellowing calves into open wagons and an old man carried a pig squalling in a sack. Shrill-voiced boys peddled glasses of tea and above it all rose the thin melody of a dozen youths fiddling farewell to a newly-married couple. Unable to speak over the din, she and Dora had clung together until Jonas prised his wife away. "Let her go now, let her go." He had pushed Salka up the three iron steps and her last sight of them was their upturned faces amongst the crowd, their cheeks wet with rain and tears.

Salka sighed and focused again on the people before her. Adele saw her distress and prompted swiftly, "And the journey? Tell us about the journey."

Gratefully Salka complied. When she described the incident of the disinfecting in Berlin, Magda recoiled in horror, her hand to her throat. Jacob had entered the room in time to hear the last part of the story, and his wife turned to him.

"*Jacob, das ist schrecklich, nicht wahr?* To treat respectable people in such a manner?"

He shook his head. "You cannot blame the authorities. By all accounts the present outbreak of cholera in Russia is one of the worst. And if it were to spread, there would be great public antagonism against the refugees even if they came from disease-free areas." He turned to Salka. "I understand Polotsk and the surrounding countryside has not been touched by plague."

"There was no word of it when I left."

16

He nodded. "You were fortunate. Just out of Hamburg, on the river, we have quarantine-houses for Russian Jews on their way to America. If they do not develop symptoms, they will eventually be able to board ship."

Tentatively Salka asked, "What will happen to the others?"

Jacob Radin pursed his lips. "The Russian refugees have given us a headache here in Hamburg. The numbers grow greater daily. Many of them sold everything to get out of Russia. They can get perhaps as far as Brody and then they're trapped, their money gone, their papers inadequate."

Adele broke in. "Papa, what can you do for them?"

"We have now in Hamburg an organisation formed specifically to help them. Many wish to stay in Germany and we help them find work. Others are determined to get to America but they do not understand the new rules. The authorities turn back those who are sick, or who have defects. Until now our German steamship lines have been forced to bring them back here without compensation, but new legislation will mean they take only those passengers who possess the return fare also." He spread his arms wide. "I ask you!"

Magda looked up from her embroidery. "I just cannot understand why they are so anxious to get to America."

Her husband laced his thumbs together behind his back and rocked gently on his heels. "They think that life will begin again for them in the New World. But I do not believe they will find much more there in material terms. Only, of course, they will have hope, which Russia denies them. Is that not so?" He raised his eyebrows and Salka nodded her assent. "So sometimes a husband goes first, works like a dog and lives like one, and perhaps he just manages to send his family their steamship tickets to join him. I wonder how many men never manage to send for their families."

Adele had been looking puzzled and now she asked, "Surely they will learn of the problems and not attempt the journey?"

"Many of them tell us they know from relatives about the hazards they face, but they continue to pour out of Russia because the situation is now so dangerous there for Jews." He looked at Salka. "I hear from your father and from many other sources that the situation is no longer tenable. Apparently the conditions of work in the towns for Jewish artisans are appalling—sixteen hours a day for only two or three roubles a week. And if they want a day off for religious observance, they must work all night before it."

Salka nodded. "Tata says if he did not work for himself, life would be too bitter to be borne."

"I begged him to leave, not just to send you," Jacob said. "I even

17

offered him money for tickets. But he is an obstinate man, and proud. For you he will accept charity. For himself, no. I asked him, what if the next pogrom claims his life, or Dora's? What use then will his pride be to him?" He stopped, checked by Magda's stern look and Salka's gasp.

"That's enough, Jacob. You're frightening us all out of our wits and worrying this poor child for no good reason." She tipped the cat off her lap and rose. "Come, girls. We will show Salka the apartment."

Over the next weeks, Salka gradually settled into the routine of the Fasanenstrasse home. The younger girls enjoyed showing her the unfamiliar sights and for a long time accompanied her every morning downstairs to watch the milk delivered: Salka was fascinated by the light cart containing milk churns from which the delivery man would fill householders' jugs and basins. It was drawn by two dogs and sometimes a mischievous boy would throw pieces of meat for them: then the girls would squeal in anticipation as the creatures lurched for the scraps, while the cans crashed and rocked ominously and the delivery man vainly shouted obscenities.

Salka found it hard to adjust to some of the customs of her cousin's house. Magda and Adele never dressed before midday, but according to German habit wore dressing-gowns and soft nightcaps until twelve. Sometimes she would watch while the *Friseuse,* the gossipy female hairdresser who arrived daily before luncheon to tire Magda's hair with the aid of frisettes, sponges, ribbons and combs, styled Adele's. The German girl was younger than Salka by six months though with her plump, full-breasted body and rounded face she appeared at least two years older. Salka, sitting on one side, would occasionally catch sight of herself in the glass and was always taken aback by her appearance. Contrasted with Adele's pink and white complexion and light curls, the unruly mass of black hair, olive skin and sombre clothes of her own reflection made her look an intruder from another world.

Salka would watch the younger girl with admiration and some sadness. She could not imagine owning such clothes as Adele's, with their pleats and gathers, the dropped waists and frilled necks. Only she longed and longed for shoes like hers. She would gaze at the thin-soled slippers of glossy black and wind her own feet, in their flat and serviceable leather boots, out of sight beneath her chair.

Jacob's household was conducted in the manner of the German middle class, of which he considered himself a part. Like lawyers, doctors, minor government officials, he kept two servants engaged always on quarter-day. Jette was responsible for the larger part of the housework and cleaning, while the cook also managed the marketing for the household and ruled over the scrubbed, brick-floored kitchen with its copper pans and hotmetal plates over the cooker.

18

As the weather became colder, the enormous white porcelain stoves, the *Berliner Kachelofen*, were cleaned by Jette. She carried in bundles of wood and the younger girls watched as she piled them up, threw in a match and let the flames roar upward. She would slam the door and then, an hour later, close the draught by drawing a little flap over the mouth of the grating, so the heated air remained in the *Ofen* to keep it warm all day.

The first evening Jacob arrived home to find the *Ofen* warm he lifted his coat tails and leaned his backside comfortably against the porcelain stove.

"Ah," he remarked to Salka, when she brought in his customary glass of lemon tea. "Some households are replacing these with cast-iron stoves to burn coal and peat: they must be mad. Such contrivances are unhealthy and unpleasant, they fill the rooms with smoke and your lungs with soot. But an oven like this"—he slapped it affectionately, as though it were alive—"gives a steady warmth to your surroundings." He stroked his heavy jowls reflectively. "They have a saying here: 'In Russia you see the cold. In Germany you feel it.' But not in my house." Swallowing the last of his tea, he handed her the glass. Dutifully she returned it to Frau Holz in the kitchen.

At first, eager to please and mindful of her mother's injunctions, Salka felt it incumbent upon her to offer to do many of the tasks she had performed at home. Magda used to thank her in the early days, then gradually it had become accepted that, unlike the Radin daughters, she was expected to work. The tasks were not large, but daily they became more numerous. Fetching and carrying, washing and drying the silver and the glass, dusting the endless array of gimcracks. The china cabinets, the occasional tables and the top of the upright piano with its short-skirted portière: all were massed with dragon candlesticks, ornately framed photographs, clocks, sprays of dried flowers.

Much of the time she did not mind, pleased to be alone with her thoughts, but there were days when she felt like the household drudge in Rosa's picture book about *Aschenbrödel*, the little cinder girl. It would have mattered less, she thought, if Adele had been similarly occupied. But in the mornings the daughter, like the mother, would wander round before dressing, chatting and drinking endless *Kaffee*, while the small girls were with the daily governess. In the afternoons there would be calls to make, or excursions to the shops, and Hannah and Rosa would be taken for walks in the Rathaus Gardens. Sometimes Salka would be invited to accompany them: more often she would be requested to perform some duty—a little sewing, stretching a pair of tight kid-gloves with the aid of a wooden finger.

At such times Salka would wander alone in the silent apartment and crave to be home in Polotsk. A craving she would try guiltily to stifle, knowing she must be grateful for the care and hospitality of Jacob's family, for without them what prospects did she have? At the railway station where she had begun her journey she had grabbed her father's jacket in desperation as he stood by the carriage door: *Don't leave me. I can't go without you.* She had seen him pause, his love for her almost breaking his resolve. He had reached up and brushed away her tears. *There is nothing for you here—remember Rosje. You have to go.*

She stood still, staring out of a window but seeing nothing. Rosje Feldman. She had lived not far from them in Polotsk, a quiet, decent girl from a strict family, a few years older than Salka. During one of the periodic outbursts of violence against the Jews of Polotsk, Rosje had been raped by a neighbour. Salka still did not quite understand what this meant but she realised it was something terrible. She knew too from Dora's whispered conversation with Jonas that it was a common enough event, that it happened to many women. Most of them denied it, for to admit being assaulted would be to lose their chances of marriage, or ruin their lives with their husbands.

But the family of Rosje Feldman were braver than most. They demanded justice and the law; they fought to bring the neighbour before the court. They did not succeed. Five weeks later, Rosje died. Salka heard her parents say it was not only her injuries which killed her, but also the knowledge that her life was destroyed. With her death, the court ruled that there was no case to answer and the neighbour walked free. And on that day Jonas had started saving, adding a kopeck to a kopeck until he had the hundred roubles to buy his own daughter a railway ticket and a future.

Salka drew a deep breath and went back to stretching the gloves. It would not be so hard, she thought, if only she did not miss her mother so much, or if Magda were a little easier to like, a little less distant. Adele followed her mother's lead and remained pleasant but cool. It was only Jacob who seemed to have any time for her, and she had soon learnt that his irritable manner concealed genuine kindness.

It was much later that she found out he had been a teacher early in his career, and still relished an interested audience when he spoke. He liked the way Jonas's girl listened when he talked over dinner about the affairs of the day. One evening he had noticed her face stiffen with boredom when his wife and daughter began on some gossip or other and had directed his conversation at her: he'd been flattered when she responded by asking him questions about the business. Intelligent questions they were, too, for an unschooled, girl, and he enjoyed the way she sparkled with excitement when he described some transaction.

She was far too thin, though, beside his robust Magda and Adele; she

20

looked insubstantial as a leaf. A real little Russian, and he preferred the German style. How did it go?' "A man may profess otherwise but what he really likes is sweet wine, plump women and the music of Strauss."

Jacob had long forgotten that he had any Russian roots. He kept in touch with the family in Polotsk, exchanged letters on anniversaries and birthdays, gifts on weddings and *barmitzvahs*, but that was mainly to please his father rather than his cousins. He did, however, undertake a great deal of work for the various organisations formed by German Jews to assist their kind fleeing persecution in Russia and Poland. Jacob believed he did so out of generosity, but in fact self-interest motivated him at least as much. Men like himself, Jews of substance with reputations to protect, hated the embarrassment and burden of the penniless refugees who arrived in Germany half-starved and exhausted, undoubtedly steeped in the medieval superstition he himself had cast aside. Rather than let them be kept on the public charge and thus humiliate their fellow Jews, Jacob and many others poured effort, time and money into sending them on their way.

Salka was impressed by this evidence of the power and influence of her second cousin, but there was something below the surface, something she sensed but could not name, which made her uneasy. During the eight weeks she had been in Hamburg she had begun to feel herself to be a superior servant, and nothing ever occurred to bolster her small self-confidence.

Because she had neither the inclination nor the leisure, she rarely glanced into the mirror in her room. Had she done so she might have seen how she was changing. Like a plant in a forcing house her new surroundings, her isolation from her parents, the need to control herself before strangers, had all worked to dispel the remnants of childishness from her features and also from her manner, so that it was a young woman's dignity which suffered as she struggled to master a new language. Not that German came hard to her, accustomed as she was to speaking Yiddish. At first she was abashed by her own clumsy attempts to express herself. But then, when comprehension was greater and she could sense the subtleties of words, something else became apparent to her. She decided, at some level beneath explicit speech, that she would have to suppress resentment at the slights she now realised frequently came her way. Nothing serious, no overt criticism, certainly no real unkindness, nothing so positive as dislike. But she knew very well that she was different.

For a long time, because it remained unspoken, Salka could not put a word to what she felt, nor define the reason for the slurs. Then, one Friday night, she heard a new word for the first time and learned what she was.

21

It frequently happened that Jacob brought one of his unfortunate immigrants home for *Shabbes* dinner, for to invite a stranger into the house for the Sabbath was a *mitzva*, a good deed. On this occasion the guest was a Russian in his early thirties, his face tense beneath the beard and sidelocks of the Orthodox, though he had abandoned the gabardine for a rusty black suit. He was working his way to America, having left his wife and two small children behind in Riga until he had established himself.

Magda seated him opposite Salka and instructed her to look after him. He responded reluctantly to her attempts at conversation, but voraciously consumed some herring, *Gries* and roast fowl, dumplings, lentils and *Mehlspeise*, for all of which he benched ardently after the meal, rocking backwards and forwards as he chanted his thanksgiving, continuing long after Jacob had finished, removed his skullcap and made ready to light his cigar.

As he stood afterwards in the drawing-room the immigrant had looked down at his feet in their worn black boots, dusty on the patterned Turkey carpet. He glanced across at Salka's flat Russian shoes and nodded to himself. He spoke in a low voice and in Yiddish.

"They are having *rachmones* on us, these good people."

Startled by his tone, she glanced at him sharply and saw his tight smile.

"In my time," he added, "I too have been in a position to show compassion to others. But not any more."

They looked at each other with understanding, both needy recipients of *rachmones*, of pity, and both of them resenting it.

She said, hesitantly, "But in America—it will be different for you?"

His answer was vehement. "God willing. But I am not in America yet. I have been held in quarantine for over three weeks now, and during all that time I have had to pay for a bed I didn't want and food I could not eat. What capital I had is almost gone and still I do not have a place on a boat. Your kinsman"—he gestured with his head towards Jacob—"is doing everything he can for me, and for that I am grateful. Only I have found out many things I had not known before about the magic land."

Salka looked at him questioningly.

"For instance," he went on, "not everyone who wishes to enter may do so. They are very careful now: they examine everyone. They check the eyes and the ears, they listen to the chest for old illnesses, they search for defects. And if they find them"—he shrugged—"then you can kiss your hopes goodbye."

Salka said thoughtfully, "There was a woman on the train—I had forgotten about her. She had two children, a baby and a boy of about five." She looked suddenly stricken. "How could I have forgotten?"

"What happened?"

"It was at Berlin. Did they disinfect you there?"

"Of course. Everyone."

"And then afterwards, the doctor?"

He nodded.

"She was crying," Salka went on, "and I asked her why. The doctor had not talked to her at all, but to an interpreter. He said the boy would have to remain in Germany, that he would not be allowed on the steamship because he had something wrong with his eyes. Trachoma, some word like that." Tears came into Salka's own eyes as she recalled the woman's face, made suddenly bleak and old.

"What did she do, the poor woman?"

"She was quite calm at first. Then she suddenly realised what it meant, that a child of five would have to remain in Germany while she and the baby continued their journey. She was going to her husband—he had sent the tickets—and if she did not go, the money would be lost and she would never see him. She rushed back to the doctor and screamed, and we had to hold her. She shouted that the child must be allowed on the ship."

"And?" He prompted her after a moment and she shook her head.

"It was no use. Of course it was no use. The doctor became much kinder then, he explained that her son had a disease which was difficult to treat, and about the island in America where everyone goes when they enter. He said that even if he went on the boat, the child would certainly be sent back from there."

The Russian asked sombrely, "What did she do?"

"I don't know, The crowds were so great I couldn't see where she went." Salka fell silent, seeing again the little boy in knickerbockers and long white stockings, his hair cut for the journey and his prayer-curls tucked up into his cap. His face mirrored his mother's distress: he clearly knew that he was its cause but the reason was beyond him. She had watched his mother trying to comfort him. *Don't worry, little one. We'll manage. If we wait a little bit, perhaps the trachomas will go away from his eyes?* She had turned in appeal to Salka and the girl had echoed her doubtfully. *Perhaps.*

When Jacob's charity guest had departed, sped upon his way by Magda with a box of pastries, Salka and Jette cleared the table. The door into the hall was open, and the Radins passed by. Salka heard Jacob telling Magda he hoped to obtain a steamship passage for the Russian within three days, then their voices faded and she caught just one word: "*Ostjude.*"

Salka had by now acquired sufficient German to appreciate the nuances of the word. It meant someone different, foreign, from the backwoods. It carried overtones of derision: *ghetto Jew.*

23

Moving slowly, she gathered up the used plates and napkins, upset and confused. If they could speak like this of a man who had come out of Russia as she had come, to escape the persecution of authority, did they then think of her also as *Ostjude*? Was that why she found herself doing so many domestic tasks, because that was all she was good for?

She was aware that Jacob never talked to her of Polotsk, never discussed the Russian side of the family. She recognised that he was German now, and successful, and rich. He and his wife, with their comfortable lives and complacent jowls, their sense of their own importance, regarded his shabby relative as another charity guest. She was *Ostjude*, like the unhappy man at dinner, like the anguished mother from the train, like all the wretched people fleeing oppression.

Salka took the crockery she was carrying into the kitchen, where by now Jette was heating pans of hot water for the washing-up. The cups and plates rattled on the tray and she noticed that her hands were shaking. She was gripped by an anger so great she doubted she could control it, a furious anger that encompassed the forces that had sent her from her home, and the patronising Radins and the deity who allowed so many to be dispossessed.

Out of her anger grew the determination that she would leave, take the train back to her parents. She went to bed feverishly devising ways of raising the money for her ticket. . . .

And woke in the small hours, disturbed by her sleeping thoughts, struggling to catch the thread. The feathers of the dead birds whirled in her head. Dead, like Rosje Feldman. Dead at eighteen, because she was a Jew in Russia.

Salka lay for a long time thinking of Rosje, and knew that there were no choices.

Chapter 3

For many weeks Salka lived in the Fasanenstrasse apartment almost as though the outside world did not exist. The city which lay beyond the calm canals fringed with plane trees remained merely a rumour for her. After that one glimpse as Jacob Radin brought her from the Central Station, she heard of it only as dinner-table conversation, saw it in the folds of Magda's new dress material, smelt it when Jacob invited fellow members of the Hamburg Bourse in to play cards and their cigar smoke wafted through the door.

It never seemed to occur to her relatives that the Russian girl might like to see Hamburg and her new-found dignity prevented her from making unnecessary requests. Alone in the apartment she would open the mahogany bookcase in the drawing-room and take out the books, handling the red, gold, and leather covers with reverence. She had just finished *The Sorrows of Werther* by someone called Goethe, and it was the first novel she had ever read.

Back in Polotsk her father had several cherished books, but they were all religious. Once, when the chapman on market day had opened his pack for a bundle of prayer-books, she had seized on a book with a cover decorated by a gold-leaf picture of a woman. *Domik v Kolomne*, it was called—"The Little House in Kolonna"—and she bought it for a few kopecks. She had struggled through the Russian by candlelight before her parents came to bed, and one day had asked her father a question about Pushkin. Jonas had been angrier than she had ever seen him. He had taught her a little Russian, he said, because to speak only Yiddish would keep her forever within the Pale. Russian was the key to freedom, in both the physical and the mental sense, but because she had the language did not mean she was to fill her head with nonsense. Weakly she had protested that the book was beautiful, and her father had torn it away from her and thrown it on the fire. "That's as may be," he had snapped, "but it's not for you to read. It's unnecessary for women, they haven't the time for it."

Apart from Jacob's books Salka's horizons remained firmly domestic, and her chief outings were accompanying Frau Holz to do the local marketing.

Frau Holz presided over the kitchen. She would arrive early in the morning, return to do her own housework in the afternoon and come back to prepare dinner for the Radins until seven at night, when she

25

would disappear bearing covered bowls which Salka soon learnt not to notice. She was a surly woman, with a rough red face from bending over her pans and hands as shapeless and puffy as the dough she kneaded. To Magda she proffered a degree of civility: Frau Holz knew she had a good place and that many another would be happy to fill it. More than that, she was well aware that in Magda she had met her match. Out of her mistress's hearing she was less sanguine and snarled her ill-temper at Jette, who was not averse to matching her curses. When Salka was around the oaths were muted, for although Frau Holz cordially hated the Russians, the English, the French and any other nationality that came to mind, she liked the little foreigner who was so willing to beat cream and egg whites for her.

Jette was a country woman who had also been with Magda for many years: she had brought up the children and lived with the family for so long she had become indispensable. When she was younger she had worn the costume of her district, the bright petticoats, black jackets and cap of muslin, the ensemble finished off with knitted stockings. The custom had declined, much to Magda's regret, although Jette would still don these garments on her Sundays off. When she was younger she would go dancing with her *Bräutigam* of the moment, and as she got older the company of young men was exchanged for that of women of her own age at meetings of her *Kränzchen*, her club in the coffee-garden.

One November day, Salka was aware that Jette and Frau Holz were giggling together with none of their usual acrimony. In the late afternoon she was sent to the kitchen to fetch a tisane for Magda, who was lying down with one of her sick headaches, and came upon an astonishing sight. Jette was sitting on a wooden chair, head thrown back, and her cheeks and closed eyelids were speckled with what looked like little brown insects.

Salka halted in the doorway as Jette brought up her head and the insects dropped off. Two remained stuck to her lined cheeks and Frau Holz shouted,

"Heinrich and Franz Guter!"

Slowly Jette stood up and another insect fell and now Salka could see they were apple pips.

"Ha!" shouted Frau Holz, "Heinrich's your man!" and she and Jette both roared with laughter. At the same moment they noticed Salka watching them in bewilderment. Wiping her eyes, Frau Holz clambered to her feet.

"We've been finding a husband for Jette," she explained, "and not before time." She reached for the kettle which stood ready on the warm stove, then turned and winked suggestively at Salka. "Shall we find one for you too, little one?"

26

Salka shook her head. She could not imagine what Frau Holz was talking about and Jette asked curiously as she bent to retrieve the apple pips, "Have you never done so? I do it every year."

Salka thought it most odd that the elderly Jette, with her veined legs and the brown mole on her cheek, should seek a husband. Reading her thoughts, Frau Holz asked slyly, "Don't they want husbands in Russia, then? The men must be terrible creatures there. Still, who'd take a Cossack to their beds?"

Jette hushed her hurriedly and fetched dried herbs for the tisane. "The mistress won't be up from her bed till tomorrow and the master dines out. So this is a good night for a maid to try and see the face of her future husband. Fräulein Adele is going to do so. Will you be with us? There's no harm to it."

Salka nodded, privately doubting that Adele would want to include her. After the initial burst of friendliness, inspired mainly by curiosity, Adele had become used to the Russian girl's presence and ceased to take much notice of her. She had friends of her own age and Salka assumed that she, too, thought of the charity guest as an inferior being. So she was surprised when Adele knocked on the door of her room later that evening.

"Will you come to the kitchen with me? We are not to wake the girls, Jette says."

Salka had been brushing her hair for the night and it hung almost to her waist in a glossy stream. She said doubtfully, "I was about to undress."

"We have to wear our nightdresses, Jette says, and carry candles." Adele giggled. "I hope you're braver than I am."

Half-reluctant, half-intrigued, Salka complied and the two girls went along to the kitchen. The room was in darkness except for two candles, and as they hesitated in the doorway Jette emerged from her poky room behind the stove, also in a nightdress with a shawl round her shoulders. She lit them a taper each, and without a word the three of them hurried out of the apartment and down the backstairs. The stones underfoot and the brown-tiled walls gave off a damp chill, and as they reached the ground floor they felt a raw wind gusting under the back entrance. Jette lifted the latch on the heavy cellar-door and it opened stiffly. A flight of stone steps disappeared steeply into darkness, and the uncertain light of their tapers showed the lower ones to be glistening wet, the rough wall on one side thick with cobwebs while the other side was open to the space below.

"What happens now?" Salka had not thought she was frightened, but found it hard to control the quiver in her voice.

"Whoever wishes to see the face of her future husband must walk backwards down the stairs and then hold up this mirror"—Jette took one

27

of Magda's silver-backed looking-glasses from beneath her shawl—"and she will see his reflected face."

Beside Salka, Adele caught her breath sharply. Jette added, "Put the taper in your right hand, and take this in your left." She held out the mirror to Salka, who shook her head firmly. "Don't you want to go down? Then will you, Fräulein Adele?" When the girl stared at her uncertainly, the woman pushed the mirror into her hand. "Go on, take it. It's the only way to see the one you'll marry."

Tentatively, Adele started forward. She put one foot on the first step but Jette caught her arm.

"No. You must go down backwards, so you do not see."

Adele turned round and, holding up her nightdress so she would not trip, began the descent. There was a tight, nervous smile on her face, and she steadied herself against the wall with the hand in which she held the taper. On the third step she stopped.

"There won't be—anything—down there?"

"No, no," Jette assured her. "Too many cats in these apartments for rats. There's just old furniture stored away.'

Adele nodded and, still watching their faces for reassurance, took another backward step, and another. She was almost half-way down now, and the taper made a flickering pool of light that disclosed bulky, covered shapes below. A sudden draught brought a smell of damp and sewers to Salka's nostrils, and she shivered. To Jette she whispered, so Adele should not hear, "I want to go back upstairs."

"*Nein.*" Jette's voice was urgent. "You cannot leave us now."

Salka wrapped her arms across her chest as well as she could, the taper still in her hand. It seemed to her that what Adele was doing was wicked: she was tempting evil spirits, dybbuks, unnameable demons by taking part in this dangerous ceremony. Salka had been born and brought up amongst people in whom fear and ignorance had bred superstition. The strictest religious codes were rigidly observed to protect against the encroaching darkness, where demonic influences were fended off by the use of amulets and incantations. To seek, as Adele was doing, to see the face of her future husband was flying in the face of everything Salka had been taught.

There was another gust of November wind beneath the outer door and Salka's taper shivered. From below came a wail: Adele's had been extinguished by the draught. Frightened, Jette and Salka stared downward. They could see Adele's pale shape, but nothing else. For a moment there was silence, then Adele gave a shrill scream.

"Something touched me!"

Jette called, "Come up. Just come up now," but they could only hear terrified sobs. Adele's figure wavered below them in the long nightdress, then they saw her twist and collapse, slithering on the damp stone steps with a despairing cry. There was a thud, then silence: Adele seemed to be lying at the bottom of the flight, but when Jette called her name she made no response. Horrified, Salka looked at Jette, but the woman did not move, just stared down with terrified eyes, her mouth open.

Suddenly furious, Salka pushed her impatiently aside. Holding her taper high and gathering up her nightdress out of her way, she clambered down to Adele. She could hear the German girl moaning softly and, as soon as she was within reach, Adele clutched her ankles like a drowning creature, nearly pulling her over.

Before she had time for thought, Salka leant down and slapped Adele's face hard so that her palm stung with the impact. The girl gasped and the moans stopped immediately, leaving her snuffling but quiet. Salka caught her shoulder and started to pull her upright, the taper in her hand threatening to go out completely.

Under her bare feet the stairs had been wet and cold, but the cellar floor felt horrible: slimy and viscous. Somewhere nearby the girls heard a thump and a loud scrabbling. Adele stiffened, ready to scream, but Salka hissed, "Quiet!" and began to haul the unresisting girl up the stairs. She knew it was only a rat, she had seen them often enough in the streets of Polotsk, but in that enclosed, dank space the sound was magnified and chilling: she could almost see the whip-like tail and feel the dirty fur against her toes.

They were nearly at the top of the stairs now, when Adele pulled back, resisting Salka's pressuring hand.

"The glass! I've dropped the looking-glass. I'll have to go back . . ."

Roughly, Salka jerked her arm.

"I'll get it. Just hurry up, will you?"

She reached the top of the steps and Jette helped her drag Adele over the sill of the door. Then she started down alone, ignoring Jette's protests, searching the steps for Magda's silver-backed glass. She was so incensed now by the stupidity of the whole escapade that she forgot to feel afraid. The mirror gleamed up at her and she bent to retrieve it. Holding it face down so there was no possibility of seeing a reflection glimmering out of the blackness, she hurried up, stubbing her toes on the stone in her haste. As she reached the top Jette was waiting to slam the cellar door behind her and ram down the latch.

Without speaking, Salka led the way back to the Radins' apartment and the welcome warmth of the kitchen, where Jette lit the gas and the three of them looked at each other. Jette's pointed nose was red and anxious, Adele's nightdress filthy, her hair dishevelled.

Salka asked, "Are you hurt?" and Adele pulled up her skirt to touch a grazed knee gingerly. Her voice was very small.

"I don't think so."

Salka surveyed them both with hostility. Stupid, the pair of them. Curtly she bade them "*gute Nacht*," and without waiting for a reply went to her room. She washed her feet and hands. She turned to look in the glass to see if her face was smudged with dust, and scolded herself for a moment's apprehension lest she should see reflected there a face other than her own. "You're as bad as they are," she thought, and saw with some surprise that she did not appear cowed and frightened as the other two had done. The exertion of hauling the plump Adele up the steps had put colour into her face and her eyes sparked with temper.

She still felt fury, as violent as that which had visited her the night she discovered she was *Ostjude*. Then she had been unable to give vent to her feelings: she had desperately wanted to make a gesture, to walk out, but duty and commonsense had prevented her.

This time she had been filled with the same anger so deep no mere words could exorcise it. Only today she had not suppressed it. Instead, she had used it. Used it to overcome her own fear and Adele's.

Salka still stared into the glass, but she did not see herself at all. She was totally unconscious of the young woman with skin of warm ivory and eyes of bronze metal, mysterious as those of some feral creature. She was unaware of the determined jaw, the new strength that had crept into her face, bringing more than a hint of self-will.

She was recalling with sudden clarity the words of the rabbi of Polotsk, with his hat of seven sable. Her father had taken her to the rabbinical school, the *yeshiva*, to receive his blessing for her journey, and the old man had come out to them, in his black-satin gabardine with a silken braided girdle, and the great, round, black hat. He had put his lined hand upon Salka's head and spoken the words of the prayer: "Be with her dear ones as she leaves . . . may it be Thy will to bring her to a safe reunion with them . . ."

When he finished, he had said, slowly, "Your new life will be very different. For us, Russia is the dark continent. But Germany is the nerve centre—it is full of movement, of growth." He had tilted her chin so that he could see her face more clearly. She had looked up at him, puzzled. He had paused and sighed as though reluctant to commit his thoughts to speech.

"It is in my mind," he had told her gravely, "that you have it in you to be the cornerstone of a great family."

Neither Salka nor Jonas ever referred to the rabbi's words during the days left before her journey. The daughter barely understood their meaning, while the father could not believe any man, however wise, could see in his child's face such a presage of destiny.

Salka had never been allowed the smallest measure of self-determination: Jonas's great desire for his only daughter was that she should grow to be a pride to Dora and himself, that she should be quiet and modest in her ways. During the time in Hamburg she had come to see that in the eyes of the Radins she was the charity guest and unimportant. Her role was perceived by them as subservient and she accepted it, knowing nothing else.

But gradually she was changing. It had begun when she heard that hateful word for the first time and realised she was *Ostjude*, a ghetto Jew. Then she had experienced an anger that was the strongest emotion she had known in her life: more violent than her unhappiness at leaving her parents, fiercer than her feeling of loneliness amongst strangers. She thought about it for a long time, what she had felt and how she had exploited it. It was as though she had discovered a secret she had not known she possessed, an inward power on which she could draw.

And it seemed to Salka as she stood in the Hamburg bedroom that perhaps, after all, she was capable of fulfilling the prophecy of the rabbi of Polotsk with his hat of seven sable.

She woke with a start next morning, knowing she was not alone, and when she opened her eyes Adele was sitting on the only chair, docile as a doll.

"What do you want?" She did not trouble to keep the hostility out of her voice.

"I didn't mean to disturb you. I've been waiting for you to waken."

Salka pushed herself up against the high pillows, then noticed that Adele's left foot was sticking out stiffly and that the ankle was heavily bandaged.

"Was that on the stairs?"

"Yes. I didn't realise until it started to swell up in the night. Jette put compresses on it." Her tone was suddenly pleading. "You won't tell Mama?"

"No."

Adele leant forward and placed a box on the bed.

"These are for you."

Salka opened the lid. Inside lay a pair of glossy black shoes. She looked at Adele in surprise.

"But these are yours: your new shoes."

"I want you to have them. Your feet are smaller than mine, but you could put paper in the toes, no?"

Salka touched the shiny leather with a finger.

"How did you know I liked them so?"

The other girl smiled. "I saw you looking. You do want them, don't you?"

"Why do you want to give them to me?" Salka smiled despite her crossness with Adele. "And at such an hour?"

With an effort Adele got up and sat on the edge of the bed.

"I wanted to apologise for being such a fool and for making you do something that frightened you. It did frighten you, the cellar, didn't it?" Reluctantly Salka nodded and she went on, "And you see, I knew it would. Mama and Papa told me that people like you, from Russia, believe in spirits and fear evil forces. They said you were more simple than us, only able to survive by clinging to old traditions; they said I should not ask too much of you." Adele paused and glanced at Salka, who watched her stonily. In a lower tone she continued, "So when Jette said it was time to see who we were to marry, like we do every winter, I agreed. Only this time Frau Holz suggested the cellar, and we've never done that before. I thought you would be more frightened than me, that's why I wanted you to be there. But I was wrong."

Salka was thoughtful. "I wasn't frightened of the cellar, or of the darkness. I wasn't even frightened by the rat, really."

"Goodness, I was."

"I think it was more that what you were trying to do was so wicked. Trying to see the face of the man you're going to marry." She paused, trying hard to be honest about her motives. "When I agreed to go with you, I did not realise quite what you planned to do. It was only when I saw the darkness and the glass that I realised it was . . . dangerous."

Adele looked amazed. "Dangerous? Why? Everyone wants to know such things, don't they? And anyway, I don't suppose anyone really ever sees a face. They couldn't, could they? I mean, such things are not prearranged. Papa says it's 'irrational to suppose there is any universal plan'." Adele exactly caught her father's inflection and Salka noted with surprise that until now she had not thought the German girl had any sense of humour.

She asked, curiously, "Do you mean they didn't tell you about the angel? You don't believe even in that?"

Adele shook her head. "I don't think so."

"It's just that ever since I can remember, I always knew about the angel. It happens for everyone. Forty days before you are born the angel calls out the name of your husband or wife. Eventually you will be united."

"And does it always happen?"

"Always. It has been foretold."

Adele said. "That's beautiful. I never heard it before. You believe that happened for you?"

32

"I know it did."

Adele looked thoughtful. "What about love? Don't you want that?"

"Of course." Salka was astonished. "Of course, but love comes later, after marriage, when you learn to know each other. How could it be otherwise?"

Adele seemed doubtful. "Perhaps you're right. Only I think one could not learn to love just anyone." She got to her feet, wincing as her bandaged ankle took the weight. "When this is better, perhaps you will walk with me one afternoon?"

Hamburg seemed to open for Salka now like a great window. "Papa calls it Germany's eye on the world," Adele told her, and she could see this was so. It was broad and spacious, threaded with canals, and she learnt that alone among German cities it was, with Berlin, a *Weltstadt*, a town of world importance. Hamburg had an atmosphere, an intensity; it did not turn inward to the rest of Germany but away, to the Baltic and the north-east coast of Europe, to the New World.

Adele now urged that Salka be taken on outings with the family and Magda, indulgent as ever towards her eldest daughter, complied. They went to see the Botanical Gardens west of the Dummtor to see the extraordinary water plants; the following week to the Grimmstrasse and one of the old Hamburg coffee-tasting rooms: the Catharinenstube was said to be the most ancient building in the city.

Salka was even taken to the first restaurant of her life: to Ehmke in the Gänsemarkt, a Victorian room where they studied the menu for a quarter of an hour first, and the food was cooked individually for them. The Radins were kosher enough to refuse meat outside their own home and ordered fish. At the next table a customer was evidently enjoying a dish called *Heidschnucke*, which Jacob told her was a speciality of the Lüneburg district. He added that it was a sheep with black spots and curly horns, and that it was being consumed with hot stewed prunes—information which made Salka shudder, much to Adele's amusement.

One mild afternoon they visited the Zoological Gardens where, to Salka's amazement, wild animals were kept in captivity. They gazed at elephants and bears, walked through the aviary and the aquarium, crowded round as the sea-lions in their stony grotto were fed buckets of fish. The noise and the smell were bewildering. After a couple of hours Salka wandered off alone and found, in a herb-garden, a bench built inside a thick old hedge, so that it was recessed and hidden. Pleased with the privacy, she sat humming beneath her breath.

"*Mirele, Mirele, zing mir a lidele, vos dos meydele vil . . .*"

It was a Yiddish song of courtship—Mirele, sing me a song, what does the girl want?—and it made her think of her parents, so that her happy

33

humming faded away. After a time she stirred: she should return to Magda and Adele; the younger girls would surely have had enough of the sea-lions by now. She was conscious that two men, strolling through the herb-garden, had paused just outside her hidden bench and waited for them to go on their way. She heard names which meant nothing to her: Norddeutsche Affinerie, Hamburger Jutespinnerei. They must be businessmen, she thought, stifling a yawn and rising, then the other said something about the Norddeutsche Bank. This, she had heard Jacob Radin say, was one of the first private banks established in Hamburg. The men were taking leave of each other and one was just walking past without seeing her when he turned.

"Oh, by the way," he added, "did I tell you the Commerzbank is moving into beet sugar? Now's the time to buy, my boy."

"Simon, I'm in your debt," replied his invisible colleague. "See you on the Bourse tomorrow."

Salka, embarrassed at having overheard them, paused until both had disappeared, then rejoined the family to find Magda remarking crossly that some people—and here she shot Salka a dark look—had no notion of the passage of time.

Next morning, as usual, all the ladies of the house breakfasted together. Magda and Adele wore their dressing-gowns and caps, and sat idly over their *Hörnchen* and coffee-cups while Salka tried, without appearing to do so, to read Jacob's copy of the *Hamburgischer Correspondent* which awaited him in his place. She was absorbed in a list of goods she found on the back page, in the shipping report—grain, oil-seed, rubber, bristles—when Jacob bustled in, announcing he would take another cup of coffee before setting off. Unusually jovial, he addressed Salka.

"Catching up on commodities for me? Excellent!" She smiled and surrendered the newspaper reluctantly. He folded it while she rose to pour him coffee from the silver pot and milk jug which stood warming on the *Berliner Ofen*. Jacob helped himself liberally to sugar, then said to Magda, "That reminds me. I won't be home for lunch today, *meine liebe*. I'm on the Bourse all morning. I've had a good tip for beet sugar."

Salka said without thinking, "Doesn't the Commerzbank have something to do with that?"

Magda hushed her, but Jacob regarded her thoughtfully.

"Why do you say that?"

Self-conscious, Salka explained about the conversation she had inadvertently overheard the previous afternoon. She added, quickly, "I didn't mean to listen—I couldn't help it."

Jacob massaged his chins.

"Mmmm. The Commerzbank has always put a lot of money into beet

34

sugar, it's true. But not lately. Now, if they are indeed doing so again, that's very interesting news. Did you see the men at all?"

"Only one, and only for a moment." Salka did her best to recollect. "The other man called him Simon. And he was very tall and fair, I think."

"Simon Hirschland." Jacob nodded in satisfaction and rose, disregarding his coffee as he hurried from the room.

Two weeks later he called Salka to his study. She had been practising the piano with Adele, who received weekly lessons and had decided she would teach Salka to play herself. The two girls spent hours now working on duets. Salka was an eager pupil, but curiosity took her happily away from the piano at Jacob's summons. He pointed to the American leather sofa. She had not been in this room before and, as she sat down, looked round with interest at the collection of miniature dovecots, dog-kennels and Swiss chalets arranged for the reception of cigars. Jacob seated himself opposite her and laced his fingers over his belly. He stared at her reflectively.

"Do you recall that conversation we had about beet sugar?"

Taken aback, she said, "Yes."

"I think you should know that after what you reported to me, I doubled my original intended investment in beet sugar. Now, I know you didn't even understand the meaning of what you told me, but the result is that I made a good deal of money. Thanks to you."

Salka said, doubtfully, "I hope I didn't do anything . . . wrong . . . in telling you about that conversation."

Jacob shook his head, and his jowls quivered in sympathy. "It was in the papers next day anyhow: you merely pre-empted them; and being alert is no crime in this city." He selected a cigar and rolled it between his fingers. "Adele thinks that in return it might please you to go out for an evening. To the Thalia Theatre, perhaps? They have excellent comedy: you would enjoy it. Or clothes. My daughter believes you might like some rather more fashionable garments."

Salka looked down at herself, at the cream blouse her mother had so laboriously pin-tucked for her.

"No," she said. "Thank you, no. That really isn't necessary. You have been more than generous already. I am pleased if I can repay a little."

He nodded his agreement. "Yes. There is that. Very well." She saw the relief on his face and nerved herself to add, in a shaky voice, "There is just one thing I would like to do, if it wouldn't trouble you: I'd like to visit your offices."

The relief changed to astonishment. He was lighting his cigar and began coughing so violently Salka jumped up.

"Can I get you a glass of soda-water?"

35

"No, no." He flapped an irritable hand and the paroxysm died away. He glared at her, his face red and apopletic. "What on earth d'you want to do that for? It wouldn't interest a slip of a girl like you. Even Adele isn't interested, and I don't believe Magda's been there more than three times in ten years." He stopped, breathless.

Salka got up and walked towards the door, deeply disappointed and wishing she had not spoken. What had possessed her to ask such a thing? Well enough she knew that a woman's place was in the kitchen while business, like the study of *Torah*, the holy law, was the province only of men. She heard Jacob say, "Just a moment," and paused obediently.

Jacob stared hard at his stubby hands with their carefully-buffed nails. It was little enough to ask, he supposed, though he could not imagine why the girl should want to visit his business premises: it was not as though she could conceivably understand what went on there. Like the good German he now felt himself to be, Jacob was of the opinion that his womenfolk were under the authority of the man of the house, and their role was clear: the management of the household, but not its purse-strings; the care of children, but not their moral guidance; the keeping of a religious home, but not encroachment upon the masculine preserve of decision-making. To expect otherwise, Jacob believed, was to meddle with the natural order of things.

And yet he considered himself a kindly man—prided himself on his generosity, his open-handedness. The girl, after all, was only in his house out of *rachmones*. And she had unwittingly done him a considerable turn. Perhaps after all he could bend his rules a little, make an exception. Be, in short, magnanimous.

"Very well," he said heavily. "If that is what you want, I will take you to the city tomorrow. Be ready after lunch."

He was not prepared for the brilliant smile Salka turned upon him. As she closed the door, it occurred to him that he had never seen such a look on her face in all the months she had spent in his home.

Chapter 4

Salka had not seen this part of Hamburg before and it seemed to her dense and promising, with its crowded, compressed streets darkened by houses which occasionally threatened to meet overhead. Multifarious shops opened on to them, their gold scrolled signs proclaiming them to be coopers and potters, watchmakers and turners, goldsmiths and pawnbrokers.

Jacob maintained a stolid silence until they reached the imposing square of the Rathausmarkt. On the second floor of a building on the north side a door bore a brass plate: SCHRÖDER RADIN. PRIVAT-BANK. Jacob tapped it with proprietorial satisfaction.

"Many times I've wished my father could have lived to see this." Without waiting for her reply he ushered her into a single room of some size. At the far end four or five men were working quietly at a long table. Jacob greeted them, and they rose politely to acknowledge Salka's presence. One corner was screened with clouded glass set into wood panels, and Jacob opened the door to his own office. A single window revealed, on the opposite side of the square, the Renaissance richness of the *Rathaus*, the Town Hall. When Salka turned her attention back to the office an anxious-looking man in gold-rimmed spectacles was lighting the oil-lamps on Jacob's desk. Introduced as Herr Diefenbaker, he bowed nervously and hurriedly excused himself.

"The unfortunate man," remarked Jacob when he had gone, "is unaccustomed to the presence of ladies on the premises."

Salka could not tell from his tone whether this was a reprimand. "It is," he went on, "quite unheard of. My wife, of course, visits—very occasionally. But then, her father was for a long time senior partner. None of my children, though, are interested." He massaged his jowls reflectively. What he did not say was that his encouragement was minimal. He liked his privacy here in this comfortable office, where in the afternoons he could sleep, unbuttoned, in his leather chair. He wondered ruefully why he had agreed to bring this girl here, but he knew the answer. He was still a teacher at heart. To impart knowledge was for him a *mitzva*, a virtuous act, and the feeling of satisfaction he derived from it was immeasurable.

As he gestured Salka towards the straight-backed chair opposite the desk, it occurred to him that it had been more than forty years since he last taught. His own father had left Polotsk for Germany as a young man and had settled in Bromberg, where he married a local girl from the Jewish community. Three sons and three daughters were raised and prospered, though none of them followed their father's profession of cabinetmaker. The second son was Jacob, who had a remarkable talent for figures, and qualified at the teachers' training college in Bromberg. The lack of qualified Jews teaching in the country meant he rapidly received an appointment to Hamburg, which had a considerable Jewish community. He liked the city and taught there for ten years. Then the father of one of his pupils engaged him privately for a little extra tuition. Jacob went to their house and was seen by the elder daughter. He was leaner then and had most of his hair. In time, the match was arranged. Magda was never a desirable woman, but she suited him well enough. More important to Jacob, who was by now growing tired of existing upon a teacher's stipend, her father was eager that he should become a business partner. He was a banker in a small firm, cautious but reliable, and Jacob brought to it industry and patience. They built up to five employees and messengers. In time the old man retired and Jacob moved into the main office.

He had done well for himself, he reflected now, very well, and he leant back in the chair which fitted him so perfectly. He saw that Salka was looking round her with deep interest.

"I don't know what the world is coming to," he grumbled. "I thought young women were concerned only with hair and clothes and matrimony. Like Adele."

Salka watched him, half-scared and half-defiant.

"I wonder which of you is the oddity," he continued. "I believe it must be you."

"I don't mean to be odd," she blurted out. "I'm sorry. It's just that—I would so like to *know* about things."

Jacob tipped his chair and studied the ceiling.

"I believe I should say to you what your own father would say if he were here: that you must not forget you are only a woman. For you, the goal of your life should be to minister to a husband and give him children. If you were a young man, then your desire to know, as you put it, would be admirable. But in a young woman it is *unbesonnen*, it is rash. Why can't you emulate Adele? She is a good girl, a charming girl. I never hear her express an opinion of her own."

Salka sighed. It was, she knew, exactly her father's view. When he had thrown her book on the fire that time, he had scolded her for reading: *For you it is unnecessary. When you're older, when you're married, you'll see there is not time for such things.*

She supposed that Jacob, like her father, was concerned with her welfare. But, she wanted to say, Adele went to school: at least she was allowed to learn something. Salka had had an education too, only of a very different sort. For two hours every morning she and a few other small girls had sat in the kitchen of the *rebbitsin*, the rabbi's wife, learned some prayers by heart and been taught the rudiments of keeping a kosher home. She knew how to detect an egg that was not kosher, which foods are *trefe* and must not be eaten. She could make the *broches*, the blessings to be offered on different occasions: upon eating and drinking, when donning a new garment, or lighting the Sabbath candles. She knew it was vitally important that such things were correctly observed. She knew, too, that it was information which fed the spirit but not always the mind.

Jacob had begun studying some papers, and after a moment she got up quietly and wandered about the room, trying to be inconspicuous. On the wall she found a framed document: "*Members of the Vereinigung von Hamburger Banken und Bankiers*" it read, and there followed a list of names and addresses. She recognised some of them: Simon Hirschland, and then M. M. Warburg and Co, 75 Ferdinandstrasse. She read further down the list. Shröder Radin, 8 Rathausmarkt. Commerz- und Privat-Bank, 9 Ness. Just beyond the list was a photograph of the interior of an ornate building with marbled walls like a palace. She peered at it. Behind her, she was half-aware of the door closing and then Herr Diefenbaker's soft voice at her back.

"That is the Bourse, Fräulein Radin—the Stock Exchange."

Salka recalled the conversation she had described to Jacob.

"Then, that is where they sell beet sugar. Is it a sort of market?" She turned to Herr Diefenbaker, her face alight with interest, and barely noticed the flush that rose from his neck to suffuse his face. He ran a nervous finger beneath his white paper collar and said stiffly, "It is an institution for the transaction of every kind of business, a place where all sections of the city's business world regularly meet every day."

"And do you go there?"

"Occasionally I am permitted to accompany Herr Radin. But I am not a member."

Salka was about to ask another question when Jacob shuffled his papers together and announced that it was time to go home. Disappointed, trying to detain him, she asked, "Would you explain to me about commercial and private banks, please?"

For a moment Jacob seemed visibly to contain himself. "Did you not comprehend what I said to you a little while ago?"

She nodded. "You said I must try to emulate Adele, and I will." A note of pleading entered her voice. "Only, I saw the list of bankers on the wall, and your name there, but I didn't understand the different terms."

As she had hoped, he was diverted. He settled himself more comfortably behind the desk and laced his hands across his waistcoat.

"Well," he said, "you should know that until around 1871, this city had a currency of its own. The Hamburger Bank was a government institution, and to open accounts with it customers deposited bars of pure silver there."

Salka glanced across at Herr Diefenbaker who, to her amazement, gave an almost imperceptible wink. She sat down quietly and gave Jacob her undivided attention.

"When the first two private banks were established," he told her, "considerable funds were lodged with them by business firms, mainly because their formalities were not so rigid as those of the Hamburger Bank. These funds were invested by the banks as bills, which was a great boon to clients, since they could be discounted by their banks more conveniently and cheaply than before."

Salka struggled to follow his words as he explained how, when the Reichsbank, the Bank of Germany, was established on the gold standard, the Hamburger Bank had to be merged with it. But the Hamburg system of bank transfers was later adopted by the whole of Germany.

"Now this," he pronounced, and Salka nodded gravely, "meant that the private banks of Hamburg were given a great opportunity. Their domain increased considerably and it was their initiative which established German banking institutions abroad."

As Jacob warmed to his theme, he forgot how he had objected to Salka's desire for information. Both as a Jew and a traditional German, he saw the role of a woman as a ministering one. His own sisters had had an education very similar to Salka's; his wife had been to a school for girls in Hamburg, though he had to admit that such education as had been forced upon her did not in any way affect her qualities as a wife and mother. Still, Jacob remained at heart a teacher: of boys, it was true, but a teacher nevertheless. When he realised this strange Russian relative of his, with her apparently untameable clouds of black hair, was desperate to learn, it was more than he could resist.

It was the teacher in him which asked her now, "Have you heard of Brazil and Chile? Of the Argentine?"

"I don't think so."

"German banks flourished particularly in these South American countries, in their big towns. So the private Hamburg banks now handled an increasing amount of overseas business, taking their cue from the enormous trade handled by the port here: indeed, they have become truly international in character."

Jacob talked to Salka for nearly half an hour, and then she followed him reluctantly to the outer office. She felt she had been within grasping distance of some revelation and now it was being withdrawn from her. Herr Diefenbaker, watching her lose the animated expression she had turned on him as he talked to her of the Bourse, waited until Jacob was speaking to one of his clerks in the outer office, then he said to her quietly, "Get Herr Radin to take you one day to the harbour. You would enjoy that," and was rewarded by her brightening face.

Jacob took her home, and she reflected that it was almost as though the incident in the bank had never taken place. He immediately assumed his customary distant civility, she her minor domestic duties. In the days that followed she thought often of that visit and the things she had learned. Each night, before she slept, she would go back over that one afternoon, taking it out and examining it, as Adele pored over her trinkets.

She had found it utterly absorbing: the talk of currency and mergers, of share prices and foreign cities. In Polotsk, in the evenings after work was finished, Jonas used to talk to her of places he had read about. She would sit with her elbows on the table, watching her father with a brooding, intense face. "Could I go there?" she would ask eagerly. "Could I see those places?" Her mother, listening, would shake her head in irritated affection.

"Of course not, child. A woman cannot do such things."

Salka would plead. "But what can a woman do, then?" and her parents would glance at each other and sigh. Dora would shrug.

"A woman's life is simple. You'll marry, God willing, there will be babies . . ."

Salka lay in the darkness of her Hamburg room and tried to reconcile her probable future with her growing longing for a life that was not bounded by the mundane demands of domesticity. She felt as though her afternoon at the Rathausmarkt had been a glimpse, through a half-opened door, into a fascinating garden. She had been allowed to stare, but not to walk into it . . . she turned over, pounded the pillow which had become lumpy from her restless tossing and tried again to sleep.

It was not until a month had passed that she had any opportunity to follow Herr Diefenbaker's suggestion. She had been experiencing toothache for several days and it had grown progressively worse despite Frau Holz's ministrations with warm mouthwashes containing bicarbonate of soda and, when that failed, oil of cloves on a small piece of cotton-wool. When it became difficult for her to eat, Magda was consulted. The dentist, it appeared, had been to the house to extract one of her teeth not long since and it would be cheaper and far quicker if Salka went to the dentist's own home. A message was sent and it was arranged that Jacob should take her in two days' time on his way to the bank, and Jette would accompany her as chaperone during the treatment.

On the appointed day, the *Taxameter-Droschke* made remarkably good time, so that Jacob dismissed it before they reached their destination. In

41

single file, led by Jacob with Jette in her best, brightly-coloured skirt bringing up the rear, they walked along the Diechstrassenfleet. It was early December and a luminous fog floated over the narrow old houses, so that their watery reflections in the narrow canals wavered out of the mist.

When they reached the house of the dentist an elderly woman answered the doorbell. She told them that he had been called urgently to an elderly patient and would not return for an hour or so; he sent his deepest apologies to Herr and Fräulein Radin and trusted they would bear with him. Jacob nodded and frowned, pulling his watch from his fob and consulting it with pursed lips. Coming to a decision, he ordered Jette to wait and beckoned Salka to follow him.

"I have a little time to spare, so we shall look for a coffee-house."

Salka, pleased, said, "Oh, yes," before she recalled Herr Diefenbaker's words. Tentatively she asked, "Are we near the port, by any chance?"

Jacob looked nonplussed. "Why, yes. It's not far. But it's a rough place, nothing but cranes and trawlers. Wouldn't interest you at all . . ."

"It would!" Salka interrupted, not caring that she was being rude and speaking Yiddish in her excitement. "Please, could we go?" Seeing his indecision she added artfully, "You told me at the bank about the trade handled by the port, and I've never even seen one."

Jacob looked thoughtful. "I suppose we have time, if we hurry. Very well." He sounded curt, and did not converse with her as he led the way along the scramble of streets. He moved surprisingly fast despite his bulk, so that Salka was breathless with the effort of keeping a few steps behind. For more than ten minutes they walked and then, turning a corner, the harbour was before them.

Salka gazed around her, revelling in the brightness and the din, the crashing of metal on metal, and the shouts of men as they guided teams of horses loaded with sacks, boxes, planks of wood and bales of straw. She had never been anywhere near an ocean in her life, and the smell of the sea was strong on the Elbe—the smell and the disconsolate screams of gulls. Out here, away from the sheltered streets, the wind blew in her face, harsh and cold, so that she gasped with the exhilaration of it: nothing in Hamburg had enthralled her like this. She thought she could spend hours staring at the masts of innumerable ships, the smoking funnels, the floating docks which rose and fell with majestic slowness. Launches tugged at their moorings; the Elbe slapped rhythmically at the quaysides. Away to her right Salka could make out the massive hulls of ships, and lightermen in blue sweaters and scarves, hands in their pockets and pipes in their mouths, watching the unloading. Stubby tugs trailed white wakes in midstream as they dashed among the homecoming ships.

42

The fat man and the girl stood for ten long minutes, watching. Then Jacob said drily, "You seem to find it interesting?"

Salka said simply, "I have never seen anything like this. Not ever."

Jacob nodded. "This," he said, gesturing across the water, "is the pulse of Hamburg. Berlin may be the capital of Germany, but Hamburg is the heart. We supply the body of the people with the blood of life—and we do so through trade."

Salka glanced sideways at him, hiding her amusement: odd to think Jacob had only come to Hamburg in his twenties.

"Yes," he went on. "In the Middle Ages, we were one of the leading members of the Hansa—that was the group of great trading cities. Later we traded with the New World, with America."

She pointed towards a grubby grey vessel surrounded by bales of goods. "What are they unloading?"

"Skins, perhaps, and hides; rubber; Chinese products. Or we bring in many things from the Colonies: soya beans and grain, oil-seed and bristles. We trade in everything and we always have."

Salka savoured the words, recognising them from the lists she read in the financial pages of Jacob's newspapers.

"And all these things . . ."

"Commodities."

"All these commodities, are they like beet sugar? Are they sold on the Bourse too?"

"Initially, yes: in bulk. It's a long process before they finally reach the market-place and I think . . ." he pulled out his watch and squinted at the face, "I think we have no time to discuss it just now."

They had walked a considerable distance along the quay, and Salka found herself once again hurrying to keep a few steps behind Jacob as he bustled back to the Diechstrassenfleet. She did not notice the streets through which they passed nor, a little later, did she even take much notice of the dentist probing and muttering to himself as he peered into her open mouth. Her mind was full of what she had seen that morning: the ships and the hint of salt on the wind, gulls and glinting water. She listened, but scarcely heard the words, when the dentist helped her off the padded leather chair and told her to apply tincture of myrrh on a pledget of cotton-wool to the affected tooth. If it did not stop paining her after two days, he would have to extract it. She nodded and smiled her thanks, and would have gone without the proffered phial but for Jette, who clucked over her charge's distraction and took it herself.

It had been a considerable time since Salka had heard from her parents. At first she assumed the always erratic postal service from Polotsk was to blame: she remembered how the children there gathered excitedly when

43

the one letter-carrier appeared in the street. Women crowded round the fortunate recipient, eager to help them decipher the news, always hopeful that it would be of some major event: a birth or a wedding, or better still—in someone else's family—a death.

When a letter from Polotsk did finally arrive it was addressed to Jacob. Salka fingered it when she passed the silver salver in the hall, running her fingers over her father's spiky handwriting. She made certain she was in the vicinity when Jacob collected his post, but that morning, as was often his practice, he took all his correspondence to the Rathausmarkt.

All day Salka told herself that her father had written to Jacob proposing that they too come to Hamburg, and by evening she had begun to believe it. But Jacob returned earlier than usual that evening. Seeing her setting the dining-table for *Abendessen*, he greeted her and hurried on, taking Magda into the study with him.

Salka finished the table, absent-mindedly. She felt perturbed—no more than that—by the way he had deliberately avoided her eyes. After a time Magda emerged and beckoned her over, her expression unusually kind. This, more than anything, made the girl suddenly aware that something serious had occurred.

Magda settled herself on a wickerwork chair and gestured for Salka to sit near her. She held the letter in her hand.

"This came this morning from your father. I'm afraid it's very sad news." She looked at the girl beside her who sat very still, back erect, her thumbnails digging deep into her palms. The older woman went on: "It's your mother, I'm afraid." She paused to scan the letter again, and looked up to see Salka's stricken expression. Hastily she added, "She's alive, Salka. She won't die. But it seems she will never be really well again." By nature undemonstrative, she strove to find something suitable to say, but managed only, "We're so very sorry."

"What happened to her?"

"She had an attack of apoplexy. It happens sometimes as people grow older."

Salka stammered, "What is that?"

Magda looked at the letter again. "Your father writes, Dora seemed to be asleep, though breathing heavily. He could not waken her and realising she must be insensible he sent a message to ask the rabbi to pray for her. When it became obvious this would not be effective, he summoned a doctor, who named the ailment." Magda stopped speaking and read on in silence.

Salka said, after a moment, "Please go on."

"I'm not sure whether you should hear what he says. It is not for young ears."

Determination made Salka's voice louder than she intended. "Please. Tell me."

Magda sighed. "Very well. But it is not pleasant." She scanned the pages. "It seems that this condition involves disease of the brain, and when your mother regained her senses she was unable to use the right side of her body."

Salka digested this. "Not at all? She can't move at all?"

"Your father says here, *My wife is able to sit propped in a chair with cushions, but for the present I must feed her with a spoon. The women round about are very good, taking it in turns to attend to her needs.*"

Salka listened, staring at a red silk lampshade. The fringe of silver beads shimmered before her eyes, splintered and fragmented. Magda, watching her, saw that she cried without a sound, the tears falling unheeded on to her hands. She put her own hand on to the girl's hair. Apart from the occasional formal exchange of kisses on the cheek required by their family connections, she had never before shown Salka any spontaneous gesture of affection.

"You said she won't ever be really well again?" The girl looked up at her with dawning fear. "Does that mean she will always be like that—having to be looked after?"

Magda said slowly, "Something similar happened to a friend of Jacob's. He remained an invalid until . . ." she stopped abruptly. "But we must pray that your mother does recover, must we not?"

"And if she doesn't, then she will always be helpless." Salka spoke half to herself. In Polotsk there had been a woman who always excited the children's derision. It was said she had neither arms nor hands, but only fins sprouting from her shoulders, that she was half-fish and half-woman, and that her deformity was the result of the sins of her parents. As Salka grew older, she wondered whether this were true, since the parents were hardworking and religious, and she found it hard to believe they could have committed any sin terrible enough to merit such punishment. She had once said as much to her mother, who had looked surprised. It was a fact, she had admitted, that sometimes babies were brought to birth less than perfect. She herself had once seen an infant born without any bones in its skull, the brain palpating visibly beneath the papery skin. After a day it had died. But the good God sent no suffering without cause, and the child had clearly borne the signs of some act perpetrated by the parents.

Salka, even at sixteen, looked at life with a clearer eye than her mother, and found it hard to accept that the innocent should suffer for the guilty. She had watched the fish-woman surreptitiously when she saw her in the town, a woollen shawl crossed over her chest and knotted at the back. It was said the fish-woman's mother had to feed and dress her: no wonder she was so wan and taciturn. And now Dora, too, had to be fed and dressed . . . her active, busy mother, with her deft hands and quick tread. And for what sin had this come upon her?

Salka's voice was barely audible. "I must go home."

"There is no question of that," Magda said firmly. "Your father says we are to tell you that whatever happens, you must stay here. On no account are you to attempt to return to Russia."

Bewildered, Salka wanted to shout in protest, but found she was still almost whispering.

"They will never come, will they? My mother could never make the journey now from Polotsk." It was not a question but a statement, and Magda did not confirm the obvious truth. Salka saw it in her face. "So if I don't go home, I may not see her again. I *must* go."

Magda shook her head and picked up the letter again.

"Your father says the atrocities in towns around Polotsk have become more terrible in recent weeks. He speaks of beatings and killings. If you were to return, he says, it would break your mother. At least she knows you are safe." She heaved herself to her feet. "Stay here for a while. I'll send Adele in to you."

So Adele was told, and tiptoed into her mother's room. She held Salka's hand, listening to her grief and guilt because she had not been there to help. It had taken this long for the Russian girl to acknowledge what her parents and the Radins had always accepted: except for some freak of circumstance, she would never see Jonas and Dora again. The distances were too great, the hazards too numerous. She would move on, grow up, live some kind of a life, and back in Polotsk the two people who loved her most could share none of it.

Salka talked a great deal to Adele that evening, talked as she had not done since she left home. Still, there were two memories she did not share with her friend—nor with anyone else, though they remained with her for the rest of her life. One was of the prediction made by the rabbi of Polotsk with his hat of seven sable. The other was of the last nights before her journey. She had sat beside Dora while she sewed frantically, making blouses and skirts which Salka finished, button-holed and hemmed: new clothes for a new life. As she worked, Dora had gazed at her daughter's face, imprinting the image on her own mind, trying desperately to absorb enough of her child to take her through the years of separation. Occasionally she would reach out to touch Salka's thick hair.

"You won't forget us, *faygeleh*? You won't forget us, little bird?"

Salka would shake her head, unable to trust her voice. Once she had caught her mother's hand and held it over her own, shutting out the light of the paraffin lamp and the Sabbath candles on the table. Softly Dora

46

had whispered, so Jonas should not hear, "If I should die while you are gone—don't forget me."

Then she had become very brisk. "Come along now. An hour you've been sitting over that bit of tucking, what are you thinking of?"

When they had finally parted on the dilapidated railway platform at Polotsk, among the baskets of red cabbages and bunches of garlic, Dora had lost control of her feelings and clung to her daughter so violently that Jonas had to prise her away. Salka had watched anxiously, unable then to understand her mother's utter despair.

She understood it now.

Chapter 5

The desolation Salka felt within herself was mirrored by the desolation of the winter city. Freezing winds, sweeping in from the Baltic sixty miles away, prohibited all but the occasional outing, and the pattern of life in the Radin household became as familiar to her as if she had been born there.

Her two brief excursions with Jacob into the world of men had not been repeated: existence was bounded by the eternal feminine preoccupations. In the kitchen the baking and boiling, the stewing and sifting, the pounding and peeling of food continued under the merciless eye of Frau Holz. The laundress came once a month on washday, arriving at four in the morning to work through the heaps of undergarments and sheets, and the kitchen fairly seethed with neighbourhood gossip. Magda and Adele concerned themselves with trivia and the *Kaffeeclack* of their small circle. And Salka practised her German by poring over old copies of Jacob's *Hamburgischer Correspondent*. She had to exercise some ingenuity to do so since Magda did not believe women should read newspapers, and as soon as Jacob had finished with one it was consigned to the kitchen. While the rest of the household slept, Salka read avidly in her room until she fell asleep over the sheets of newsprint, waking with a guilty start in the early hours to extinguish her light.

On sunny Sunday mornings the family occasionally braved the biting cold in order to visit the Rathaus Gardens. They would walk along paved pathways beside ornamental railings fringed with icicles, towards the high, painted wedding cake of a bandstand where a red and gold military brass band played bits of *Tannhäuser* and *Lohengrin*. Salka loved the plump eider-ducks pecking hopefully at the grass bristling with frost, and the way the sharp air carried the music with such clarity that it was audible even before they had reached the park gates.

They would return to the Fasanenstrasse for a massive luncheon to which several of Magda's sisters and their families would be invited. The meal would last for several hours as they lingered over the pickled salmon and black bread, roast veal with *Klösse*—tiny dumplings—served with lentils, sauerkraut and home-tinned vegetables which Frau Holz had variously pickled and spiced with cinnamon and nutmeg before they were put into containers and hermetically sealed by a solderer.

Salka measured the passage of the weeks, as she had since childhood,

48

by the festivals. When Christmas came the Radins celebrated Chanukah, the Feast of Lights. Magda set the heavy, eight-branched silver candelabra in the window. For eight nights they kindled them, adding one each time, until all had been lit by the small *shammash*, the servant candle, and the heat that emanated from them made the air uncomfortably close.

She knew the year had turned when Purim arrived. In Polotsk she had liked the story of the girl Esther saving the Jews from the evil machinations of the Persian Haman, and on Purim morning in synagogue, when the Book of Esther was chanted to a special melody, she surreptitiously joined in when Hannah and Rosa, together with the other children of the congregation, stamped their feet excitedly at the mention of Haman's name, in derision of the arch-enemy.

Then it was the Passover, the spring festival, when the Hebrew slaves were freed from Egyptian bondage and moved into the desert. Her father, appreciably more Orthodox than Jacob, had always taken her to *schul* the day before, when first-born sons fasted in memory of the passing of the Angel of Death over the homes of the Israelites to slay the Egyptian first-born. Jonas always said, because he had no son, his daughter should observe the deliverance. Salka wondered whether Jacob would do the same, as the father of three daughters, but no reference was made to the occasion.

As the evening neared she grew silent, conscious that at home she would have been given the task of searching the house for leaven bread which had to be burned; her mother always hid a couple of pieces for her to triumphantly find. In Jacob's house, Magda merely asked Frau Holz to take home what was left before they made the *matzos*, the flat sheets of flour and water which tasted so delectable spread with lemon curd.

As the *Seder*—the service preceding and surrounding the Passover meal—began, Salka found its fifteen elaborate sections almost unbearably painful. Every word of the prayers conducted over the dinner-table by Jacob reminded her that she, like the ancient Israelites, was in exile, homeless, rootless. She tasted the bitter herbs—the *maror*—horseradish tart on her tongue, for the bitter lives of the slaves under Egyptian bondage. She dipped her piece of parsley in salt water—greenery for the spring, salt for the tears of the Jews. She put her little finger four times into her wine glass for the four expressions of redemption, and all the time she felt a fierce longing to be home, sitting at the table her father had carved, helping her mother serve the festive meal.

She looked across at Adele, in her own home with her family, and envied her. Adele, catching the look and almost recognising it for what it was, quirked her lips in sympathy, for she and Salka had begun to understand each other very well, different as they were. At the affectionate gesture Salka's eyes filled with tears and she bent her head to hide them.

49

As she did so, she noticed the gleam of Adele's patent slippers on her own feet and felt, absurdly, cheered.

In May Adele confided excitedly that her father planned to take them to Austria where he had business for two days in Vienna. Salka listened and smiled politely, assuming she would be left with the two younger girls in the care of Frau Holz and Jette. Magda and Adele discussed clothes interminably, visited the dressmaker to have garments "made over" and freshened, and purchased ribbon and artificial flowers to trim the new hats. Tarlatan and yards of trimming went into an evening costume for Adele, while Magda's alpaca coat was freshly edged with fancy cord.

The week before they were due to leave the conversation at dinner turned to the journey. Jacob glanced across at Salka, who was quiet. Although they had talked little since their visit to the harbour, he had not forgotten how impressed he had been by her interest.

"And you," he asked her now, "are you also prepared for our excursion?"

Taken aback, Salka looked at him. "But I am not to come with you."

"Not? Do you dislike travel?"

Salka glanced at Magda, who pursed her lips over her soup. "Under the circumstances, I didn't think . . ."

"Is that right, my dear?" Jacob lifted his eyebrows at Magda, but before she could answer Adele had intervened: "Please, may she come with us, Mama, may she?"

In the face of the direct appeal, Magda agreed that Salka should accompany them. A few days later she was again standing on a station platform, though with rather more composure than she had felt last time she did so. As Jacob shepherded them to the luxurious, fabric-hung ladies' coupé, they passed the fourth-class carriages, with the hard wooden benches Salka remembered so well.

She had come a long way, and not only in distance, she reflected; no one seeing her now amongst so many fashionable travellers, sitting at her ease with a novel on her lap, would ever know she was not one of them. She raised a hand to smooth the feathers of the humming-bird on her toque. It had belonged to Adele but that fact in no way lessened the charm of this, her first hat. For a brief moment she thought of the headsquare she always used to wear outside the house, low over her forehead so that it modestly hid her hair: she had taken it off one day after the discovery that to be a Russian was somehow demeaning, and hidden it in a drawer.

The route into Austria was a popular one, and at appropriate times hampers, ordered beforehand, were presented at the carriage door filled with local delicacies. Salka had never imagined travellers could be so

50

cosseted. All the same, she would have enjoyed one of her father's acid drops. She smiled to herself, remembering the bag he had pushed into her hand as she boarded the train so many months before.

When they finally reached Vienna it was dark, and they caught only tantalising glimpses of illuminated buildings, shop-fronts and theatres before they reached Fillgadergasse 4, a kosher boarding-house in a sedate section of the city. They saw little more next day, for Magda woke with an appalling headache and was confined to bed. Jacob disappeared to fulfil his business engagements leaving the two girls to attend her, and sit in the communal drawing-room. There was an abundance of stiffly arranged wickerwork chairs; near the window a writing-table was screened with trellis-work so heavy with ivy the room was bathed in a greenish, underwater light which Salka found deeply depressing. It seemed hard that this was to be all they could see of Vienna, a city even she knew to be one of the most beautiful in Europe.

In the evening Jacob took Adele with him to dine with a colleague since Magda could not accompany him, and Salka remained with the invalid. She helped Adele into the new costume and watched her go a little sadly; by the time they returned she had gone to bed, and listened drowsily as Adele whispered about the magnificent apartment where they had been entertained, and of the people she had met. She was still talking as Salka fell asleep.

The following day saw sunshine and Magda "perfectly restored" as she announced at breakfast, so it was decided that Jacob would take them all to the races.

They drove in a hired fiacre down the wide stretch of the Hauptallee, chestnut trees above their heads pinpointed in brilliant white. The Freudenau was thronged with racegoers, strolling towards the enclosures, placing their bets with gesticulating bookmakers, squiring soignée women in pale frocks. Jacob led them into the "Gulden" seats on the stands. Below them, in the twenty-kreutzer section, they could look down on students and bank clerks out for the day and making a good deal of noise about it.

Salka gazed across the circular track with its hurdles and ditches, bounded by the white fence and circumscribed, in the distance, by dark woods. On the edges of the track, waiting for the next race, men stood in congenial groups, some with binoculars round their necks.

She pointed. "Who are they?"

Jacob shrugged. "Who knows? Professional gamblers, a lot of them, men who make a living from the horses. Counts and cavalry officers. Businessmen and bounders."

Just then she noticed a line of horses stalking on to the track, the animals' coats gleaming beneath the vivid silks of the jockeys, which were

51

slashed by red, blue or gold sashes. She stood on tiptoe to see them move easily into place behind a white bar, stamping and throwing up their heads, chafing against their bits.

The crowd grew quiet, sensing the tension on the track. Salka saw a blue flag flash and fall, then the bar lifted above the horses' heads and they were away, brown and black bodies surging forward, oiled hooves reverberating on the turf.

Enthralled, Salka watched them take the first hurdle, necks stretching and reaching, gleaming haunches rising and falling in unison. On the next, one animal checked and turned, its rider hurtling forward over its head. Two more horses immediately behind side-stepped the prone figure and lost their momentum, colliding with each other. The crowd stopped cheering and held its breath, and then the jockey struggled to his feet and they cheered again.

By now the leading horses were almost out of sight, silhouetted against the pale blue sky as they raced full out on the flat, sweeping round in a tight wedge of colour to the home-stretch. She saw that they were separated, strung out; the strain was visible in their corded necks and the jockeys' whips flicking their heaving sides. And then they were at the finishing line and the blue flag flashed again as the shouting, jostling people swept forward to glimpse the winner.

While they were waiting for the next race, Jacob caught sight of an acquaintance and took his wife and daughter over to introduce them. As Adele was led away she shot Salka an apologetic look, and the Russian girl realised again that for all his kindness, Jacob was too much of a social snob to wish to introduce his shabby relative to these Viennese socialites. *Ostjude*. She had not thought of the ugly word for weeks.

On an impulse she turned her back and threaded her way through the crowds, moving towards the empty green space she could see beyond the stands. Reaching its comparative peace—it was deserted save for a few couples strolling arm in arm and two youths walking heavily blanketed horses gently to and fro—Salka wandered over to the fence. She stood in an angle between the white bars, looking towards the Prater trees and the distant Hungarian flatlands. The air was cool and damp from the invisible Danube nearby and she inhaled deeply, relishing the smell of hay, stall and meadow mixed with women's perfume.

The day had grown warmer. She was still wearing the clothes she had brought with her from Polotsk, aware by now how unfashionable they were, but having no choice in the matter. Her jacket and long skirt were dark grey serge, but beneath it she had on a favourite blouse, white broderie anglaise with a high, lightly-boned collar. Though it restricted her movements slightly she took great pleasure in the feel of the crisp

52

material scratchy against her skin. Round her neck on a narrow black-satin ribbon hung a minuscule bottle of perfume. All the young girls in Hamburg were wearing them, Adele had said, and gave her one for her birthday: it released the warm and dusky smell of chypre.

Salka removed her jacket and folded it over her arm. With the other hand she attempted to smooth her hair back into the coil she had managed to achieve that morning. It was already escaping, springing in curly tendrils down the nape of her neck, and she gave up in despair. She relaxed, leaning both arms on the fence, the sun hot on her back. She let her mind drift, thinking of nothing, content as a cat.

"Of what are you dreaming, *süsses Mädel*?"

The voice close behind her was low and masculine. Salka froze. There was no one else near her but the man who had just spoken, and she was deeply disturbed. Perhaps it was being so addressed. "Sweet girl", she knew from Frau Holz, was the term used by men for little dressmakers and chorus girls; it assumed they were available and willing. It was not a term Salka had ever expected to hear applied to herself.

She did not respond in any way hoping that the man, whoever he was, would realise he had made a mistake and leave her alone. There was a long silence, but she knew he had not stirred.

"You must surely be thinking of a lover, to be so engrossed in your thoughts."

This time the voice was harder, though still as low; still—and this she found most disquieting—as intimate. It was as though the two of them, she and this unseen man, were alone in a room. It was a Viennese accent, she recognised that from the people she had heard in the hotel, and cultured: it gave an impression of wealth and confidence, breeding and good looks. Salka was not accustomed to such voices.

She did not move. She was by now almost unable to do so. Again, he spoke, curt. "Turn around. Please. I do not care to address my remarks to a lady's back."

Without complying Salka said, nervousness making her voice more husky than usual, her Russian-accented German stronger: "I do not wish to speak with you."

"Such an intriguing accent." She heard mockery now, amusement. She continued to stare ahead at the tranquil trees but she did not see them. In a sudden flurry of anger at being so importuned she swung round, her back to the railing. She started to say, "Will you please leave . . ." but then she saw the man who stood before her and the words stammered to a halt.

He was quite short, not much taller than she, and broad. He had on a grey suit and the rounded collar of his shirt was held by a heavy gold pin. His cheeks were smoothly clean-shaven, the sardonic curve of his lips

53

emphasised by a dark beard. Salka wanted to evade his eyes but it was impossible: she looked at him with reluctance and then, inexplicably, with half-recognition. There was something so intensely familiar about him that she could scarcely breathe for surprise. He, seeing her expression and misreading it, stepped forward so that there was almost no space between them and she could see nothing but him.

Nothing but that compact body and the wide shoulders, the aggressive tilt of his head. He looked at her in a way no man had looked before, as if there was nothing he did not know about her, no thought he could not read, no secret place he could not invade.

Shocked, she made to move back, but the bars behind pressed into her flesh. He put one hand on the railing beside her and even in her panic she noticed, ludicrously, the manicured nails. She realised she was trapped, for on her other side was the sharp angle of the fence. The stranger was not smiling now, his face was intent, and she tried to call something, anything, but no sound would come. It was ridiculous, her thinking mind told her, that in broad daylight, with hundreds of people near by, she was unable to get away.

He spoke again—something she could not hear—and she shivered at the timbre of his voice. Because she was just eighteen and totally inexperienced, because she belonged to a religious group and a social class which rigorously protected their young girls, Salka knew very little of the relations between men and women. So she had no way of recognising the voice of desire. But her body recognised it.

He put out a hand and very delicately touched the iridescent phial of perfume at her throat. She leant back still further, out of his reach, and at her abrupt movement he withdrew his hand, and in doing so brushed against the curve of her breast in the white broderie anglaise. At the slight contact she felt, somewhere between her thighs, a thud of pleasure.

She knew it was pleasure even though she had experienced nothing like it before. Horrified equally by his action and the force of her involuntary response, she flung up an arm to ward him off, turning away from his knowing, challenging gaze, but there was nowhere to go. Desperate, she ducked beneath his restraining arm and sprang away from him, running back to the groups of laughing people, to the steadily walking horses, the stands.

"And just what have you been up to?"

Magda was standing in front of her, one hand on her hip. "What were you doing down there?" She gestured with her head. Salka stuttered, breathless, torn between relief, embarrassment and fear.

"He . . . someone tried . . . to talk to me. I'd gone to look at the woods—just for a moment—and he was behind me . . ." She stopped, seeing the disbelief on Magda's face.

"Really? It seemed to me that you were leading him on, standing up against him like that for all the world to see."

Salka tried to protest, but the older woman would not listen. In sharp tones she issued reprimands, speaking of duty owed, of decent standards to be preserved, of examples to be followed. Salka tried not to hear but fixed her eyes on the brooch Magda wore on her bosom. It was circular, of black onyx, set with what appeared to be small pearls, oddly shaped with flattened surfaces. She had asked Adele about it once, who had laughed and said they were the milk-teeth shed by herself and her sisters when they were small, which Magda had had mounted. Salka stared at the brooch and was conscious of the now-familiar anger welling up inside her. Jacob appeared and hastily drew Magda away, while Adele took Salka's arm and walked her towards the waiting fiacre. As they went, Salka could hear another race, the pounding hooves and the roars of encouragement from the crowd. Only now the sounds had lost all their charm for her, the baying racegoers screamed in her ears and the brilliant colours of the May afternoon were tarnished.

She did not know what had happened to her. She knew only that it had been out of all experience, that it had somehow taken her over the borders of her childhood. What she could not foresee was that the Radins' reaction would change a chance encounter into a calculated escapade, and her own innocent involvement into the behaviour of a cocotte.

The only person who tried to understand was Adele. Although more worldly than Salka, more apparently sophisticated and poised, it was only a surface gloss, a veneer. Though less prone than her Russian cousin to believe what Jacob called "superstitious mumbo-jumbo" she had instead a conviction that the formalities of everyday life were of overriding importance. What one said, and wore, how one behaved, whether all the proprieties were observed, attending synagogue at the appropriate times—it sometimes seemed to Salka that Adele did everything for effect.

The truth was that she clung to such things obsessively because they gave her confidence. Basically shy and nervous, she was inclined to chatter and giggle—tendencies upon which both Magda and Jacob frowned. Then she would blush furiously, her pride hurt, and glance under her eyelashes to see if her younger sisters had noticed her discomfiture: they always had. Even Salka—though she would have been astonished to hear it—made her feel anxious. Salka, when uncertain, had learnt over the last few months to keep silent: it was the best protection she had found in a world of strangers. But to Adele she seemed cool and aloof. The incident on the cellar steps had begun to bring them together and despite their differences they had grown fond of each other, for they were of an age but in no way rivals.

After the shocking incident at the Freudenau—Salka had never so described it, but it was now accepted as such by the Radins—they returned to the boarding-house and, the following day, to Hamburg without reference to it. Or indeed to anything very much at all, since Salka and Magda, each disconcerted by the other's behaviour, would not speak.

But once home, Adele's kindness, combined with her intense curiosity and Salka's need to confide in someone, encouraged the Russian girl to describe the few minutes she had spent with the stranger. She explained why she had walked over to the fence, how he had spoken, and she demonstrated the way in which he had moved in on her, too broad and implacable for her to escape.

She did not ever manage to tell Adele the whole truth, although she really thought she had. She had forgotten, in her panic, that extraordinary moment when she felt she knew him—that man—from some other, half-remembered time. And although she told how he put out a hand to touch her, she went no further for she could not be sure, now, that he had actually done so. She thought he had, she could still feel her skin scorching from his fingers, but surely no civilised person—and his voice proclaimed him as such—would have done such a thing?

Adele, trying hard to absolve Salka from blame, reported this to her parents. The effect of the abbreviated version was to leave Magda, especially, more positive than ever that Salka had somehow engineered the incident and led the man on. Both she and Jacob were convinced that the little Russian was a scheming creature and not to be trusted. Magda concluded that she was an undesirable influence and urged Jacob to complete the arrangements he had begun for his daughter.

Less than a month passed by before Jacob and Magda took Adele into the study and told her they had arranged a match for her. Jacob's contacts were numerous and it had not been necessary to employ the services of a marriage-broker as was the normal practice.

Adele, telling Salka about it in her room, was ecstatic. She had already met her prospective husband although at that time she had known nothing of her father's intentions. He was the son of the banker with whom Jacob and Adele had dined in Vienna while Magda was unwell. Salka nodded, vaguely recalling Adele's excited whispering about the grandeur of the apartment, the number of courses served and the elegance of their host.

She asked, a little sadly, "And what did you think of him? Of your *Verlobten*? Your fiancé."

Adele went pink. "Papa says he is a man of the world. He is older than me, of course, and he didn't say much. But oh, he's like someone out of those books we were reading by Fanny Lewald. So distinguished, and his clothes cut just so, and he took my hand most elegantly but did not kiss it, and you know how in Hamburg people ignore the conventions . . ."

Salka listened to Adele's enthusings and tried to untangle her own confused feelings. She knew she should be happy for her friend, only it was hard to think Adele would be living so far away in Vienna; but it was not that thought which worried her. She said nothing that day to spoil Adele's mood, waiting until, two days later, they were walking together beside the canal near the apartment. Magda, who now kept a watchful eye on Salka, had been distracted by the younger girls and was behind them.

Salka said, thoughtfully, "I meant to ask you the other day. Do you remember after the cellar"—Adele shuddered—"how we talked about love? You said you could not learn to love just anyone."

"Then I had not seen Leon," retorted Adele. "No woman could help loving such a man."

Salka stared into the green waters of the canal, watching a shoal of quicksilver fish changing direction in perfect unison.

"Anyway," Adele went on, "he and his father will visit us next week, to take tea and discuss the arrangements. You will meet him then, and tell me if I'm not right."

Magda, however, had other ideas. As the day of the visit neared, she began her preparations. Jette was set to cleaning silver and turning out the rooms, she herself washed the silk lampshades. The muslin curtains had already been cleaned for the spring the moment the *Berliner Ofen* was no longer in use. Now she decided the drawing-room needed painting, and within two days dozens of workmen had arrived to carry out her orders. And amidst all this activity she found time to explain to Salka that it would be more suitable if she were to be present only briefly at this first meeting: perhaps she would care to assist Jette in handing the cakes?

Salka agreed quietly. She knew well enough that the present amity between herself and Magda was merely an uneasy truce. Unbidden, the ugly word came into her mind again. *Ostjude.*

On the Thursday afternoon, Adele was in such a panic that she begged Salka to help her dress. She had chosen to wear green mousseline taffeta, trimmed with lace dyed to match. The sash had to be secured separately and, infected by the other's excitement, even Salka's fingers fumbled with the patent fasteners. While Salka was busy Adele glanced down and asked, "But why are you not wearing my black slippers?"

"I don't think your mother wishes me to dress up."

"Of course she does. You must put them on, to please me."

Salka had not worn them since Vienna, and was reluctant to obey: she had not intended to do anything to draw attention to herself. Not that it would make any difference, for on Adele's day no one would even notice her. She stayed in her room, reading, long after she heard the doorbell chime and the scurry to admit the visitors. When she did finally go to the kitchen, Jette was still full of admiration.

"Such splendid gentlemen," she said. "The father has on a cashmere coat so light you wouldn't believe, and a briefcase of Russian leather. And the young man is really *schneidig*—such a suit!" She and Frau Holz exchanged looks over Salka's head.

"To them that has," Frau Holz observed, taking a batch of cinnamon cakes from the oven, "more shall be given. I imagine he'll pocket a dowry to keep him warm for many a year." She pointed to the cakes. "Help yourself," she added to Salka. "I doubt you'll be invited to join them."

The two German women had never been under any illusions about the Russian girl's position in the family. With the infallible instinct of long-time servants, they knew she was not quite acceptable to the Radins, and assumed that today she would be kept in the background.

Salka nibbled the spicy cake thoughtfully. It was interesting how quickly Adele had decided she loved her fiancé—what was his name? Leon?—when she had been so briefly in his company. Perhaps her own ideas were wrong, as they seemed to be on so many things in Germany. People thought differently here, events occurred more swiftly. What was it the rabbi of Polotsk had said to her before the journey? Something about Russia being the dark continent but Germany—that was it—being a place of movement and growth.

She wiped her lips thoughtfully. The taste and smell in the kitchen filled her with longing for home, for her mother hurrying home from the underground bakery with the plaited loaf for the Sabbath, egg-cakes and oil-cakes and gingerbread piled neatly beneath a napkin . . . but not any more. Everything had changed.

Salka was aware that her own attitudes were changing also, as she came to realise how many of the beliefs she had held since childhood were based on ignorance and superstition. Still, she would never want to part with some of them, and thought how Dora used to tell her, like a fairy story, of the angel who called the name of her husband forty days before her birth. Salka remembered how odd Adele had found that, and yet it must have happened because the man was in the house at this very minute, and the formalities were taking place. She wondered when it would happen for her. It never occurred to her that it might not do so. She had once asked Dora, "What if I don't marry?" and her mother had brushed aside the very idea. "Of course you'll marry. We exist in the world in order to be married." Jonas had looked up from his polishing and nodded agreement. "A single Jewish girl would be unnatural. A little death."

Salka's musings were interrupted by Rosa, the younger sister, who came into the kitchen asking for a brush and pan. When she brought them back, the pan held the remains of a smashed plate.

"What happened?" asked Salka.

"It was the betrothal ceremony. There were presents for Adele, lucky thing, and then Leon's father stamped on the plate and everyone shouted *Maazel Tov* and Mama whispered to me it wasn't a best plate."

Jette interrupted. "Time to take in the trays, if you please." Salka followed her carrying the second one loaded with pastries. She was so busy finding space on the table to set it down that she did not see Adele for some time.

The room was crowded. Not only Jacob and Magda and the girls, but several members of the Hamburg family were present including three of Magda's sisters and their husbands. Salka had met these ladies briefly but had never seen them so dressed up as they were today, with feathered hats and bosoms laden with brooches. There was an older man, very tall, to whom Jacob was earnestly talking—that must be the Viennese banker.

Jette poured coffee and handed the delicate china cups to Salka to distribute among the guests. When she reached Jacob, she handed a cup to the tall man who gave her an absent *"Danke schön"*, clearly assuming that she was a member of the staff.

Jacob said, "Take a cup to Adele and Leon and introduce yourself," before turning back to his conversation.

Salka obediently collected two more cups and moved over to Adele, who was on the far side of the room beside the bookcase. She was holding the heavy illustrated copy of the *Haggadah* containing the Passover service that had been a wedding present to her parents, showing the delicate hand-painted pages to the man who stood beside her, his back to the room.

As she crossed the Turkey carpet Salka saw Adele drop the book in her nervousness, her neck reddening self-consciously beneath the carefully piled curls. The man leant to retrieve it for her and the room became suddenly silent—one of those curious silences that falls upon a crowd when, as Dora used to tell her daughter, the angel of death was passing overhead. She gave a little shiver at the recollection. As the man straightened he said something to Adele, his words breaking the hush.

Salka did not register what he said. She was conscious only of the distinctive tone of his voice. The green and gold coffee-cups rattled on the tray as she looked at him properly for the first time: the broad back, the thick dark hair, the high white collar. She did not need to see his face to recognise him.

The man who had accosted her at the Freudenau.

Chapter 6

She did not know how she got out of that room, away from the blur of pale faces turned towards her, away from Adele's surprise, Magda's sharp look. She could only see his face as he noticed her for the first time that afternoon, at first inquiring—she realised afterwards that she must have uttered some sound of distress—then with growing consternation as she thrust the tray into someone's hands and hurried out. She tried to tell herself he had not realised who she was, but she had seen again, with the same shock of recognition, that melancholy and strangely familiar expression.

When all the festivities were over Adele came to her room, asking anxiously what had happened. Salka had apologised: her tooth had been troubling her again and had suddenly given a violently painful twinge. Reassured, Adele had fetched the tincture of myrrh for her and filled one of the stone hot-water bottles so that Salka could wrap it in a shawl and put it against her face for relief.

Salka let her fuss around, her mind in a turmoil. She did not know what to do: whether to tell someone—Jacob perhaps—that it was Leon who had spoken so offensively to her at the Freudenau, or whether she should not say anything, and trust that he would be equally anxious to be discreet. For though she knew she was blameless she was sharply aware that Magda, especially, believed she had deliberately engineered the incident. At the time, she remembered, Magda had not met Leon and had anyway barely seen him. Certainly she would never recognise him again. No, Salka decided, she would say nothing.

Having reached this decision she finally fell asleep. But in the morning she had a fresh anxiety. How could she let Adele enter innocently upon marriage with such a man? Salka longed to be able to turn to someone for advice, but she knew she must not speak of it to any of the Radins. For days she brooded over what she should do.

Then one afternoon she found herself alone with Frau Holz in the kitchen, helping to prepare *Abendessen* for the family. The cook stirred the cream sauce for the partridge she was roasting, staring into the copper pan in gloomy silence. After a while she started muttering to herself, a habit with which Salka was familiar. She knew no response was required and only the occasional word filtered through her own thoughts. But then she caught one phrase—"chasing other women"—and despite her distaste, found herself listening. Frau Holz appeared to be talking about her husband, by trade a porter in the meat-market, and judging from the monotonous tirade Salka now followed with some interest, his behaviour was far from satisfactory. "Running around after that bit of skirt" was an expression quite incomprehensible to Salka. "Keeps his brain between his legs" was another.

When finally the grumbling stopped Salka asked tentatively, "Has he always been like this?"

"My Walter," replied Frau Holz heavily, "thinks as he's God's gift to women. When he was younger, well, then he had something to offer, or I'd not have taken him. You couldn't blame him then, or them either. He came back from the war with all those medals, and made free with anyone. Many nights he'd not come home." She wiped the back of a floury hand across her forehead and her face was coarse and weary.

Salka was puzzled. "But if he behaved so badly, if he forgot about you, why did you stay with him?"

"Three small children and another on the way, and ask yourself what choice did I have in the matter?"

"But surely, if he was like that, you couldn't have loved him any longer?"

Frau Holz stared at her. She said, and there was surprise in her voice, "It's hard to explain, but there's some men you want no matter what. I've known women whose husbands . . ." she shot a look at Salka and modified the words on her lips, "whose husbands knock them about so you wouldn't believe, and still those women wouldn't change their men. I'm near fifty now," she gestured down at herself, "and fat as a house, and if my man fancies a pretty face still, and she fancies him, it makes me angry, but I can't blame him. In the end, he comes back to me, and that's just the way it is."

Salka listened. Perhaps this Leon, then, was also such a man, and perhaps Adele would not blame him, either. If that was the case, it seemed to her, relationships between husbands and wives must be more complex than she could have imagined. It was all very confusing. At any rate, she would say nothing about the Freudenau.

As it transpired, her decision proved unnecessary. The following week Jacob Radin appeared in the doorway of the dining-room with a face so thunderous Magda scurried after him without even her coffee-cup. Adele and Salka heard raised voices and then a roar from Jacob.

"Never let me hear the name of Leon Salaman in this house again."

Adele went white and ran out of the room. The door of her father's study slammed behind her.

Much later, Adele showed Salka the letter that had so incensed Jacob. It was written on thick cream paper, in a spiky hand oddly like Jonas's. It

61

apologised profusely to Jacob for causing him and his family—particularly Adele—unhappiness and embarrassment. "I am deeply hurt that my own son has proved capable of such heinous behaviour, and ask you to believe that I have done everything in my power to make him see reason. The fact is, I must beg to withdraw Leon from the marriage-contract into which our two families have entered." It was signed, Sandor Salaman.

Salka looked up from the letter at Adele.

"Does this mean—that you . . ."

"Papa says," answered Adele quietly, "that Leon is breaking off the match."

"*Why?*"

"We don't know." Adele was mechanically straightening an antimacassar. "Mama says it is incomprehensible. It is not as though he hadn't met me before this was decided. Leon knew when we were in Vienna that this was in the air, although I had been told nothing. Nothing," she repeated, and her voice was flat and small. "I thought perhaps . . . he did not care for me, but Mama says that is foolish. Both my parents are of the opinion that this has little to do with me. Indeed, Papa is sure Leon has a relationship about which his father was unaware."

"You mean, he wants to marry someone else?"

"Oh no. Not marry. A mistress." Adele winced at the word. "Apparently Viennese behaviour in such matters is different. Light love-affairs are commonplace, even among people like ourselves." She shook her head. "My parents say it is better this way than to sustain marriage with a man who does not value me."

"I am sure they're right." Salka watched her friend with compassion. It was in her mind to tell Adele at last of the incident at the Freudenau, but she found herself reluctant to do so. It might prove to Adele that Leon was a philanderer—this was a word she had heard one of Magda's sisters use, when she had not known Salka was in the room, about a famous opera singer they were discussing—but it might simply make her more unhappy. As she had learnt to do over these last months, Salka remained silent.

For a week or two Adele behaved remarkably well. Too well. She sent back the many engagement presents she had already received, with formal notes of regret dictated by her mother which only approximated to the truth. She cancelled appointments for the dressmakers, got rid of the samples of material for wedding-dresses collected from department stores and tore up the lists: of wedding guests and seating arrangements, the number of carriages to be ordered and possible menus for the wedding luncheon. She did all these things with determination and some composure, and afterwards she began, like a plant in shadow, to fade.

For a time, this was not apparent to her parents, who carried on their lives more or less as usual. Listlessly, Adele let herself be taken about, but she could not manage to participate, remaining always a passive bystander. Magda put aside her annoyance with Salka and encouraged the older girl to keep her daughter company, so that gradually they became inseparable. Adele was unhappily quiet even with Salka, but she was comforted by her presence and the Russian girl learnt to converse without expecting any response.

In a curious way Adele's dejection matured Salka. She saw clearly that it was the less admirable traits in Adele's character that predisposed her to such despair: her careful observance of the proprieties, her concern over appearance, all militated against her recovery from so public a humiliation. Her mother's attitude accentuated this: several times Salka heard Magda bewailing to one or other of her sisters the problem in ever finding now a suitable husband for Adele in Hamburg. On one occasion the two girls were crossing the hallway after returning home early from a walk, and heard Magda's voice from the drawing-room.

"We face a very real difficulty," she was saying, and they could tell she was crying. "Jacob had boasted of the match to everyone he knows, and you know how people gossip. Adele was the innocent party but there will always be those suspicious that everything was not as it should be." She started sobbing in earnest and Salka hurried Adele on, but she could tell from her friend's stricken expression that she too had heard.

Adele seemed to be falling into a lethargy from which she could not shake herself. The colour drained from her skin and she neglected her appearance. For someone so fastidious to forget to smooth her hair or wash her face, to let her nails grow out of their pretty ovals and her clothes look uncared-for and carelessly chosen, meant more than any outburst. She had not cried at all when the engagement was broken off, nor did she do so now. It was as though she had been so shocked by the event that she could not then respond to it. Only weeks later was the cost made visible, and it was higher than anyone had foreseen.

One morning Salka saw that Adele's dress had a tear under one arm. She pointed it out but Adele merely said indifferently, "Never mind. No one will notice."

"Of course they will. You must change."

Adele shrugged and complied. Later that week she wore the dress again, still torn. Another day the lace frill from her petticoat trailed on the ground as they walked out, picking up leaves and grime. Then she was reprimanded by her mother for putting on a blouse with two buttons missing from the bosom, the gap haphazardly pulled together with a brooch.

Salka went to Magda, who arranged that the seamstress would come in to go through her daughter's clothes, but before long the rips and tears began to appear again.

Magda's reaction was to try to keep Adele out of sight. Where previously she had urged her to attend afternoon concerts or select coffee-parties, now she found excuses to leave her at home.

One afternoon Salka was reading aloud to Adele from a popular novel by Frau Marlitt: it was pleasant, but she would have preferred to go on with the life of the philosopher Moses Mendelssohn which she took from the drawing-room bookcase when the Radins were out. Glancing up, she was struck by the way in which, though Adele was sitting quite still, her hands were in constant nervous movement, touching her face, her collar, the arms of the chair, thin white creatures desperate to escape. With an effort, Salka went on reading, but now she had observed this, she saw it all the time. It was obvious to her that something terrible was happening to the younger girl, unobserved by anyone but her.

So she went to Jacob, not Magda, and told him everything: about the clothes and the silence and the frantic hands. Jacob nodded, his eyes on his cigar.

"You have told Magda?"

"About the clothes, yes, and she knows how sad Adele has become. Only she seems to want to pretend"—it took an effort to say this to him—"that nothing is really the matter."

Jacob sighed. "That is because she doesn't know what to do. And no more do I. None of us understands why this unhappy situation has come about, but we must deal with it as best we may." He drummed his fingers on his desk. "I am much to blame for this: I've seen little of Adele for weeks. However, I'm sure a tonic is all she requires."

"No." Salka's response was firm. "It isn't a doctor she needs. She doesn't appear to be ill, she isn't starving herself. Only she isn't interested in doing anything but seems always tired. And you know how she used never to stop talking? Now she says hardly anything, not even to the little girls."

Jacob's cigar had gone out. He trimmed it carefully and relit it from an oil-lamp kept on his desk for the purpose.

"You're talking in riddles," he said, irritated. "You say Adele is behaving in this uncharacteristic fashion yet you don't think she needs a doctor."

"Not in the usual sense." Salka stared down at her hands. Adele's were pale and tapered, the backs dimpled. Her own were square and practical, peasant hands. Salka had been brought up to believe an illness was physical. An ulcer on the tongue, a twisted ankle, precipitated her mother's sympathy. Vague feelings of discomfort, headaches, did not.

Even so, she was astute enough to see that Adele was enduring emotions without the resources to bear them.

"I read a medical article some time ago in one of your newspapers. I hope you don't mind?" she added swiftly. "I didn't really understand all the words, but it spoke of a new discipline, and how people can be emotionally sick, not physically so."

Jacob jerked upright in his chair. "You are referring to psychiatry?"

"Yes."

"You realise that psychiatry is the most despised branch of medicine, and no reputable doctor will have anything to do with it?"

Salka felt her colour rise. It wasn't easy to argue with Jacob. "I know. The article in the *Hamburgischer Correspondent* said so. But it also said that a growing number of young doctors in Germany are forsaking the reputable ladder of internal medicine in favour of psychiatry."

"You realise they frequently use hypnosis to treat their patients, don't you? Would you want to subject Adele to that?"

Salka tried hard not to sound defiant. "The newspaper spoke about Krafft-Ebing and hypnosis, yes. Only it seems that there are new ideas now. Some doctors are becoming dissatisfied with hypnosis and instead encourage their patients to talk about their problems, and even about their dreams."

Jacob stared morosely at his cigar. He read his newspaper with respect: if they were right on the stock-market, they were likely to be right on other matters also. Still, it was not easy to admit that his own daughter could need the attention of these newfangled doctors, these young dabblers in the occult . . . He snorted angrily to himself and Salka quietly got up and left the room.

Jacob Radin, cautious and pedantic as he was, had always admired those who took risks. It came to him now that his brother-in-law Max, himself a doctor, had been talking of some Jewish fellow he'd come across who had literally put his medical future in jeopardy. He was a Viennese, Jacob thought—couldn't remember his name—and he was apparently defying medical and academic circles alike. Now he considered it, perhaps that was the man Salka had been talking about. Not that Adele needed such treatment, of course, but . . . Jacob decided he would have a word, no more, with his brother-in-law.

Within the week it was decided that Adele did indeed require qualified help to overcome her state of mind. With unexpected firmness, Adele refused to go to Vienna again and Magda would not allow her to be treated in Hamburg where the situation might easily become common knowledge. It was finally arranged that she would take her daughter to the Salpêtrière in Paris, and it would be given out that the trip was purely for pleasure.

Salka was kept busy for days helping with preparations for the journey. Adele would do nothing for herself, so Salka packed the cabin-trunks. As she folded dresses and coats, kid-gloves and street ensembles, hats and shoes, Salka reflected that for two or three months Adele was taking five times the amount of luggage she herself had carried for a new life. Three dresses, she had brought, half a dozen blouses and three nightdresses. Her coat and shoes she had worn. And if her wardrobe now looked less scanty, that was due entirely to Adele's generosity.

Magda and Adele were gone for over a month before letters started to arrive. Brief at first, bleak little notes, they gradually became more and more discursive. In one, when Adele sounded quite herself again, she described how she and her mother had attended a soirée.

It was so elegant, she wrote, *and everyone so charming. It was held in a great house belonging to a financier called Levin. The wife is German born and Mama knows her family. I cannot tell how many people were there, but I believe writers and artists and even some people from the theatre attended. I looked well and was introduced to many young people. One gentleman asked if he might call. I hope he does so.*

When, after twelve weeks, the two women returned, it was immediately apparent that Adele was transformed. Her hair was cunningly arranged, her clothes immaculate, and she chattered in the old way. Hugging her, Salka realised with a pang that during a whole year in Germany, Adele was the only person who ever held her close. Even Magda appeared happy and rested, though heavier than ever. "All that delicious French patisserie," Adele said, patting her own corseted waist when they were in her room later, unpacking her boxes.

"You look so very happy," Salka observed affectionately, "that I can scarcely remember the reason for your journey."

Adele's eyes flickered slightly. "All that is behind me now. It might never have happened. Only if it had not, I should never have gone to Paris; and in Paris, I met someone."

"*Adele*. Tell me."

"It has still to be announced, but if all goes well I am to be married. Very soon. His name is Paul Sauvel; he's a violinist and a composer. My only complaint is that I am to live in Paris, and I will so miss you all."

Salka caught her hand. "I am so happy for you. Was he your gentleman caller in Paris, then?"

"The same. And this is quite different to . . . last time." Adele's eyes flickered again, and then she squeezed Salka's hand. "When I met him, I thought of you and your angel giving the partner's name before birth—do you remember? Well, I knew then that my angel spoke Paul's name."

"When is the wedding?"

"As soon as possible. Mama is against an engagement this time, and as we are both so sure of our feelings there is no need for delay." She had been riffling through a travelling-bag as she spoke and now pulled out a small parcel in red paper. "Here, this is from Paul and me. Because if you hadn't realised something was wrong with me, all this would not have happened."

Hesitantly, Salka pulled off the paper. Inside a flat morocco-leather box bore a name she did not know: Cartier. She pressed the catch and gasped at what she saw on the dark velvet: a narrow gold bracelet, intricately worked to resemble an ornate strap, set with blue turquoises. She could only stare.

"Go on," Adele urged. "Try it." Still Salka did not move. So it was Adele who opened the clasp and slid it on the Russian girl's wrist for her, where it gleamed against her olive skin.

Overcome, Salka said in a voice made even more husky than usual, "I never had any jewellery before."

"I know. But you've missed something," and she showed Salka where, on the inside of the band, a message was inscribed: *Salka. From Adele and Paul.*

The marriage took place four weeks later, from the Radins' apartment. The groom was older than his bride by twelve years, a tall and thoughtful man with a gentle face and soft brown hair that fell over his forehead in a quiff. They were, thought Salka when she saw them together, a matched couple. Adele chattered excitedly and Paul watched her with evident adoration. The rest of his family seemed equally pleased. The mother, a widow, was a slim woman dressed in deep purple, for her husband had died the previous year. Her elder son looked like Paul but had an air of great authority. He was in the diplomatic service—an unusual post for a Jew to hold in France at that time. Salka found him intimidating, though he and his wife went out of their way to talk to her.

The wedding-day was almost as much of a whirl for Salka as for the bride. Afterwards, she could recall only the long quiet minutes when the photographs were taken and the family posed stiffly with the couple, their features carefully composed for the photographer beneath his black hood.

Afterwards the newly-married pair planned a month-long wedding tour of Europe. They would spend some time at a health spa where Jacob and Magda, together with Madame Sauvel, were to join them for a week. To Salka's amazement Jacob invited her to accompany them, and the realisation that it was at Adele's insistence in no way affected her pleasure.

Duly, a month after the wedding-day, she found herself travelling to Strassburg, from where they went by local train the last thirty miles to Baden-Baden. During this part of the journey she hardly spoke, staring out at the dark evergreens of the Schwarzwald rising so cleanly from the forest floor it seemed as if it must daily be swept, only exclaiming as she saw thatched farms in patchwork meadows.

As the train started its haul up the side of the Schlossberg they left the Black Forest behind them. By the time they reached Baden-Baden the sun was low and long shadows lay across the squares and parks, the covered walks and handsome buildings. They were booked into a small hotel some distance from the newly-weds, the Rheingold on Fremersberg-strasse. That first evening, Jacob ordered dinner to be served in their rooms rather than go out to dine, but afterwards he grumbled that the otherwise excellent food had become chilled as it was brought through the streets from the restaurant.

Salka woke with a start next day, surprised out of her sleep by the brilliance of the light through the white curtains after her dark Hamburg room. She stepped over the warm floorboards to the window and peered through. Early as it was—it seemed to be around six o'clock—men and women were already passing along the street, all headed in the same direction. Many had towels over their arms, some wore white towelling robes.

It was only later she learned that the custom in Baden-Baden was for most people to take the prescribed quantity of thermal spring-water, usually three eight-ounce glasses a day, of which the first two were taken before breakfast. It was then possible to bathe half an hour after the morning drinking, and subsequently anyone who wished could retire to bed for a time before taking breakfast.

Adele told her all this when they met in the afternoon. She led the way down a narrow passage leading to a wooden bridge over the narrow Oosbach River. It gave on to an esplanade which reached from the Hotel de Baden to the Lichtenthaler Allee half a mile further on. Along this promenade, bounded at the back by a green hill, Adele pointed out the various Cure-houses, the Conversation-house and the *Trinkhalle*.

"Come and try the waters," she urged, and they walked up a broad flight of stone steps leading to a raised terrace, from which great columns reached up, forming a covered walk. A doorway in the middle led to the central hall, square and beautifully proportioned, the roof supported by a single marble column. At its base was a circular sunken basin surrounded by railings into which the waters of the Ursprung bubbled. The *Brunnen-mädchen*, the young woman who served the mineral waters, presented them with two cut-glass Bohemian tumblers: Salka was fascinated by the way the sides of hers were immediately dotted with minute effervescing bubbles.

"That's the carbonic gas," explained Adele as she sipped her water and Salka followed her example.

"It's hot!" she exclaimed. "I didn't think it would be so hot."

"They say it would scald a fowl," Adele agreed. "D'you want whey to cool it?" Salka decided she preferred the taste as it was, unexpected but agreeably brisk on her tongue. When they had finished they walked through the *Trinkhalle* to the esplanade and Adele headed for the Friedrichsbad to book cabinets, the luxurious private bathrooms, for early next morning. While she waited Salka read a booklet which claimed that next to the bathing establishments at Aix-les-Bains and Bath, the Friedrichsbad was the most complete in Europe providing "all the methods for the application of mineral waters according to the requirements of modern balneology."

At seven o'clock the following morning Adele led the way up a flight of stairs to a gallery which ran the length of the building, partitioned off at one point to form a conversation-room where, she explained, patients and friends could rest or amuse themselves whilst waiting for the baths. It appeared empty but as they turned to go a woman's voice hailed them. Madame Sauvel, almost unrecognisable in her voluminous towelling robe with hair knotted on top of her head, rose from a deep chair. She had just been to the *Trinkhalle* and awaited her turn in the *Gasbad*.

"I'm a little nervous," she confided in her charming, French-accented Yiddish. "But my physician recommended it for rheumatism in the shoulder. Won't you both come with me to bolster my confidence?"

Adele said eagerly, "I've always wanted to see how a gas-bath was effected," and when the attendant tapped on the door for Madame Sauvel, both girls followed her along the gallery to an inner room. This contained an extremely large wooden box, about five foot high. Madame Sauvel was directed to get in, clothes and all, and when she had done so the attendant covered the box with a lid through which the lady's head protruded. An air-proof cloth was carefully arranged about her neck. The attendant inquired if she was comfortable, and then turned a tap in a tube attached to the gasometer which led inside the box. After a minute's immersion Madame Sauvel declared that she felt a glow of heat spreading through her.

When she was released from the contraption, the attendant exhibited the apparatus for applying gas-douches to the afflicted parts of the body by means of a flexible tube with brass fittings. Each of these was especially designed to perform a particular function: one was shaped to spread gas over the surface of the eye, another to introduce it into the ear passage. Madame Sauvel was shown how to direct a suitable end-piece on to her shoulder, which her physician had instructed her to do for not more than ten minutes, and Salka and Adele left her looking nervously at the apparatus.

Adele hurried Salka past the *Damfbad*, taking a moment to peer in at the glass cupboards in which the patient lay full-length upon a perforated wooden shelf and by means of an iron lever permitted as much steam vapour as desired to pour through a trap above his head.

Salka asked in some trepidation, "We're not going to do that, are we?"

"We're having hot saline baths, which are quite different." Adele showed the way back down into the main hall, and thence to a series of small compartments along the rear of the building, where a short woman took charge of Salka, bustling her inside. The compartment was furnished with a sofa, several blankets and a wash-basin, and it was almost unbearably hot. The attendant glanced at her, noting her obvious discomfort.

"This is your first visit? Don't worry, you'll soon get used to it." She removed a wooden cover and Salka saw a very large wooden tub sunk in the ground, the bottom thinly layered with sand. A broad pipe admitted the hot spring-water.

"As you're new to it, we'll keep the temperature to just over ninety degrees. When you get accustomed, you can go as high as a hundred and six for a full bath."

Salka said doubtfully, "That sounds tremendously hot."

"So it is," the woman agreed cheerfully, laying out towels on the rack provided. "There's nothing like a good hot saline to set a body up. Now you just pop in there and I'll be back in half an hour."

When she had gone, Salka undressed and stepped gingerly into the water. It felt hot but not disagreeably so, and she sat down, then lay back so that the water lapped round her shoulders. She yawned, and let her body relax. Her arms drifted against the painted wooden sides of the tub and she thought about Adele and Paul, and how happy they were together. She reflected on the accidental way they had met, but did not let her mind reach back far enough to recall the cause of Adele's strange illness. She had put all that and the unhappy incident at the Freudenau out of her head. Hard to believe that had all been five months ago.

She inspected her fingers and found they were wrinkled from their long immersion. Enough was enough. The attendant had suggested she finish off with an all-over douche, the *Strahlenbad*, but she decided to forego that experience for the present. She was almost dry when a knock on the door preceded the entrance of the attendant, who clicked her tongue disapprovingly.

"A cure is a cure. You need every minute in there you can get."

"I feel a bit shaky."

"You should always wrap up well after bathing," she was advised, "and take a rest. By this evening, you'll be amazed how well you feel."

Salka did as she suggested, and dozed for at least a quarter of an hour. Then she made her way to the great reception-hall of the Friedrichsbad. She had thought it oppressively warm when she entered but now it seemed cool. Light flooded through the arched glass roof, and on the tesselated marble floor banks of palm trees made discreet alcoves for horsehair sofas. Adele joined her and they wandered through to the conservatory, where the air was damp and smelled of camellias. Other bathers, still in their white robes, sat at wrought-iron tables with coffee and crescent-shaped rolls before them, idly observing newcomers and speculating about them. They watched the two young women with appraising eyes. Adele Sauvel was already known to some of them, but not her companion. They would scarcely have noticed her in street clothes for her rather drab, colourless garments so poorly cut would not have excited their interest. But in the white towelling robe, her heavy dark hair wound tightly under a turban, Salka for the first time in her life caused a stir when she entered a room. The smooth olive skin, the winged black brows over eyes the colour of golden stone, the single piece of jewellery set with turquoises, caught everyone's eye. She looked, was the general consensus of opinion, like somebody.

Yet later that afternoon, when Salka accompanied the newly-weds on a walk round the old town, many of the same people failed to recognise her, seeing only a good-looking young woman in a plain costume. She herself was unaware of their scrutiny on either occasion.

Paul took his wife upon his right arm and offered his left to Salka and they spent an hour in the Lichtenthaler Allee, making small purchases from the booths which lined each side and effecting slow progress among the parties of fashionables. They strolled at leisure along paths cut in the green hillside and shaded by shrubberies; they admired the view of Baden and the grey ruins of the old Schloss; they sat beneath a striped awning to drink raspberry vinegar and stone-bottled local beer for Paul. Salka found herself listening to a group of *Kurgäste* seated behind them. One of the visitors sounded like a doctor, she thought.

"The springs here," he was saying, "are well adapted for treating chronic rheumatism, asthenic forms of chronic gout and minor degrees of scrofula." He paused to sip his drink and went on, "They may also be useful in chronic bronchial catarrh, but in view of the somewhat variable nature of the climate, the benefit to be derived from them by those suffering from this affection is questionable."

Salka noticed that Paul was watching her with some amusement. "You look quite horrified," he told her. "Did you not know that people visit the spas to cure illness?"

She shook her head. "I had thought they were purely pleasure resorts." She gestured at the crowds around them. "Everyone looks so very *fein*."

"That's because August and September are the most elegant months here. The English come then because their Houses of Parliament are in recess, and taking the waters is very much the thing to do. But the season

71

runs from April to October, and you see more genuine complaints then. People come to the spas for all sorts of things, because they suffer from dyspepsia or anaemia, if they're too fat, or nervous, or hysterical." He took hold of Adele's hand. "It's one reason we decided to make a stop here, isn't it? And then, the cure is said to be good for asthma and even for back problems."

"Goodness! Are all these things cured by bathing as Adele and I did, and drinking some water?"

Paul laughed. "Nothing so simple. The baths you had were the most basic form. Different spas provide all sorts of variations. You saw the gas- and vapour-baths, didn't you? You can be bathed in peat or thick mud, in carbonated saline water or sulphur. There are wave-baths and jet-baths and inhalation rooms . . ." He desisted, chuckling, only when Adele gave a little scream and put her hand over his lips.

One evening the family party attended a concert in the *Kursaal*. The grand saloon took up the centre of the buildings, red marble columns soaring up to support a gallery that ran round the upper walls. The ceiling was divided into square casoons, richly painted and studded with gilt rosettes, and from these hung a dozen chandeliers glittering with cut glass. The saloon hummed with talk as carefully-adorned women preened themselves for the benefit of the other *Kurgäste*, while their escorts gathered in congenial, cigar-smoking groups.

Gradually the talk and laughter faded, and the profusion of velvet chairs and sofas were occupied. Salka sat with the Radins, while Adele joined Paul and his mother on the far side of the saloon. A spattering of applause had heads craning, and Salka wondered that the unprepossessing, bespectacled figure that appeared between the double doors at the far end of the room could be the great Zuckermayer. He bowed with an abrupt, graceless movement and made his way to the great polished Steinway in the centre of the floor. Dwarfed by the instrument, he settled himself upon the stool, waiting until the final throat-clearing and scraping of chairs had ceased.

Salka knew he would be playing Haydn, but she was totally unprepared for the impact of the music. This was the first concert she had ever attended, and it bore no relation to Adele's pleasant melodies on the instrument in the Fasanenstrasse. She was seated a fair distance from the pianist, and slightly behind him, so she could perfectly see the curve of his back as he leant into the music, and the way his hands alternately caressed and attacked the keyboard; she marvelled that so slight and insignificant a man could produce such compelling sounds. The whole vast saloon was awash with the music: it rolled over the gilt chairs and the rapt listeners like clouds over fields of wheat, and swiftly decayed so the air trembled with its passing.

When the first half of the recital was over and the perspiring Zucker-mayer had accepted his applause and departed for a brief interval, Jacob suggested a glass of wine or a bowl of ice to the ladies. Salka declined and walked across to the long windows. She could see her own reflection in the glass: hair drawn tightly back, the boned collar of her white blouse making her hold her chin up and her back very straight. Still in the grip of the mystical voice she had heard in the music she started to turn the handle of the window, intending to walk through the illuminated garden, through the phalanx of flowers, to where the Oosbach river flowed in darkness.

Then a man's arm was in her way, impeding her, and the door was pulled close, and she heard another voice. It was only the third time she had done so. First at the Freudenau, then in the Hamburg apartment and now here, just as low and curt. How could she have forgotten the sound of it?

"*Wait.*"

Chapter 7

She waited.

In truth, she could do nothing else, for he so surprised her that she could neither think nor move. She stood staring at the reflection of the room in the window and now she saw Leon Salaman standing slightly behind her. He took a step forward into her line of vision and reluctantly she transferred her gaze to him, seeing with the now-familiar start of recognition the intense dark eyes, the aggressive tilt of the head. He said nothing, only watched her with that knowing, amused look until she could no longer bear the silence.

"What . . . are you doing here?" Her voice sounded thin and small in her ears.

He shrugged, very casually.

"The same as yourself, I imagine. I am taking a course of the waters because it is the fashionable thing to do."

If Adele were to see him, she might be upset: Paul had intimated that her stability was still fragile.

She said, her tone hard, "There are many watering places from which to choose. And yet you came to this one, at the very time we are here."

"A matter of chance, I do assure you. Though perhaps the fact that it is so convenient for Iffezheim did influence me somewhat."

"Iffezheim?"

He smiled, dropping into that intimate tone that so disturbed her, as though they were quite alone.

"They're racing there this month. But I thought you were a connoisseur of such events."

She felt herself colour at this reminder of their first encounter at the Freudenau and took a step away. She glanced back into the room, suddenly fearful that the Radins would return and see her talking to him.

He sensed she was about to move away and added, quietly, "I want to speak with you. Don't go." There was a pause and he added, "Please," as though he were not accustomed to using the word.

She said, "I have nothing to say to you, Herr Salaman. You must excuse me."

"I came here tonight especially to see you."

"You could not possibly have known where I was."

"One has only to consult the list of *Kurgäste*, Fräulein Radin. Then I went to your hotel and they told me you were at the concert tonight. My information is of the best."

"Did they tell you also that Adele was here?"

"Adele?" He was momentarily disconcerted. "No, I didn't know that."

"Yet she is."

"Her name was not on the list." He sounded more aggressive and Salka answered in the same tone.

"She is not Radin now, but Madame Paul Sauvel. So you see, your information is not so good as you think."

He said, musingly, "Perhaps I should look for her to proffer my congratulations."

Salka gasped. "No! You must do no such thing. I think you should leave at once. She has only been married a few weeks and you have no right to upset her."

He stared thoughtfully into the saloon, then came to an abrupt decision. "Very well, I will leave if you want me to. But only on condition that you meet with me later. I told you, I want to see you."

Salka said firmly, "I'm sorry. But no."

He shrugged his shoulders again and the gold bar glittered on the pale silk necktie. "As you wish. Madame Sauvel, did you say?"

Salka cursed herself for a fool. She should never have mentioned Adele's married name. She thought rapidly.

"I will wait for you at our hotel later on."

"Not good enough. Walk to the end of the street. I will pick you up at the church on the corner a few minutes after ten o'clock tonight."

He gave her a nod and walked away. Salka moved back to her seat and sat down gratefully, seeing with relief Leon Salaman's back vanish through the outer door. By the time Jacob and Magda rejoined her, she had regained her composure. The second half of the concert began and she waited for the music to wash over her as it had done earlier. She could hear as well, as easily see Zuckermayer bent under the burden of sound he carried upon his thin shoulders; but wait as she would, she could not find the mystical voice that had earlier spoken to her out of the music.

Another voice, more human, filled her mind.

When the concert was over, the Radins joined the Sauvels. Paul suggested coffee, and they eventually managed to secure a table outside the Conversation-house. They waited a long time before catching the eye of the sweating *Kellner*, who managed to deliver the beverages without either spoons or sugar tongs, and it took almost as long to pay for the refreshments as it had to obtain them.

By nine o'clock the crowds had begun to disperse, returning to their rooms and their beds in preparation for the strenuous day ahead, though

75

many preferred to end the evening at the gaming-tables: the play here, Paul had said, was higher than at any other spa.

Salka went to her room. She sat at the window, looking out on to the street and the small groups of visitors now sauntering to their hotels arm in arm, cheerfully discussing their evening's entertainment. She was conscious that in the next-door room the light had been extinguished, and she heard the bed creak through the wall: Magda and Jacob had retired for the night.

At ten o'clock she got up and put on her jacket. As an afterthought she got out a hat, a toque that Adele had given her. She pulled the finely-spotted veil over her face: it would be better if she were not recognised, although she felt sure no one else she knew would be up at what, by the standards of the place, was an ungodly hour. She pulled on a pair of dark-grey kid-gloves that Adele had passed on because they had stretched and were too large for her, quietly opened the door of her room and walked down into the foyer.

It was empty but for the night-porter, an old man painstakingly wiping over the floor wth a damp mop. He did not hear her until she was almost level with him.

"Can I get you anything, Fräulein?"

"I can't sleep. I am just going to take the air for a few moments."

He nodded. "Stay close to the hotel, then. Don't walk near the river so late."

"No, I won't."

She let the door swing behind her and started as a nearby church chimed the hour.

She walked to the end of the Fremersbergstrasse. On the corner was the church whose bell she had heard and she stopped at the bottom of the steps, uncertain. It was almost dark now, even here high on the Schlossberg, and the sky was painted with distant streaks of purple and red which deepened as she watched. A couple were approaching her, then two men deep in conversation. Behind them, a figure alone—but she quickly saw he was too old and slow-moving. She wondered briefly whether perhaps Leon had changed his mind and would not arrive. He must have thought better of this madness, she decided. She stood for what seemed an interminable time, and then suddenly resolute, started back the way she had come. As she did so she heard hooves behind her, and a closed fiacre trotted past, the heavy curtains drawn against the night chill. It stopped, and the door opened. A man climbed easily down and stood, one foot on the metal step. Leon Salaman took off his hat as she came up to him.

"Would you care for a turn around the town?"

She hesitated momentarily, wondering what her mother would say to this little escapade. Her impulse was to refuse, but she remembered his veiled threat about Adele. She was quite sure he was capable of carrying it out, and that could not be permitted.

He took his foot off the step but stood very close as she climbed up. The vehicle swayed and rocked on its spring. She grabbed the cord handle to support herself, felt his steadying hand on her elbow, and then he was in beside her, slamming the door shut. She had somehow supposed it would be dark inside but a brass paraffin lamp was alight on the partition with the driver's box. It illuminated the worn leather seat, the polished wooden sides of the carriage and the musty velvet curtains.

Leon lifted the speaking tube and ordered the unseen driver to make a circular tour for half an hour. Then he leant back in his seat.

Salka by now had moved into the furthest corner of the carriage. She found she was trying to take up the smallest possible space and that she was quite literally holding her breath: she forced herself to breathe out.

Leon seemed very much at his ease. He hummed a tune she recognised but could not name, a pleasant, frivolous little sound. The fiacre was fairly bowling along the deserted streets, and for a second she wondered, could it be that the driver had been given previous orders, and was in fact driving off with her? The thought made her sit up even straighter, and just then she heard the man's voice, tinny on the speaking tube: "D'you wish me to drive down past the Nunnery, sir?"

Leon grimaced and picked up the tube. "Wherever you like," he said shortly. "We're not interested in the scenery."

Reassured that they were indeed merely driving about quite aimlessly, Salka permitted herself a sidelong glance at her companion. He did not appear to be interested in her at all, but was sitting with his eyes shut. Without opening them, apparently feeling her look, he asked, "Won't you lift your veil? It's very becoming, but somewhat superfluous within the confines of this carriage."

She said shortly. "If you don't mind, no."

"As you will." The shrug was in his voice.

Again there was a silence except for the creaking of the leather and the occasional stone ringing as a hoof struck it. Despite her intense nervousness, Salka felt tired. It had been a long day: the bath at seven, the walk in the Lichtenthaler, the concert and now—this. It was too much; she had been a fool to come. But if she had not, she risked Adele's unhappiness. Who did Leon Salaman think he was, with his orders and demands and threats? What kind of man behaved as he did?

As though she had spoken aloud, he suddenly said, "You're wondering why I wanted to see you." His eyes were still closed.

Stiffly she said, "I suppose so."

"I felt I owed you an apology."

Salka drew a deep breath and twisted round to look at him. She could feel the old, familiar anger again. *Use it*, she told herself.

"You owe me nothing. I want nothing from you. But to do that to Adele was unforgiveable. You humiliated her. You made her ill."

He stirred and opened his eyes. "Ill? I didn't know."

"And you didn't care. I don't suppose it ever occurred to you that she suffered because of your behaviour, did it?"

He sounded almost subdued. "I had no choice but to act as I did. The match with Adele was not of my making—I'm sorry for her unhappiness, but it was best that way."

Salka frowned. *Best for you*, she thought. She was honest enough to admit that Adele, for all she had been through, seemed now quite incredibly happy. But that was no thanks to this man. She said, "I'm tired. I don't want to talk. Please take me back to the hotel."

"I thought you were enjoying our little jaunt. You didn't have to accept."

She stared at him in genuine amazement. "Do you really think I wanted to drive with you at night? I'm here only because you said you would talk to Adele, and you mustn't. She and Paul are very happy—leave them alone."

Leon was looking at her now, "Do you truly believe your motives are so pure? I think you accepted because you wanted to. You wanted to ride with me, in the dark. Didn't you?"

Salka lifted the dusty velvet curtain and peered out although there was nothing to see in the blackness: she wanted to give herself a moment to think. She heard in his voice the same nuances that had so disconcerted her at the Freudenau—as though there were a complicity between the two of them, an understanding. She had been taught to be frank with herself, and when she heard him say she had wanted this meeting, she had to admit that perhaps he was speaking the truth, although she had not acknowledged it before. Only, why did she want to see him alone like this, knowing the kind of man he was?

She felt him move along the worn leather seat, closer to her. He put his hand on her upper arm, turning her towards him. With his free hand he reached up to lift the veil from her face. She felt his competent fingers as he gathered up the fine mesh, and leant back away from him. But now, in the thin light from the paraffin lamp, she could see him clearly and experienced again that extraordinary conviction that he was known to her. But how could that be? She had seen him, fleetingly, three times. There was no possibility that their paths had ever crossed, for her experience of meeting young men was virtually non-existent. At home in Polotsk, when any man had called to visit her father, she and Dora had always retired to the kitchen as a matter of course. Not because they were unworthy, as her mother was at pains to point out, but because the conversation of men was held not to interest them. And in Hamburg she had met only a handful of people, none of them even vaguely like Leon Salaman. *And yet she knew him.* She stared at him, her eyes wide with anxiety and alarm: she must be losing her reason.

He was smiling at her now, watching her with amusement and that knowing, challenging look she remembered so well, that look that told her she had no secrets left, no defences. Her anger had totally ebbed away; she felt helpless and uncertain, as though she had lost all power to act or think, mesmerised, like the wild rabbit she had seen on the edge of a field near the railway track on the journey from Russia. The train had been stopped for nearly three hours—they never knew why—and she noticed the poor creature hypnotised with fear as a white, sinuous animal with a black tip to its tail crouched before it, weaving its head from side to side as it waited for the moment to strike.

He was speaking to her, though by now she was in such a state the words made little sense.

"I think you know what I want," he was saying. "I believe that you do. Don't you, *don't you*? Don't pretend to me, *kleine Russin*. Little Russian."

She swallowed desperately and shook her head.

"I don't. I don't know. Stop it."

Only he wouldn't stop, but went on and on, saying those things she didn't understand in that voice he had used to her before, the low and private voice that had such a terrifying effect on her, that made her want to run and hide from him.

At that moment she heard a shrill whistle and then the tinny voice spoke through the brass tube: "Want me to go on driving, sir?"

Salka was quicker than Leon. She grabbed the speaking tube and said into it.

"Back to the Fremersbergstrasse, please. Quickly."

"Quickly? Am I so dangerous?" Leon's voice mocked her panic. But the interruption had halted him and he sat back in his seat. Nothing more was said until the fiacre stopped outside the hotel, rocking to a standstill. Leon opened the door and climbed out first, waiting for her to descend. She paused on the first step, unbalanced as the fiacre swung with her descending weight. In the darkness she could not see what Leon was doing: he seemed to be holding the skirt of her costume to allow her foot to find the step. She was wearing new boots, of grey leather, with high, laced tops: Magda, grumbling, had bought them for her when her old ones had split.

Then, to her utter astonishment, she felt a hand grip her leg just above the ankle, where the boot finished. For a moment she could not believe it, but then she saw that Leon was watching for her reaction as he circled

79

her leg beneath her skirt, his fingers warm on her skin through her fine stockings. Appalled, she jumped down the last two steps to the ground, breaking his grip and landing awkwardly on the side of one foot so she half fell. She recovered herself and without a backward glance crossed the pavement, pushed open the double doors and ran into the hotel. The old man was just finishing the floor, and as she picked her way across the damp patches she heard the church clock striking again. It was only the quarter-hour to eleven.

Salka stood in her room without putting on the light for a long time. She did not know which had shocked her more: the brazen gesture Leon Salaman had made—or the wild excitement it had roused in her.

She dozed fitfully that night, and by four o'clock knew she would not sleep again. By five she was padding round her room in bare feet, and within the hour she had dressed, slipped an explanatory note beneath the Radins' door, and taken herself through the passageway to the promenade. In the stand-house the military band was already playing, the metallic music carried on the early morning air like a chain of gold. Among the chestnuts she saw a group of boys playing four-corners, and stopped to watch them as by cajolery, feints and stratagems they established themselves beneath their chosen trees.

Early as it was, the walks cut into the hillsides were already in use, as visitors marched up one *allee* and down another, preparatory to taking their morning waters. Salka followed their example and, coming upon an elevated moss-house furnished with seats, paused to enjoy the view and admire the turfed sides of the pathways gemmed with flowers of bright-blue Centaureum.

Lack of sleep made her movements languid, and after the tumult of feelings she had experienced the previous evening she was tranquil, almost as though by seeing Leon Salaman again she had in some way exorcised his presence. She thought about that for a while: "exorcised" was the right word, she decided. It implied that he was like the multitude of demons which Dora believed peopled the night and threatened happiness. Yet, in the clear morning light, how absurd such fancies seemed. Leon Salaman was just a man like any other, Salka told herself. But she could not quite believe it.

She was beginning to feel hungry: it must be near breakfast-time, she decided, and started to stroll back towards the river and the promenade. She had reached the right angle where it was crossed by the Lichtenthaler Allee and noticed that already the booths which lined it on either side were open for business, selling small trifles—drawings of the Nunnery of Lichtenthal and the old Schloss, and paintings showing sagas of the Black Forest. Two women near her were looking at porcelain figures of ugly little dwarves while a child played beside them. She was no more than four years old, dressed in white with yellow sash, and she was spinning a *schmätterling*, an aerial top, its brightly painted vanes rotating high in the air like a wheeling butterfly.

Salka was watching her with real pleasure, for a moment forgetting her own preoccupations in the child's delight. The light toy blew towards her and veered downwards on the breeze. Salka caught it as it careened past and crouched down to the child's height.

"Here," she said, "It's *hübsch, nein?* It's pretty."

The child said shyly, "*Danke,*" and held out a small hand. As she gave back the toy, Salka glanced up. On the far side of the Allee, apparently purchasing something from a booth, was Leon Salaman.

Slowly she straightened, the top still in her hand. The child, thinking she had removed it, started to cry, and the mother glanced up from her shopping and said something to her companion. Confused, Salka apologised and when she looked again he was still there. She noticed now that he was dressed for travelling and carried a small valise of Russian leather. He was going then, thank God; he had kept his word. She let out a sigh of relief and turned away.

Coming towards her along the promenade was Jacob Radin, wheezing with the effort of his walk.

"There you are," he called, breathlessly. As he drew level his face became concerned. "What's the matter with you? Look as if you've seen a ghost."

"I have. Leon Salaman is over there somewhere."

Jacob's face grew livid. "What's that young reprobate, may his skull grow dark, doing here?" he demanded. "Were you talking to him?"

"I only just saw him. I've been up there," she waved a hand towards the moss-house on the hillside. It seemed best not to mention the previous evening for the moment. Jacob caught her arm and hurried her back the way he had come.

"I want no truck with him," he said breathlessly, "and nor do you. If he's around, I don't want Adele to know it."

"He was wearing travelling clothes," Salka said. "He's probably leaving."

"I'll check the list of *Kurgäste* after breakfast. If he should plan to remain here, Paul and I will pay him a visit." Jacob's tone was grim, and Salka, hurrying beside him, felt a sense of relief. They would deal with him: she should have told Jacob yesterday he was here. She had handled this badly, she knew. Leon Salaman's presence had a deeply unsettling effect on her.

As they sat down to luncheon, Jacob quietly confirmed what she already knew: young Salaman had left by the first train of the day, apparently bound for Strassburg.

"I propose to say nothing of seeing him this morning, and I want you to put it out of your mind. Least said, soonest mended. We've only another two days here, and I want to make the most of them."

After the meal, Salka returned alone to the hotel. She was tired after the disturbed night and had said she would lie down for a while.

On the table beside her bed stood a small cardboard box. Surprised, she sat down on the bed and picked it up: it weighed little, and was unaddressed. She opened it. Inside was an even smaller box, covered with gold stars and topped with a bunch of mauve violets cut from velvet. A white card lay on top of them. It bore no name, but written in dark blue ink was a message: *I did not know my heart had any door, until you opened it*.

Inside there were half a dozen handmade sweetmeats, such as were sold in the booths of the Lichtenthaler Allee.

Hamburg seemed a desolate place without Adele. Salka took up her duties again on her return with a reluctance new to her. After the week at Baden-Baden, the pleasure of seeing Adele so happy with Paul, it was harder than ever to return to the shadowy existence of the Fasanenstrasse, the cleaning and clearing and polishing. She looked about her with distaste at the over-ornate rooms she had once thought so impressive and found them gloomy and fusty-smelling. After the fresh air of the Black Forest, everything seemed quiet and dim: sunshine was muted through the heavy nets at the window and cries from the street outside were muffled by distance. Salka retreated into silence. Magda and Jacob, now that their elder daughter was gone, seemed to have less than ever to say to each other at meal-times, and often the table was quiet for long periods but for the steady chomping of food. To be fair, Salka had to admit that Magda chatted to her a good deal, asking her opinion on purchases and hairstyles in a way she never had before. But the Russian girl felt this was due less to the fact that Magda valued her opinion than that she had no one else to ask.

Adele's departure had signalled the end of the piano lessons, which Salka missed. She tried to keep up her practising, but Magda interrupted her several times with extra jobs to be done, and the message was clear. The girl did manage, though, to continue working on her French. When Adele had begun learning the language many months before, she had urged that Salka be allowed to join her and the Radins had finally agreed. Now the tutor was cancelled, but Salka had kept her books and her interest, writing laborious letters to Adele in French.

82

The days went by, and the weeks became months. Salka thought that now nothing would ever change.

And then everything did.

One Saturday morning the family went, following their custom, to synagogue. The girls and Magda sat in the gallery with the women, while Jacob prayed below them wrapped in his white prayer-shawl. Salka glanced down once or twice and saw that he was watching her—which was odd—and that he had a frown on his face, for which she could not account.

When they got home she was about to go to the kitchen to help serve the meal when he said, abruptly, that she should wait for him in his study. She was eyeing the bookcase, wondering whether Jacob had bought anything new, when he came into the room and the door crashed close behind him. He seemed fairly to stamp towards his desk—unusual for him. Like so many fat men, Jacob's movements were normally neat and precise. He squeezed into his chair and glowered at her over the top of his glasses. She looked mildly back, which seemed to make him even more cross.

"Well, young woman," he demanded, "and just what have you been up to?"

She racked her brains. "Nothing much. I spent yesterday cleaning the silver for *Shabbes*, and then early this morning I . . ."

"No, no, no." Jacob flapped an irritable hand. "I'm not interested in that nonsense. I mean, what was going on in Baden? Magda and I thought it very odd that young Salaman should turn up there, and now, I see, you and he apparently got together behind our backs."

Salka was nonplussed. "I don't understand. Why are you asking all this? What's happened?"

"What happened? What happened?" Jacob glared. "*This* happened." He flung a sheet of heavy writing-paper down on his desk and then, as she leant to pick it up, snatched it back and wagged it at her. "This is from that young *pisher* Salaman. It seems he hasn't finished with me yet."

Salka, taken aback by the vulgarism, said nothing. She couldn't imagine what Jacob meant. Was it about Adele?

"He's back for what he can get again, and I don't know how he finds the gall to ask it."

Salka found her tongue. "Ask what?"

Jacob slammed the letter down and crashed his fist after it. "He wants," he said, and his tone was ominous, "he *still* wants—to marry into my family. What do you think of that, eh?"

Salka said, "But it doesn't make sense. Adele's married now, the other girls are too young, so who . . ."

83

"It isn't Adele he wants. It was never Adele he wanted. Leon Salaman wants to marry *you*." Even as she stood with her mouth half-open in amazement, he leant forward and thrust the letter under her nose. "What did you do to warrant this, I ask myself? What happened between you two?"

Salka groped for a chair and sat down. Her mouth was dry and she shivered.

Jacob got up and opened the door. After a moment Magda came in. Both of them bristled with hostility. It was Magda this time who asked, "Well? We'd like to know how you managed this."

Salka found her voice at last.

"I did nothing. Nothing. I don't understand what's happening." She turned to Jacob. "That man doesn't really want to marry me, does he? He can't be serious: people don't behave like that."

"It seems he does." Jacob's hand holding the letter was quivering. "We're waiting for an explanation, young woman."

She shook her head. "There isn't one. I did nothing to lead him on or . . ."

"Nonsense," Magda admonished her sharply. "Don't you play the shy little girl with me, miss. It's plain for all to see that you've been up to something behind our backs, and we mean to find out what."

Salka longed to block out the sight of their fat, angry faces, their accusing eyes. She could see that they had already made up their minds. It would be impossible to convince them she had not contrived this. Ever since the incident at the Freudenau Magda, especially, had been suspicious of her, and Leon Salaman's presence in Baden-Baden must seem to them proof. Now this letter was final vindication of their fears.

She crossed her arms defensively across her chest. They were still waiting. She tried to keep the tremor out of her voice.

"I didn't do anything wrong," she said. Even to her ears, her words sounded feeble. "I would never hurt Adele. At Baden, Leon said he would approach her if I didn't talk to him, and I was so afraid he would upset her. But nothing happened to make him think . . ." She gestured at the letter still in Jacob's hand.

Jacob massaged his jowls. "In all my days I've never come across anything like it. A man contracts to marry my daughter and then without any reason changes his mind. And a few months later he had the insolence"—he used the Yiddish word *chutzpa*—"to ask for you."

Magda added, maliciously, "A little Russian *parech*. A sly little nobody who has taken advantage of us . . ." She stopped as Jacob frowned at her.

"Enough. For the sake of my cousin I will not have his daughter

84

insulted in my house, even by you." He looked again at Salka. "I do think, however, that you owe us an explanation."

Salka said, in a whisper, "I wish Papa were here," and Jacob's glare softened a trifle. She was, after all, very young. He sighed, tapping the letter against the side of his nose, and watching her reflectively. His anger had been so great he had not decided what to do. He said abruptly, "How old are you now?"

She said quietly, "I will be nineteen in four months' time."

He was surprised. "I thought you were younger than Adele. Nearly nineteen. Time you were married."

Salka kept silent. She began to feel very afraid.

"Yes," Jacob went on musingly, "you can't go on living here for ever, can you? You need a life of your own." He turned to Magda. "It's my feeling we should agree to this"—he flicked the letter with a disdainful finger—"this match. What do you say?"

Salka said loudly, "No!" but Jacob ignored her.

Magda had turned very red. "You mean you want to let her marry him? Leon Salaman? The man who refused your own daughter? It would be a scandal." She fanned herself with a plump hand in her agitation. "We'd be a laughing-stock."

Jacob, all his anger gone now, raised his eyebrows.

"You think so? I believe we could survive that; and consider the positive side. Salka will never get an offer like this again. He's the son of a good family with a fine business. She will want for nothing."

Salka said again, almost shouting this time. "*No*." Neither Magda nor Jacob paid her any attention, intent upon their argument. Magda got up, hissing with temper.

"Jacob Radin, if you do this, I'll not forgive you. To give this girl a station in life she doesn't deserve, one she's stolen from your own daughter—it's shameful, that's what it is." She gave Salka a spiteful look and took herself from the room.

Salka also stood up.

"I will not marry Leon Salaman. I didn't steal him from Adele and I don't want him. I don't even like him, and I have no idea at all why he's done this. It's as much a shock to me as it is to you. I'm perfectly well here, and if you don't want me then I'll go back to Polotsk. But I will not agree to this."

Jacob tilted his chair back and laced his hands across his stomach. His mind made up, he had become genial.

"And why not, you little goose? Sit down a minute. Look, I don't know whether it's true what Magda says about you—and you know as well as I do what she thinks. But whether it is or not is water under the bridge now. Adele is over her troubles, she's happily married with everything

85

she could want. Maybe she wouldn't have been suited after all to young Salaman. It certainly seems that he's eager enough for you."

Salka held her hands down in her lap to stop them trembling.

"But I don't like him. I *hate* him."

Jacob laughed. "Nonsense. If you know so little of him, how could you hate him? We know he behaved badly. Well, perhaps he's learnt his lesson. Men can change."

"You said to Adele that he broke off the engagement because he already had somebody—a woman—in Vienna. You told Adele that life with a man like that would be unhappy. What if he's still got her, whoever she is?" Salka stared at Jacob in desperate appeal. "What about me?"

Jacob said soothingly, "Now then, my dear. Now then," and Salka thought bitterly that he had never before so addressed her. Only now, when he thought he was getting rid of her. Jacob seemed almost to have sensed what was going through her mind.

"I know what you must be thinking," he said. "You feel we're not concerned over what happens to you. But I assure you that isn't the case." He got up and walked round the desk to sit beside her, placing a pudgy hand on her arm. His tone was placatory, as if he were talking to a cross child. "Try and see it sensibly. Leon Salaman is a personable young man, or I wouldn't have wanted him for Adele, would I? For some reason, he felt that the two of them were not suited. I don't know why, I admit that—and he behaved very badly. But he says as much in his letter. Now he wants you. He knows the situation, that you've come from Russia with nothing; and between you and me, the dowry Adele would have brought him means very little in terms of their wealth: the Salaman bank is a very considerable empire."

At Jacob's kind tone, Salka's eyes started to sting with tears. Now she said, sniffing, "He—frightens me."

"Nonsense. Once you get to know him, once he's your husband . . ." he felt the tremor run through her arm at the word, "then there'll be no need for fear. Salka, I stand in lieu of Jonas. I must do the best I can for you, since your father can do nothing. This is too great an opportunity for you to turn down. You'll have a man by your side, be mistress in your own home. No more carrying to table, eh? No more running round after Magda." He took out a handkerchief and pushed it into her hand. "Dry your tears, then. Think what you'll have: clothes—finer than Adele's, I expect—furs, servants. Later on there'll no doubt be children. And all for the little girl from Polotsk. Not bad, eh? Not so bad."

Salka shook her head. She supposed that Jacob was genuinely doing his best for her. But she knew that in his opinion material possessions mattered more than personal happiness. His own marriage showed that. Salka was observant: he and Magda got on well enough, but she never so much as saw them embrace each other the way her own parents used to do.

It also remained that her own opinion in this mattered not at all. Adele had been told, not consulted, about the first engagement, and that the marriage to Paul had been arranged as it had was due only to the illness she had undergone. If a woman's place in German Jewish society was slightly more advantageous than in a similar group in Russia, Salka was all too well aware that it was still subordinate. She was not expected to have her own ideas, opinions and certainly not desires: she remembered how appalled Jacob had been when she first asked to go to his business premises.

She remembered how, back in Polotsk, she used to ask her parents longingly, *What can a woman do*? Dora would tell her: *You'll marry. Please God there will be babies . . .* But that was not what Salka had meant. She had wanted to know, can I travel? Can I read books? Can I learn? Now she was getting the old answer again, from Jacob Radin, and it was still not the one she so desperately wanted.

Engrossed in her thoughts, she had stopped listening to Jacob, but the name "Jonas" jerked her attention back to what he was saying.

"I see it as my duty"—he was droning now, in his schoolmaster's voice—"to do what my cousin Jonas would wish under the circumstances, and I know that your dear parents, may God's light shine upon them, would eagerly grasp this opportunity for their only child . . ."

Salka sat and let him talk himself out, which took some time. What was the point of arguing? She had always been a realist, like her father, and her stay in Hamburg had served only to reinforce this trait. She could perhaps, in time, earn enough money—though heaven alone knew how—to pay for a ticket back to Polotsk; but what then? All her father's letters over the last months had insisted that he and Dora were only happy when they thought of her and her new life, her prospects. Jonas would be both angry and disappointed when he learned that she had run away from a future such as Jacob was now describing to her. No, her parents would never forgive her. They would remind her that they had made sacrifices in vain. They would think of Rosje Feldman, and tremble for the future.

There was something else as well, something she found it difficult to accept. When Jacob announced Leon Salaman wanted to marry her, she felt disbelief and then a growing fear, as she recalled his experienced hands turning back her veil, the staggering shock of his fingers gripping her ankle. But behind her instinctive recoil she was forced to acknowledge that he had induced in her unnameable sensations: dark emotions which both thrilled and appalled her.

Salka had learnt the hard way to be self-contained, and in the months of Adele's absence this had become even more necessary. Now she longed for Dora, for a woman in whom she could confide, who would tell her if other women felt like this, experienced the same urgent needs of which she had so suddenly become aware.

In the crowded, airless Hamburg apartment Salka began to feel like a creature caged. She wanted to pace to and fro, as the wolves had done in the Zoological Gardens, their eyes bright with longing. She looked at herself in the bedroom glass, seeing her heightened colour and the way her own eyes shone gold with tension, so that she appeared as wild as they.

She fingered the velvet violets Leon Salaman had sent her. *I did not know my heart had any door until you opened it*. Was it love he felt for her? Or was this the way he behaved with his other women? She wondered if he planned to become engaged to her and then walk out as he had deserted Adele, until commonsense told her this could not be the case. No man, whoever he was, could seek to marry every woman he met.

She put the violets into a drawer and slammed it shut with a violent gesture. Why did he want to marry her? Why her, when he had rejected the pretty Adele, with her dimpled hands and ample dowry? Why her, who had neither family nor fortune to put against his? Why her, when at the Freudenau he had accosted her as if she had been any little dressmaker?

Anyway, she didn't want him. She loathed him, surely, with his curt commands and his arrogance, the way he made her both frightened and furious? Even to herself, she found it almost impossible to admit how powerfully he affected her.

She thought she hated him. She did not know, then, how close love and hate could lie.

Chapter 8

They dressed her in white for the wedding.

It seemed foolish to Salka, so much money for a dress she would only wear a few times. She would have preferred—having so few clothes—a more practical colour. But Adele had insisted. "Everyone of any note now," she wrote, "wears white to be married; you simply cannot do otherwise, or people will talk." Innocently, Salka had asked in the Fasanenstrasse kitchen, why white? Jette and Frau Holz exchanged a meaningful glance. They had grown chary of saying too much before her, now that she was affianced to an influential family.

"Innocence," said Frau Holz. "White's for innocence." Privately, she and Jette had discussed the probability that Salka, for all they were so fond of her, had indeed been carrying on with the Salaman fellow. Though when and where she'd had the opportunity it was hard to see.

Salka sighed, thinking of weddings she had attended in Polotsk, where the brides had worn brilliant colours. She turned her mind to Dora and Jonas: they had written sending their blessings, an ecstatic letter full of their hopes and prayers. They would be eternally indebted to Jacob for arranging such a marriage, and would give anything they had in order to be able to attend it, but it had been decreed otherwise and they must accept the inevitable, blessed be His name. Soon, they hoped, Salka would be able to visit them with her husband . . . .

Pleased with his own magnanimity, relieved that at least he would be free of his obligations, Jacob had announced he would provide Salka with a trousseau. She had at first protested fiercely that she had no need of one, but he had ignored her: no member of his family should be seen in want by the Salamans, when any Jew knew that in every peasant community a collection ensured that the poorest bride had a wedding-dress and clothes.

Magda had submitted with ill-grace to her husband's decision and taken Salka shopping several times. She so resented what she saw as Salka's totally unwarranted good fortune that she found it hard to be civil to her and neither of them took any pleasure in their purchases, though Salka would have done so simply because it was such a novel experience for her. "*Dürftig*," she had heard Magda muttering beneath her breath. Indigent. She had glanced round in embarrassment lest any of the

89

assistants in the department store should have heard, but if they did they gave no sign.

There was worse to come. Magda was now convinced that she had been justified in her accusations after the incident at the Freudenau: Salka was an experienced little trollop who knew more than she ought and had somehow managed to ensnare young Salaman away from Adele. For all her righteous indignation, however, Magda was a woman of iron principles. Some things had to be done no matter what, and before the wedding she took it upon herself to impart to Salka the wifely duties and obligations which would be hers. But she did so in such a way, employing so many euphemisms, that the Russian girl was barely able to understand what she was talking about and shifted from foot to foot wishing that the older woman would stop. Before Adele's marriage, she and Salka had discussed the ritual bath that preceded the wedding-day and the long list of laws she would have to observe in order to preserve a Jewish home. If only Adele were here now, she could explain what Magda was talking about—but the Radins had decided that it would be best if Paul and his wife did not attend the wedding.

Salka knew from their correspondence that Adele attached no blame to her and regretted that they would, now, be permanently separated. Although perhaps, one day, they could visit each other. Salka had thought of this and closed her mind to what Magda was so interminably saying. She had tried to imagine a life in which she would have the means and the leisure to travel to Paris, but she might as well have tried to weave a rope of sand. The future that awaited her in Vienna with Leon Salaman was as impossible, as unimaginable, as Hamburg had been when she journeyed from Polotsk. It was true that now she was older, a little more worldly and better read. She still felt ill-equipped, unwilling to admit that now she had the answer to her eternal question, *What can a woman do?*

The Radins had brought her to Vienna for the wedding at Magda's insistence: she wished to keep the whole affair as quiet as possible, and avoid the talk among her friends and acquaintances in Hamburg when they knew that the same man who had jilted Adele was now marrying the little Russian relative. It would be impossible to keep it entirely quiet, but this way she hoped at least to avoid the *Kaffeeclatch* of her circle.

For the same reason, the Radins had agreed with Leon Salaman's father that the engagement should be in name only: neither family wished to repeat that particular formality.

Sandor Salaman had written at length to Jacob, but Salka had not been permitted to see the letter. Jacob had read out parts of it to her, peering at it through his spectacles and pausing often as he paraphrased for her benefit. Salka was left with the distinct impression that he was disconcerted, and keeping something from her.

Whatever it was had not prevented Jacob and Magda, together with the two younger daughters, from journeying with Salka to the same boarding-house where they had stayed on their previous visit. They arrived the day before the wedding and Jacob went alone to talk to the Salamans. He returned late and Salka, lying in bed, could hear the rumble of his voice through the bedroom wall.

She couldn't make out the words, but he obviously had a great deal to say. On and on he talked, until she was thoroughly awake. What could he be saying, what had Leon's father told him? Restlessly she twisted in the strange bed, then on an impulse got up and lit the bedside lamp.

Inside the half-open wardrobe hung the wedding-dress, swathed in a muslin cover. She lifted a corner and stared with hostility at the white *point d'esprit* net with its lace insertions.

She had not tried it on when it arrived from the dressmaker: she had not wanted to, she said in answer to Magda's questions and the girls' blandishments. Now she stepped into it, the *glacé* silk foundation sliding cold against her skin, shivering at this donning of a fancy costume, ritual preparation for a mystery.

It was impossible to do up the closely placed row of hooks and eyes at the back, so she left it gaping open and knotted her hair on top of her head, securing it firmly with pins: it was so thick she could do it tomorrow herself without any pads or frames to fill out the swathed puffs round her face. The veil she secured with flowers supported on fine wire which had to be woven into the hair. The flowers were of mother-of-pearl: she looked at them sadly and a phrase of her grandmother's came into her head. *A woman may have pearls round her neck though she have stones on her heart.* When she had finished she moved towards the light and stood by the bed. She looked into the hand-mirror and saw there a stranger's face, unfamiliar and compelling, skin emphatic against the white net, eyes tawny-gold in the artificial light.

She stared at the image which was her own and yet not her own, and thought of another night when she had watched her excited face in a different room: the night when Adele had tried to foresee the future. Very slowly, Salka lifted the hand-mirror so that it reflected the shadowy room behind her. She could not immediately find the courage to look into it. But there was nothing. No movement, no unexpected shape, no glimmer of another face. She did not know whether she felt relief or regret. Who had she thought to find? She looked again at herself, and knew beyond any doubt that she had wanted to see Leon Salaman.

For the truth was that she was still in thrall to the superstitions of her childhood. She had inherited her father's practical nature, certainly, but for all the years she could remember Dora had filled her mind with stories she had learned from *her* mother, stories of magic and mystery, of evil

91

spirits, *dybbuks*, of angels and the thousand and one abracadabras which could be used to invoke good fortune. Now that she was distanced from Russia, Salka had begun to see that the supernatural played so large a part in daily life because it offered the only release from hopelessness. To believe in the miraculous was the only possible chance of change in a world of wretched poverty and continual terror. Dora's word had sunk deep into her daughter's consciousness so that even now, in a new environment, the feeling for mysticism ran in her too deep ever to be eradicated by common sense or reason.

Salka wanted to see Leon Salaman in her shadowed glass because that would have meant he was intended for her, marked out for her, that it was his name the angel had called out forty days before her birth. Frightened and uncertain, the Russian girl was seeking confirmation that this strange and sudden marriage was not the result of one man's whim and another's ambition, but also her preordained destiny. She was no fool. She knew in her heart that she would not receive any affirmation, that what was about to happen to her was indeed a matter of chance: chance that Leon Salaman had happened upon her that day at the Freudenau; chance that it had been him of all men selected for Adele's husband. But knowing this made no difference, afforded her no consolation.

Salka took off the wedding-dress, heedlessly let it drop upon the floor and climbed clumsily into her bed.

By morning she knew she was ill. Her skin burned so the bedclothes hurt where they pressed upon her and she could not stop shaking. When she forced herself to get up in response to Rosa's call, daylight throbbed in her head as she pulled back the curtains. Her throat was too dry and tight to swallow even the flaky pastry on her breakfast-tray and the strong coffee tasted bitter. She wondered vaguely if the wedding could be postponed, and when Magda looked in to see if she was dressing, told her how she felt. Magda briskly touched her forehead and wrists, noted her flushed cheeks, and said she was suffering from nerves. Salka could not summon up the will to resist, though her bare feet seemed to feel each tuft of the carpet as she stood unsteadily beside her bed.

She bathed, and though the hot water made her head spin she thought she felt better. She wrapped herself in a blanket to keep warm while she did her hair, only her arms ached so much she was not able to style it, but pulled it back tightly from her face. The pins would not hold it up this morning, and in despair she left it to fall loose down her back, secured with the pearl flowers. The maid who had brought her breakfast had tutted in disapproval and picked up the wedding-dress from the floor. Fortunately Magda had not commented upon its creases, and Salka did not care. The *glacé* silk that had made her shiver last night felt so icy

92

against her hot skin that she gave a little sob as it went on, and when she began she could not stop, so that Rosa and Bertha found her crying when they came in to do up the dress for her. With fumbling, childish fingers they struggled with the fastenings and tried to console her. "You look beautiful," they told her, for they could not see it was fever which made her eyes huge and shadowed and heightened her colour. She could scarcely see for the tears but, "Brides always weep," said Jacob, as he took her arm and bundled her into the cab, and she wasn't able, somehow, to find the words to explain that she was ill.

She stared out of the window and heard Jacob telling her this was the old city, but his voice seemed to be coming from very far away. When they reached the Seitenstettegasse the cab stopped outside a five-storied, many-windowed building, unlike any synagogue Salka had ever seen. She was hurried across a small courtyard, up some steps and along a passage. Magda came forward to inspect the dress and give her a stiff embrace before Jacob took a grip on her arm and a man dressed in beadle's livery opened another door.

By now Salka hardly knew were she was. She felt as though someone else was moving inside her body and walking beside Jacob, eyes submissively cast down to the mosaic floor. What was happening was important, quite hugely important, the most momentous event that had ever occurred in her life. Only it wasn't happening to her, it was someone else stepping quietly in this amazing place, which was like something out of the Arabian Nights, with its Moorish arches and carved wood and marble.

Her eyes were smarting with tears she must not shed, and when she glanced up at the raised platform ahead of her, with the great Ark of the Law beyond, she was dazzled by the cupola of golden scales reflecting the flickering light cast by torches on either side. She could smell the burning gas, and something else, a fainter, familiar smell, of the olive-oil which fuelled the great brass lamp before the Ark. The Eternal Light. Salka stared so hard at it that it was like looking at the sun, and when she felt Jacob's hand urging her up the steps to the platform she could not see where she was going. She was aware only that the figures standing beneath the wedding canopy turned at their approach, but could not discern their features. She stumbled on the last step, catching her foot in the trailing wedding-dress, and one of the dark figures moved forward quickly and took her other arm. The effort of climbing the six steps made her head whirl and swirl, and she knew she was going to faint. Her hands were cold and her face burning, the smell of olive-oil was making her feel violently sick. She swayed visibly and the men on either side of her tightened their grip and looked at each other with concern.

"I must sit down," she managed to mutter, and a chair was hurriedly placed behind her.

She heard Magda saying near her, "Pull yourself together," and tried feebly to protest, but no words would come. She was vaguely conscious of anxious faces peering up at her and then a woman she did not know waved a small bottle under her nostrils; a sharp smell made her draw in her breath and cough. She felt a bit better after that, as if she were inside her skin again, and managed to stand up.

"Let us proceed," someone said and from somewhere to the right came a shimmer of sound from a hidden harp; then it was joined by the round notes of an organ. Jacob took two steps forward and Salka found herself beneath the ornate silk-and-velvet canopy. The music faded and a man's authoritative voice began to speak.

She heard the marriage service from a great distance, sometimes clearly, sometimes muffled, as though she were standing in a cave listening to the sea outside, threatening but never reaching her. The reiteration of phrases heightened the sensation of unreality: *Blessed art Thou, O Lord, who has created joy and gladness. Blessed art Thou, O Lord who didst make man in thine image after Thy likeness, and didst fashion woman to be his helpmate evermore. Blessed art Thou, O Lord, who fillest the hearts of bride and bridegroom with joy. Blessed art Thou . . .*

As she stood, swaying slightly, she became aware that Jacob's solid bulk beside her had gone and someone else was there. Someone at once alien and yet deeply familiar, the dark hair and the wide shoulders, covered now with the fringed prayer-shawl. He was speaking, following the words of the rabbi, holding her cold hand in his and sliding a wide ring on to her first finger.

"Behold," he said, and startled out of her torpor by the tone of his voice, she looked at him properly for the first time. "Behold, thou art consecrated to me with this ring . . . ." She thought, *He sounds as though he means it; how extraordinary*.

Then the rabbi held out to her a lighted candle, and another each to Jacob and Magda. The three of them were then directed to walk round Leon seven times. The silent synagogue watched them enact the ancient practice of the cabbala, the medieval movement of mysticism, as they made the circle to shut out the demons who resent happiness.

As they completed the final circle, Salka could feel the ground giving under her feet, and started helplessly to waver: the candle points quivered before her eyes, one moment swollen globules of light, the next shrunk to distant dots. She was conscious of faces watching her, of an arm that must be Leon's holding her up. But the face of which she became suddenly and strongly aware was that of Leon's father, Sandor Salaman. She recognised him easily from that single meeting in the Fasanenstrasse apartment: the dominant nose, the decisive mouth that on Leon became somehow sardonic and slightly self-indulgent, the groomed and silvered hair. What puzzled her in her fraught and bemused state, what she could not understand either then or later, was the expression as his eyes rested on her.

She had spared few thoughts for the man who was to be her father-in-law. She knew that his letter had disconcerted Jacob for some reason, but she was so obsessed with what was happening to her that it seemed unimportant. Last night, as she heard Jacob's voice talking endlessly, it had still not seemed a matter of any moment, what this scarcely-known man had said. Now, beneath the blazing golden roof of the Ark, she saw that he towered by at least six inches above the other men present, a fact which of itself gave an aloof air. He was watching her and she realised with that sudden sharp shock of recognition that it was from Sandor Salaman that Leon had those melancholy and haunting eyes that so disturbed her. But the expression in them was different. Leon's expression she could read, even if her innocence made it hard for her to decipher.

In the eyes of Sandor Salaman, as she returned his look with bewildered surprise, Salka found a deep dislike.

For what felt like many days she lay in bed in a darkened room. Magda came in occasionally, and she saw Jacob's red and flustered face, but mostly she was tended by a middle-aged woman she did not know, who talked to her consolingly in a singsong country voice and sponged her with cold compresses. On the third morning she opened her eyes and knew she was better: the furniture no longer changed shape as she looked at it, and the bed had become still.

The door opened and the woman came in, holding a covered basin. She saw Salka looking at her.

"*Guten Morgen*, Frau Salaman. You seem much improved today."

Salka remained silent, and the woman chatted on as she set down the bowl and opened the curtain. It was only then Salka realised it was she who had been addressed: *Frau Salaman*.

She lifted her left hand and saw the confirmation, the bright band on her fourth finger. It fitted perfectly, for a Hamburg jeweller had measured her finger and Jacob had written the size to Leon. Unused to jewellery, it felt cumbersome, a constriction.

She started to speak, but found her throat so dry, her lips so parched, that no sound would come. The woman uncovered the bowl of hot water to wash Salka's face and hands, and fetched food: something warm in a basin which she spooned between her lips. Only then did Salka manage to ask, her voice more hoarse than ever, "Where am I?"

"You're in the Salamans' apartment. In your own home." She saw the girl's puzzled expression. "You do remember?"

"Not much. How long have I been here?"

"Three days now. The Herr Doktor says it was a fever brought on by overexcitement and you're not to talk too much."

Salka lay and thought about this. She wondered whether she had managed to get through the rest of the wedding ceremony: certainly she could remember nothing about it, nor anything afterwards, though she knew there was to have been a reception. The woman went away, and eventually Salka slept.

When, later in the morning, she had bathed with help and was back in bed, she asked tentatively, "Where is . . . Herr Salaman, do you know?"

"Why at the bank as usual. Oh, but," the woman laughed at herself, "you'll be meaning Herr Leon, won't you? He's out for luncheon." She stood for a moment, watching Salka, then clearly overcome by curiosity, asked, "Do you remember what happened when he came in to see you?"

Salka shook her head. The woman opened her mouth to say something and thought better of it. Salka frowned.

"Why? What did happen?"

"Oh. Nothing really. You were just . . ." Obviously embarrassed, the woman started to fiddle with bottles of quinine and a jar of powdered morphine and ipecacuanha.

"Just what?"

"It's not my place to say, *meine Frau*." Red-faced, she took herself to the door. "Please to ring if you require anything."

That afternoon Jacob and Magda, in travelling clothes, presented themselves at her bedside.

"We didn't want to leave until we knew you were recovering," said Magda, and it seemed to Salka that both she and Jacob smiled more warmly upon her now that she was out of their jurisdiction. Jacob patted her hand upon the bedclothes, and told her to get in touch with him should she need any advice.

As they were taking their leave, Salka said, "What happened when Leon came to see me?"

She saw the look that flashed between them, before Magda answered smoothly, "You were overwrought, and no one holds you responsible."

That sounded worse than Salka imagined. "Responsible for what?"

"Nothing, nothing," Jacob hastily assured her, hoisting himself laboriously to his feet. "I'm sure he's forgotten all about it."

When they had gone, Salka felt suddenly, appallingly, alone. She realised that she did not even know where she was, or what lay beyond the room she occupied.

After a while she got out of bed, surprised to find how insubstantial her legs felt. She managed to put on the dressing-gown Adele had sent from Paris, a pretty garment of soft éolienne with strappings of pongee silk which fell from pleats on the shoulders. She washed and brushed her hair

96

back from her face, the bristles harsh on her scalp. Then she opened the door and slowly walked round the apartment.

She saw no one, though she heard low voices when she opened a door into what was evidently staff quarters. The main rooms, of which there seemed an inestimable number, opened one out of another, each seemingly more sumptuous and ornate than the last: tapestries; paintings in encrusted frames; velvet drapes of garnet and sage; great pieces of furniture in a style she had not previously seen, bulbous and yet delicate, inlaid with tortoise-shell and mother-of-pearl.

Awed, Salka passed through the rooms which glowed like pictures she had seen on the magic box the children were sometimes allowed to use in the Hamburg apartment: they would turn down all the lamps and the box would show an enlarged picture upon the wall, the colours rich and jewelled. She came to the final drawing-room and crossed to where long windows reached the ground. Outside gilded railings protected them from the balcony beyond. She seemed to be on the first floor, and drew in her breath sharply at the vista before her: the wide and formal street, the measured buildings. To her right, she could see that the road curved in a huge circle with more streets radiating from it like the rays of a star, with yellow lamps pricking the mauve dusk.

Salka stood like a child at the window, on tiptoe, as the evening closed in and the room darkened around her.

She was too absorbed to notice footsteps behind her and when Leon said, "I am pleased to see you on your feet," she could not at first make him out clearly in the fading light. When her eyes became accustomed she saw that he wore his habitual, slightly mocking expression. She turned from the window and stood a little stiffly, holding the collar of her dressing-gown high round her neck and trying to conceal her bare feet beneath its hem.

"Yes," she said, her voice deep from nervousness. She cleared her throat. She felt at a disadvantage due to her lapse of memory about the wedding-day, and this was exacerbated by the hints she had received about her behaviour towards Leon when she was ill.

He asked, "Should you be walking about?"

"I only wanted . . . to see where I was."

He said, suddenly more gentle, "You really don't remember anything much of these few days, do you?" When she shook her head, he added below his breath, "That wretched woman should have told us how ill you were. It was criminal to put you through such an experience in that state."

"Wretched woman?"

"Your cousin's wife: Magda."

Salka found herself for some inexplicable reason defending Magda.

97

"I'm sure she meant well. She was only trying . . ."

He broke in. "She was trying to make sure she and Jacob were not inconvenienced."

Reluctantly, Salka conceded to herself that he was right. He went on, "So you obviously have no recollection of the reception party after the ceremony? It was held here, and I showed you round the apartment afterwards, before you collapsed."

"Did I?"

"It was most spectacular. One minute you were sitting in a chair, the next you were flat out on the carpet." He took a step towards her. "Have you acquainted yourself with your new home?"

"This is . . . where we will live?"

"For the present. It is the family apartment, but as you can see it is vast and most convenient for the bank." He was beside her now and gestured towards the street below. "That's Praterstrasse and beyond is the Prater, the forest in the city. You can't see from here, but there are meadows and woods—it's the imperial hunting reserve. Over there"—he pointed— "d'you see that structure? That's Riesenrad, one of the landmarks of Vienna, and very new. Behind it are the Prater amusements. Rather too many beer and sausage stands for my taste. Still, it's very pleasant, particularly in summer."

She gazed obediently out but gathering darkness made it impossible to see far. Leon had moved to the wall, she heard a loud *click* and the room was immediately flooded with light from a dozen sources upon the walls, a harsh glare that removed all shadows and hurt her eyes. Seeing her discomfort, Leon explained with some amusement and a touch of condescension, "We have electric light here. I forgot that in Hamburg you were accustomed to paraffin lamps."

Affronted, she said, "I have seen electric light before, you know, I'm not a barbarian. All the Hamburg stores have it. I just wasn't expecting it in a private house." On the impetus of her annoyance she added, breathlessly, "No one will tell me what happened when you came to see me while I was ill."

She saw his face change, harden. But he just said, "Sit down. You look pale." He went over to a butler's table and poured something into two glasses. "Drink this." He swallowed his measure in a single draught while she spluttered on the fiery taste. "Go on," he said, "it's only brandy. It'll do you good. Take it slowly."

She sat on a buttoned leather-chair and held her glass in both hands. As he passed behind her, Leon put out a hand as if to touch the hair that crackled down her back, promising to be as lively and springy to the touch as an animal. He checked the impulse.

He stood in front of her, one hand in his trouser pocket. He looked relaxed and master of himself but she noticed that his thumb, holding the glass, twitched convulsively. She was watching him, she realised, as she might a stranger—and that, of course, he almost was. A stranger, but also her husband. The thought frightened her and she tried the brandy again.

Now it was Leon's turn to clear his throat. He spoke to a point somewhere above her head, avoiding her eyes.

"I just want you to know that I do intend to respect the feelings you clearly harbour concerning me. I told you you didn't know what you were saying; I believe that's true. But even so, I think you were nevertheless expressing yourself accurately. The unconscious mind is more truthful than the conscious one."

"What did I say?" It must have been something terrible, she thought, and the question was nervous.

He considered her thoughtfully. "The words weren't important. Their meaning was unmistakable. You feel I married you against your will." He set down his glass, and smoothed his beard with one hand. "I am not accustomed to seeing myself as a monster, though you have left me in no doubt that that is how you view me. I have given the matter a good deal of thought while you have been ill, and I think the only solution is for us to consider ourselves married in name only until such a time as you feel inclined to look at our relationship in a less hysterical light." He reached out towards her and instinctively she stiffened, but he merely took the empty glass from her hand. "And now, I have to go out. I suggest you return to your room to rest. In a day or two, you will no doubt feel able to join my father and me for dinner."

Salka had listened to him carefully, but illness had dulled her mind, and she needed to consider the implications of what Leon had just said. She stared up at him from her chair, suddenly conscious that she was in a situation far more complex than she had imagined. She nodded. Then she got up and without a word made her way back through the labyrinth of rooms to her bedroom.

Leon Salaman watched her go. As she passed him, he caught the warm smell of her body beneath the thin robe, the dusky echo of chypre he had noticed that day at the racecourse.

If he remembered, he gave no sign.

Chapter 9

Leon gave no sign at all in the days that followed, no indication of his thoughts or feelings. He behaved with punctilious correctness, exhibited the most elaborate courtesy, and this forced Salka also into the same pattern of exaggerated formality. Like actors in some highly stylised play they circled each other uttering empty lines and meaningless phrases, stiffly and self-consciously performing roles they did not know.

The sensation of putting on a performance was heightened for Salka by the presence of a third party. Sandor Salaman spent little time at home: he was a man for whom work was the breath of life. He hurried to it early each morning and returned, reluctantly, late at night. The apartment was large enough for his own suite of rooms to be separate, and he met with the young couple always by prior arrangement. But it remained his home, his furniture, and the force of his personality was such that Salka was deeply conscious of her father-in-law wherever she went, until she became so inhibited by his invisible presence that she ceased almost entirely to use the main rooms, confining herself to her bedroom and the little dressing-room during the day.

She had nothing to do; nothing at all required of her. She barely saw the servants who ran the great apartment with practised efficiency. The housekeeper was a middle-aged widow who relished being in charge of a male household and had no intention of allowing her hold on it to be lessened by a slip of a girl from Hamburg with a strange accent—she was even rumoured in the kitchens to be a Russian, though the housekeeper doubted this, since she understood all Russians to be barbarians and the girl seemed subdued enough and civil. Well-dressed, too, though not in the Viennese style. The new mistress she may be, but she gave no orders and expressed no wishes, so the housekeeper continued to plan the menus as she always had, order the staff, arrange the furniture as she thought fit and if she had any queries she went straight to Herr Salaman with them. Nor had any arrangements been ordered concerning a maid for Herr Leon's wife, so she had just sent up whoever happened to be available at the time and there had been no complaints yet. It all seemed to be working out in an entirely satisfactory manner.

It had occurred to Salka that she ought to take some sort of a hand in the running of the apartment, but her illness and subsequent uncertainty produced an inertia she did not even try to overcome. She did not feel like a wife—she had no reason to feel like one—but like a little girl, sitting quietly in her room, speaking when she was spoken to, putting on her best clothes for dinner with the grown-ups.

It was, more than anything, her equivocal situation which concerned her and made it easy to relapse into unthinking passivity. She was married to Leon Salaman, and yet she was not his wife: her voracious reading of Leon's books had told her that, under any country's law, the marriage was not valid as things stood between them—and if she was not his wife, how could she take a wife's part in the household?

It sometimes seemed to her, sitting at dinner beside Leon and facing his father across the table with its cloth of white damask covered with almost invisible silver flowers, that even if all had been perfect between them, the older man's dominance of his home, his surroundings, would have precluded any hope of her assuming the normal duties of the woman of the house.

She was overawed by Sandor Salaman, by his seigniorial presence and his sonorous, metallic voice. She knew very little about him, but Leon had told her that Sandor's father had been a *chazzen* leading synagogue prayers, and she could hear echoes of that when he spoke. His massive personality would have made it hard enough, she reflected, had he liked her.

As it was, she would even have welcomed his indifference. It had rapidly become clear to Salka that her first impression had been right, and that the expression of active dislike she had seen on his face in the synagogue had been neither a trick of the light nor of his features. He disliked her: sometimes she even felt he hated her. Not that anything was said by him, either to her or to anyone else, to tell her this. His behaviour, like his son's, was impeccable. He talked to her of day-to-day matters, of the weather and such politics as he thought she would understand, if he included her in his conversations with Leon. He rose when she entered a room, and when she left it; he regularly inquired after her health.

But sometimes, when she glanced at him unexpectedly, she caught a burning, fierce look in those eyes so like Leon's, which she could not understand, for it seemed to her she had done nothing to earn it. She doubted whether he knew of the state of affairs between herself and Leon, for she was certain that Leon's pride would forbid his speaking of the matter. She supposed it was because she was not his own choice for his son's wife, only he surely knew that was none of her doing. The cause of his antagonism remained a disturbing mystery.

It was a strange time for Salka. She felt as she had those first lonely months in Hamburg, friendless in a foreign country. Leon continued to act towards her as he had proposed and she found that, after all, she did not feel the relief she had expected at this unlooked-for respite from his attentions. Before their marriage, Leon had pursued her against her will. Now he exhibited polite indifference, and she found this both offensive and frightening. For some inexplicable reason, his behaviour made her think of a cat stalking a bird, keeping utterly still to lull the silly creature into feeling safe before it pounced. It was to be a long time before she realised how apt the simile was, and only then did she acknowledge that it had given her the first real insight into Leon's nature.

As she became accustomed to the Salaman household, she started to venture out into the city. The first few afternoons she spent in Vienna were with Leon, who offered to take her for an occasional drive on Sunday. Apart from that, they did not go out together. She supposed that he received invitations from friends and business associates for himself and his new wife, but he rarely mentioned them, and she knew he gave her ill health as an excuse. She felt annoyed by this inaccuracy, but no more than that, since she did not feel confident enough to cope with social situations when she felt so emotionally uncertain.

She contented herself with her brief excursions into the city, nervously undertaken and always alone. It was January and the air was raw on her face, the only part of her she could not muffle against the bitter cold. She wore the tight sealskin jacket and matching pill-box hat that Jacob had bought her, overriding Magda's protests, and heavy velvet dresses in colours that reflected the sombre skies. She thought, catching sight of herself in shop windows, that she looked like a real society-lady, and felt cross with herself for her pleasure.

Her days she spent without companions or occupations. As she recovered from her strange illness, as her energy and will-power flooded back, she began to experience again the emotional tension that had so disturbed her in the Fasanenstrasse apartment. She knew she was no longer a child, and yet she was not a woman either. She never thought to ask herself if it was love she wanted. She had no vocabulary for the urgings of the body or the promptings of the heart. Within the vacuum of her little white dressing-room and her pearl-grey bedroom she waited, taut and strained, for something to overtake her.

One afternoon she decided to go for a walk. She searched for her gloves before remembering that the previous evening she had left them in a jardinière in the hall, when she had excitedly seized a letter from Adele. They were still there, and she was smoothing them when she noticed a man standing before the fireplace in the small saloon, one elbow on the velvet-draped mantelpiece. He was smoking a pipe and she watched him with astonishment: he seemed very much at home. She gave a muffled exclamation of surprise and he turned.

He was, she thought, a medium sort of man: quite tall, quite young, though his brownish hair was thinning and fading, making him look older than he was. He had a slightly stooped look, as though he were perhaps a teacher, accustomed to bending over desks and small pupils. As he walked towards her he took the pipe from his mouth and carefully laid it on a silver tray. Then he gave a slight bow.

"Salka. I hoped to find you in: I was wondering how you were getting on."

She felt flustered at the familiar address, and her voice was deep with nervousness. "I'm sorry. Do I know you?"

He looked startled. "We met at the wedding—surely you remember?"

"I can recall almost nothing. I wasn't well."

"Indeed you weren't, but I hadn't realised how bad it was." His expression turned to sympathy. "Are you better now?"

"Thank you, yes. Only I still . . ."

"Of course. How confusing for you." He gave a sudden smile, and for a moment looked so like Sandor that she was not at all surprised when he said, "I'm Leon's brother, Friedrich. Older brother, needless to say."

"Leon's not at home."

"I know. I didn't come to see him, but to call on you."

She started to take off her gloves again and unpinned her hat. "How nice of you. Will you take coffee?" With a poise she did not feel she touched the electric bell on the wall, and when the maid answered ordered coffee. It came accompanied by a silver cake-stand covered with rich pastries which Salka observed with amazement; Friedrich followed her look.

"My father is averse to such rich foods, and I believe normally they aren't served. But the staff know my weaknesses, I fear, and as you see indulge them." He dropped his voice, conspiratorially. "Won't you join me? We daren't send them back with only one gone."

She giggled. "Why not?" It was odd. She did not know him at all, yet she felt far more comfortable with Friedrich than she did with Leon. While they ate he told her about himself. He had completed Gymnasium and University in Vienna, took his degree in mathematics, and had gone into the bank as Sandor wished. Three years later, Leon had followed him. But Leon had proved far more adept than he at absorbing the atmosphere, the facts and figures, the whole ambience of banking. Gradually, Friedrich had realised that he lacked any facility for what he was doing and began to lose interest. His best subjects had always been the sciences, and now he felt drawn more and more strongly towards more abstract ideas and problems than those which faced him every day over the leather-topped desks of Salaman und Söhne.

At first, Sandor wouldn't contemplate such a defection and refused even to listen to him. It took months before Friedrich's obvious unhappiness so

103

proclaimed itself that he could no longer ignore it, and then he made reluctant concessions: Friedrich could attend university again, to read science this time, but he was to give it up if he did not gain first-class results: better an indifferent banker than an incompetent scientist. Perhaps this was the spur Friedrich needed; at any rate he acquitted himself brilliantly, and within a year of taking his degree he had a laboratory of his own in the science faculty, with a small staff of technicians and a comfortable stipend on which to work. As a research chemist his work was laboriously slow but fascinating; at the time Leon was contemplating marriage, Friedrich was contemplating the possibility of a simple, widely available pain-killer which could be taken in tablet form.

Most of this he explained to Salka that first afternoon, the rest followed when he took her to Prinz-Eugen-Strasse, to the Belvedere garden palace. They walked in terraced gardens, peered in at luminous and airy halls where Prince Eugene of Savoy once held magnificent banquets, and passed grassy plots, beds of flowers and fountains. Near a small artificial lake, under a weeping tree, Salka noticed a statue of a youth. There were statues everywhere in the grounds of the palace, only this was not lifeless white marble but warm bronze, burnished as though many hands had smoothed it. There was no plinth or pedestal; it stood free on the wet grass, the tree drooping over it protectively like a grey mesh veil only it— he—scorning sanctuary, stared out with the insolence of perfection at the watcher. Arrested, Salka forgot Friedrich, who was talking at her side, forgot to move, forgot everything as she gazed back at the waiting, naked figure. She must touch him, feel the gleaming curve of the shoulder, and she was about to take a step towards him when Friedrich laughed, breaking the spell, and asked if she had fallen asleep. Feeling oddly guilty she turned reluctantly away, but not before she had given that half-hidden figure a last look.

As they walked away Friedrich said, teasingly, "You would have shocked Maria Theresa, you know. She took exception to naked figures in the Belvedere and ordered them all melted down. But the sculptor hid them instead, and at the beginning of the century they were all restored."

She observed, "You love the city, don't you?"

He gave a half-bow, and said gallantly, "In the right company."

Another time, Friedrich accompanied her to Praterstern, where they walked slowly along the main avenue to the *Lusthaus*, the circular pleasure-house at the eastern end. They sat there for a while on a white bench and watched the nursemaids with their small and solemn charges. On the way back they passed the show booths and merry-go-rounds Salka had watched longingly from the apartment windows but feared to approach alone. She could hear the harsh squeaks from the Puppet Theatre, and they pushed through the crowd to where they could see the tall striped puppeteer's box mounted on the cart and the hideous mannikins jerking on their hidden strings. Salka laughed with pleasure and Friedrich looked at her with an odd expression in his eyes: she had seemed so reserved, so solitary, and here she was laughing like a country girl.

He forgot that she was Leon's bride, and thought only that he was in the company of a desirable woman. When she said, pointing excitedly, "Doesn't it look wonderful to be up there," he gazed with her up at the Riesenrad, with its fifteen rotating gondola-cabins on the great wheel.

"We're very proud of that," he told her. "It was designed by an English engineer only a few years ago. Do you want to go up? It's over two hundred feet high, and the views at the top are unparalleled."

"Have you been up?"

"Not for some years. But you want to try, don't you?"

"Oh. Please."

Indulgently Friedrich bought tickets, and when the wheel came to a stop they waited for the occupants to descend, pink-faced and laughing. Then he handed her into a cabin and sat opposite her, enjoying her excitement and her sparkle. Slowly the Riesenrad began to rotate, and the gondolas started ponderously to rise. In five minutes they were at the top of the wheel, swaying in the light wind. Below them Salka saw the wintry trees and ornamental walks of the Prater park, the fair-ground bustle, heard the grinding music of the hurdy-gurdy on which perched a sad-eyed monkey hunched against the cold in its green and scarlet jacket. Beyond the park she could see the city, the broad throughfares and the ornate buildings, the parks and squares. Gradually their gondola started the descent. Friedrich gave her his rare smile.

"*Gut, nein?*"

She spread her hands in an expansive gesture, hoping he would read in it her pleasure and gratitude for taking the time and trouble to give her such a treat. He understood perfectly, and gave a sigh of exasperation. What was the matter with his fool of a brother, taking so little notice of a woman like this?

Oblivious to anything but the pleasure of the moment, Salka gave a little gasp as the gondola jerked suddenly downward. She felt it shudder and swing so that her stomach turned nervously and she grabbed Friedrich's arm for reassurance. They were almost at the bottom of the wheel now, and her gloved hand was still on her brother-in-law's arm when she looked across the paved square surrounding the Riesenrad to the protective railings beyond.

There, in his grey shawl-collared cashmere coat, a gold-topped cane in his hand and his face hard and set, stood Leon.

* * *

105

Friedrich helped Salka from the gondola and escorted her across the square. The brothers exchanged a look incomprehensible to her. Leon said, his tone caustic, "Really, Friedrich, I'd have thought you could have found a more suitable place to take the air."

Friedrich said to Salka, "Your husband is reminding me that the Volksprater is no place for a lady, being the haunt of the lower classes. He would have preferred the Hauptallee, which is full of fine horses and fashionable toilettes."

Salka said impulsively, "But no! I wanted to come here and you . . ." Disconcerted, she realised that Leon was watching her with eyebrows raised, lips compressed in anger. Friedrich bowed and excused himself but she scarcely noticed.

"I love my brother, Salka. I do very much hope that you will not attempt to come between us."

Leon's voice was as tight as his expression.

She tried to keep her own from shaking as she answered.

"We merely walked together, and I wanted to go on the Riesenrad. He has made himself pleasant, that is all. What did you suppose?"

"The evidence of my eyes suggests that you are not averse to his company."

Salka felt a flare of her old, familiar anger. Good.

"And why not? He is my family now, is he not? He at least does not seem to find my presence as distasteful as you do."

He caught her arm and started to lead her away: she was aware that she had raised her voice considerably and that Leon was keeping his deliberately soft.

"I think, my dear, that the boot is on the other foot. It was you who found my company objectionable. So objectionable that you screamed at me in your delirium to get away from you, to leave you alone. In front of your relatives—and my father—you flung up your arms and implored me not to touch you. Me, your husband of one day. How do you suppose that made me feel?"

Salka stopped walking, and blindly put out a hand to a low balustrade to steady herself.

"*Did I say that?*"

He mocked her. "You naturally remember nothing of it."

"But I don't." Her anger had evaporated completely. "I don't." It had become very important to make Leon realise that she was in earnest. "I would never knowingly have behaved like that."

"I seem to remember saying to you that the unconscious mind is more truthful than the conscious one. You behaved in your fever as you could never have done in your right mind. But you revealed your true feelings towards me."

106

Salka had her back half-turned, one gloved hand on the stone balustrade. He saw her clear, stern profile, the matt olive skin and the abundant black hair beneath the silvery sealskin turban. She looked suddenly foreign to him, elusive, apart.

There was silence between them. Leon stared at this girl he had thought to dominate easily and who had so swiftly disabused him of this idea, hurting his pride and wounding his vanity, so that he found it almost impossible to forgive her; and Salka stared into the bleak future she had conjured up during the past days spent alone, a future where she and her husband, bound irrevocably together, shared nothing but a few rooms and a name.

She straightened her shoulders and removed her hand from the wall, turning to face Leon. He had brought about the marriage: well, now she must ensure their union was not a disaster. For her own sake as much as for his. When she spoke her voice was deeper than ever, husky, so that it made Leon think of some furry creature suddenly granted the power of speech.

"I may have felt like that then. I don't know. But you gave me very little time to get to know you; you must realise how much of a shock this marriage was to me." She looked at him questioningly and he nodded slightly in assent. "I can only ask you to remember that I was ill in a strange place, and," she added simply, looking directly at him, "you frightened me."

He swallowed. "Do I frighten you now?"

Her voice was a whisper only. "Yes."

He reached out and took her hand, the kid-glove smooth to his touch.

"Come home." His tone wasn't cold any more, nor mocking, but had that caressing, intimate, suggestive sound that had so disturbed her at the Freudenau and in the music-room at Baden. "Come home now."

He watched her open her collar and take out the stud which fastened it to her blouse. She undid the buttons and the clasp of her wide leather belt, and let her skirt drop to the floor. She loosened her petticoat and it fell on top of the skirt. She stepped out of them both, leaving them in a pool on the carpet. She shrugged off her blouse and it joined them. She could not bring herself to look at Leon but stood in her narrow knickers that fitted to just above the knee and her pink satin corsets, her head averted.

He said, hoarsely, "Go on."

Obediently she undid her suspenders and the corset was thrown on top of the other clothes. When she glanced at him from beneath her lowered lashes she saw that he was staring at her flesh where the top of the bronze stockings reached her thigh. She gave an involuntary shudder of apprehension and the strap of her flimsy chemise slipped from one bare shoulder. Hastily she drew it back into place and seated herself quickly on the side of the fully-made bed.

They were in Salka's room, in the half-darkness of late afternoon as the sky outside began to redden with the lights of the city. Within, everything was pale, drained of colour: grey curtains, dove-coloured walls, carpet of taupe. Leon had dropped their coats and hats carelessly over a chair and now he sat in his formal suit on another. He had seated himself at an angle, his arm thrown across the back of the chair, but she knew that despite the casual pose he was as tense as she.

Grateful for the rapidly failing light which blurred their features and softened the outlines of the furniture, Salka tried to slow her rapid breathing. When she looked nervously at Leon, she could now make out only his dark beard and the shadowed eyes. He started to rise and she said quickly, "Someone . . . may come in."

He crossed to the door and locked it. The click of the key turning was loud in her ears. He walked to the bed where she sat. With oddly gentle, almost feminine care he started to draw out the little amber combs which held up her hair, so that it fell below her shoulders. He ran his fingers through the tangled weight of it, feeling it warm and springy as an animal beneath his hands, as he had known it would be. He bent his head and smelled it, inhaling the dark, dusky scent of chypre. Salka sat utterly still, willing herself not to move, hands clenched on her thighs.

Leon looked down at her. His voice was so low she could hardly hear it.

"I'm not going to hurt you. I'm going to teach you what it is to want someone."

He was on the bed beside her, still holding her hair, pulling it softly so that she was forced to turn towards him, to see the face she knew hardly at all and which she nonetheless *had known*, somehow, before, in some distant time. She felt strangely detached, conscious that what would happen now was irrevocable. He reached out and began moulding the rounded tops of her arms, smoothing the olive skin of her shoulders, pushing aside the straps of pleated linen edged with Malines lace that held up her chemise. She gave a little gasp of alarm as he stared at her body half-veiled beneath the muslin. He put one hand on her back between her shoulder-blades, the other pressing hard against the faint rise of her breast as though he wanted to crush it flat beneath his palm. She tried to protest but there were no words any more, no defence, no protection against his eyes and his hands, and his voice which was saying such things to her that she wanted to block out the sound, to stop the panic that was closing her throat and making it so hard to breathe.

Leon was leaning across her now; she could feel the hardness of his chest and the horn buttons of his waistcoat were hurting her, so that she tried to squirm away from his weight. Only that seemed to excite him: he pushed her back further until she lay across the width of the bed and then he started greedily to kiss her nipples through the thin material of the chemise. When he did that, she felt with a shock the deep thud between her thighs that she had experienced when he brushed against her breast at the Freudenau racecourse that May morning. Knowing so little, she had even then recognised it as pleasurable. This time the sensation was sharper, more urgent, and she had to stifle an exclamation.

At the muffled sound, Leon stopped kissing her and lifted his head. She saw on his face a look almost of triumph.

"You want me now," he said, in that low voice that so disturbed her. "You want me now, don't you, *kleine Russin*? Little Russian."

She stared up at him. The room was almost dark. Only his white shirt gleamed and his eyes. She closed her own to evade his gaze but he would not let her escape so easily.

"Open your eyes. Look at me."

She did as he said. He kissed her mouth, the first time he had ever done so. His lips were unexpectedly firm and cold, his short beard soft on her skin. One hand was tangled in her hair, the other stroked her leg above the stocking top. It slid round, to the place her thighs were shielding, and she quivered and tried to break free, to protect herself, only he became more determined. Unable to move beneath his weight, pinioned by his chest and his arms and his mouth, she felt his hand assaying her, and pressed her thighs together. But he persisted, rubbing and caressing her there, and she found that his exploring fingers produced a different sensation, a shrill pinpoint of feeling, so that even as she resented what he was doing to her, she did not want him to stop, to shatter the shivering spiral on which she was climbing, climbing . . .

She felt herself on the very brink and struggled to hold back: her pride did not want Leon to witness the shameful pleasure he was giving her. Then it was too late. She made a harsh sound deep in her throat and struck his hand away as she reached the top of the spiral then felt it disintegrate in a fluttering spasm that left her legs trembling and tears in her eyes.

Above her, Leon was still. Waiting, watching. She hated to think that he had been looking at her face through that. She felt drained and vulnerable. Nothing was said for a long time, then Leon whispered into her hair, "You liked that? My little peasant, did you like that?"

She would not look at him. She could not deny the intensity of that lonely excitement, but she knew it was insufficient. It had left her empty and craving, depleted and unhappy. She stared straight ahead out of the sombre depths of her thoughts.

Leon smiled his faint, mocking smile, but his voice was serious. "You see?" He pulled the lace-edged strap into place on her shoulder. "You're learning already what desire means." She felt him move beside her, sit up. "You'd better get dressed in a minute. It's almost time for dinner."

He fumbled on the wall for the switch of the light over the bed: the sudden harsh glare made her fling an arm over her eyes. She became aware that Leon, smoothing his thick dark hair, was looking at her again, and that in the light her chemise was now nothing but a creased and flimsy rag. With a groan, she caught the edge of the heavy satin bedspread and pulled it over herself: it was icy against her flushed skin, as cold as her satin dress had felt the night before the wedding.

Leon was standing beside the bed, pulling down his waistcoat and settling the heavy gold chain of his pocket watch, shooting his cuffs. Vainly she scanned his face, trying to read in it some emotion, but he showed none. She knew she must have done something wrong. Was he angry with her? How had she failed? Surely this was not all there was. Goodness knows it had been hard to follow those things Magda had said to her, about her duty and marital rites, but Adele had whispered to her in Baden-Baden that it was wonderful. It did not seem wonderful to Salka: she had almost hated the way in which Leon was able to produce feelings in her over which she had no control, while he himself remained unmoved.

He was still beside her, and she longed for him to go, to leave her alone to collect herself. He put out a hand and caressed her shoulder.

"You don't find me so objectionable now, do you? You wanted me to touch you. Say it. Tell me." His hand tightened.

"*Ja.*"

"And you're not frightened now, are you?"

This time she did not answer.

Later, at the dinner-table, she sat while Sandor discussed with Leon the London banking system. Normally—though she was not included in the conversation, which was considered too substantial for her—she would have listened avidly to what was being said, taking in names and places as she crumbled her bread, storing facts in her retentive mind for the sheer pleasure of hoarding them. But tonight she did not bother to listen. She traced the silvery flowers on the damask cloth with the point of her fruit-knife and wondered helplessly what manner of man she had married.

110

Chapter 10

That Leon Salaman was an enigma to his new young wife was due as much to geography as to temperament. She was Russian-born, with a veneer of hardworking Hamburg bourgeois behaviour. He was Viennese, and his philosophy, emotions and perceptions were shaped and moulded by the city in which he had spent his twenty-nine years.

> *Es gibt nur a' Kaiserstadt,*
> *Es gibt nur a' Wien.*
>
> There's only one Imperial city,
> There's only one Vienna.

So went the adage, but it was no longer accurate. Vienna, the heart of Europe, was in reality two cities. The old Vienna was aristocratic, with a vast army supported by a grandiose civil service. The Emperor Franz Josef lived at the Imperial Palace of Schönbrunn and used the Hofburg for official business; there was glittering ceremonial, pomp and pageantry. Then, in 1855, as Franz Josef walked along the city walls, an assassination attempt was made: in reprisal he tore down the walls and built in their place the Ring, an open boulevard intended to facilitate the dispersal of crowds by grapeshot fire.

The Ring was resplendent with beautiful buildings: the Parliament house, the Burgtheater, the Opera were all Imperial classical, the Town Hall and the Votivkirche fine examples of Gothic revival, and forty buildings were designed by Otto Wagner, master of art nouveau. Beyond the Ring the new Vienna flourished, with its population largely drawn from the lands of the Monarchy. A great proportion of them were displaced Jews. Driven from much of Europe during the later Middle Ages, restrictions were lifted after the revolution of 1848 and the ambitious went to Vienna where, assimilated and wealthy, they gave the city a large middle class it had not previously possessed, and made the capital into a cultural melting-pot.

These new Viennese went into finance, and the Bourse achieved international importance. Newspapers such as the *Neue Freie Presse* flourished, and the University, its medical school and the school of history achieved new eminence. Psychology, philosophy, political economics and sociology all thrived. Theatres were packed, and above all music was made, played and listened to, and out of the famous past—Haydn, Mozart, Beethoven—rose the revolutionary world of Webern and Schönberg.

The new Viennese did not look to Berlin or Frankfurt for their foreign influences, as the old Vienna had done, but to Paris, and their German was laced with French words and phrases. Where the Germans drank beer, the Viennese drank coffee; their social life was sparkling, their ideas original and their wits quick.

Vienna was elegant, sophisticated, fashionable and frivolous; the Viennese themselves were sentimental, emotional people. Leon Salaman was very much one of them. His mother came from the old Vienna; his father from the new. The family of Baron von Saar had lost their money, and it was financial considerations above all that rendered the prospect of a Jewish son-in-law tenable. Sandor Salaman married Anna von Saar when he was already established as a banker. Two sons were born to them, Friedrich and Leon. A third child died, Anna also. The boys were brought up strictly, their lessons dictated by tutors, nervous young men with exquisite handwriting. As soon as they were old enough, they attended the Akademische Gymnasium, their straw hats secured to their jackets by means of a black ribbon round a button.

They were not happy there. Although neither of them had ever been conscious of being in any way "different", they soon discovered that the professors, while not unfair to Jewish pupils, would pronounce their names with a subtle derision, and this had its effect on the treatment they received from other pupils. The word "anti-Semite" was scarcely heard in those days. Leon was fifteen before he realised its implications for him, and it angered rather than upset him.

His mother's two younger brothers, twins, were cavalry officers; handsome, moustached men with all the arrogance of the old aristocracy. They were curt with those they considered inferior and could be vicious to their men. Only to their horses and dogs did they show real kindness. The young Leon thought they were wonderful and did his best to imitate them. This presented some difficulties, as Sandor would have no animals in or near his home. Leon had to content himself with behaving most unreasonably towards his gentler brother, punishing him for imagined misdemeanours and issuing sharp orders which involved much marching up and down stairs and standing to attention for long periods while Leon forgot and wandered off on other pursuits. By the time he reached the later years of his adolescence, Leon was also attempting to emulate his uncles' behaviour with regard to women, so far as he could ascertain it. Both men were single, though it was common knowledge that they had kept many women in their time. (Frequently sharing one between them,

112

though Leon did not know this. Or not then at any rate.) What he did know was that their attitude towards all women they considered beneath them was cavalier: women took what they could get, and were grateful for it. They had to be pretty, preferably extremely young—though not so young they did not know how to take care of themselves. The von Saars had their share of bastards, but even illegitimate children could make certain claims, and the twins did not care to be hindered in any way.

Leon remembered his mother scarcely at all. Though he had a good relationship with his father, who was a demonstrative man, he was unused to the company of women and shy of them. Also, he was a romantic. His first sexual encounter took place at the age of sixteen, when he told his father he needed two gulden for books and wandered round Praterstern till he found a pretty pigeon of a girl and followed her, he thought discreetly. When they reached a doorway in a small square off Kärntner-strasse, Stock-im-Eisen-Platz, she stopped the swaying walk that had so fascinated him, turned, smiled, and left the door open behind her. She was waiting for him when he reached the top of the dark stairs which smelled of mildew, and even in his confusion he noted gratefully that the room was clean. She was not much older than he, perhaps eighteen, and her skin had the blue-white tinge of skim-milk. She lay on the bed while Leon, suddenly breathless, leaned against the wall still fully-dressed, twisting his straw-hat in his hands. After a while, still without touching her, he gave her the two gulden and went away.

The following week he returned. That time, though she had earned it, she would not take the payment.

Through her, and the many others who followed, Leon came to realise that women were more necessary to him than he had ever imagined possible. It was knowledge that took some time to acquire, for his early experiences were necessarily limited by his lack of money; but by the time he was eighteen, Leon Salaman had changed.

It was not only a physical change, though that had been considerable. The rather plump youth had broadened and hardened; the little-boy belly and the tentative gestures had gone. His features had been those of a soft-faced boy too young for his years; now the snub nose had a decisive curve and the dark eyebrows had thickened; the mouth that had been girlish had become sensual. He had the poise of a more mature man and the assurance of one seldom faced with rejection. He had all the graces of a young man in society: he had taken lessons in drawing, dancing and gymnastics; he frequented the fashionable stables and became an expert horseman.

His father, a loving though remote figure deeply engrossed in his work, eventually woke to the fact that Leon's sexual education was further advanced than he had supposed. His first reaction was astonishment that his younger son should be the cause of anxiety when his elder brother Friedrich had never given a moment's cause for concern. This was rapidly followed by a more practical response. He called Leon to the study one evening and described to him the effect of syphilis and attendant diseases of the skin. He spoke of paralysis, blindness, softening of the brain, insanity and worse. He showed horrific pictures in a medical book. Leon was appalled by the weeping sores, the hairlessness, the tumor-like gummata, and for a month had graphic nightmares. He could not reconcile so abominable a penalty with so sweet a sin. For that month he was chaste. He had promised Sandor that he would never seek the favours of a prostitute, and he was scrupulously honest. Instead he took the first of a series of mistresses.

Leon Salaman had just begun to read mathematics and economics at the university, and for the first time had a small income. Although he was still not his own man—he continued to live at home, like his contemporaries and his elder brother—he now enjoyed a freedom of movement he had never had before. It was possible to miss the odd lecture, make assignations for meetings when he should be studying. So Sandor was satisfied for a few years. By the time he realised what kind of a man Leon had become, it was all too evident that he could not change him.

Leon Salaman had an insatiable sexual appetite. He wanted women, he needed them, he desired them. And he attracted them. He had only to walk into a room and stand still as only he could, taut with restrained male energy, and it was as if he gave off some scent that warned them of his presence. He disturbed women, they became agitated and fussed over their clothes, smoothed their hair, broke off their conversations with distracted expressions and nervous little laughs. They would try to act as though unaware of his presence, but the sidelong glances they risked showed their acute consciousness of him. They responded to his looks, to that brooding air that made them long to console him; to the black hair that would crisp beneath their fingers and the broad back that would be sleek under their hands. Above all, they were drawn by the way he watched them with intensity and absorption, and a touch of amusement . . . and knowledge. They sensed instinctively that nothing could be withheld from him, for there was no desire he could not rouse and slake.

During his university years Leon Salaman had many acquaintances among the elite of the new Vienna: the youths who would be the lawyers and physicians, the scientists and professors of the future. With them, in the evenings, he would frequent coffee-houses and taverns, to drink absinthe, or go to cafés where they played cards and billiards.

Few of them, though, became close friends, for Leon Salaman was not a man who required friendship. As his prowess with women became notorious, he elicited from his contemporaries either joking admiration

114

("Salaman," observed one wryly, "evidently possesses the penis of a god.") or aversion. The latter would watch with contempt as yet another woman eyed him covetously, and would have been hard put to it to say whether they felt nervousness or envy for him.

But like all men who service many women, Leon Salaman did not really like them. "No woman," he remarked sadly, "is capable of intimacy." He could not see that his own behaviour precluded this: that his challenging, aggressive manner towards them put them always on their guard. Had they felt secure, certain of him, they would have responded and taught him what he still did not know: that men and women could be linked by bonds closer even than those of the flesh.

By the time he was twenty-seven, Leon Salaman had established a style of life which, if it did not totally satisfy, at any rate suited him. He lived in his father's apartment, the two of them maintaining their own privacy, and also kept a couple of rooms in the Bohemian area near the Café Central.

He was doing reasonably well at the bank, while not, in his father's opinion, fulfilling the promise of his university days. It seemed that he was a brilliant theoretician who lacked the ability to put his ideas into practice. He did not possess the infallible instinct for political nuance, for shifts of tension and power, which had earned his father the description, voiced by Baron Albert Rothschild, of being "one of God's bankers".

Even so, he was far more adept with figures than his brother Friedrich, who by now had returned to the university and his chemistry. He had voluntarily ceded his position in the bank to Leon, saying jocularly that in exchange, all he wanted was a promise that Leon would always pay for any book he needed to buy. In fact, the bank continued to give Friedrich an income. He was three years older than Leon, and when he reached his thirtieth birthday Sandor had to concede reluctantly that his elder son required his own establishment. Friedrich bought an apartment on the nearby Circusgasse.

The two brothers were exceedingly close despite the differences in temperament. Friedrich was quieter, thinner, less defined than Leon; his voice lighter, his hair brown where Leon's was black, his eyes blue and quizzical instead of his sibling's dark and melancholy gaze. Despite the colouring, they looked alike and were clearly brothers. They gave the curious impression that Friedrich was the sketch, Leon the painting.

Friedrich regarded Leon's sexual proclivities with a mixture of despair and awe. He had himself, from the age of twenty-two, been engaged for three years to a charming girl of good family for whom he felt deep affection. She had died of complications following an ear infection, and he had been inconsolable. Friedrich had had intercourse perhaps a dozen times in his life, though naturally never with his fiancée. He had enjoyed

115

the experience but it had not shaken him to the depths as it had Leon. He was afraid, too, of infection. (It had been Friedrich who, when his own warnings fell on deaf ears, persuaded his father to talk to Leon when he was eighteen). Friedrich had always been more interested in his mental than his physical state. He intended to marry some time but had refused several suitable partners over the years. At present, his work was the most pressing interest in his life.

So when Jacob Radin approached Sandor Salaman with the suggestion—put forward with carefully concealed trepidation—that they should arrange a match between Adele and Leon, the banker discussed it in confidence with his elder son. Friedrich was enthusiastic, seeing it as the only solution to Leon's philanderings and their possibly disastrous outcome. Sandor was less sanguine, but he too hoped against hope that a pretty, home-loving, Jewish wife would give Leon stability. He urged the match upon Leon, painting a picture of domesticity and the probability of heirs.

Leon's first reaction was a smiling refusal: he lacked nothing, why would he want a wife? But Sandor persisted, and Friedrich added his voice. Leon was influenced despite himself: he rather liked the new conception of the seducer as a patrician, appearing in public with a well-dressed wife upon his arm, tyrannising his numerous children . . . Then, too, there was the very real consideration that it was what his father wanted.

Leon Salaman had gone through a period in his late adolescence when he hated Sandor. Or rather he hated what he was: a man of commerce, belonging to richly furnished rooms, poring over columns of figures, fond of cigars and good wines—and, above all, a Jew. That was when Leon, conscious suddenly that he and Friedrich were the butt of derision from the professors at the Akademische Gymnasium because of their father's religion, desired nothing but to be like his uncles, with their captain's uniforms, their glossy boots, their horses and dogs and women, and their impeccable if impoverished lineage, aristocratic and Aryan.

As he grew older, Leon saw the von Saar twins differently. Saw them in fact, as Friedrich had always done, as swaggering braggarts. He acquired new admiration for Sandor, who had never admonished him for his lack of filial respect, but merely waited for him to recover his perspective. Leon in his twenties saw that his father was a man of remarkable talent, a self-made man. But beyond that, he recognised for the first time the strength of Sandor's character: he could watch his son's defection with pain yet bear no resentment, comprehending completely the misery of a youth torn between Christian and Jew, between the old Vienna and the new.

With this knowledge of his father came the desire to please him, and

116

this finally made him agree to the match with Adele. It was arranged that she and her parents would dine with them in Vienna before any commitment was made: Leon found her agreeable enough, with her plump white arms and soft bosom, her open, candid face. The engagement was planned and took place in Hamburg. It was then that Leon began to feel deep disquiet. It had been one thing to meet Adele and her father in the setting of the Viennese apartment. It was another to go to the Fasanenstrasse, to that stuffy, middle-class, over-furnished room with its horsehair and woolwork; to meet the well-fed family, the numerous relatives, to listen to the talk of weddings and dowries, of clothes and houses.

What had shocked him most of all was that much of the conversation had been in Yiddish. Even Sandor had looked nonplussed. Though he could speak it—it had been the language of his childhood—he very rarely did so. In their circle, it was simply not used. Yet here were all these people, who seemed to him to be shouting at the tops of their voices, gesticulating and interrupting each other, and Leon could scarcely begin to follow what they said.

On the journey back to Vienna the next day, Leon had been sunk in thought. On the second day after their return he waited two hours after his usual time of leaving for Sandor to conclude his business at the bank. Sandor's new motor-car drove him to the bank, but he preferred to walk home: it was the only exercise he took and it refreshed him to pace the damp streets and shed the day's anxieties. But that night, walking home with Leon, he had listened with increasing dismay as his son told him that he could not go ahead with the marriage.

"I'm sorry. I'm *sorry*. But I cannot tolerate those people."

Sandor had remonstrated.

"It is the daughter you are marrying, not the parents."

Leon had rounded on him.

"But don't you see, Papa? She is like them. In a dozen years she will be a replica of her mother! Better looking, I grant you, and better dressed because I'd see to that! But with the same values, the same attitudes, the same ideas."

Sandor had sighed.

"I hate to think how unhappy it will make Adele, to break off this match now. She has her heart on her sleeve for you, no?"

Leon had shaken his head in frustration. "I know. I *know*. But what am I to do? I swear I did not realise how it would be, what sort of people they were . . ." he shot a sudden sharp glance at his father, "and nor did you. Am I right?"

Sandor had answered heavily. "I had been a little afraid. But I did not listen to my apprehensions, because I thought this match would be a good

117

one for you. She is a lovely girl. Don't throw her away because you think she is beneath you."

"Not beneath me. Just different from me. From us." They had been silent for a while, as they walked along Franz-Josefs-Kai. Then Leon had burst out: "You haven't forced Friedrich into matrimony, and he is older than me. I don't want to go against your wishes, but I cannot contemplate the rest of my life with this unsophisticated little girl from Hamburg."

Sandor had stopped walking, and leant upon his gold-topped cane. For a moment he looked like a stooped old man. "Where is the woman you *could* marry, eh? Does she exist, the one who could suit you? I very much doubt it."

Leon, who had just seen Salka so briefly for the second time, had judged this an inappropriate moment and had not answered. Two days later, Sandor had written to Jacob Radin. It had been a long, apologetic letter. In it, he explained that perhaps he had presumed in pressurising his son towards the marriage he himself desired. He begged the forgiveness of the Radin family and Adele in particular. Privately, in a separate note, he added a postscript to Jacob. It accompanied a draft for a substantial sum to be added to Adele's future dowry.

I believe you will understand when I tell you that I cannot stand upon my dignity and command my son to carry out my wishes. He and Friedrich are all that I have. If I try hard to be indulgent now, it is because I bitterly regret the years of their childhood when I was too unhappy myself to see their small sorrows.

After that, the matter was dropped by the Salamans. Sandor, informed by Jacob when Adele married, told Leon what had taken place. Leon nodded, but did not enquire who the man was. Sandor sent a handsome gift, an art nouveau vase of burnt umber glass. Tactfully, only his own name was on the card.

Life continued in the Praterstrasse apartment without event, until Friedrich called in one evening gaunt and harassed: a friend of his, a manufacturer with whom he had been at university, had died. Thirty-one years old, said Friedrich bitterly. A talented Alpine climber, skater and fencer—and dead in an asylum. He lifted his head and stared at his brother's half-turned back as he poured brandy.

"It might have been you," he had said, hoarsely. "It could as well have been you."

He did not need to say any more: Leon knew the man. One memorable evening he had been seen at Leidinger's, drinking his way through two bottles of champagne to help him recover from the effort of having made love six times during the afternoon.

Bullied by Friedrich, Sandor diffidently broached with Leon the subject of matrimony once again. This time, Leon was ready. He had decided on a wife, he said. He hoped Sandor would consider her suitable. At first, Sandor felt nothing but relief that it was a Jewish girl his son wanted, when he had feared it might have been some little milliner or even chorus girl. It would be difficult to approach Radin again, certainly, but still . . .

It was only when Sandor Salaman learned more about Salka, learned about her Russian background, that he conceived his violent antipathy towards her. She thought it was because he also regarded her as *Ostjude*: a ghetto Jew.

It was a long time before she found out how wrong she was.

Chapter 11

Every day at eight sharp Dieter Stüdler rang the bell of the Praterstrasse apartment. Every day, including Sundays, he would be greeted by one of the maids and make his way to a dressing-room set aside expressly for his own use. He was a barber, with his own flourishing business nearby, but summer or winter, he never missed his appointment at the Salaman household.

Stüdler removed his hat and coat, carefully smoothed the grey wings of hair that were now all that was left to him, and laid out his instruments on a clean white cloth: the folding, straight-edged razor with its ivory handle that fitted so comfortably into his palm after fifty years of use; the helmet-shaped pewter bowl in which he worked up a stiff lather; the three pairs of scissors.

He always shaved Herr Salaman first, the young gentleman being one for rising later. Though with *his* money—Stüdler gave the razor an extra honing on the leather strop as he thought this—he'd not open the curtains till gone midday, and be damned.

When Leon finally took his place in the chair he seemed morose, merely grunting his "*guten Tag*" and making no comment as Stüdler lathered him up with the soft badger's-hair brush. The barber hid his smile. So disgruntled, and with a new little wife such as he had . . . some people were never content.

Under his well-trained hands, Leon relaxed. He enjoyed the lathering and shaving, the snipping and clipping of his beard. He could positively feel the tension going out of his shoulders and neck as the familiar hands massaged his jowls. He began to think about Salka. His mind had shied away from thoughts of her this morning. He supposed it was because she always managed to disturb him, and he was not accustomed to a woman having any such effect.

He closed his eyes under the pleasurable sensation as old Stüdler pressed hot towels over his face. Normally he drifted into a light doze at this point, but today his mind was too alert—uncomfortably so. He felt—and it was not an emotion with which he was familiar—bewildered.

Leon Salaman could not, at that precise moment, have explained why it was that he had chosen to marry Salka Radin. He could, after all, have had his pick of young women in Vienna. The Salamans were one of the ranking Jewish families. His own profligate behaviour would have been no problem, though he supposed any prospective father-in-law might have frowned upon it after the marriage.

It was one of Salka's virtues that her parents were so far away and her nearest family merely a second cousin in Hamburg. But he knew that had not mattered. From the moment he had spied her in that old-fashioned white blouse of hers at the racecourse, standing with her back turned to him, so absorbed and self-sufficient, he had been on his mettle. When she spoke, in that dusky voice with the break in it that was peculiarly inviting, and looked at him with those stormy golden eyes, he had wanted her. To find her again like that, in his fiancée's house, had seemed a sort of omen, and one that could not be disregarded.

He recognised the effect she had on him but not the reason for it. Due to circumstance, only his mother's Aryan family were known to him. Sandor rarely referred to his own parents or his Russian background, so that despite their name, Friedrich and Leon did not consider themselves part of that line. It was not a conscious rejection, merely that Sandor had chosen not to present them with their patrimony. In marrying Anna von Saar he had allowed himself to drift even further from his roots, not because of embarrassment at the disparity between his background and that of his wife, but out of his great love for her. He did not want there to be differences between himself and Anna; he desired only similarities and cohesion.

As a result, Leon had grown up a Jew in name only, unaware of his heritage. Then Salka, with her sensuous, Semitic features, her hair as dark as his, the Russian still sounding in her voice, touched in him a blood-memory too deep for understanding to reach.

The towels were off now, and Stüdler had opened the boxwood case and brought out a bottle of blue lotion which he poured into the palms of his hands and then applied with brisk pats. Leon preened himself under the barber's ministrations and went on with his thoughts.

If he were forced to say what it was about her that made him determine on marriage, he supposed it was the fact that she so very evidently didn't want him. Not that she was unresponsive: he knew from her look and that breathless little sound she'd made at the Freudenau just what an impact he'd had on her. But she didn't want him anyway. That had surprised him. He was used to women who walked away and trailed their glances invitingly after them, transparent as dropped veils; or girls like poor Adele, who'd so clearly thought he was wonderful and would probably never have questioned her first impressions.

But Salka intrigued him. He had meant it when he put that note on the box of sweetmeats in Baden-Baden. *I did not know my heart had any door until you opened it.* Perhaps, for the first time, he would find whatever it was he searched for. Certainly no other Jewish girl had ever aroused his interest as she had done. She was entirely different from the indulged and pampered young women he met socially in Vienna. Safely chaperoned, kept in ignorance, trained to comply and obey: there would be no challenge, no excitement, no vibrancy in such a marriage.

It was marriage, then, that he had chosen. Leon was no fool and he knew well enough the price a man could expect to pay in the end for the sort of life he led. He wanted a wife for many reasons, most of them selfish: because his father desired it, and as emotional ballast; to satisfy a need he felt now for children, and to prove to the world that he was a solid figure capable of shouldering responsibilities and inspiring love.

Leon had never considered the feelings of any woman, and he did not do so now. The marriage was arranged without reference to Salka and he assumed she would be as eager for him as all the other women were: how could it be otherwise? He had decided he would love her, would even give up little Greta for her sake. All these good intentions had been shattered by his Russian bride (and Leon gritted his teeth at the recollection, so that old Stüdler felt the grimace beneath his fingers).

Salka had rejected him fiercely even in her delirium, had shrieked out her rebuttal of him. It had been a public humiliation, and it had wounded Leon deeply. He had become stiff and angry, cold in his pride and distant, determined to make her as unhappy as she had made him. But yesterday, seeing her laughing like that in Friedrich's company, animated as she never was in his presence, he had felt a mixture of jealousy and lust. What had happened in the late afternoon was calculated. His self-esteem required that she should acknowledge desire for him—and he knew, none better, how to waken desire.

Stüdler had nearly finished: he was opening the white box of pomade, which he applied lightly to Leon's beard to keep it in place. Then he whipped off the protective towel and flicked his brush over the suit collar and shoulders. Leon thanked him, examining his reflection critically. He made his way toward the hallway, patting his pockets to check his watch, his chased silver matchbox on its chain.

In the hallway, he noted that, as usual, his father's hat and coat had gone. Sandor left punctually at 7.30 a.m. and arrived at the bank before any of his employees. Leon smiled to himself, remembering how a friend of his father's, the banker Max Warburg, used to admonish Sandor for this. "Betrays your origins, my dear fellow," he would say. "Shows you're a peasant. Now when I worked in London, as a young man, Lord Rothschild didn't arrive at New Court until mid-morning. 'A perfect gentleman never comes to the office before ten o'clock in the morning. Or stays after four in the afternoon.' That's what he always said."

During the retailing of this story, Sandor would listen attentively. Then he would wink at Leon and Friedrich. All of them knew that Max Warburg worked prodigious hours—but not as long as Sandor's.

Leon buttoned his coat and adjusted the white silk scarf at his throat. As he did so, he leaned his silver-headed cane against the Chinese jardinière, with its myriad of scarlet tulips made of porcelain so fine the flowers moved on their slender stems at the slightest draught. He had been fascinated by this phenomenon as a child, and would touch it surreptitiously when no one was about. He did so now, with the old feeling of daring. Then he noticed, among the luxuriant green ferns the jardinière held, something dark and glossy. Curious, he investigated further. And brought out two soft little leather gloves. Salka's. She was always doing that.

He held them for a moment, reflectively smoothing the creased kid, full of tenderness, the way he might have felt for a child. After all, this was all his doing. He had found her, chosen her, brought her to Vienna. She had no family here, no parents or friends, and she was his. She might reject him, but in the end she would have to accept him, for he was all she had. She had no protector, no defence, no recourse but him.

Leon let himself out and set off briskly across town. He found he was humming the overture from *William Tell*, and was surprised how light-hearted he felt.

Salka read the words on the menu before her. *Bauernschmaus. Backhuhn. Rotkraut.*

It was New Year's Day. For the first time, Leon had taken her out, visiting his married friends with gifts and cards. They had driven out to a white villa in the elegant suburb of Grinzing, to a town house on the Kärntnerring, to an apartment in Pasqualatihaus, in the queer old quarter near the University. Salka had been introduced to a dozen friends and acquaintances of Leon's, and twice as many of their children, to whom she had given boxes of sweets.

She had never seen Leon like this, charming and slightly garrulous; she had not imagined him capable of such informal behaviour. Then he had ordered the motor to take them to Leidinger's, where they now sat. Moreover, he had clearly planned this in advance, for the *Ober* had immediately conducted them to what was almost a small room on its own at the back of the restaurant, where they sat in a deep recess hung with curtains, able to watch the other diners but almost unseen themselves.

Salka had spoken scarcely at all during the afternoon, but had been content to nod and smile and respond briefly when spoken to. Reticence in a young bride was not only permissible but desirable, since it gave other ladies the chance to dispense advice and exhibit their homes. Only one of the older women, wife to a physician, had seen the bleakness in the girl's eyes when she thought no one was watching her.

She sat now looking at the menu listing dishes she did not want to eat. More than ever, she was confused by Leon, by his switches in mood. Yesterday, after the incident on the Riesenrad, he had been coldly angry and then, suddenly and inexplicably, had rushed her back to the apartment and her bedroom. What had happened then she did not want to even think about, but Leon had been affectionate. *My little peasant.*

She studied him surreptitiously while he read the menu: the rather heavy, masculine features beneath the thick dark hair with the little flecks of silver she noticed for the first time. Absently, he raised a hand to adjust his tight collar, a broad hand with square nails, and Salka flinched, remembering the reluctant and perverse pleasure he had given her the evening before.

He said, without looking up, "What will you have? The roast quail and snipe are excellent." He waited a moment, then added, "They're game birds. Very good."

Salka flushed. She had not known what they were, but hoped to conceal her ignorance—though it seemed impossible to keep anything from Leon. Only yesterday, she had believed that if she tried hard enough, their marriage would be a real relationship, not something that existed in name only. But Leon seemed to delight in making her feel totally inadequate, as though she did not know *anything*. Furious with herself and him, she ordered a chicken dish and excused herself. Upstairs she washed her hands, splashed cold water on her hot face and smoothed her hair. When she felt calmer, she returned to the dining-room and the odd little curtained room Leon had called a "*cabinet particulier*". He'd said they were a speciality of Leidinger's, and had laughed when she asked why. Now, she realised there were three or four such alcoves, and she couldn't be sure which was theirs. She hesitated, looking about for a waiter to ask, but none was in sight, and she became suddenly self-conscious about diners at other tables. Hurriedly, she pulled open a door and took a step forward.

In the same instant she realised it was the wrong alcove and saw that a man and a woman were inside. On the table were the remains of a meal: napkins thrown down, glasses of liqueur and wine unfinished. The chairs were pushed aside and in the dim light Salka received a confused impression of two tumbled bodies on the studio bed. She whispered an apology and stepped back hurriedly, but not before she caught soft groans and panting she would rather not have heard, glimpsed what she would have preferred not to see: the woman naked to the waist under her hastily pushed up skirts, bare legs twined over the back of the man who bent over her, *into* her, moving up and down and up . . . Salka closed the door and stood in the space between it and the heavy velvet curtain, in the merciful dark, her breathing as loud and irregular as theirs.

She felt revulsion and relief: *that's* how it is. Everything she'd heard and been told made sense now. Magda's ill-defined injunctions concerning duty and marital rites, Adele's murmuring about pleasure, and something Frau Holz had let fall one day in the kitchen as she muttered sullenly to herself about the hapless Walter. "Making the beast with two backs," Salka thought she'd said, only it had meant nothing at the time.

Salka pressed her forehead against the panel of the door and tried to order her thoughts. Why had Leon not even attempted this with her last evening? Perhaps she had done or said something quite wrong, something that betrayed her ignorance again. And why had he brought her here, to a place like this? She was quite sure that the couple she had just witnessed were not married. It was a place for assignations, for liaisons, for the kind of life she and Adele had so fearfully supposed that Leon Salaman led.

"Salka."

It was Leon, behind her. She took a deep breath and turned.

"I thought you'd got lost . . . did you mistake the room?" She nodded and pushed past him. He followed her next door, a faint smile growing on his face. "Why so angry?"

"Why not?"

He shrugged. "I imagine from the reaction that you glimpsed somebody engaged in amorous activity. One should never open strange doors."

"Obviously it was a mistake. I did not think that people would behave so in a public place." She felt herself growing more and more angry, the old familiar anger that she knew how to use. "I should not have thought any respectable person"—she fairly spat this out—"would have brought his wife to such a, such a . . ."

"Den of iniquity," he supplied, but she swept it aside.

"I have done everything I can. I apologised for what I said to you in my delirium. I have tried to behave properly. But you mock me and laugh at me and make me feel an imbecile." She stopped, breathless, and found she was crying tears of rage. She smudged them from her cheeks roughly with the back of her hand.

"Leidinger's is an excellent restaurant, as it happens." Leon spoke absently, an odd expression on his face. He had never seen anyone cry like that, the tears welling and falling but without any contortion of her face. They formed and fell and rolled down her cheeks as though she were crying rain.

He put out a tentative hand and touched the side of her face where the skin was wet. Then, very slowly, he put his fingers to his lips and tasted her tears.

125

When he did that, she felt as though her heart turned over, so physical was the impact of his gesture upon her.

She stood absolutely still, her eyes blurred.

She remembered his fingers enclosing her ankle outside the hotel in Baden-Baden, and the secretive caresses of the previous evening. She thought of the couple in the adjoining room in their heedless embrace, and desire moved in her, a dark animal stretching itself in a hidden cave. She could have opened her mouth and wailed aloud, like the mating cats she used to hear prowling the walls of the Fasanenstrasse in the early hours.

Leon watched her with that brooding intensity she found so disturbing, and needed no words to understand. He did not touch her. He rang for the *Ober* and paid for the meal they were not going to eat. Hats, coats, and they were in a cab. He sat on one side, she on the other, separate.

"Are we going home?" Her voice more hoarse than ever from her tears.

"No."

He took her to the apartment he kept near the Café Central.

She scarcely noticed where they were: the trim entrance marked No. 28, the stables on either side, the narrow staircase, the little door at the top leading into the chilly two-roomed apartment. The salon smelled oppressive, unused, with the windows firmly closed behind their heavy curtains. Salka did not ask why he kept the apartment, or how often he visited it. She did not, at that moment, care.

White with hunger and apprehension she took off her coat and waited as Leon turned on lamps. Through the doorway she saw the bedroom, and a divan covered with a cream spread of crocheted lace . . . . It was scratchy under her hand, that lace, as she sat and watched Leon unbuttoning his jacket, and its feel reminded her of the white broderie anglaise blouse that also scratched her skin.

The room was warming up as the gas fire turned from blue flames to lilac pink, and she began to relax as the heat reached her. The only light came from the hissing gas-jets and the open door. In the shadowed room, Leon methodically emptied his pockets, placing his watch and chain, his match-case and leather cigar-holder, carefully on a table. He removed his shoes and stockings, then undid his braces.

When he turned towards her she felt for an instant afraid, for she had never seen a man's body before, and she was grateful for the concealing shadows. It was with amazement she discovered how beautiful he was— more beautiful than the statue that had so moved her in the Belvedere garden—his chest lightly fuzzed with dark hair, the smooth olive skin of his arms, the narrow hips and shapely legs. Naked, he looked taller and moved differently out of his stiff formal clothes, so that he seemed younger and less intimidating. He was quite unselfconscious, he knew how he looked, and it occurred to Salka that many women must have seen him like this, waited for him like this.

He crossed the room.

"Let me into bed. It's cold."

She stood and pulled off the lace, bundling it on to a chair.

"Now you," he said.

Salka hesitated. She glanced round the room and saw the wash-basin behind a screen. She undressed there, carelessly dropping her clothes on the floor in her haste. She left on her chemise for modesty and stood for a moment, shivering. There was a mirror on the bureau next to the water-jug and basin but she had no need, this time, to search the silver recesses of the glass for a face other than her own. She pulled the amber combs from her hair and it fell around her shoulders.

Leon held back the quilt for her and without a word she got in beside him. She felt light-headed from the Madeira she had sipped during their afternoon visits and the bed was freezing. A foot briefly touched hers.

"You're like ice. My icy little Russian." Leon's voice had assumed that disquieting intimacy and she tensed.

He felt her movement, reached out an arm to pull her close.

"I'll make you warm. *Kleine Russin*." He had turned his head, and breathed the words into her throat. "I'll make you warm."

He held her to his chest so she felt his heart thudding beneath her arm. He held her for a long time, rubbing her cold feet with his own, until she warmed and softened against him. All her anger and antagonism dissolved and disappeared, all her uncertainty was lulled by this new, gentler Leon.

Very delicately his hand on her back traced the spine down to the curve of the buttocks. She stiffened but, undeterred, he smoothed her skin until she relaxed again, mesmerised by his caresses. He started to move his chest against hers, brushing against her breasts until the little ends stood up. He touched one, hesitantly at first, then with assurance; he rolled the nipple between his fingers until she wanted to protest. But even to her ears the groan she uttered sounded like assent. Then it *was* assent, and her insides were dissolving like sugar. He sensed the change, and moved back a little. He weighed her breasts in his hands, and murmured swift words as he had the previous evening. Only this time she did not want him to stop, because the words were about her, and what he was doing to her. He had his right thigh over hers and she felt a stirring there, where she had not wanted to look. He pulled her hand from the back of his neck and guided it down, tugging when she resisted, and placed it on that part of himself that was lifting and moving blindly.

"Hold it," he whispered. "Stroke it."

She obeyed, and to her wonderment her shrinking touch found him

127

silky warm and unbelievably smooth. As she circled him with her fingers she could feel his excitement growing. His fingers were tangled in her hair and he pulled her head down so he could reach her lips. He kissed her, and his mouth was hard. It moved to her throat, her shoulder and further yet, a nipping, sucking mouth she could not evade, that made Leon at once child and lover, that made her writhe and cry out in a voice rasped with pleasure and pain.

Even in her confusion, Salka was aware how Leon matched his responses to her own, how every move complemented hers so that, gauche and unaccustomed as she was, her movements melded with his in absolute harmony. Almost beyond thought now, it came to her with sudden clarity that discord with Leon lay in discussion. Like this, in bed, where words were only tiny instruments to further delight, his body was articulate and expert, guiding hers so that she also became fluent in this new language.

He shifted his weight so that he lay full upon her. "Now," he said, quick and urgent. "Open your legs."

She let her thighs fall apart and he fumbled for an instant. Then she felt it, that smooth part of him, hard now and determined, pushing its way into her, invading her, transfixing her, hurting her so that her hands on his back clawed into that smooth olive skin which clung so tightly to his bones and sinews.

In answer, as though she had spoken aloud, he freed one of his arms and showed her how to move her legs, settling them around his waist. She thought of the couple in the *cabinet particulier* and imitated the woman, clasping her ankles together for support. When she did that, Leon moved more strongly and she held her breath as he forged deeper inside her, and then withdrew silently for the next stroke.

After a little while—something odd had happened to time—she became accustomed to the rhythm of his movements and even began to like the sensation, which was acute and made her breathing jerky, but which she found hard to equate with the words she had read in books. Was this ardour, then? Was this passion? She craned to look at Leon's face and in the faint gaslight saw it was closed, intent, voluptuous. He seemed to have forgotten her entirely, though considering what he was doing, she didn't see how this could be.

He was moving faster now, harder, his body slamming into hers and hurting her. She tried to push him away, make him stop, but that only seemed to make him more determined. Just when it seemed to be almost unbearable, he arched his torso away from her and his whole body stiffened as he threw back his head with a harsh, choking cry as though he were in pain.

Alarmed, she kept absolutely still. She could feel his tremors somewhere

128

deep inside her as he succumbed alone to some ecstasy she could not share. He gave a deep sigh and collapsed on to the pillow beside her. He did not speak, and after a short time seemed to be asleep.

The covers had slipped off and she was cold; as she squirmed to free herself their skins stuck together with a faint slippery sound. Her struggles roused Leon. He opened his eyes and smiled, a slow, sated, sensual smile. He reached down and pulled up the quilt over both their heads, and lay back with his cheek on the tangled mass of her hair. He murmured, "Go to sleep," and because he was still inside her his voice reverberated softly through her body.

Salka lay entwined with him in the darkness, hearing his deep, even breathing. She lay submissively, in the attitude of sleep, feeling his weight on her arm, his face on her hair, her thigh aching under his. Her mind whirled and darted, a moth dancing to a flame, until she thought her head would burst with her thoughts.

She had seen Leon's face as he reached the climax of possession and he had been unknowable, caught up in a rapture she had not shared. She had not felt even that shamed intoxication he had given her in so calculated a fashion the previous evening. Therefore, since she had not experienced this mysterious emotion, she supposed she did not love him.

In two nights, Leon had begun to teach her what her body had been seeking for a long time, and she realised that for the rest of her life she would be burdened by the demands and mysteries of the flesh. Salka neither welcomed nor resented this realisation. Women were subject to the physical as men could never be, receptacles for conceiving and carrying, bearing and rearing. She accepted the fact without question . . . and she accepted Leon. He was her husband, and they would live together. She thought, lying in that warm bed, that she could be married to Leon and still remain free.

But love came in its own time, treacherously.

Chapter 12

One morning, Salka found a hidden room.

The February day was grey and wild; gusts of rain spattered the drawing-room windows and she could see people clutching their hats and coats as the wind bowled them along Praterstrasse. She drew the morning-gown she wore higher round her throat, and gave a little shiver of pleasure at being inside in the warmth. Turning to go back to her own rooms, she noticed that one of the velvet drapes on the far wall had been pulled aside, revealing a door she had not seen before.

It must be some sort of cupboard, she thought, and on an impulse crossed the room and opened it. The room beyond was small and prettily proportioned, with two arched windows: it was papered in pale greens and yellows with a faint art nouveau pattern like an elongated lily embossed on what looked like silk.

On an impulse she went in and shut the door behind her with something like awe. It was not simply that she had never suspected there was another room in the already vast apartment, but that this was utterly different. In those first moments she could almost have believed herself in a garden. Everywhere she looked there were fragile blossoms. They wreathed round looking-glasses, entwined candlesticks and picture-frames, ran riot over the small chandelier. Pale pinks and blues, subtle greens and gold; lilac, lavender, lemon, lime.

She thought at first they must be of spun sugar. Then she noticed that the walnut cabinets with glass fronts against the walls contained yet more of these exquisite confections. Of course, they were Dresden porcelain. Ethereal shepherdesses in mob-caps, their skirts edged with lace frothy as foam, flirted with curly-haired swains in peach-coloured ruffles. On an occasional table a tea-service in the same colours stood on a silver tray. Beside them a matching vase held a bunch of small white flowers.

Very carefully, feeling that a hasty movement might shatter something, Salka walked to the table and picked up the flowers. They were yellowing slightly and gave off the melancholy perfume of decay. Then she knew what the room reminded her of. It was a shrine, like the roadside niches in Russia where a painted icon would show a smiling woman with a child, a candle lit before it and a field posy. But a shrine to what? She stared around her again.

At the farthest end of the room, between the two windows, hung an oil-painting in an oval mahogany frame set against black velvet. It was of a woman in her early thirties, wearing a dress of unfamiliar cut, with a fluted collar. Her pale-gold hair was elaborately styled: parted in the centre and pulled back into a high chignon. The artist had posed her so that she looked out of the painting over one shoulder, slightly askance. It could have been coy, but the green eyes were veiled and imperious; the tilt of the head challenged the watcher.

Of course, she was Leon's mother. It was not his face, for it was Friedrich she could see when she looked at the painted features. But the expression was unmistakable. Sandor Salaman's wife. This must have been her sitting-room, and all this priceless china would have been given by Sandor. How he must have loved her, to keep the room like this.

Salka stood in the centre of that amazing room and felt ashamed. She saw for the first time that something tragic must have happened for this woman—who would have been her mother-in-law—to have died so young. She had come into this apartment—*her* apartment—and scarcely thought of its previous occupant. She had once asked Leon about his mother, but he had answered abruptly and she had let the matter drop. In all these months it had not occurred to her that it must be hard for Sandor, to see her virtually in his dead wife's place. Perhaps that explained his dislike of her?

Salka twirled the slender vase reflectively between the palms of her hands. She must have seemed totally unfeeling to Sandor. Only he had given her no opening for any personal conversation at all: he did not seem to want to hear anything she might have to say. She sighed, and put down the flowers. He had appeared to her remote and severe, an ageing man who cared only for his bank. But this silent room, pathetic and poignant, spoke of another Sandor, who still cherished a woman long dead.

Salka closed the door softly behind her, not to disturb the memories.

Gradually, Salka and Leon settled into a pattern of life which, if it was not on her part ecstatically happy, was at least harmonious. She was still wary of him, still intimidated by his worldliness, his mocking expression, his sarcasm. She felt sometimes that she woke each day to a hazardous new venture, an uncharted path that could safely be negotiated only if she used all her care and cunning.

The nights were different. Then Leon wooed her with his lips, his hands and his body. He possessed her completely, but she did not trust him. He lavished on her all his experience, all his expertise, and she knew he had used these arts on many other women. Her innocence aroused him more than coquetry could have done; he exhausted and extinguished himself in her, then buried his face in the black undulations of her hair.

Salka responded to him because it was impossible to resist his desire and

131

his violence, the pleasure and pain he brought her. She was discovering in herself a disturbing sensuality. She craved his caresses, she implored him with her eyes, she could have wept for wanting him, and the things they did together wove a dark enchantment.

But in the cool light of morning, she blushed at the tumbled white expanse of their bed, and smoothed away with a hasty hand the tell-tale signs before anyone could see. She braided her hair tightly and appeared before her husband once more cool, quiet and aloof, her own woman.

Leon, who had left her sprawled asleep in sheets redolent of their night, satisfied that now she would be like all the others, tamed and gentled, watching him anxiously, eager for his approbation, was bewildered by her apparent duplicity, and even more determined to make her wholly his in the only way he knew.

Every night Salka surrendered to him . . . and every morning she evaded him. If she had been an experienced woman cleverly plotting to enslave a man, she could not have succeeded better.

For the truth was, Leon was a predator. He was strong and fierce, and thought only of himself and his need. What he wanted he took, and he had taken Salka. He had thought, at the beginning, that because she was young, unformed, innocent and, above all, an alien in a strange country, he could subjugate her as he had all the others, so that they were besotted by him and bereft when he left them. What he did not see was that the women he had chosen in the past were no match for him. They had been chorus girls, milliners, the wives of minor civil servants, pretty, empty-headed and flirtatious, who entered upon affairs expecting them to be as light and frothy as Viennese pâtisseries, and discovered too late that they were victims of a man who desired them but did not particularly like them.

True to his nature, Leon, like any predator, relished the chase at least as much as, and probably more than, the capture. The swift appraising glances, the conversation full of innuendo, the little gifts of flowers and chocolate, the hasty meetings . . . Leon would prolong the delightful preliminaries, consciously putting off for as long as possible the inevitable moment when the woman who had seemed so different, so charming and, above all, so unknown, would take off her clothes and lie down for him, becoming just like all the others.

How well he knew the flat despair that enveloped him once the climax of possession had subsided, and he lay in silence while the woman by his side, smug in her satisfaction, chattered happily. There would be other meetings, other hours on the divan in his rooms, but, lacking the spice of anticipation, they did not retain the savour of the first days and quite soon the affair would fade. The women were always hurt and bewildered, for he had pursued them with such determination and proved quite unmistakably his fervour for them. They could not be expected to understand that Leon found his image of them infinitely more provocative than the reality could ever be. They would invariably attempt to recapture his interest, sending letters (on paper smelling faintly of violet pastilles) first entreating him and, when that provoked no response, threatening suicide. The bolder ones would place themselves deliberately in his way in public places, but he was accustomed to that: he would be initially regretful and gentle then, if they persisted, smilingly insult them in his seductive voice.

Leon was aware of all the wiles women could wield and inured against them. So he was unprepared for Salka, who used none, and acted without premeditation. She had attracted him because she was so unlike all the others. Most of Leon's mistresses had been of a certain type: fair, fluffy creatures, curvaceous and graceful, with minds sufficiently sharp to bestow their pretty bodies to the best advantage.

Salka, in contrast, was as dark and intense as Leon himself, and he did not understand her. He mistook the stillness with which she hid her lack of assurance for passivity, and thought that since she spoke little she had nothing to say. Because her body yielded to his, compliant and biddable in the dark, he failed for a long time to notice that he succumbed alone to that final, shuddering ecstasy, leaving her lost somewhere in his wake. He did not know how to give her the rapture he felt, and the veiled gaze she turned on him afterwards seemed to be an accusation of his failure.

While she held back from him that final proof of his possession, while something in her eluded him, Leon felt the thrill and exhilaration of the chase. As long as she did not respond utterly to his body and his will, he wanted her.

When they had been married three months, Salka found she was carrying his child.

As the weather eased, Salka discovered another passion: Vienna. Each day she went a little further, and the city, initially hostile in its grandeur, its vast avenues and severely classic buildings, revealed unexpected pleasures.

At first she confined herself to Leopoldstadt, the district on the northern side of the Danube canal in which Praterstrasse and Taborstrasse were the main arteries. She chanced upon two synagogues, one in Tempelgasse and then another, the Synagogue of the Turkish Jews, situated in Circus-gasse, and found that this had been the Jewish quarter of Vienna since the seventeenth century.

She investigated the cobbled streets with the old ghetto houses, where the shop-signs read "Moritz Grünberg", "Rosenberg", "Winternitz"; where S. Scheim sat on the pavement waiting for custom, second-hand overcoats suspended from rails behind him, and D. Rumberger's hats were displayed outside his small shop in glass cases. Street traders, trays suspended round their necks on leather straps, hawked trinkets: ribbons and needles, cotton and sewing silk. Once, she came across a group of women, immigrants from Galicia by their dress, sifting through a heap of garments in a flea market. One of the women, no older than Salka, must have felt she was being watched and looked up, holding in her hand a pair of shabby shoes. Their eyes met, and the woman took in Salka's fashionable clothes, the close-fitting sealskin jacket and turban, the gloss of good grooming. Salka turned away with a pang, as though she felt again on her own feet the shapeless, bulky Russian shoes she had so hated when she saw Adele's black patent slippers.

Salka moved away from the crowded Jewish district and ventured as far as the suspension bridge, its buttresses adorned with statues, which crossed the canal to Schottenring. The following day took her along Franz-Josefs-Kai beside the canal to the Aspern-Brücke and thence to Ringstrasse: she found these two great streets girdled the Inner City and revelled in the spacious boulevards, the planned vistas.

She plucked up enough courage to travel on the electric tramway, squeezing her way into the crowded cars and occasionally travelling so far that the one she caught for the homeward journey would show the blue lamp signifying it was the last on the route that day. In this way, she discovered romantic old streets in the heart of the Inner City and the extraordinary fascination of Viennese baroque: the old houses which lined Annagasse and Johannesgasse; the masterpiece that was the Winter Palace of Prince Eugene in Himmelpfortgasse.

The tramway opened the city for Salka as nothing else could have done. She rarely took the one- and two-horse cabs, for eighty heller to go a short distance seemed to her excessive, and the taximeter cabs charged even more: two kreutzer for an hour-long journey. Leon made her a generous allowance and there was plenty now in her purse: bronze one- and two-heller pieces; ten and twenty heller in nickel; gulden, the gold florins now becoming rare. But she was unaccustomed to spending freely, and the habits of a lifetime were not broken in a few weeks. So it was by using public transport—which would have horrified Sandor and Leon— that she explored the shops of the Kohlmarkt, Graben, Kärntnerstrasse and Stephans-Platz. She looked at leathers in J. Weidmann on Babenbergerstrasse and admired the oriental carpets stocked by Haas and Sons on Stock-im-Eisen-Platz. She glanced briefly at the jewellery in Brandeis on Singerstrasse and lingered over portraits on porcelain at Rädler on Breitgasse. Ladies costumiers interested her—Seegold on Kärntnerring, Jungman and Nephew on Albrecht-Platz, but she bought nothing. She admired hats in Demelbauer on Singerstrasse and in the end purchased only a slim umbrella from Schaller.

Far more absorbing were the fish market in the Ober Donaustrasse and the fruit market in Elisabeth-Brücke, where she watched the rapidly gesticulating auctioneers and then went home to read the stock-market prices in the newspapers, as she had done in Hamburg. Not long afterwards, by chance, she came upon the Exchange in Schottenring, with its Renaissance-style vestibule, and went in far enough to catch a glimpse of the great hall. That started her on the other vast buildings, like the Imperial Vault and the Treasury, and then the museums: the Ephesus, and the Museum of Art and Industry. She found there were lectures there every Thursday and attended several. That led to others: at the Geological Institution, and then at the Zootomical Institute. After that she went to talks in the hall of the Society of Engineers, and at the Society for the Promotion of Scientific Knowledge in the Akademische Gymnasium.

On her way home one afternoon, walking through Prinz-Eugen-Strasse, she stumbled and turned her ankle on the uneven pavement. An elderly female passer-by helped her to the entrance of a nearby building. Salka went in to find a chair where she could rest for a moment. Fortunately it appeared to be a library: beyond double glass-doors she could see a vast, dim room, the walls filled with rows of books, and long desks where, beneath individual shaded lamps, absorbed figures read and jotted down notes.

Salka was watching them with something close to envy for their industry and concentration when she realised that a disparate group had gathered near her. Some of the men looked like students, their clothes shabby but their faces eager. Others seemed to be professional people, and one or two had a raffish air and smoked incessantly. There were a few women, somewhat older than herself. Two of them wore round gold spectacles and had their hair drawn back uncompromisingly so that they appeared stern and dedicated: they stood a little apart from the others. A third, plump and untidy, had the chapped hands of a manual worker. They talked among themselves, but so quietly that Salka could not hear what they said, until a cab stopped outside, a door slammed impatiently and one of the older men paused beside Salka.

"He's here, let's go in."

As he spoke a man strode through the door, clutching a document case. He was slight, with a full beard and hair receding at the temples. He looked unremarkable, and yet all eyes were on him.

Intrigued, she stood up, wincing a little as she took the weight on her injured foot, and followed the others along the wide corridor. About three dozen people had gathered in a reading-room, where newspapers on wooden frames were stacked in random heaps. Everyone found seats

135

where they could, perching on desks or leaning against the panelled walls. The tall man stood behind a wooden lectern, nervously fingering the papers piled in front of him. But once he started talking he never consulted them. He talked like a man possessed, and Salka, sitting uncomfortably on the end of a long bench, listened and noticed the pronounced squint that gave him such a piercing look.

After about fifty minutes, he bowed slightly to his audience.

"I suggest a short break for ten minutes, and then I'll answer any questions you'd like to put."

There was a spatter of applause and some of the men went out into the corridor to smoke. One of the shabby young men, who had been casting surreptitious glances at Salka during the speech, edged closer to her.

"He's magnificent, *nein*?"

Salka nodded fervently. "Oh yes. I've never heard anyone talk like that." She hesitated, not wanting to appear ignorant. "Have you heard him before?"

"Heard Theodor Herzl? I should think so. And you?"

"No, I'm afraid not." To excuse herself she added, "I haven't lived long in Vienna."

There was a pause, then the young man inquired, "Do you know anything about him?"

For the next ten minutes he told her how, since Herzl's first visit to the headquarters of the Zionist group in Rembrandtstrasse, he had revitalised the community so that Jewish culture was now blossoming again in the city. Writers, students' associations, all had appeared to revive Judaism in Vienna.

"There's even a Jewish athletics organisation now—we've always been excluded from membership of the existing ones—and he's just started a newspaper: *Die Welt*. They'll sell copies at the end of the meeting."

When she arrived home, Sandor was in the hallway removing his cashmere overcoat. He looked a little perturbed as he acknowledged her, but made no comment. He waited until Leon and Salka had joined him in the saloon after dinner before asking her whether she had been out so late alone.

"I was by myself, yes. But I didn't mean to be so late. I hurt my foot and it took me some time to get back." She didn't like to mention Herzl in case Sandor for some reason disapproved.

Sandor turned to Leon and said testily, "I don't think your wife should be allowed to wander around by herself."

Leon looked nonplussed. "I don't see why not. She hasn't come to any harm."

"That's beside the point. It isn't fitting that a woman of our family

136

should not be accompanied. Your mother always took her maid with her when she went out."

"Papa, for goodness sake. It's 1897. You can't be serious."

Salka listened to this conversation with her mouth open in disbelief, which changed rapidly to extreme annoyance. The thought of being always followed by a chaperone was appalling; she could not surrender the small pleasure of wandering alone around the city.

She interrupted sharply.

"I am here, you know. You need not discuss me as though I were deaf. You're very kind," she turned to Sandor, her tone belying the words, "to worry about my welfare. In Hamburg, before I was married, Adele and I were frequently unaccompanied if Magda was busy and Jette had her afternoon off. I'm nineteen now: I don't need looking after."

Sandor, who had been looking at her, seemed suddenly to notice the newspaper she was holding, intending to show it to Leon.

"What have you there? It looks like that Zionist paper."

She held it out to him.

"I bought it today." Relieved that the matter of the chaperone seemed to have been forgotten, she added, "I heard Herzl speak."

The two men glanced at each other. Leon said, "The authorities are not fond of Herzl. Where did you go to hear him?"

"I was in a public library. I somehow got caught up in this group of people."

"Who were they?"

"I don't know: students, a number of professional people, some women."

"And a government agent or two, I'll be bound."

She said, defensively, "He didn't say anything subversive. He talked about his vision of a state of Israel with German theatre and German opera, and Viennese coffee-houses. It was fascinating."

Sandor asked thoughtfully, "What else?"

"He spoke of the problems of assimilation and anti-Semitism."

"Did he mention duelling?"

She thought for a moment. "Yes. He said he had a high regard for it and wanted to introduce it into the new state of Israel."

"Herzl was an expert and dangerous fencer, like many Jewish students: they became so good to protect themselves from provocation and attack from the Burschenschaften, the German National Association who had many members among the students. His skill was one of the reasons he had to leave Vienna a few years back when there was a wave of anti-Jewish feeling."

Salka digested this for a moment. She said, thoughtfully, "I didn't

137

know that. Is it like this all over Austria? I was never conscious of Jacob talking about such feeling in Hamburg."

"I think it's generally accepted both in Germany and Austria that Jews are second-class citizens. They themselves, of course, frequently feel that they are totally German, and are bitterly shocked when they receive verbal abuse and physical violence, both of which certainly occur in schools and universities. In public life, of course, anti-Semitism becomes a little more subtle. An unbaptised Jew cannot become a higher civil servant, for instance, a diplomat or a ranking army officer. However, that hasn't prevented them from becoming industrialists and university professors, as well as writers and publishers."

Salka stared at her father-in-law, speaking so calmly and intelligently about what to her parents had been a terrifying reality: they had only to hear the names of certain towns—Konotop was one, she remembered, and Kiev—for their faces to become white, their eyes haunted. She had a hazy recollection of hiding, crouching somewhere when she was about twelve years old, and hearing wild shouts and then screams. Afterwards, there had been many funerals, and people had wept in the streets, and Rosje Feldman had died.

Because of that reality, a few years later, she had been forced to leave her home and Dora and Jonas, everything and everyone she knew and loved. Her eyes smarted, and she bit the inside of her cheek to keep back the tears. She stared at Sandor Salaman with scorn, sitting so comfortably in this magnificent place, his bank set at his back, his sons beside him. What did he know of pogroms and pandemoniums, of death and mutilation?

Sandor correctly interpreted the expression in her eyes and started to speak. Then he stopped, and sighed. He got up heavily.

"If you will excuse me, I'll say *gute Nacht*."

He went to his suite. Without turning on the light he sat down on the edge of the high bed where for many years he had slept lonely as an armoured knight upon a tomb. He felt cold and saddened. He should have opposed this marriage of Leon's, not tolerated it. This girl touched too many chords in him, brought back with painful clarity too much that he had forced himself for many years to forget.

Sandor switched on the lamp beside his bed, and started methodically to empty his pockets: the gold watch on its chain with entwined initials engraved on the back which his wife had given him; the heavy linen handkerchief; the eyeglasses in their embossed silver case which he now needed for reading. How she had looked at him, that girl; what withering scorn those eyes had held . . . .

And what eyes they were. They reminded him of an icon he had seen once, as a youth, carried in procession in Pinsk in honour of some saint.

138

He had never forgotten the impact that had on him, even though he'd turned and hurried away from the sight. Salka's eyes were the same remarkable colour, almost golden, as the varnished eyes that had stared straight at him out of the painting that day. He could still see them, mysterious and sorrowing, something to do with the shape the artist had given them. He sighed. Curious that he should remember with such clarity so brief a moment.

He undid his collar-studs and took off the stiff neck-band. He opened the silk shirt, his fingers fumbling for the buttons and stopped, fixed in a reverie.

How could he tell her—the little Russian girl who was his son's wife, who thought the Salamans so impressive, so secure in their money and status—how could he tell her that he knew, as well as she did herself, every painful step she had taken from Polotsk?

Chapter 13

Sandor's father was a timber merchant in a small way of business, living twelve miles from the Russian town of Pinsk in an area that a hundred years before had been part of Lithuania. In Ozer Salaman's time it was within the Pale of Settlement. The Jews there were cobblers, tailors, peddlers. Many of them still held to the traditions and cabbalistic symbols of their mystics, the white stockings, caftans and long cheek-curls. Most were illiterate and spoke only Yiddish, the language in which they felt safe, the intimate code of their condition, with its pathos and irony. It was a harum-scarum language, a street tongue, a *zhargon*. It expressed their own rootlessness, based as it was on Rhenish and tenth-century German, containing a little Slavonic as it reached the Pale, scattered with Russian and some Polish. It had not in Ozer's time standardised its syntax nor completed its vocabulary: it was only beginning to produce a rich literature. The Jews did not speak Hebrew: that was the language of pioneers, of the Promised Land. Nor did they have Russian, for they never used it, dealing only with their own kind.

Ozer Salaman was a *maskil*, a follower of the Hebrew Renaissance, anxious to bring his people into the present. He knew that Russian was the key to social and economic emancipation, and was not content that his children should only know "enough Russian to placate a policeman". Sandor, like his twelve brothers and sisters, learnt it at Ozer's insistence. But Ozer was aware that many Jews who had escaped the Pale, gone to Moscow and St. Petersburg and become lawyers and doctors, journalists and government officials, had put not only their place of birth behind them but their Judaism also. He was determined his sons and daughters should not lose their faith. Before any son left home, he had to promise Ozer and Gitele, their mother, that they would shelter only under a Jewish roof. They were expected to avoid Gentile contacts except for business reasons.

Ozer could not afford to educate all thirteen of his children, but Sandor was the third eldest boy and was sent to the local ghetto-school to be taught by scholars who believed that all the world's wisdom lay in the *Talmud*, that great body of Jewish oral lore and literature codified in the fifth century of the Christian era. The boy was promising enough to go with his two elder brothers to a school in Pinsk, where they boarded with the Strauss family. Maier Strauss was Gitele's brother and ran a thriving

140

bakery; his house seemed always to be warm and smelled enticingly of hot bread. Sandor was the same age as Maier's own son and they became inseparable. Maier decided to send his son to the Polytechnic in Darmstadt, where he had cousins, and urged Ozer to let Sandor go as Nathan's companion.

It was not a difficult decision for Ozer and Gitele to make. Reluctant as they were to lose Sandor there was little else they could do for him. The two elder boys would run the business with Ozer and Sandor would anyway have to make his own way in the world. Ozer was fired by the idea of his son travelling so far: it would have been impossible even a few years ago. But under the benign rule of the present Tsar, Alexander II, Jews were now allowed an unprecedented freedom of movement and opportunity.

The little Hessian capital of Darmstadt was scarcely more than a large village, appallingly slow but lying a bare fifteen miles from Frankfurt. The town had neither commerce nor industry of any kind, yet in 1853 a concession was granted for the establishment of the Bank für Handel & Industrie. This, known as the Darmstadter Bank, was the first German *crédit mobilier* bank, formed to finance and float companies and issue their shares. There was also the Polytechnic at which Sandor—by now seventeen—was to study. Ozer chose law for him, for he had always had a hankering for the legal profession—in his case quite unrealisable. But Sandor's heart was not in it. He spent his days poring over dry points of law, his evenings at first listening, then talking to Joseph Strauss.

This was the elder of Maier Strauss's two cousins, a partner in his own business of *Geldwechsler*, a money-changer and trader of bills. "Und Strauss" was Walter, the younger brother, a pompous man who occasionally asked the young Salaman to lunch with his family on a Sunday. His invitations to the shabby young man were not entirely altruistic, for he had a daughter to marry off.

Gradually, Joseph became more and more interested in Sandor. He liked the self-possessed and silent youth and was amused by his growing fascination with the world of money. He began to give him small errands, and then entrusted him with messages including carrying money for transactions. Sandor became obsessed with the meticulous detail of the financial business, the neat handwritten rows of figures in the great ledger, the talk of currency and interest and, above all, the importance of the transactions. Joseph talked to him of the great names in banking—the Baring Brothers, Oppenheim, Torlonia and Aguados.

Eventually, with Ozer's approval—for Sandor, even outside his father's orbit, was a dutiful son—he left the Polytechnic and became Joseph's clerk. For three years he displayed industry and discretion, qualities much appreciated by a cautious and reliable firm such as Strauss und Strauss. So

141

when the agent of Rothschilds—in Darmstadt finishing business transactions which involved Joseph Strauss—broke a leg and was unable to travel, it was Sandor Salaman who was entrusted by Joseph and Walter to return the papers to Frankfurt.

With some trepidation Sandor made his way to Frankfurt, for his German was still less than proficient and travel full of pitfalls. Before he set out Joseph Strauss had given him a piece of advice. *Always sit with your arms folded when travelling in public conveyances. Should you fall asleep, no one will be able to steal the papers you will be carrying.*

Sandor found the house in Fahrgasse without difficulty. It was far from impressive, and he could scarcely believe this was the residence of the wealthiest businessman in the world, though Joseph Strauss had told him that Rothschild kept his offices in the house, where they had always been, out of superstition. He was shown into a poorly-lit waiting-room where he sat stiffly on a hard chair rehearsing what he would say. When a brisk clerk in his early thirties came in, Sandor explained his business and handed over the papers. The man nodded and told him to wait. Ten minutes later he returned and asked Sandor to follow him.

The room in which Sandor found himself was long, narrow and woodpanelled. At the far end a raised dais supported a desk at which sat a middle-aged man, plump and somewhat unkempt, his coat falling negligently about his shoulders. But despite his unprepossessing appearance he sat like a Padishah while at his feet secretaries and clerks worked busily, and agents and clerks bustled about. When they reached the platform Baron Maier Karl Rothschild, his eyes still on the papers before him, beckoned Sandor on to the dais. The Russian obeyed and stood awkwardly, unsure what to do.

The Baron continued working for three or four minutes, while the youth before him grew increasingly nervous. Then he looked up, gazing mildly at Sandor.

"I understand that Strauss und Strauss have done us a considerable favour."

Sandor cleared his throat. It seemed as if the whole room had fallen attentively silent.

"It was most unfortunate for your agent, sir."

"The correct address is Herr Baron," the clerk hissed in Sandor's ear, so that he added hastily, "I mean, Herr Baron."

"He is progressing well, I see." The Baron, oblivious, consulted Joseph's letter. "It would appear from these papers that he was unable himself to complete his business in Darmstadt."

"He is confined to bed, Herr Baron, and will be for the next two weeks at least."

"So we have you to thank for acting on his behalf?"

"I was merely carrying out the instruction of your agent and Herr Strauss."

"Nonetheless it was well done, and I am grateful to you—and to your employers. There was, after all, no profit for them in handling these transactions on our behalf."

"Herr Strauss was not seeking to make a profit out of your agent's accident, Herr Baron." There was reproof in Sandor's voice. Baron Rothschild pushed his half-spectacles back on to his nose and stared at Sandor through them. He nodded slowly.

Sandor knew that the Baron held many titles, but the only decoration he wore was the ribbon of the Hesse Court. It was hard to realise this quiet, genial figure belonged to a family that had financed countries. The Baron noticed his eyes on the ribbon and smiled.

"What about you, young man? Are you going to follow your employers and be a bill-broker?"

Taken aback, Sandor answered nervously, "I don't know, Herr Baron. I studied law at Darmstadt, and my father is still anxious that I should continue with legal training."

"What is your own inclination in the matter?"

"I believe I should like to be a banker, Herr Baron." Sandor felt foolish. What must the Baron think of a penniless clerk like himself making such a declaration? But the Baron seemed to see no cause for amusement.

"The pursuit of any aim," he said thoughtfully, "demands above all things a concentration of one's forces on a single point. Concentration is the characteristic of a genius. Stick to one business, young man, and you may achieve any ambition."

At the front door the Rothschild clerk handed Sandor a sealed envelope. When he opened it outside, it contained seventy-five gulden: more than he had ever before possessed.

That day he walked the Frankfurt streets with money in his pocket and his eyes open. There were glowing theatres and great shops, buildings of awesome size and cool parks, and it became apparent that many of the people entering those theatres, using those buildings, were Jews like himself. He saw in Frankfurt what three years in Darmstadt had not shown him: that his father had indeed been right, and that the Jews of Russia were a century behind their brothers in the west. Here, deep in Germany, the Enlightenment had reached every corner of the ghetto and the Jews were emancipated and well-educated: there was nothing they could not achieve. He thought of Baron Maier Karl Rothschild and his title of Official Court Banker, and it seemed to him that he, too, could aspire to greater heights than becoming a *Geldwechsler* in Darmstadt.

Acting on impulse—rare for him, who weighed and carefully considered

143

the smallest decisions—he walked into the next tailor he passed and inquired diffidently about ordering a suit. The man measured his young customer and showed him materials. They agreed a price and the tailor asked him to return in a week's time. Horror-struck, Sandor explained that it would be impossible, since he must return to Darmstadt next day. Whereupon the tailor sighed, contemplating a full night's work for himself and his wife.

The following morning Sandor put on the suit, and in the dim and fusty shop saw a new man in the pier glass. Twenty years old and beginning to fill out, thanks to the good meals provided by Frau Strauss, so that he scarcely resembled the narrow youth who had arrived in Darmstadt clutching a German dictionary and a cardboard suitcase. The expression was still a little wary, but no longer uncertain: strong features were emphasised by the brief, dark beard, and the pale skin and compelling gaze gave him the look—though he had no basis for comparison—of a Rembrandt.

Before he returned to Darmstadt, Sandor purchased new shirts and a supply of stiff collars, a pair of boots and—this took the last of Baron Rothschild's beneficence—his first umbrella. Wearing these clothes, he walked in the hopeful spring sunshine of the Frankfurt streets on his way to the station and made the journey home in a state of wild elation. He could not envisage what he would be able to achieve, or by what means he would do it. He knew only that he was filled with an intense energy which crackled in his fingertips and made his muscles quiver. His eyesight seemed preternaturally sharp and every sound was magnified. In such a state, men go into battle and prove themselves invincible. In such a state they undertake acts of great hazard and show themselves courageous. Sandor Salaman confronted Joseph and Walter Strauss and demanded that he be made a partner.

The brothers stared at their young clerk with amazement and amusement. He faced them with his new-found determination and they said they would think about it. Over the next few days they considered him carefully: his astonishing ability with figures; his grasp of their business. They mused over the letter they had just received from the Baron Rothschild and saw that their young clerk had overnight assumed an authority.

Both brothers had families, but no son to take over in their stead. Joseph's daughters were all married, but their husbands were in different occupations and well settled; his only son was a smiling, blank-faced child of sixteen. Walter's son was a rabbinical student, much to his father's gratification, and only the youngest daughter still remained at home. She was a puny girl of thirteen, and even though Walter discussed the possibility of making her marriage part of their agreement, it was decided this would have to be postponed. (Joseph did not admit that his real reason in opposing the match was that he felt Sandor might then be better disposed to his father-in-law than to himself.) All in all, the brothers were not averse to the idea of Sandor succeeding them.

For the next few years, until he was twenty-seven, Sandor was content to work hard and learnt all that the brothers had to teach him. He became an impressive figure. He carried himself with assurance. Above the sober suits he wore and the high white collars, his beard was full and glossy, his eyes dark and magnetic as ever. His German was now impeccable, almost all trace of the Russian accent having vanished. With his confidence had come a vitality previously hidden by uncertainty. He was a man who knew his destiny and his every energy went into his work. He would be at his desk in the morning before the clerks and the messengers had even arrived, and it was always he who locked the main doors at night.

As the brothers delegated more and more to their young partner, Sandor began to implement long-laid plans to move the Strauss business gradually from bill-broking to becoming a merchant bank.

Like all German banks, Strauss, Strauss, Salaman bought shares in different enterprises and thus became part-owners. Sandor liked to think of merchant banks as being "the family doctors of finance", and he was not unlike a doctor himself. He inspired confidence and acquired a reputation amongst the Darmstadt merchants for being approachable and giving sound advice: he seemed to possess an infallible instinct for recognising a sound venture.

In 1873, when he was twenty-nine, the bank was doing so well that the three partners discussed the possibility of setting up a second establishment. Joseph and Walter, while approving the idea in principle, felt that the competition in most cities would tell against them. At the same time, their resources were now such that they could with ease finance another business.

After a long consideration, Sandor said, "I think we should go to Vienna."

The brothers stared at him, appalled.

"Has something addled your brains?" Walter inquired tartly. "They're calling this the year of terror in Vienna, or had you not noticed? The slump has brought panic, share quotations dropped by three hundred million florins overnight, there are reports of numerous suicides . . . and you want us to go to Vienna?"

"The banks and mercantile houses that were ruined in May had lamentably weak foundations. They were bound to fall at the first financial crisis. But I believe Austria offers a promising field for financial activities. There are possibilities for industrial development there and the country

145

has little capital now. I tell you, money can still be made in, and out of, Austria."

"I don't like it," Walter grumbled. Joseph cleared his throat.

"Oh, I don't know," he said, cautiously. "I think the proposal warrants judicious thought. . . ."

Within a year Sandor had opened the doors of a new bank in Vienna. The city was a revelation for him. If Germany was at its industrial zenith, Austria was at a cultural equivalent. Science, art, music, literature were all there for the taking, and though for the first year or two he kept his mind assiduously on his work, it became impossible for him to resist all the lures of the city.

His circle of friends became wide and included many prominent men: Sandor would listen to their talk of disciplines other than his own—science, medicine—with absorption. He would go to concerts and theatres late at night. He patronised art exhibitions and the ballet, where he saw a young Russian dancer called Pavlova who brought tears to his eyes. He heard his first opera, the new and brilliant *Rhinegold*, and read the translation of an extraordinary book, recently published by a man called Jules Verne: *Twenty Thousand Leagues Under the Sea*.

Everything around him fed his mind: nothing touched his heart. He was almost thirty now and he wanted to be married. He had known only a few women and his brief encounters with them had been largely matters of chance, for since he reached maturity he had been too set on his future to let himself be distracted by promptings of the flesh. Then, too, the teachings of his parents had sunk deep. He was a responsible and kindly man. His religion was important to him, although it was a private rather than a public affair: he went infrequently to synagogue, upon the High Holy days, but had never eaten meat that was not kosher, nor stayed under any but a Jewish roof.

The men who were his friends were Jews, but since they were mostly Viennese, their behaviour when it came to women shocked him. The liaisons, the little bed-companions, the light relationships so freely entered upon and so easily relinquished seemed to him tawdry and cheap.

He went eventually to a *shadchen*, a match-maker, but none of the young women suggested roused his interest: they seemed to him too plump and powdered, too bovine for his taste. At a dinner to which a friend invited him he met a young woman, a cousin from Berlin. He went twice to the house and held brief, chaperoned conversations with her. He was seriously considering her when he met Anna von Saar.

That he should have done so at all was chance again. He had been shopping in Zacharias where he always bought his gloves, just as he always purchased hats from Habig. It was early evening in November, and as he left the shop he collided with two young women hurrying along

146

deep in conversation and not watching where they were going. One slipped on the greasy pebbles of Seilegasse and would have fallen but for his quick response. She leaned against him for a moment as she recovered herself and he felt the curve of her waist against his arm. When she looked up at him, green eyes in a creamy face, he was seized by longing. Apologetic, flustered, he saw her and the companion to their cab and stood sadly upon the pavement, forlorn at the thought that he did not know who she was. When she wound down the window and bade him goodnight in a soft voice, he hastily took out his silver case and pressed his calling card into her hand.

She wrote telling him that her mother held an At Home on Thursday afternoons, if he would care to attend. He waited two weeks before he did so, and during that time he discovered that her family were minor Austrian nobility, now so impoverished that all that remained of their once-vast estates was a decayed country-home and a town house in the old aristocratic quarter near the Imperial Palace.

By the time his name was announced, and he stood in the arched doorway of the crowded, once-grand room with its peeling gilt and faded tapestries, he knew that Anna had twin brothers, cavalry officers with unsavoury reputations, and that there had been a small scandal involving Anna herself. Sandor's informant—one of his fashionable customers—could not remember the details, but thought that an engagement had been broken off because of her behaviour. "They're all tarred with the same brush," he had said disparagingly.

All this was in Sandor's mind as he stood on the edges of the thronged room, amongst minor court-officials, diplomats, and members of Vienna's old aristocracy. It was not the sort of gathering in which he could feel at ease and tension crept through his neck and shoulders. He wondered what on earth had possessed him to attend such an occasion and turned to go.

Anna von Saar stood in front of him, small and slight, her skin pale even in the warm room, those drenched green eyes the colour of leaves under clear water. She smiled demurely.

"I am so pleased you are here." She beckoned to a manservant. "Would you care for wine?" When he declined, she took him to meet her mother. The Countess was a tall woman, slim, with iron-grey hair and an imperious expression, who stared at him with slightly raised eyebrows. She extended her fingertips to Sandor who bowed over them politely. When she heard his name, she withdrew her hand.

"Salaman?" she asked. "And you are . . . ?"

"Herr Salaman is a banker, Mama," Anna said at his shoulder.

"Ah. Commerce. How interesting." The Countess gave him a chilly smile and drifted away. He looked sharply at Anna, but her expression bore no trace of condescension. She sat next to him on an uncomfortable chair and chattered charmingly about inconsequentialities; he heard only her voice, but not a word she said registered. Once—apparently without noticing—she touched him, and the skin on the back of his hand burned where her slim fingers had rested. Then it was over and he was walking away, wrapt in his thoughts and careless of the drizzle which he usually hated.

It would be a disastrous marriage—even if she would have him—a mismatching. She was part of the old Vienna, with her pedigree of resonant names. He thought of how she had taken the initiative by inviting him and recalled the look in those eyes, and he could well believe that some scandal attached to her. She was wayward, Gentile and poor— he had not missed the state of that room, nor the worn livery of the servants. The dress the Countess wore had looked dowdy, even to his eyes, and she had offered him a deliberate slight. *Salaman*? She had dismissed him as not belonging to her world. *Commerce*, she had said. *How interesting*. She had clearly seen he was a Jew. He wondered whether Anna had also realised. If she had, she appeared not to care. But what of her twin brothers, with their reputation for womanising and violence? No. The whole thing was absurd: he was a fool even to be considering it.

He strode on, hunched into the caracul collar of his coat, his spirits black as night. He hardly knew this girl. Their paths would never have crossed in the normal way. They *had* met, however, and she had already shown she was not averse to him. He stepped off the kerb into a puddle and swore. He wished he had never seen her. No other woman had ever reduced him to such a state. He was like a lovesick youth.

What Sandor could not see was that the thunderclap of emotion which had so suddenly struck him was exactly that. Where other men he knew had spent their early twenties dreaming of and pursuing women, he had had neither the time nor the inclination. He had desired only success, and he had achieved it. Behind his desk he was mature and decisive. Away from it, he was as inexperienced and naive as a man ten years his junior.

What disturbed him now was the strength of his desire for this Gentile countess: the fragile look of her, skin so fine he swore he could see the blue veins in her wrists and green eyes in which he could lose himself. His hands remembered how slight she had felt when he caught her in Seilegasse and the way she had swayed against his arm. He groaned aloud at the thought and a couple near him turned and stared thinking he was ill.

Sandor returned the next week to the Countess von Saar's At Home. This time, he was received with greater civility by the mother, and by the daughter in such a way as to leave him in no doubt of her feelings: it was evident she had spoken of him to her family. Now he was near to panic.

He knew what such a marriage would do to his parents, who cared so passionately for Judaism. But he was far removed from them both physically and emotionally. He visited them more often now that he could afford the journey, but even so it could never be lightly undertaken, that voyage into his past. However, all his brothers and sisters had married as their parents wished, and if he made a different decision, he did so in his maturity.

He made up his mind and felt there was no time to waste. Just a month after that first meeting, having spent two afternoons in Anna's company, he wrote to the Count von Saar requesting an audience. He had not set eyes upon him until he was shown into his study, and was slightly disconcerted by the very size of the man. He was well over six foot, with the thickset shoulders and muscular arms of a practised horseman. His colour was high, and his eyes, under their reddish lashes, the same extraordinary green as Anna's. He wore, even here in the city, country clothes: heavy trousers of stout cord and long boots polished to a high gloss but with much-mended soles. Beside the desk stood a spittoon which he used discreetly before he rose to his feet and place his half-finished cigar on the edge.

The Count did not offer his hand to Sandor, but asked him to be seated. Sandor said, firmly, "If you don't mind, Herr Graf, I prefer to stand." He clasped his hands behind his back.

The Count seated himself with difficulty and winced as he sat down. In explanation he said, *"Die Gicht."*

Sandor nodded sympathetically. "Gout must be most unpleasant for an active man."

"It's a damned nuisance and that's a fact. Now, Herr . . ."

"Salaman."

"Herr Salaman, you wished to speak to me?"

"Yes, Herr Graf. I hope you will not find me presumptuous since I am unknown to your family and you are unaware of my circumstances. I am a banker, a junior partner, but I intend in time to buy out my associates and move the main house here from Darmstadt. You have only to ask any of the established bankers here and they will vouch for what I say. My family are all in Russia and I have no responsibilities." He drew a deep breath. "I seek your permission to ask for your daughter's hand."

The Count did not look at him, but stared out of the window on the other side of his desk. The silence lengthened and became almost intolerable: Sandor had consciously to restrain himself from blurting out his passion for Anna, pleading for her.

Still without moving his gaze, the Count said, "You are a Jew, are you not?"

The words had an ugly sound, though Sandor had been expecting them. He said quietly, "I am, Herr Graf."

"I've never had much to do with Jews, y'know. When I was in the army they had a corps specially for them: Moses' Dragoons. They could really use a sabre, those fellows. Had to, of course. Got called out so often. D'you fence?" He glanced across at Sandor, who was ridiculously conscious of his formal suit, his sober appearance. *Commerce*. He shook his head.

The old Count said, regretfully, "No. You wouldn't." He added abruptly, "My daughter brings nothing with her to a marriage, you realise that? A couple of horses from the estate, a wedding—but no house and no land." He sighed. "She needs a man with money—and you, it seems, have it." He started to struggle to his feet again, then pointed at Sandor.

"Pour us both a brandy, will you? I take mine with seltzer."

Sandor found the glasses and decanter on a dented silver tray. Handing the Count his glass he asked, diffidently, "If you need more time to consider, Herr Graf, I . . ."

The Count swallowed some brandy.

"It's not I who needs to consider, but my daughter. If it's what she wants, and if you can support her properly, then you'll not find me saying you nay, for all you're a . . ."

What Sandor was disappeared in the next gulp of brandy. It seemed hardly an enthusiastic reception, but his suit had not been refused. He set down his glass almost untasted.

"If you will excuse me, Herr Graf, I'd like to speak to Anna at once— if she's here."

"Here? Of course she's here. Been waiting in the music-room." The Count gave a wheezy laugh and took up his cigar, tapping off the cold grey ash. He waved a hand towards the door. "Go and put your case, Herr Salaman."

So Sandor asked Anna von Saar if she would become his wife. For answer she stood very close to him and laid her head upon his shoulder in a gesture at once submissive, tender and calculated, so that he held his breath and smelt the lemony scent of her hair. A long engagement suited no one, and they were married six weeks later. The Countess organised a theatrical entertainment for the *Polterabend*, the evening before the marriage, and the ceremony itself was a civil one only. This caused the Countess some chagrin, but Anna did not care. "It's only the civil service which matters," she said practically. "The rest is just tears and pretty words."

When it came to the point, Sandor was surprised to find how much it hurt to make his vows before a civil dignitary and not a rabbi. But he told himself he could not have both Anna and his religion, and Anna had become so vital to him that without her he did not think he would be able to breathe.

On their wedding-night it became apparent that his bride, though eight years younger than he, was infinitely more experienced. It mattered to him not at all. It seemed part of the sophistication, the self-confidence, the tone of her voice, even the faded splendour of the house she had that day left for him; all these proofs of her position thrilled and excited him. She came from a very different world to his, and her acceptance of him was the final, irrefutable proof of how far he had come from the outskirts of Pinsk.

Two children were born during the first five years of their marriage. The elder boy, Friedrich, looked a little like Anna, with the same fine bones, but it was the younger, Leon, who was truly her child. He resembled his father, but his spirit was hers, as was his way of walking into a room and standing very still, almost as though waiting to be admired.

Throughout these years, Sandor's relationship with the von Saars underwent a fundamental change. He had never been under any illusions about how they regarded him, and knew that it was only his money which had secured this unlikely alliance—although, as he once pointed out with deceptive mildness to his father-in-law, theirs was not the first aristocratic Austrian family to ally themselves with the Jews of Vienna, and would not be the last. Even so, the family viewed him with some disdain.

The day came, as Sandor had known it would, when the von Saars needed his money. The Count had no business acumen. He had lost a good deal of his capital in the financial crisis of 1873 and never managed to recoup himself. After a bad harvest, he spoke to his daughter and she asked Sandor if he could help. He lent them the money they needed, of course, but unlike other small banks, who financed the aristocracy and charged them exorbitant rates of interest, Sandor merely asked that he be paid back when they could find the money, though he knew they probably never would. He was not doing it for the old Count and Countess, but for his adored Anna.

The twin brothers, the arrogant cavalry officers so alien and inexplicable to Sandor, called him "the merchant" even as they settled their bills with his gulden. The parents deprecated their son-in-law while they used his wealth to shore up their decaying estate. "He is of the Mosaic persuasion," the Countess would say, though never in his hearing.

Then the old Count suffered a stroke and was confined to his bed. The twins could offer no practical help to their mother when it came to managing the houses, the estate and the servants, and she turned to Sandor, who did not fail her. He spent many hours advising her and making improvements, sending in accountants and estate managers. The von Saars looked more and more to Sandor and by the time Anna had been married for ten years, their disdain had turned to dependence. He took no pleasure in this volte-face, but only in his dealings with the twins did he permit himself a measure of sarcasm, which they never recognised.

When Friedrich was nine years old and Leon almost six, Anna became pregnant again. She and Sandor were delighted, and hoped this time for a girl. It was a girl, but by the time they knew it had ceased to matter. It was a cross-birth, the child lying obliquely across the womb and the pelvis. When the accoucheuse saw that the doctor—the best gynaecologist in Vienna—would have to be called, Anna's body was so exhausted that her womb had ceased to contract and he could do nothing but use his gleaming instruments to lacerate the child's body and remove it in unrecognisable segments.

Anna survived her baby by only twenty-four hours. When she died Sandor was so dazed and shocked that he had no recollection of those terrible days, of the mourners who came to his house to see her for the last time, of the funeral cortège with the dark horses, the black ostrich-plumes and the single drum that beat, over and over and over, the message that his love was gone.

For a year the apartment in Praterstrasse was muffled and quiet, and the unhappy little boys wore black clothes. Sandor's grief was so great even his children could not rouse him from his torpor of misery and, once the first months were over, they avoided him, frightened and embarrassed as all children are by great emotion.

With the passage of time, Sandor began to recover himself. The bank had been neglected for a year and there was a great deal to do. He reverted to his old habits, changed since his marriage, of arriving there before any of his employees and leaving long after them. His social life before Anna's death had been sparkling—her connections, his money—but now he steadfastly refused all invitations not involved with the bank. He had no desire for frivolity, no wish to meet other women. He had only ever wanted Anna, and it was over. He never ceased to grieve and work was for him the only anodyne.

He did not revert to his religion after Anna's death: if there was a God He had betrayed Sandor. His parents were by now dead, and he had no thought any more for the Pale, the unpaved roads, the crowded, convoluted streets, and the smell of garlic and old clothes.

Then Salka came into his house, bringing his past with her.

Chapter 14

Leon Salaman was not an unkind man, merely an unthinking one where women were concerned. Throughout his boyhood and adolescence there had been almost no feminine company at all. His mother had died when he was only six years old and he could recall only half-forgotten moments he had spent with her: grasping her hand tightly as they passed the limbless old soldiers who begged so pitifully in public places; inhaling her special lemony scent when she consoled him after a fall. He was not given to self-examination, or it might have occurred to him that he sought her again every time he embarked upon a new adventure, lured by the promise of softness and sympathy. But he had idealised his mother in his mind to the point where no one, however perfect, could even approximate to her, and so every attempt to replace her was doomed before it began.

He grew up without learning that women could be friends and companions. He saw them in terms of their looks, and what they thought or felt did not interest him. He did not let them know this, of course, and his impeccable manners and innate charm were more than enough for most of them, even without his physical appeal and financial status.

All these attributes continued to serve him well—until Salka. In the past, he had pursued until he possessed: the act of love marked for him the beginning of the end. She, unlike any other woman he had ever known, gave only her body. Her mind and her heart she kept from him. He failed to see the irony of it, that he had married the only one who did not fall at his feet.

He began to comprehend the depth of his yearning for Salka only after they had been married for many weeks, and he had at last become aware that she was still resisting him. For the first time in his life, he was in the grip of the emotion he had so casually aroused in others and he did not know how to deal with this painful new experience. It reduced him from his customary role of sovereign and he suffered visibly. The confident amorist became anxious and uncertain, as pathetic in his own eyes as the unwitting husbands he had so frequently and heedlessly cuckolded.

He started to woo Salka. More assiduously than he had before, he paid court to his own wife. He sent her expensive, out-of-season flowers and absurd delightful gifts—spun-sugar mice, a carved ivory pen, combs for her hair set with tiny diamonds. He wrote daily when he was away on bank business, and composed poems which he left for her to find beside

153

her bed. He took her out to the Opera and to classical concerts, to sophisticated plays by Schnitzler and the music hall. He arranged intimate dinners in discreet restaurants and, across candle-lit tables, exerted himself to be witty and amusing. He wanted her exclusively for himself and she soon learnt that if she chatted too long with an acquaintance, Leon would become sullen and silent. If, as occasionally happened, friends attempted to join them, he made no pretence at civility and could barely conceal his impatience until they went. Alone again with her, he would hold her hand or caress her cheek in public, not caring who saw, oblivious to the amusement he gave to those who knew Leon Salaman as a cynical seducer.

Salka herself was at first amazed by this unprecedented behaviour and then—when she realised he was sincere—moved by it. She could not easily reconcile his new tenderness for her with his earlier conduct, and it was a long time before she could permit herself the luxury of believing she was greatly loved.

What convinced her, finally, was Leon's reaction when she told him she was pregnant.

Salka was deeply affected by the discovery that she was to bear a child. At first, she had not wanted to tell Leon, as though her position with him was still too precarious to risk. She did not even write to her parents. She confided only in Adele, sending a long letter to Paris as soon as the early signs alerted her, for she had no woman in Vienna to talk to. Adele, now the mother of a six-month-old son, had replied immediately. If the menses still did not appear the following month, there was no possible doubt. So she waited three long weeks until her hopes were confirmed.

Even then, she was inexplicably reluctant to make her condition public. While the baby was still hers alone, its presence merely a promise, she was warmed and strengthened by it: her cherished secret. Her happiness was mixed with wonder and panic, for she had virtually no experience of babies. She was unable to see beyond the image of a helpless little creature, demanding, dependent and, above all, hers.

She felt, too, although she knew it was irrational, a superstitious fear: as long as she did not speak of this child, it would be safe from malignant spirits. She thought of Dora's multiplicity of fears and how her father used to tease her: *Where there are many women, there is much superstition.* Still, she would have to tell Leon soon, or he would see for himself. Already she was conscious of changes in her body. Not that she was gaining weight—on the contrary, her wide leather belts were cinched on their tightest notch—but her breasts felt full and hard, and so tender that she shrank from Leon's touch at night. She knew from Adele that morning sickness was to be expected, only she had never felt better.

Lying in the bath one morning she calculated she must be about thirteen

154

weeks gone. She was now conscious of a thickening round her waist and made up her mind to tell Leon that very day. Absorbed in her thoughts, she lay for longer than usual in the hot water. When she finally stood up and reached for the towel, a wave of nausea rose in her throat. Her forehead felt clammy, but not from steam, and her feet as she clambered clumsily from the tub were cold. There was a rushing sound in her ears; she tried to call someone, but everything went soft and black and impenetrable. She surfaced again, bemused, to find Leon pinching her cheeks while the housekeeper waved a burnt feather under her nose. She shook her head: the singed fronds smelled offensive. Leon looked relieved.

"What happened? Did you slip? Have you hurt yourself?"

"No, no." Her voice cracked. "I felt dizzy; I don't know . . ."

Leon helped her to her feet, the towel round her, and put her into bed. She heard the housekeeper talking to him in a hurried voice, then he came back and sat on the edge.

"You look terrible." His fingers traced the black shadows beneath her eyes. "What's wrong?"

She closed her eyes. "Nothing."

"I don't think it's nothing. I think it's something. You're thinner, you've no appetite, you faint for no reason. This good lady suggested that you are probably in an interesting condition. Is that right?"

She answered, "Yes," but so low he thought it was a sigh.

"But this is excellent. Excellent. Why did you not tell me sooner?"

"I . . . wasn't sure."

"Do you know when it will be?"

"I think in early October."

"So." He looked at her with unconcealed emotion, so that she saw the delight and the pride.

She asked, unnecessarily, wanting to hear him say it, "Are you pleased, then?"

For answer he embraced her. "How can you ask, my little peasant? It's the most important news a man can receive, no?" He tightened his hold. "I'll keep you very safe, and you will make us the most beautiful baby in the world."

She laid a finger on his lips, filled with sudden dread.

"Shhh! You mustn't say such things aloud."

He laughed. "As you wish. But you must take care now. We're bringing you a warm drink and you're to stay in bed until you feel better. In a day or two, when I've had time to arrange things, we'll see about putting the house at Döbling in order."

She looked puzzled, and he went on, "We've been every summer since I was a child. You'll love it. You can spend months there: the air will be good for you, and the greenery."

Salka listened to him with gratification, warmed by his caring, and when he told Sandor that evening, his happiness was unmistakeable. As he spoke to his father, he put his hand possessively on the back of her neck. It was a gesture he frequently used and she always resented: did he expect her to fawn beneath this masterful caress like a pet dog? Usually she made an excuse to move out of reach—a dropped skein of silk, a forgotten article to be fetched. This time, she made no such evasion, finding joy in what was, after all, a sign of affection.

Sandor behaved impeccably. He smiled, he congratulated them both, he opened champagne . . . and yet, when he turned away to pour it into the shallow glasses, Salka saw a shadow of something she did not understand pass across his face. When he straightened up to hand out the glasses, it was gone. He had seemed both saddened and somehow apprehensive. She puzzled over it later, that expression, but could make no sense of it.

On a day that smelled of rain and spring, Leon drove Salka out to the pretty residential suburb of Döbling, where trim villas stood in their acres of ground. He stopped the Mercedes outside a house barely visible from the road, hidden behind a manicured hedge.

Leon removed his heavy leather gloves and she unwound her thick veil. She followed him up the immaculate short drive, their feet crunching on the chipped stone. The house was built in the style of the Tyrol, with many small windows and wooden balconies. Behind the dark wooden door the interior was shadowed and quiet, all the windows shuttered. The floors were wood also, highly polished, and she could imagine how pleasant it would be in summer, protected from the heat by the surrounding trees. Now it struck cold as she followed Leon dutifully round, admiring the simple furnishings: carved tables, armchairs beneath their dustsheets, and the kitchen with its scrubbed work-tops bleached almost white. The bedrooms were cottage-like with flowered walls and low ceilings, the windows set into embrasures deep enough to take window seats covered with cretonne.

They spent the afternoon planning small changes and mentally rearranging rooms. Everything seemed perfect and yet, as they drove back into Vienna, Salka sat silently immersed in thought. She was experiencing a niggling unease. The house was charming, she could not deny that, and the countryside refreshing after Vienna; but Salka was totally urban. In Russia she had been used to life in an overcrowded, bustling town. Hamburg and Vienna, with their parks and gardens, carefully groomed and confined expanses of green amongst the buildings, had suited her completely. This house was not, of course, far from civilisation, but nonetheless it was remote enough, silent enough, to concern her.

And Leon, instead of being merely a matter of miles from where she was—the Hoher Markt was a lengthy walk, no more—would now be hours away. She blinked away a furtive tear. Something was happening to her, something of which she was as yet scarcely conscious but which nevertheless was already beginning to affect her. Her body was changing to accommodate the baby, not only in visible ways—the glowing skin, the darkening nipples—but invisibly. Her heart enlarged to meet the demands that would be made upon it; the ligaments began to soften in preparation for delivering the child safely.

There were other changes, too. Her emotional balance became unpredictable. She felt uncertain and frequently tearful, so that alone in her room she would briefly weep without cause. Where so recently she had held herself aloof from Leon, wary of his determination and power, unwilling to be dominated by him, now she sought that domination. As the child swelled in her, all her equivocal feelings towards her husband vanished, her uncertainties slid away. She wanted nothing so much as to be near him.

She slept more lightly now. The previous night, awakening for no reason, she had lain drowsy and warm. Leon had come to her bed and his body touched the length of hers. She had lifted herself on an arm and looked at him, lying on his side with his fist clenched on his chest. Tentatively, she had cupped her hand round the curve of his shoulder, as she had wanted to do with the bronze boy in the Belvedere gardens. Under her palm Leon's skin was satisfyingly smooth over muscle and sinew. She had never been so conscious of his body. On an impulse she had leant forward and put her lips to the base of his throat where she could feel the pulse beating quick and urgent. She was filled with disbelief at her blindness. Leon no longer seemed sensual and strange but necessary to her, vital to her well-being and happiness. She had caressed his shoulder as he slept, and could not comprehend why it was that by her own intransigence she had risked losing so much.

Salka thought she would remember that night when she could remember nothing else. She had discovered that she loved Leon and she was filled with wild exhilaration. It was him—it had always been him. She understood at last that shock of recognition she experienced when she first saw him at the Freudenau: it was his name the angel called forty days before her birth, his face she would have seen reflected in the silver glass.

But she did not know that love had come too late.

Salka found that her relationship with Sandor also was altering in subtle ways. She assumed it was because of the expected grandchild. In fact, it was due more to his growing awareness that she merited attention. He had observed her behaviour, both alone with himself and Leon and when they entertained: if she felt at a loss or nervous she did not behave as many other women would have done, giggling and blushing, but waited, gravely composed, until she knew which utensils were used for a dish foreign to her, or how to address some titled dignitary Sandor was entertaining.

Sandor did not for a moment imagine that being married to Leon could be easy for her; he knew his younger son too well to be sanguine about his behaviour. So he was interested to note that she appeared to have tamed him. Leon came home every night now, and on all evidence was eating out of her hand.

She had started to ask more questions, too, about the bank, and to his surprise—and certainly to Leon's—she was not uninformed. He presumed she'd picked up something from Jacob Radin, but she was certainly capable of intelligent questions. Her reading was also unlikely. Most of the women he knew, wives of friends and colleagues, read only family journals such as *Die Gartenlaube*, the bower, or the popular novels of Frau Marlitt, which depicted women as simple, unworldly, modest creatures. Salka, he had noticed, did not concern herself with such material. He had on various occasions found her with a life of Moses Mendelssohn, the philosopher, Fontane's *Frau Jenny Treibel*, which he understood was largely about an emancipated intellectual, and *Effi Briest*, a critical view of marriage between a mature man and a young wife. She was now reading—he glanced across at her to ascertain the title—*Die romantische Schule*.

"Are you enjoying that?"

She was so absorbed, he had to repeat the question, and she said diffidently, "Very much." Then, not wanting to sound rude, she added with more enthusiasm. "I find some of the German a bit difficult still, but beautiful."

Curious, Sandor asked, "What made you read Heine? Or did you find him by chance?"

"No. I was reading a biography of Rahel Levin. Do you know of her?"

Sandor shook his head.

"She was an extraordinary woman," Salka said eagerly. "She was the daughter of a Jewish merchant from Berlin, and her home was a meeting place for the most unlikely people—musicians, artists, Prussian officers, princes. Goethe went there, and Heine said gaining access to her salon was superb good-luck. So then I thought I should read something he wrote."

"It was Heine, was it not, who considered that baptism was the entry ticket to European culture?"

She hesitated. "I hadn't known that."

"And despite the sarcasm of that remark, which was made in reference to a lawyer named Eduard Gans, Heine found baptism to be necessary, which is perhaps less than admirable considering his devotion, painful though it was, to Judaism." Sandor paused. "What about Goethe? You've already read him, of course."

Salka flushed, hearing the note of amusement. She sat back in her chair and tried not to sound defiant.

"Yes. One of his plays, *Stella*, and *Trilogy of Passion*."

Sandor's eyebrows shot up.

"Indeed you surprise me. I had not imagined your tastes to be quite so eclectic. Did your parents encourage you to read?"

Salka was quiet, thinking of the time her father had wrenched the treasured, tattered Pushkin from her hands and flung it on the fire. *It's not for you to read. Women haven't the time for it.* She said sadly, "No. My father taught me a little Russian, but that was because he believed to speak only Yiddish would be a limitation. He never anticipated that I would use it."

Sandor started to say something and abruptly changed his mind. Instead, he asked, "Has Leon spoken to you about a maid?"

She looked at him with apprehension. "No."

She had thought this issue had been forgotten. But Sandor seated himself beside her and continued, confidentially, "I had a word with the housekeeper. It appears she has a young relative, a niece I believe, who is seeking a new domestic post. She is coming here next week, and we very much hope you will like her. You'll need someone to take care of the baby, too, and this young woman sounds ideal."

Salka looked mutinous, but contented herself by thanking her father-in-law politely and returning discreetly to her book. She felt certain the girl would be a typical bumpkin, scarlet-cheeked and yellow-braided. If she were impossible, it would surely not be beyond her ingenuity to get rid of her. She was therefore disconcerted to discover, when the niece finally arrived for an interview, that she was about a year younger than Salka herself, with a clear country skin and an impish face. She found she was smiling back at Bette, liking her spattering of freckles and tightly curled hair. The knitted stockings and the polished buckles on her substantial shoes. The vision of a sharp-eyed chaperone receded.

As the summer approached, Leon and Salka went several times to the Döbling house. They acquired extra furniture—a mahogany, marble-topped chest of drawers for the master bedroom, on which to stand a water-bottle and glasses, sponges and brushes, and a pretty japanned tub, for the house had no bathroom, a convenience Sandor had long since installed in the Praterstrasse apartment. Superstitiously, Salka would not look at furniture for a child's room before it was born, although a cumbersome parcel had already arrived for her from Paris, which proved to be a carved wooden cot on rockers, complete with pillow and coverlet made by Adele herself and trimmed with fragile lace to match the white hanging curtains.

I wish I could have brought this myself to you, wrote Adele, *but I cannot travel at the moment. Louis is teething and fretful and I do not want to leave him. God willing, I will see you when your baby is born.*

In May the couple, together with Bette, moved into the house. A local woman was engaged to come in daily and cook, and the elderly gardener Leon had known since he was fifteen had already filled the window-boxes and tubs with geraniums. His wife had cleaned the house from top to bottom. She had polished the banisters and opened the shutters so that the pale sunlight warmed the rooms, gilded the mirrors and put a shine on the parquet floor, lighting up the patterns of medallions in the coloured woods. Salka walked around in quiet satisfaction: it felt like a house in which to be happy.

For the first month Leon travelled daily to the bank. Then, in June, he announced one morning that he would stay overnight at Praterstrasse, since he had a meeting early at the bank the following day. Salka felt slightly perturbed at the idea that she and Bette would be alone in the house, but put her anxiety aside. She told the cook not to bother to prepare the leg of mutton she had ordered for the evening, since she would prefer clear soup and fruit: as she became more burdened with her pregnancy, she found it easier to eat lightly and frequently rather than follow the Austrian habit of consuming vast meals.

The following week a similar thing happened, and Leon again stayed in Vienna for part of the week. On his return he was full of talk about an acquaintance who had recently married, about another whose business was doing badly and needed finance. He described, during dinner, how David Landesmann's company, a manufacturing plant producing locomotive parts, was severely undercapitalised and unable to acquire new equipment as necessary. When the meal was over they walked round the garden, admiring the trimmed hedges and bright borders. Leon had his arm around her waist, and Salka felt the small separation well worthwhile if it brought him back in so good and affectionate a mood.

He yawned suddenly, "I've eaten too well. I'm exhausted. Let's go to bed soon. I had a late night on Wednesday."

It was as if a cold finger had touched her skin. Keeping her voice light she asked, "Did you?" and pointed to the sweet Alpine strawberries hiding beneath their protective leaves. All the time her mind was jumping. How could he have had a late night at Praterstrasse? Sandor frowned upon anyone visiting after nine and had the doors locked by ten-thirty during the week, winter and summer, in deference to his habit of rising early. It was the only cause of annoyance for Leon in living in his father's house.

They went to their room and made love carefully, and Salka forgot her apprehension. He had entirely lost the mocking, challenging manner he used with her in the early days. He was considerate, attentive, more affectionate than he had ever been.

It took five weeks more for her to perceive that Leon had also become elusive. A pattern developed whereby he spent part of each week living in Vienna, and though she disliked being so much alone, she could see that in the heat of summer the long drive would be wearisome. But she knew there was something beyond that though for a long time she refused to admit it to herself.

Then, in early August, when Salka was in her sixth month of pregnancy, Leon decided she needed some mountain air. They went by train to Styria, through the lucid green valleys and vineyard hills to Lake Altaussee lying in a high valley. Their hotel, Die Goldene Spinne, looked on to the Dachstein glacier, an endless, extraordinary spectacle, always the same and yet changing constantly with the light.

Salka watched it with fascination, sitting in a wicker chair in the garden of the hotel, occasionally embroidering the fronts of diminutive nightdresses, or reading the new novel by Lou Andreas-Salomé, *Ruth*. This writer fascinated Salka, for she also was Russian-born and many of her stories were set there. But always Salka's eyes were drawn back to the glacier, glittering in the hot sun which could not touch it and making the lush green foliage round the lake more brilliant by contrast. Sometimes Leon would walk with her beside the Altaussee: they would watch dragonflies hover and dart, and hear the cool sound of fish breaking the still water as they leapt for insects. More often, though, he walked alone, in stout shoes, his jacket over his arm, returning in the middle of the afternoon in time to nap before dinner.

It was a peaceful time, suspended, out of real life, and Salka relaxed. With her mat, olive skin she scorned the use of sunshades, unlike the pink-and-white German and English women at the resort, and after an hour outside she would remove the protective straw-hat. Because of this exposure to the sun combined with her pregnancy, an odd thing happened. From her nose over her cheeks a deeper colouration had appeared, shaped like the wings of a butterfly, so that it seemed almost as if she were masked. Within this dark decoration, her eyes looked all the more remarkable; made of golden metal, mysterious, enigmatic. Her body blossomed with the coming child, her hair became so luxuriant she was conscious of balancing its weight as she walked. She looked smoothed and glossy, ate strawberry torte with whipped cream and basked in her new-found security. Only one thing marred her contentment: before they left Vienna a letter had come from Jonas. Dora was failing now, despite all the care he could give; she shivered when they carried her outside to sit in

161

the sunshine, and the light hurt her eyes. *She asks*, Jonas wrote, *Will I live to see my grandchild?*

One morning Salka woke at dawn to find the high valley swimming in mist, the Dachstein glacier hanging like an opal above a limpid lake. A great bird—she thought it must be a heron—stood motionless on the water's edge, hunched and waiting, and beyond him the dark shapes of fishing boats drifted in and out of the mist, insubstantial as a Chinese watercolour.

Salka winced as she felt again the strenuous kick that had disturbed her sleep, and pressed both hands against her abdomen. The first time she had felt the quickening, well into the fourth month of her pregnancy, it had been difficult to believe that the light flutterings were the child's movements. Now she could clearly feel it squirm; sometimes, when she was holding a conversation, a particularly violent kick would cause her to stop short, her train of thought completely disrupted.

Sometimes the child was quiescent for long periods, up to twenty-four hours, and initially this had concerned her, until she realised that it must be asleep. When it awoke, she felt it more vigorous than ever. It had been very quiet all the previous day and was now evidently awake and lively. She leant against the deep windowsill, watching the trees and bushes emerge from the receding mist and humming under her breath. *Mirele Mirele, zing mir a lidele, vos dos meydele vil . . . .* She wondered if the baby could feel the reverberation in its hidden, globular world.

It seemed that at last she had the answer to the question she had so anxiously asked her parents: *What can a woman do?* Dora had smiled at her father, shrugged. *A woman's life is simple. You'll marry, God willing, there will be babies. . . .*

Salka had never believed her, had yearned for something beyond the merely domestic life her mother had so serenely led. In Hamburg that day Jacob had taken her to the Rathausmarkt and talked of currencies and share prices, of Brazil and the Argentine; she had seen another world, absorbing and enriching. Then there was the chance visit to the port in Hamburg, where she had smelled on the wide river the scent of the sea, seen bales of goods from unknown countries waiting to be sold. How she had longed to learn more, how she had pestered Jacob and how little encouragement she had received. Everyone had believed as her parents did, and only now did she perceive that they were right after all.

Leon stirred in his sleep and flung out an arm to where she had been lying.

". . . are you?" he muttered.

"Here." She sat on the edge of the bed and eased herself in, bulky and cumbersome now with the extra weight she carried. He grunted and pulled her towards him. She smelled his warmth and expensive tobacco and the mixture of citrus and leather that came from the cologne he used so lavishly. She inhaled these particularly masculine scents—pregnancy had also sharpened her sense of smell—and reflected on the way in which Leon, with all the self-absorption of an elegant male cat, would spend longer than she on grooming himself.

He didn't look elegant now, with his hair tousled and his nightshirt unbuttoned. She adjusted her body to his, and started to kiss him: the complicated mouth, the strong throat beneath the beard. She kissed the fur on his chest where the buttons were opened and he groaned, sleepy and voluptuous, as she caressed him with a secret and audacious touch. Before he was quite awake they made love: she happy and passive, protective of the child; he confident and practised, sure now of her assent. He invaded her with power and control, so that she shook to his rhythm, unable to resist the sensation that was gripping her, stiffening her limbs, making her head roll from side to side on the pillow as though she were in anguish. She opened her eyes. Leon's face beside her was closed, intent, absorbed as he rode her to her climax. Salka tried to delay the pleasure that threatened her, unconscious of the sounds she made, the seductive, rasping slivers of sound deep in her throat as she tried to hold on. She clenched herself against him and then it was flooding her, filling her, and she broke against him in waves.

When she opened her eyes again he had fallen back into sleep, spent and relaxed, one leg sprawled over her thigh, the trace of a smile on his lips, a hand cupping her breast. She felt complete, as though an urgent question had been answered. Flowered curtains filtered the incipient day, and Salka let herself drift to the very edge of sleep.

Then, abruptly, she was wide awake, eyes open, mind sharp as broken glass. She knew, with terrible certainty, that Leon had been making love not to her but to some other woman. She knew it more clearly than if he had admitted adultery because her body, not her mind, was aware of the subtle differences. He had murmured to her words that were not her words, used caresses calculated to arouse the ardour of a different woman, gestures that were unfamiliar to her.

It seemed to her that he had given no hint during the previous weeks of anything untoward. He had been . . . preoccupied. That was the most she had noticed. He had hesitated before answering some comment of hers, perhaps, or changed the subject. She had made excuses, assumed he was tired, or working too hard. Loving him, she had not let herself see or hear anything that might bring hurt.

Only her body could not be fooled. Even at the peak of pleasure it had known, even as they succumbed together to what Leon had taught her was called the "little death", it was not deluded.

Salka lay as she had lain a few minutes before, only now everything was

163

different: even the room seemed darker, as though the mist outside was cold and threatening, where twenty minutes before it had been the landscape of a dream.

Leon assumed her long silence while they took coffee and rolls, butter and honey, to be just another manifestation of her condition, and at eleven disappeared to walk as usual. He kissed her goodbye, expecting her eagerly proffered lips and finding instead a cool cheek: he curved his fingers beneath her chin and turned her face to him, but could read nothing in her opaque golden-brown eyes.

In his absence she struggled with her thoughts. For a long time, she had been aware of Leon's character. He had wanted her so much whilst he felt she still was not his. As long as she did not capitulate entirely to him, as long as he sensed in her some reservation and knew there was a place where he could not yet reach her, then he was still the pursuer, and all his pride demanded that he capture her.

She could see, now, that the very form of such a love—if love it could be called—contained the seeds of its own destruction. He had worked to win her with all the ardour he could command, and in the end he had succeeded. She had stopped resisting him, she had come to love him, because he seemed so genuinely to love *her*. He had brought her to it despite herself—and then he must have found, as he always had before, that it was the chase and not the object of it he so passionately desired. So it had begun again, the pattern he repeated so many times. Only now she, Salka, was caught up in it.

Small things she had scarcely noticed at the time came back to her, assembling themselves into a chilling pattern. There had been fewer shirts in Leon's mahogany wardrobe with the glass-fronted shelves and the ivory handles. When he dressed for dinner one evening he had been unable to find a particular pair of his cuff links. Last time they visited Praterstrasse, Sandor had said nothing about Leon's staying there during the week, and when she had started to speak of it, Leon had swiftly interrupted. All sorts of things, unremarkable in themselves, suddenly became damning evidence that Leon was either using again the rooms to which he had taken her on New Year's Day, or had acquired others. She was in no doubt as to their purpose.

She stayed in her room through the heat of the day, walking up and down, up and down, feeling as caged by her situation as she had done all that time ago in the Radins' Hamburg apartment. In the afternoon, tired and depressed, she lay on the bed and slept. Waking two hours later, she found that it was dusk, and Leon had not returned.

She levered herself off the bed. Holding her wrapper closed, for it would no longer fasten over the baby, she pushed the window that stood ajar and stepped out on to the narrow balcony. The garden was deserted, the cane chairs left haphazard and a sunshade lay open on the grass beside a child's toy soldier and a crumpled newssheet. The air was tepid, moist on her skin.

When she was dressed for dinner she walked through the empty hotel rooms—everyone must be eating—and across the damp grass. She followed the twisting gravelled path that led down to the water's edge, through bushes of deadly nightshade and the twining red convolvulus. She reached the precarious wooden jetty where, amid clumps of water iris, a couple of dinghies were secured for the night. Leon had warned her not to walk on it: deliberately she stepped on the slippery old slats and with childish bravado made her way to its farthest end. She stared out across the Altaussee at the distant glimmer of the glacier. Clouds of gnats danced on the waters; she could hear the whirring of stag beetles in the undergrowth. She stood as still as the heron she had glimpsed only that morning, as still as the nocturnal creatures she had frozen in their tracks as she passed them in the long grass. Her eyes gleamed gold in the strange, butterfly mask of her skin so that she too seemed camouflaged for the coming night.

She tried to summon her anger, that had proved in the past to be her ally, that could carry her through as it had before, but it would not come. She was too vulnerable, for now she was two people, not one. Burdens of the flesh—she almost smiled at the irony. At the beginning of the day she had revelled in that burden, convinced that only by submitting to the traditional feminine fate had she found contentment. Now, a few hours later, it seemed that she had engineered her own downfall. She called herself a fool because she had not possessed sufficient wit to dissemble, to prevaricate, to lie to Leon and thus ensure his fidelity.

Instead, she was the victim of her husband's complex sexual life. Common sense told her that, if she were the most involved with him, she was still not the only woman he had hurt. But she did not care what they had suffered. She did not want to know who they were or anything about them.

For all that slow summer day she had been learning a new emotion, enduring the spasms of the heart with which she was to become achingly familiar.

For the first time in her life, she was jealous.

165

Chapter 15

After that, the days jumbled themselves together somehow, and only the steady growth of the child she carried marked the passing of the weeks.

She remained at the Döbling house for the summer and spent much of her time in the long garden-parlour, half-lying in the swing-chair, staring out towards the empty road and watching the chestnut trees make chequered shadows on the grass through hot afternoons. For the baby's sake she tried not to think, but she could not always hold it at bay and the pain of her thoughts was like being scratched by a diamond: shrill and needle-sharp.

She did not speak to Leon of what she now knew, for no confirmation was necessary. He had quickly appreciated that she was aware of his infidelity but saw no reason to modify his behaviour: he was, after all, only doing the same as many men in his circumstances. He was discreet and careful—what more could she ask?

He did not neglect Salka, either. She did not go about much during the day and never at night, since women in her condition were not expected to appear in society. Instead, he bought her books and told her about the bank; at weekends he would urge Friedrich to dine with them, for he knew how much she liked his brother. And—within the bounds imposed by her condition—he made love to her often.

To her own surprise, Salka found she wanted him despite everything. Even when she thought she could not bear to have him touch her, when she planned and intended to reject him as she had before, she could not resist him. It made her almost ashamed of herself: it seemed undignified. She meant to be cool and distant, but when he looked at her with his eyebrows lifted in an unspoken question, when his voice dropped into that low and intimate register, she knew that knowledge of what was to come was written plainly on her face. When he put out the light at last and turned to her, she welcomed him with small, despairing sighs of consent as she surrendered to the endless craving he roused in her, hostage to the pleasure of her senses.

She could not change the love she felt for Leon now, the love that had seized her when she thought she was free. She could not change it, but she suffered from it and the jealousy it brought was drawn tightly like a stricture round her heart. It seemed to her sometimes that her jealousy changed everything, coloured by its strength whatever she looked at, every emotion she felt. She endured it day after day, and it never grew less.

Just the opposite. It was as though each of her senses was refined so that she was constantly on the alert, wary as an animal guarding its young. She noticed with something like horror that some days when Leon came home, she could actually smell another woman on his clothes: a trace of powder, the faintest hint of perfume.

Salka found she could no longer drink coffee, which gave her heartburn. Instead, Bette made her herbal teas, gentle infusions of gentian, peppermint, ginger or dandelion root. She dutifully ate a good deal of parsley, which her mother always said made beautiful children and the cook used coriander in dishes for Salka, which would make a boy-child muscular.

One afternoon, when Salka was lying on the sofa in the shuttered salon, telling herself she was resting and trying without success to relax her taut limbs, Bette knocked on the door.

"Excuse me, *gnädige Frau*, I thought you might like something to drink."

Wearily, Salka pushed aside the shawl that had been covering her.

"How did you know I was awake?"

Bette gave her a compassionate glance.

"You don't sleep well even at night now, do you? You're looking very tired. This might help: it's limeflower this time, to strengthen the nerves."

"Do my nerves need strengthening?" Salka laughed as she spoke, but Bette took the question very seriously.

"It'll maybe help with your worries just now."

Salka sat up and took the proffered cup. Of course Bette knew she was unhappy. They were of an age, they lived very closely together, and she was an observant young woman: there was no point in pretence.

"What am I going to do, Bette?"

She hadn't meant to ask the question. It took both of them by surprise, and the girl was nonplussed.

"It's not my place to say, *gnädige Frau*. But I don't think you should be out here on your own now, it's getting near to your time."

Salka said slowly, "I hadn't thought. Go back to Praterstrasse, you mean?"

"Yes. The apartment has so many conveniences we haven't got here, a proper room for bathing, even, and I'm sure I don't know how *die Hebamme* is to get to this house."

Salka was astonished. "The midwife is booked for a week before the birth. She'll be here, won't she?"

Bette shook her head. The Frau knew so little.

"Most babies come at night. All my mother's did, and my elder sister

167

had all three of hers after dark. If the baby comes early, and there's only you and me here . . ."

Salka considered.

"You're right, Bette. As soon as it gets cooler, we'll go back to Vienna."

Late in August they closed the house and drove to the city, to the baking heat of the pavements and the sudden chill cast by the shadows of tall buildings. They returned on the Friday: on Sunday Salka slipped out alone to walk the deserted summer streets and feel the cool air wafting from the Danube Canal. She was by now in her thirty-second week, she thought, and Adele had written that pregnancy lasted forty weeks. Her movements had lost their decisiveness, and the swift, swaying walk had given way to a rolling gait.

As she walked, her mind was on Leon. It was clear to her that, pregnant, she interested him less and less. She had seen on his face when he looked at her an expression she did not like to recognise, for she knew it to be triumph. He felt that now she was entirely subjugated and safely confined by impending maternity. She was his, the mother of his child. He did not have to strive any longer for proof of his power over her: he had it.

Salka had to keep pausing for breath and she had a constant dull ache beneath her ribs, so it took her a long time to get home. As she let herself quietly into the apartment, she heard Sandor's voice. He sounded angry: she had never heard him speak with such vehemence. Well, it was none of her business. She crossed the hallway to their side of the apartment, and just then an inner door was opened and it was impossible to miss her father-in-law's words.

". . . show no thought, no concern. What kind of man displays such indifference? You must be deranged. I am ashamed of you."

Leon's voice muttered some reply she could not catch and then it was Sandor again, his words rapid with temper.

"I don't understand. You cannot claim I urged this match upon you. Why choose Salka, of all women?"

Salka stood still, knowing she was a fool to let herself listen but desperate to learn what Leon would say. There was a pause before he answered and then he was so quiet she could only just hear him.

"She had—has—a quality that touched me. I don't know what, exactly. Not just the way she looked. It was as though she was someone I'd known long ago and and always wanted."

Silence fell between them, then she heard the sigh in Sandor's voice.

"That I can understand. Something like that happened for me when I saw your mother for the first time—for her, too. But that is a rare thing. Most marriages are mundane, matters of convenience and propriety, to suit business interests or social obligation." The acid was back in his voice. "I thought you had it. For months you scarcely left Salka's side. Yet now, when she really has need of you, you cannot even tell me where she is, so little do you care."

Now she could hear exasperation in Leon's raised tones.

"Do I have to seek permission to live my own life? I love Salka, yes, but that doesn't tie me to her twenty-four hours a day, for God's sake."

"No one's suggesting that." Sandor's voice rose in exasperation. "You're deliberately choosing to misunderstand me. What upsets me is your lack of fidelity. You appear to have no sense of honour, and that is not a trait you have inherited from me."

"I have never pretended to myself that I could love one woman to the exclusion of all others." Leon had his voice under control now. "Papa, you'll never understand. You've told me often that my mother was the only woman for you. I'm not like that. I'm not capable of such single-mindedness."

"How do you know?" Sandor was tart. "To the best of my knowledge you've never attempted to put a rein on your lust. Sin is sweet in the beginning, but bitter in the end, and the day you realise that will be the day it is too late for repentance."

"And if I don't repent?" Salka had never heard Leon speak to his father in such a way.

"Then you'll lose Salka," said Sandor, grimly. "She's not the fool you appear to think. She loves you now, and she lets you see it. But you're mistaken if you believe she'll continue to do so in the face of your behaviour."

Salka had started move, but was arrested by hearing her own name. Then Leon said, drawling his words, "You had no particularly high opinion of her when we married."

"I didn't know her then. I do now, and I believe she deserves a better man than she's got in you." Salka recognised the contempt for Leon in Sandor's voice and walked hurriedly away, but not before she heard Leon say, "You don't know her if you suppose she'd leave me."

Salka put her hand to her face. How well Leon could read her feelings, to be so certain of her. She opened her own door with relief, but she was too late. Leon, his face white and set, had already stepped into the hallway. He called to her, his voice abrupt, "You didn't tell me you were going out."

"Would it have made any difference if I had?"

"It might have avoided this . . . scene."

"I've only just come in. I don't know what's going on."

"My father is expressing the opinion that I take insufficient care of you because I didn't know your whereabouts."

169

"Oh." She opened her door and Leon followed her inside. She reached up and took the hatpin out of the light straw she was wearing, and placed the pin with its ivory-flower head carefully in the tulipwood box on her bureau. In one corner of the box she glimpsed the bunch of dark velvet violets Leon had sent her in Baden-Baden. Beneath them lay the note that had accompanied them. *I did not know my heart had any door . . .* It was the only love-letter she had received in her life, and it had proved meaningless.

She wanted to walk into his arms, to feel his face in her hair, his body warm and muscular against her own, something to help her carry the weight that burdened her. But she had learnt long ago in Hamburg the value of silence, and she used it now. She took off the pale straw hat and dropped it on to the bed. She turned to look at Leon, and in the bright afternoon light the butterfly mask was more noticeable than ever, her eyes gleaming against the dark skin like bronze metal. Stirred, he took a step towards her, and she saw the excitement in his eyes. She gave a gasp. "*No.*"

But he ignored her, reaching for her shoulders, the white linen collar of her dress. She wrenched herself away.

"We can't," she said: "not now. I'm too near my time."

He dropped his hands: "Of course," and gave an elaborate yawn. "I think I'll go to my room and have a nap before dinner."

When he had gone, Salka sat slowly on the edge of the bed and bent to rub her swollen ankles. It appalled her, the sudden realisation that Leon only wanted her when she resisted him. It seemed perverse and cruel that he was drawn to her when she was fighting him, fending him off. If she admitted she loved him, behaved naturally as her emotions dictated, he treated her with indifference and went his own way. She found tears were dripping from her lowered face on to her hands and then she was really crying as she had not done since she discovered his infidelity, crying for what she had so briefly possessed.

There was a knock at the door. Expecting Bette, Salka sniffed and said without moving, "*Komm herein.*"

It was Sandor. He stood for a moment hesitating in the doorway, clearly as embarrassed as she. He muttered, "*Es tut mir leid.* I'm sorry," and started to pull the door closed.

On an impulse Salka called, "Please. Please come in," and he entered, his face furrowed with worry.

"Is Leon here?"

"He's just gone."

There was anger in Sandor's face now.

"Did he do this?"

She shook her head.

170

"No. Not really. It's just that I wonder sometimes what I'm doing here."

Sandor looked at her tear-stained face and the anger on his own disappeared. He looked older, suddenly, and tired.

"May I sit down."

"Of course." She was surprised when he seated himself on a chair close beside her, and even more so when he put a hand over hers in a consoling and protective gesture. Head still bent, she stared at that hand, big enough to cover both her own. It was carefully tended, the nails shaped and buffed, and on the fourth finger of his left hand was a ring. She knew he always wore it, but she had never taken much notice before of the handsome translucent agate in a heavy gold setting. She thought his wife must have given it, and her mind turned to that extraordinary room, the porcelain and the painting. She was still crying, but in a curious way she was crying now for Sandor and the empty spaces in his life, quite forgetting her concerns.

Sandor let her cry until he saw that she was recovering, then he lent her his large white-linen handkerchief. When she had composed herself he took her hand again, smoothing it under his own, conscious of the still slightly reddened skin from the housework she had always done at the Radin apartment, though he did not know that she had made herself cold cream of oil of almonds, white wax and rose-water to whiten them.

"I cannot make apologies for Leon," he said, "because though he is my son no man speaks for another. I can't explain him to you, since I do not understand him myself. He has so much and gives so little of himself to others."

Salka said, hesitantly, "So you know how he behaves, then?"

"Since he was a very young man. I can't pretend I was the first to recognise him for what he is. Friedrich was far more astute than I, though at the time he was several months short of eighteen. Even then, Leon was incapable of resisting women, nor did he want to. There is something in him that is, I think, ungovernable."

Sandor gave his daughter-in-law a rueful smile. "For a long time I felt I was to blame. Oh yes . . ." he brushed aside her protest, "yes, I feared I had given him a poor inheritance. My wife's brothers were—and are, I may say—profligate where women are concerned, and when he was younger I believed their example must have influenced him. But example alone cannot be held responsible for him now."

"I had no idea you realised what he was like. I thought I had to keep it hidden." Salka's voice was so low Sandor could hardly catch her words.

He asked, curious, "How long did it take you to find out yourself?"

She withdrew her hand from under his and sat up straighter.

"Always. I always knew."

171

"Then either you are exceptionally perceptive or you're a witch."

She managed a smile at that. "Neither: I . . . met Leon by chance, before his engagement to Adele." She told Sandor briefly about the encounter at Freudenau. When she had finished, he nodded.

"So that is why you displayed such antipathy to Leon." His tone was dry. "And to think I supposed it was planned. I owe you an apology, my dear."

She had never heard an endearment from him before, and looked at him uncertainly: was he being sarcastic? He saw her expression and hastened to reassure her.

"I somehow got the idea that you were behaving with calculated cleverness. I had never seen Leon so . . . tamed, and it seemed to me that you knew exactly what you were doing."

"No." Fatigue and despair flattened her voice, and painful self-know-ledge hardened it, so that she sounded like another, older woman speaking. "No. When I resisted him because he frightened me, he put every effort into making me love him. And then, when I did, when I couldn't help myself, when I really, really loved him, then it wasn't enough. It wasn't what he wanted." She took a deep breath. "Now I feel a stranger here. I can't explain to you what its like, not to belong. If I thought Leon loved me it would be hard enough. But as it is, I just want to go home."

"To Hamburg."

"Hamburg?" she replied scornfully. "No. Home to Russia. I knew you wouldn't understand."

Sandor started to say something, then checked himself. He stood up.

"It's almost time for dinner. Will you be all right now?"

"I'm not hungry. I'll just have soup brought in."

His tone was sharp. "You will do no such thing. You're not to hide away from Leon. It is he who is at fault, not you. Don't give him the satisfaction of seeing you in distress."

Her head jerked up and she stared at Sandor with disbelief, and then with growing understanding.

"So bathe your eyes," he said, "and do your hair." He walked to the door. "And remember, *I* won't let you down."

He made her a brief salute and they smiled at each other—like comrades . . . or conspirators.

The first week of September brought no change in the weather, no relief from the languid heat that rose from the pavements and filled the nostrils with fine particles of dust. The air was pungent with the scent of overripe fruit and half-dead flowers, a sweet, heavy smell which made Salka feel

172

sick. Bette said crossly that it was the drains and had a word with the housekeeper: then the apartment smelled for a time of lysol.

Salka, now almost at term, felt all her energy was concentrated on the baby, as though it were the only reality and everything else shadow. She did not feel its movements often now because it had no room to turn or kick. For long periods it rested and she imagined that it slept to gain strength for its impending journey. Above the rounded stomach, Salka herself had become thin. Her limbs had always been slender, and now her face had lost the plumpness of early pregnancy, her cheeks were hollowed and exhaustion fingered delicate purplish bruises on her lids. The strange and beautiful butterfly colouration round her eyes had further intensified, so that she looked as though she were decked for some elaborate masque. She rarely went far from the apartment, though she liked to walk in Praterstern. Sandor had decreed that she must no longer go out alone in case of any accident so Bette usually accompanied her. She insisted on walking a few decorous paces behind her mistress though Salka constantly forgot etiquette and waited for her to catch up. Bette watched the slow figure before her, saw how the women would glance at the bulging folds of her dress with discreet sympathy and how men would look at her face—and look again, their eyes alert with interest. Salka noticed none of them, her mind full of anxiety over Leon, and longings for the baby. She walked on like a woman in a trance, moving with the oddly assertive dignity of the heavily pregnant.

One afternoon they returned home later than usual. It was hotter than ever, a moist heat that beaded Salka's upper lip with sweat and made it hard to breathe. She and Bette had lingered under the Praterstern trees to catch the breath of a breeze trapped there, reluctant to face the unyielding pavements and the airless apartment. Darkness came a little earlier each evening, and by the time they started for home wide lilac and grey clouds were rolling in with the night.

Salka felt uneasy, nervous as a cat who scents a distant storm. She could feel her hair prickling and every movement of her dress grazed her skin. She ate little at dinner: poached fish; a sorbet. Sandor was not at home so she and Leon dined alone, exchanging only desultory remarks. They took their coffee at the table, and then Leon said, with deceptive nonchalance, "I believe I'll go out for an hour or two. Don't wait up for me, you must be tired."

"Where will you go?" She kept the question deliberately mild.

"I said I'd drop into the Café Central around ten. Landesmann will be there. We'll probably have an absinthe and maybe a game of cards." He did not look at her as he answered.

Forty-five minutes later, when he had gone, Salka was discovered by a concerned Bette in the long drawing-room overlooking Praterstrasse, pacing up and down, up and down.

"*Gnädige Frau*, are you all right? Is there pain?"

Salka turned unseeing eyes to the girl.

"Where does he go? Do you know? Where does he go?"

Bette was shocked. "I'm sure I don't know Herr Leon's movements." She put out an anxious hand. "Won't you sit down? You've been on your feet all afternoon, and in this heat I don't . . ."

Salka ignored her. Restlessly, she went to the window, staring down at the street below where the gas-lamps made pools against the encroaching darkness. She was waiting for something—and then it came, a white streak that ripped across the sky, lightning that was followed after long minutes by a distant grumble of thunder.

"It's miles away yet," murmured Bette with relief but Salka did not hear. As though the arrival of the storm had been a trigger, she was feverishly searching for her bag, her keys. She moved as fast as she could through the apartment to the front door, while Bette hurried after her.

"You're not going out? At this time, alone? *Gnädige Frau*, what will your father-in-law say?"

Deaf to Bette's anxious pleading, Salka descended the stairs, holding on to the railings for support. Bette did not even stop for a jacket, but pulled the door shut and followed. In Praterstrasse Salka walked on the edge of the pavement, searching for a cab. One stopped eventually, an old-fashioned horse-drawn fiacre, and she ordered it to the Café Central, fuming at the painful slowness with which it negotiated the bridge to Franz-Josefs-Kai and then followed ill-lit streets to Herengasse. Bette hovered nervously in the doorway, but Salka was beyond caring. Conspicuous by being a woman alone and made more so by her condition, she stood beside one of the grand staircases, and tried to see Leon amongst the crowd: she scanned the marble-topped tables where people played chess, read newspapers in wooden frames or chatted over their glasses of coffee. The lights were dim, curving brass lamps hanging from the glass ceiling.

A man rose from his seat near one of the tall, exotic plants which flourished heedless of the smoky air, and came over to Salka. He gave a formal bow.

"Frau Salaman. You should not be here alone. Can I be of service?"

Salka looked at him uncertainly, then managed a smile of relief.

"Herr Landesmann. My husband told me he was meeting you tonight. Is he still here?"

David Landesmann glanced behind him, worried. "Why, no. He was only here briefly. . . . Perhaps I could accompany you home?"

"I'm not going home. I want to find Leon." Salka's voice was louder

174

than she intended and people sitting at nearby tables had dropped into interested silence. "Did he say where he was going?" she persisted, and David Landesmann swallowed in evident anxiety.

"I'm so sorry. I . . . I couldn't say."

Salka stared at him and he licked his lips nervously. "I see," she said, in a flat voice. "Thank you. Please don't let me detain you."

At the doorway she paused. Bette came forward and behind her, sitting in his high-backed leather chair, Salka saw the doorman. He stood up.

"Would you like a cab, *meine Frau*?"

"Yes, in a moment. But I'm trying to find someone—Herr Salaman. I believe he left here about half an hour ago. I thought perhaps, if he went by cab, you might have heard him state his destination?"

The doorman said dourly. "Couldn't do that, I'm afraid."

Salka sighed. "Of course. Well, if you would call one for us . . . ?"

Bette, who had not spoken, turned to the doorman, a bright smile on her lips, and asked, in the slightly whining Viennese dialect Salka found so hard to follow, "Oh, please, it would be so very kind of you. My lady, as you can see, is in no condition to go rushing round looking for a man who isn't at home where he should be. I'm sure you have children of your own, you'll understand."

The man paused for a moment, shoving back his cap to scratch his head. Then, grudgingly, he said, "Several came out at once, so I can't be sure. I think he went to Saphir's. I'm not certain it was him, mind."

"Thank you." Salka fumbled in her purse and handed him a coin. When he had moved into the street, ready to whistle for a driver, she whispered to Bette, "Saphir's?"

"I don't know. I never heard of it." She caught Salka's arm. "Please come home. You shouldn't be going around such places in your state. It's not right."

Salka shrugged her off, not ungently, as if she were a bothersome child in an adult world. As they stood in the doorway lightning slashed the sky again, making them jump, and breathlessly Bette counted the seconds before the thunder.

"It's much nearer. Oh please, let's go home—it's dangerous to be out in a storm."

She could have saved her breath: Salka was oblivious. She ordered the cab to Saphir's, and the driver peered down at her with a smirk on his face which only Bette noticed. In the musty interior she said, nervously, "I don't think it's a good place, whatever it is."

"I'm sure it isn't." Salka sounded grim.

Bette tried once more to deflect her.

"What are you going to do when we get there?"

"I've no idea."

175

Saphir's proved to be in a shabby street near Circusgasse, where the cab drew up outside a door marked only by a gas-lamp on the wall. A couple of men lounging nearby eyed the two women as they got out of the cab, and one of them called something in a hoarse voice which made Bette blush and move closer to Salka. The door was opened by a girl of about fourteen in a white cap and apron, who let them into the overwarm entrance foyer and then scurried away. After a moment a middle-aged woman came out to them. Even under the inadequate lighting they could see the high colour of her cheeks, and against the solid, dark bulk of her dress shone a necklace of showy stones. She smiled, showing a mouthful of bad teeth, and raised an eyebrow.

"My ladies. What can I do for you?"

Salka's voice was hoarse and deep. "Herr Salaman—I believe he is here?"

The woman smiled again, bland. "I don't believe I know the name."

"I *know* he's here."

"Of course, our gentlemen sometimes prefer to use assumed names— one never knows."

"Do you want a description of him?" Salka asked abruptly.

"No, no," the woman said hastily. "If you will give me a few moments . . ." She went out through a long passage leading to the back of the house. Left alone, Salka and Bette stood quietly. They heard footsteps above, a door slamming. A man descended the narrow staircase, hat in hand, buttoning his coat. As he passed them Salka caught the smell of liquor on his breath, and another, different scent that spoke of warm flesh and amorous activity. Catlike, she sniffed the air when he had gone, and her suspicions hardened into certainty. This was a place like the restaurant to which Leon had taken her that New Year's Eve, only worse.

The woman returned, her bland smile intact, and told them that no, there was no Herr Salaman on the premises. Indeed, the name meant nothing to her. . . . She thought that now the ladies should leave, and her eyes lingered visibly upon Salka's thickened waist as she suggested this. But even as she spoke, Salka had moved, pushing past her, heading blindly down the dark corridor while behind her the woman first protested, then lifted her shoulders in resignation.

At the first doorway Salka paused for a fraction of a second: memories of that *cabinet particulier* with its sweating inhabitants dissuaded her. She hurried on, through a doorway hung with a curtain made of beads that clinked softly in her wake, then past an archway leading to a dark garden surrounded by high walls. She paused there for a moment: it smelled of the kitchen and cheap perfume. There was a shrubbery on one side and as she looked two shadows detached themselves from it, becoming a man in evening dress and a woman straightening a sleazy satin frock. For a

176

moment she thought, *Leon*? and then she heard the voice and turned away.

Like a sleepwalker Salka moved on, hearing and sense of smell made hypersensitive by jealousy, her steps silent and rapid. She came to a back staircase and climbed it slowly, panting with the effort. At the top she found herself in a long room, dimmer even than the rest of this peculiar house. The only light seemed to come from lamps almost at floor level, and then she perceived that along the length of the room people were lying on low divans or else on heaps of cushions. Some were alone, others in pairs, their faces and hands illuminated by the golden glow of the oriental lamps beside them. As her eyes became accustomed to the gloom she saw a woman bending over a brazier in the centre of the room to light a spill, which she carried back to her supine partner. She used it to ignite a long, slender pipe which she then handed him, and lay down beside him as he started to draw on it.

Salka became conscious now of the smell. The overrich, sickly, cloying odour reached inside her throat and made her cough, so that she had to support herself with one hand on the newel post. No one took any notice of her: it was as if she—or they—did not exist. The movements of the smokers and their partners were slow and gentle. She saw another woman rise and drift away with somnambulistic ease, as though the air were water.

So this was why the doorman had been so reluctant to direct her to Saphir's. Women like her did not go to such places. She knew—everyone did—of their existence, knew that beneath the gaiety and glamour of Vienna lay this other, dissolute world where men could indulge any perverse and sensual pleasure.

She did not know how long she had been standing in that heavy atmosphere and she had forgotten the storm outside when suddenly the room was filled with a cold flash of lightning, which showed her that it was an attic, its high windows covered with flimsy curtains, the wooden floor bare but for an occasional square of patterned carpet.

The attic was again enveloped in darkness, rendered more dense by the preceding brilliance, and out of the silence, somewhere on the gallery above, Salka heard the beginnings of a sound both foreign and familiar, something between a song and a sob. It took her a few moments to identify the involuntary broken murmurs and cries of a woman on the very brink of pleasure.

Salka stood transfixed by the rhythmic little cries. She wanted to run, to put her hands over her ears to block out the voice, only she could not move. It was not prudery but pain. The sound of the unknown woman's ecstasy had tightened her chest and made her gasp for breath. Until this moment she had known that Leon was unfaithful, and she had suffered.

Only now, for the first time, she was forced to realise that he was unfaithful to her *with other women*. Worse, perhaps it was not many women, briefly known, but one in particular, whom he loved. She had been jealous enough before she wondered about Leon's partners. Hearing the unseen woman on the gallery above, Salka was seared by the thought that it could be Leon who was the instrument of that sensuous pleasure.

Her head reeling from pent-up emotion and the overpowering haze of the opium, she turned to go, stumbling down the stairs, fleetingly lit up by another sheet of lightning which tore the sky apart, and along the narrow corridor, past the odorous garden, to where Bette patiently waited by the door. Then she was outside, panting, her throat raw from unshed tears. It had begun to rain at last, a warm downpour that immediately soaked through their light summer clothes.

Salka stood outside the closed door of that place, rivulets of water running down her face, her heart pounding with the effort of the last few minutes. Like a lunatic, she clutched her hair, the neck of her dress, her already sodden skirt, in the grip of an anger fuelled by Leon and the woman on the gallery, and the fate that had shown her love and then so swiftly disinherited her. Lightning struck again, and Bette saw Salka's anguished face, blue and livid in its light, and heard her scream into the storm: *"Why did he marry me? Why? Why?"*

Chapter 16

It was midnight before they reached the Praterstrasse apartment and Sandor was waiting.

Without a word of reproach he opened the door to the two sodden women, and caught Salka's arm as she swayed against Bette. Together they got her to her room, and while Bette pulled off Salka's soaking dress and put on her nightclothes, Sandor heated water in the kitchen to fill a stone hot-water bottle and mixed two glasses of brandy and seltzer. He listened while Bette explained where they had been, then gave her a brandy and sent her to bed. He held the door for her. "Thank you," he said, "for all you have done."

He pulled a chair forward, sat beside the bed and looked at his daughter-in-law with compassion. Her eyes were closed, her hair hung damply round her shoulders and her skin was yellow from exhaustion, so that the butterfly mask was more emphatic than ever. She appeared young and forlorn, and Sandor watched over her with a tenderness he had almost forgotten: like the boy in the Hans Christian Andersen stories he used to read to his sons when they were small, he felt as though the icicle that was his heart was melting.

Conscious of his gaze, Salka said, "I'm sorry," her voice deep from tiredness. "I'm a fool. It did no good."

"I assume you tried to find Leon. He has still not returned, so I presume you didn't succeed."

"I don't know. I think I found the place where he was. But I didn't see him, I couldn't . . ." She twisted her face away in evident distress.

Sandor waited a while, then asked gently, "Do you want to tell me about it?"

"There's nothing to tell. He wasn't at the Café Central. David Landesmann knew but wouldn't tell me where he'd gone, so I asked the doorman. We tried . . . a house. But he wasn't there."

"A house?"

She said, "Don't ask me about that. Please."

Sandor sighed.

"I have no need to ask, my dear. I can imagine all too well."

She sniffed and tears slid from under her closed lids.

"You can't. Nobody could imagine such dreadful things."

He smiled despite himself.

"I have lived more than twice your lifetime. Do you really think I would be shocked by anything now?"

She turned her head towards him at that, and he saw with a start the golden eyes that evoked so many memories. She lifted her hands from the cover, letting them fall back on the bed in a hopeless query, and repeated to her father-in-law the question she had screamed in that shabby street.

"Why did Leon marry me? Why me?" There was no emotion in her voice now, it was flat and quiet.

He could have answered, because you are unusual, different, because you are strong enough to resist him, because a beautiful woman arouses the desire to beget children. All he said was, "There was never anyone else Leon wanted. You know the match with Adele was arranged by Radin and myself. Until you, Leon refused even to discuss matrimony."

"You didn't want him to marry me." It was not an accusation, merely a statement. Sandor pressed her hand in apology.

"I was mistaken."

She remarked in that exhausted voice, "You know, I've always had the most extraordinary feeling about Leon. From the very beginning, from the time he spoke to me at the Freudenau, I felt as though I knew him from . . . before. I don't know how. But the feeling was so strong, it seemed to me I couldn't refuse. Nothing to do with loving him, or even liking him. But it was as though he was always meant for me. It's absurd."

Sandor said mildly. "Not at all." He paused, and picked his words carefully. "People from a similar background are often drawn to each other. It would explain everything."

She gave a half-smile. "It would if our backgrounds were not so wildly different. I come from a poor Russian town. My people live frightened lives. I didn't think so when I lived there, but I see now how small their hopes were, and even those were never realised. But you"—she waved a hand which took in the exquisitely furnished apartment, the discreet servants, the elegance of his own clothes—"you inhabit another world."

He was silent for so long that she feared she had offended him. Then he stirred, and said, "I'll let you sleep now."

"*No*. Don't go." She looked thoroughly alarmed. "I can't sleep yet. Please stay, just for a little while."

"There is a story I'd like to tell you. Would that be too tiring?"

"A story?"

"A true one, as it happens. But one I have not spoken of for many years." He told her, then, of his father's house near Pinsk, and his twelve brothers and sisters. Once he had begun, he found he remembered things he had buried so deep within himself he thought they had gone for ever: the noise of market-days; the smell of the streets; oil-cakes; spice-boxes; bath-houses.

180

He spoke haltingly at first, as he felt his way back into his childhood, then with growing confidence. Salka listened, contemplating him with astonishment and a new understanding as he showed her the past they shared so closely, nodding when he touched a chord for her, finding herself near to tears when he spoke of his parents, of the noisy household where there was always a new baby and his mother combed their hair on the doorstep in preparation for the Sabbath.

Sandor forgot the time, forgot where he was. He was conscious only of the young woman who lay propped on her pillows, utterly absorbed by his revelations of their mutual consciousness. He talked with an animation he had not displayed for years; his dark eyes glowed with emotion. All the studied calm, the assured dignity he carefully cultivated for his role as a prosperous banker, fell away. Salka had seen Sandor as a distant, powerful figure, inspiring awe but not affection, not a man in his own right but merely Leon's father. For the first time she noticed that the thick hair which grew like Leon's was still dark except for the heavy wings of silver at the temples. As he gestured and strode about the room in the excitement of his story, it became apparent to her that his body was supple and straight beneath the confines of his immaculately tailored suit and waistcoat, and the dauntingly high white collar of his starched shirt. As he explained how he had met Rothschild, all those years ago, she could see exactly how he must have been that extraordinary day in Frankfurt when he bought a suit and found a future: she saw the strength of purpose, the magnetism, the incredible vitality that had carried him so far from the country of his birth.

It was the early hours before he had finished speaking, and he left nothing out. To no one—least of all his sons—had he ever spoken of the pain that Anna's death had been to him. He revealed to Salka something that he had not admitted even to himself—that he had an irrational and primitive fear that her death had been a punishment, that he should never have forsaken his faith and forgotten the god of his fathers.

When he had nothing left to say, he gave Salka a rueful smile and ran his hands through his hair in a way that reminded her of Leon.

"I've talked too much. I've worn you out. But I wanted you to know. Mine is not, you see, a different world to yours."

She said simply, "I am so glad you told me. It changes everything." On an impulse she reached out for his hand and held it to her cheek, the agate in its gold setting smooth against her skin. She felt immeasurably happier as though a void had been filled. It lifted her loneliness, to know that Sandor bore the same burden of memory as she; it softened her longing for Jonas and Dora—and it assuaged another hurt. It had been a long time since the ugly word had crossed her mind. *Ostjude*. Ghetto Jew.

But even that had lost its power to wound now that it applied also to Sandor Salaman.

Hesitant, she asked, "I still don't really understand why you wanted to leave Russia. I was forced to go. Cholera had spread to Polotsk and my parents said that the pogroms would follow as sure as night follows day. Did that happen to you also?"

He made a wry grimace, lifting his shoulders in a gesture of resignation that was age-old. He thought of Ozer's helpless fury at the economic harassment and legal humiliation under which the Jews of Russia laboured. He remembered listening, as a bewildered little boy, while his elders whispered anxiously of accusations levelled against them concerning ritual blood-murder. Scarcely had that horror passed when the whispers began again: Jews were being forcibly expelled from villages where they had lived for generations. The Salamans, like all their neighbours, were haunted by the spectre of the pogroms, and from the age of seven Sandor endured a recurring nightmare of a courtyard filled with people, all with huge white bandages wrapped round and round their heads where they had been clubbed by mounted police.

But all that paled beside the worst whispers, about a cousin he had never seen, from a village in the province of Vyatka. Dov was nine years old, like himself. He was taken, the whispers said, torn from his family by the soldiers, conscripted for twenty-five years by order of the Czar. In one dreadful day forty children were seized from that village alone, hustled into clumsy soldiers' overcoats and marched away in straggling ranks. Marched for ten hours a day, mourned the whispers, while Sandor lay rigid in his bed, his brothers snuffling in their sleep beside him. Given nothing but biscuit to sustain them, no word of comfort, no warm hand to hold. Helpless, went on the whispers, ill, exposed to the icy wind that blows from the Arctic Ocean. The whispers went on and on and on about that other boy of nine. Coughing, they sighed, coughing his little heart out. Going to his grave, along with all the others. Even now, fifty years later, Sandor felt tears sting his eyes as they had that night.

He said slowly, feeling his way among all those images and whispers, "It was so many things, gathering and gathering throughout my father's life and *his* father's life, and mine, until I had to leave, for all of them. Do you see?" He glanced across at the window, where beyond the light summer curtains they could hear the rain streaming. The lightning had passed, but they caught the distant rolling of thunder many miles away. "What finally made me leave," Sandor went on, musing, "was something huge and powerful, impossible to resist: a storm wind that ripped me out of my place and carried me away."

Salka nodded, thinking of the physical and emotional storm through which she had just passed herself, and recalling the hectic days of her journey from Russia and those first strange weeks in Hamburg.

"A storm wind." She repeated it, thoughtful. "It was like that for me, too, only I never gave it a name. A storm wind."

There was a companionable silence for a few minutes, before Sandor stirred and said, "I must go. You need to sleep, and it is most improper for me to be in your room. You know now how very correct and conventional I am, thanks to my immaculate Austrian background." They smiled at each other. By the time he closed the door she was almost asleep, but her dreams were full of the zither in the Café Central. Only now she was sitting in the darkness, on her carpet-bag on the train from Polotsk, and at the other end of the carriage a group of Poles were singing. She could not understand the words, but their meaning was unmistakeable: it was a song of loving and leaving and loss.

She wept, in the dream, as she had wept on the train; her head ached from lack of sleep and her back from sitting upright for so long.

When she woke next morning, long after her usual hour, she remembered her dreams instantly, reminded by the pain in her back. After several minutes it disappeared and she rang for Bette to bring her rolls and *Kaffee*.

The girl pulled back the curtains, chatting brightly about the morning and casting quick little looks at Salka. Sunshine spilled into the room; trees and buildings had been refreshed by the downpour.

"Herr Salaman has gone to the bank as usual," Bette said, casually, "and Herr Leon is just finishing *das Frühstück*."

Their eyes met, and Salka said quickly, "Don't mention . . ."

"As if I would." Bette pushed another pillow behind her back. "I shouldn't go out today, if I were you. Take things quiet."

Salka drank her coffee."All right. I'll do some sewing"—she looked round the room, feeling exhausted but somehow energetic at the same time—"and I'll . . . I'll wash my hair, if you'll help me."

Two hours later she stood in the empty drawing-room, gazing through the gilded railings of the balcony, out over the Praterstrasse to the parkland beyond, and rubbing her hair. She was thinking about Sandor and the revelations of the previous night, but keeping at bay thoughts of that shadowy house, the oversweet smell of opium and the ecstatic sobbing of that unseen woman.

Without any warning, she was suddenly aware of a warm gush between her legs. She gave a little wail of startled embarrassment. Her bare feet and the carpet were wet with a clear, colourless fluid, absolutely scentless and beneficial as rain: it took an entire thunderstruck minute for her to realise the waters had broken and she must tell someone.

It was only much later, reflecting upon the events of that September day, that she noted with sadness that her instinctive reaction had been to summon not her husband—not Leon—but Sandor.

The old Academician's voice had taken on the assured, rounded tones of a professional speaker in full flow. Sandor Salaman breathed heavily into his beard and silently allotted him precisely ten minutes. Through the hum of his thoughts he caught the occasional well-turned phrase: "generously donated this magnificent library . . . nurture the young minds in our midst . . . financing culture no less than building business empires gives us the foundations for the future . . ."

Surreptitiously he put a hand inside his waistcoat, withdrew the heavy gold chain and let the watch fall into his palm. Holding it shielded he glanced at the time: five-and-twenty minutes to five. The watch was cool in his hand, exact to the minute as it had been these twenty-odd years— Anna's gift. As he thought her name, a small grimace of pain crossed his face. The message about Salka's confinement had brought it all back to him: his wife's stifled cries that terrible night, the formless bundle he had not been meant to see, and Anna's eyes looking at him, not green now but dark with suffering. He shook his head to clear it: he must get home. The Academician's tone had changed, becoming more elegiac, and Sandor composed himself for the end of the speech, the soft spatter of gloved hands in well-bred applause, the murmur of appreciative comments. The Academician was turning to him, gesturing to the rostrum. He must be quick. Another time, another day, this would have been a moment to linger over, to savour—not today. He moved briskly across the platform to speak.

When he had finished, he politely forced his way through the out- stretched hands—shaking one here, another there—and the smiling congratulations to make his way to where Leon stood.

"Have you heard?"

"Nothing yet, Papa."

"We'll go straight home; the motor's outside."

Leon said, diffidently, "I'll be there as soon as possible. I've one or two things . . ."

Conscious of being watched, Sandor tempered the tone of his voice, contenting himself with saying dryly, "I cannot imagine they are more pressing than Salka's business at this moment."

Leon had the grace to look ashamed, but did not answer. Sandor turned sharply and moved away, taking more proffered hands as he neared the doorway. He was almost there when he saw he was about to come face to face with the Mayor, Karl Lueger.

Sandor hesitated just for a fraction of a moment, then keeping his hands firmly at his sides, he gave a slight bow. The majestic figure turned towards him and duplicated the courtesy. Neither smiled. Sandor had supposed he would be there, though he would greatly have preferred the man's absence: as Mayor, he had little choice but to attend the opening of so well-found a library, especially when it was the gift of a private firm like Salaman und Sohn to the University. But while Sandor knew well enough that Lueger—whom he admired as a tireless and intelligent administrator—would be prepared to be civil to him in public, he had no intention of allowing such civility. Lueger had been elected Mayor after a considerable struggle, for he fought on an anti-liberal, anti-Jewish policy, and he exploited the grievance of the lower-middle class by ranting against the "Jewish press" and insisting they must be "conquered". Sandor was well acquainted with Vienna's unhappy record towards its Jews: he knew that his connections with the aristocratic von Saars bought him some immunity, but he was damned if he'd shake the hand of "handsome Karl".

For the sake of the old Academician, now bumbling happily beside them, he exchanged a few meaningless words with him and the Mayor, then excused himself. His driver was waiting, good man, the door of the motor already open.

"Can we do it in half an hour?"

"Sir."

Once they were moving, he closed his eyes. He was exhausted: by lack of sleep these two nights, by worry for Salka, and by anger towards his son, so heedless, so careless of what was his. Last evening, when Leon had taken himself out after dinner, apparently quite capable of leaving his wife in labour, Sandor raised his voice—something he rarely did—"Lust and reason are enemies. You are possessed by folly!" Leon had stood very still—just the way Anna used to do—and looked at him with those fathomless eyes of his, then he had shaken his head slightly and gone. Sandor wished very much that it had been his elder son, the gentle Friedrich, who had married Salka. Though, he had to admit, she'd undoubtedly be too much for Friedrich. She had a mind of her own, that girl.

When they reached the apartment, he had the door open before the vehicle had even stopped, was out and half-way up the stairs by the time the driver had got out. The apartment was still ominously quiet. He stopped at the door to Leon and Salka's rooms—nothing. Then he heard Doktor Schindler's voice, slow and soothing, and Salka groaned deeply. It was still going on, then. Forty-eight hours. He went swiftly through to his dressing-room, with its walls of mahogany cupboards, and rang for hot water. A maid answered the bell, a young girl he didn't know, her face under the tightly-braided plaits red with excitement. When she brought the jug of hot water he said, "Would you ask Bette to see me, please."

"I'm sorry, sir, she's with the mistress. Is there anything else?"

"No, no, thank you." As the girl turned to go, he said, "Has—anything happened, do you know?"

"I don't think so, sir. No one's come out for half an hour now."

"When Herr Doktor or Bette comes out, tell them that I am home."

When the girl had closed the door, Sandor took off his jacket and waistcoat, removed his shirt and washed. Then he dressed in fresh clothes, used cologne liberally and felt better. He went into the drawing-room and tried to read that day's copy of *Neuer Wiener Tageblatt*, but the words glazed on the page before him. It had been an hour and a half since he got home. Someone appeared and asked if he wished dinner served and he said no, perhaps later.

He went back to his own room, and from the top drawer of his bureau removed a drawstring bag of embroidered linen. He sat for a long time on a straight-backed chair, the pouch on his knee, fingering it meditatively.

He had been most unhappy with Leon's choice of a bride, he freely admitted it. It had been nothing personal, but he had grown far from his Russian roots. He had become an Austrian, a successful banker, and he would have preferred a girl such as Adele, of more settled, German background. So when Leon prevailed, he had made no attempt to make his son's Russian bride welcome: he had viewed her from the first with an arrogant disdain of which he was now heartily ashamed. She had gained his respect gradually by her intelligence and the dignity with which she had comported herself. But she had done more than that: she had looked at him with the golden eyes of an icon, and brought him face to face with his buried past. Now she was in danger, as Anna had been all those years ago. In his despair, and because his wife was Christian, he had not dared offer any words to his god on her behalf. Afterwards, he thought he had gone beyond that, had deemed himself too sophisticated, too much a man of the world, to need the simple comfort of prayer. He was older now, he had suffered much since then, and yet until this moment he had continued to neglect his religion.

Very slowly, Sandor opened the linen bag and removed the two long leather thongs with a square, black-leather box about the size of a calling-card case fixed to each. He balanced them on his hand, feeling both trepidation and relief. Though they were sealed, he knew that inside were tiny parchments carrying Hebrew texts: *And it shall be a sign unto thee upon thine hand, and for a memorial between thine eyes, that the Lord's law may be in thy mouth.*

He went through the elaborate process of donning the *tefillin*, the old ritual designed to focus the mind on the devotions. He placed one box on

186

his left arm, on the inner side which would be nearest his heart when he prayed, and coiled the strap seven times about his forearm. The other box he put in the middle of his forehead, on the hairline, winding the strap about his head and knotting it, bringing the ends over his shoulders in front. Then he wound the armband strap three times round his wrist and upper knuckle.

The physical act of binding, the touch of leather on his skin, calmed him as it was intended to do. *Hear O Israel, the Lord your God, the Lord is One. And you shall love the Lord your God with all your heart, and with all your soul, and with all your might.* He smiled as he remembered his father telling him that God Himself wears *tefillin.*

Sandor hunted in the linen bag for another, smaller pouch—of silk this time—and took out his *tallis,* the long prayer-shawl banded with black, to mourn forever the destruction of the Temple. As the cool folds warmed round his neck, smelling faintly of sandalwood, comfortable and comforting, he wondered how he could have been guilty of such negligence.

He turned to face east and started to pray, the familiar litany flooding his brain. He found words of repentance coming unbidden, words he had not uttered in three decades.

I have turned away from Thy goodly precepts.
Take me not hence in the midst of my days.
I am but a clod of the earth, a worn dust of the ground;
A frail mortal, a fleeting shadow, a wind that passeth away and returneth not.
What am I? What is my life; what my powers; what my righteousness?

Sandor prayed for a long while rocking quietly back and forth on his heels, the timeless chants, the repetitions, melodies and grace notes holding him rapt. He continued until he found he was no longer using the Hebrew incantations, but merely asking, over and over, that Salka be brought safely through her confinement with the child.

He removed the *tallis,* kissing each set of fringes swiftly before he did so, and unbound the phylacteries from his forehead and his arm. Then he put on his jacket and went to sit in the hallway near Salka's bedroom. He was still taut with anxiety, but also elated, as though he was at a turning-point he could not yet clearly see.

It must have been twenty minutes before anything happened and he waited patiently, straining to tell from the faint sounds what was happening behind the door. Then it opened, and Bette hurried out, her once-crisp apron limp and stained, her white cap awry. When she saw him she stopped short.

"Herr Doktor says, please to step inside."

187

Sandor leapt to his feet, and found his legs were trembling. For two nights and a day he had been waiting. Once he had glimpsed Salka for a moment, looking totally unlike herself, absorbed in the business of birth.

"Is it here?" He could read nothing in her face.

For an answer, she pushed open the door for him, and Sandor stepped inside . . . and stopped.

The long room, with its substantial dark-wood furniture, grey walls and rose-flowered curtains, was unbearably hot, for at the far end a fire burned in the marble fireplace. Near it stood the cradle, hung with white. It was empty. He turned to the bed, and Doktor Schindler stood back so that Sandor could see his daughter-in-law.

Salka was lying very still in the wide bed with its rounded mahogany headboard, and Sandor realised that the end of the mattress had been raised slightly, so that she was tilted at an odd angle. Her eyes were closed and she seemed to be asleep. He asked Doktor Schindler: "What . . . ?"

"Everything is splendid, my dear sir. We raised the bed purely as a precaution, you understand: she lost a little too much blood. But she will be perfectly herself in a week or two, and the baby . . ."

"Where is the baby?" His voice cracked with strain. Salka opened her eyes. He saw how pale she was, the butterfly mask an enigmatic shadow about her eyes. She held out her hand and he moved to the bedside.

"Are you all right, my dear? I've been"—he swiftly amended this—"we've been so worried. I'm sorry, but Leon . . ."

She shook her head, an almost imperceptible movement.

"I don't want to hear it." Then she glanced down and said to him, "*Look*" and there was a note in her voice that had not been there before. As she spoke she moved and he saw what he had not previously noticed: cocooned in the curve of her right arm, swaddled in a white shawl, was a shape smaller, surely, than any child could be.

Salka, watching his face, said softly, "Sandor. Here is your granddaughter." She lifted the bundle and his arms curved instinctively to take it.

He gazed down at the child. Very carefully he pulled back the shawl to see more clearly the crumpled features, the closed eyes, the lightly-fuzzed head where the quick pulse beat. As he watched in delight the child moved, its mouth opening in a minuscule yawn; and while he stood there, holding with unaccustomed arms the frail new body, he experienced a sweep of emotions.

Protectiveness was there, for this innocent, helpless child, and anger towards Leon for his lack of feeling and concern for his wife. Also he felt an immense, passionate gratitude to Salka for giving him again what he thought he had lost forever. There was something else, too, an awakened recollection from his own childhood, a memory that had caught him

188

unawares, summoned up by the arrival in his family of Salka herself and prompted by her questioning about Russia.

It was as though this birth completed an unfinished sentence. He could see his father, sitting at the head of the Sabbath table on Friday night, the braided loaf before him covered by an embroidered cloth, the goblet of wine beside it, the candles. Ozer would stroke his beard and look round him with amused pleasure at the excited faces of his thirteen children.

Pride in the family had been imperative for Ozer, a reason to hold up his head in a hostile land. The name of Salaman was amongst the oldest of Jewish families. They were mostly small merchants in Eastern Europe. Many were scholars, studying the *Talmud*. A distant cousin had reached England, they believed, though nothing had been heard of him for fifty years. And throughout their history, rich or poor, that one dominating precept had been handed down from father to son: *Your family are your tower. They are all that you have. Keep them close, defend them at all costs. And in return, they will become your own defence.*

Sandor had left Russia and the family behind him, drifted imperceptibly away from the rites and rituals of Judaism. Then he had married Anna and felt himself assimilated, of the new Vienna. He loved his children, but they were Anna's also, of the line of the von Saars. Even at the time of their birth, he had not wished to make them Jews.

It was only now, with the warm weight of his grandchild in his arms, the scent of sandalwood from his *tallis* still clinging to his clothes, that the truth of Ozer's words came to him. He had made the name eminent as it had never been before. It was his, that tower. The tower of Salaman. The only real promise for the future.

He said, stumbling over the words, "She's beautiful. What a beautiful child, Salka."

Salka gave him a tired, radiant smile and held out her arms for the baby. Sandor stood watching as she smoothed the child's cheek with an experimental finger. He looked at this young woman who had brought life when he thought everything was over, and it seemed that the room must be ringing with the sound of his joy.

Chapter 17

Leon arrived too late to see Salka that night, for she had already been left to rest. She heard his low voice answered by the nurse in the next room, some time after eleven, and then the woman opened the bedroom door a crack. Salka feigned sleep. She had no wish to talk to her husband just then. She was tired as she had never been before, every muscle protesting against the huge effort she had made over the last forty-eight hours. Her neck and shoulders ached as though still corded and straining, her throat was sore and the tendons in her legs quivered with fatigue.

The apartment gradually quietened and all sound ceased on the Prater-strasse, but still she lay awake. She felt calmer than she had done at any time during her pregnancy, as though some invisible balance had been restored. She was spent, like a soldier after a victorious battle: utterly drained but so elated it was impossible to sleep. It seemed as if she had never been so alive, every sense sharply alert. She could feel the floor shake as the nurse moved next door, and the tiny, muffled kitten-cries from the nursery were as loud in her ears as if she had been bending over the crib. She could smell the ether Doktor Schindler had administered through the clumsy mask. At first she had refused, disliking the rubbery mass pushed against her face, but later she had been glad of the numbing sensation it temporarily afforded her.

The act of giving birth had shown Salka something she had not come to terms with before. It had not been an exertion of her own will, but of a power outside herself that dictated what her body would do. Many times during the interminable hours of labour she had longed for it to stop; sweating and breathless she had struggled for control. Finally she realised that she was in the grip of a force so great, so implacable, so powerful that to deny it would be perilous.

Only then, when she acceded to the inevitable, regular contractions of her own muscles, when she accepted that she was nothing more than a vessel for the child, that it *would* be born despite her cries and pro-testations—only then did she become conscious of the momentum of birth, the surge and cessation of sensation, and dominating it all, deep and dark, mysterious as music half-heard at night, the recurrent drumbeat of pain.

She shifted slightly to change her position: the binder they had pinned round her hips after the delivery gripped tighter than any corset. The child was perfect, Doktor Schindler had assured her: not a mark, not a blemish. She had astounded Salka, with her tiny, squirming body that had almost disappeared in the big red hands of the midwife, and the angry cry she had let out when Doktor Schindler held her by her feet—how could he do that—and gave her a brisk smack. Salka had propped herself on her elbows to see and scarcely noticed the doctor dealing with the afterbirth, so absorbed was she by the things they were doing to her baby: the linen ligature tied round the cord, so astonishingly thick, when it ceased to pulsate; the bandage they wrapped round the baby to hold the pad of scorched cotton in place over the navel.

They had shown her the baby before she was washed, just wrapped in soft flannel, her hair plastered down and slippery with vernix. A few minutes later Salka held the light body for the first time, and marvelled at the minute and perfect features. Then the child opened her eyes and in the middle of that bright room, bustling with activity now the birth was over—the doctor, the midwife, Bette, pink and excited, one of the maids gathering up sheets and towels—it was as though the two of them were quite alone. The baby's as yet unfocused eyes were a deep blue, even the whites were blue with startling health, and Salka felt again the shock she experienced when first she saw Leon, the extraordinary knowledge that someone totally unknown was nevertheless inexplicably familiar—and despite the colour of her eyes, the child did indeed resemble her father: the well-defined mouth, the shape of her face were his.

If only Jonas and Dora could be here now, instantly, to share the first days. She smiled to herself, for she knew exactly what her mother would say, what she had always repeated when a neighbour or a relative gave birth: *One is not enough.*

Salka's thoughts blurred and slowed, her breathing deepened. In the chilly hour before dawn she was conscious of a rustle of movement throughout the apartment. Her baby wailed briefly, then subsided; a floorboard creaked and a man coughed softly. In the Praterstrasse she heard the rattle and clatter of a motor vehicle on the cobbles, and the slam of a distant door: in the silence an authoritative voice ordered, "*Westbahnhof, bitte.*" Someone must be catching an early train, to Germany perhaps, or Switzerland. A journey. A long journey. *Be with her dear ones, whom she leaves, and may it be Thy will to bring her to a safe reunion with them. Hear our petition for Thou, O Lord, hearken to prayer and supplication.* . . . Good heavens, she could still remember the words of that old man who had blessed her before she left Russia, his hands on her head as cool and pale as parchment. What was it he had said? *I believe you have it in you to be the cornerstone of a great family.*

Salka dozed fitfully and dreamed of her parents, and gingerbread, and the old rabbi of Polotsk with his hat of seven sable.

Leon stood beside Salka's bed next morning, holding flowers—heavy-headed roses and babies'-breath—and looked at the child in the crib, where only the curve of a cheek was visible between shawl and lacy wool-bonnet. He appeared so dark and sleek, so groomed and self-sufficient, that she felt frail and battered by comparison. She subsided against her pillows. It seemed almost an insult, that the events of the past forty-eight hours, which had so shaken her, had left him untouched. He smiled and congratulated her, kissed her closed lips and told her Doktor Schindler had let him know how brave she had been. She made to lift the child from the crib but he prevented her.

"No. Don't wake it up on my account."

"You must see your daughter." She had not meant that to sound as it did, like a plea. Ignoring the small reluctant movement of his hands she placed the white bundle in them, watching his face. For a moment it was frozen, expressionless, and she held her breath, her heart in her throat, willing the child to succeed where she had failed.

Leon sat absolutely still, holding his daughter. She stared up at him with wide, unfocused eyes, in concentrated wonder—and Leon melted under that gaze, softened and gentled. Unwilling to let Salka see the effect that look had on him, he handed the baby back to her after a moment with a brusque gesture, but all day his arms remembered the extraordinary new sensation of holding the baby, the sweet insubstantial weightlessness of her.

That afternoon he went straight home and Salka, going silently into the nursery on bare feet, found him standing beside the crib, hands laced behind his back, his expression a mixture of satisfaction and concern. He looked up as she crossed the room to him.

"She's making funny noises. Nothing's wrong, is there?"

"Of course not." She bent to listen. "She's just snuffling a bit."

"The nurse is competent?"

"She looked after all Emma von Ephrussi's babies. I think she's excellent."

"And you. Should you be on your feet? I understand you're to spend at least three weeks in bed."

Salka said, feeling guilty, "I just wanted to make sure . . ."

Leon's voice was authoritative.

"Come along. I met Bette earlier, about to mix up a magic infusion of red raspberry leaves for you to drink. She said it would ensure you made plenty of milk."

Salka paused only to tuck the quilt more tightly round the tiny bundle in the crib, then took Leon's hand and went with him. This was yet another side of his mercurial character, this sudden thoughtfulness, and she wondered wryly how long it would last. Climbing back into bed, suddenly incredibly tired for no apparent reason, she was perplexed again by his unpredictable behaviour. His callous attitude towards her over the last few days—she had been aware, during the long hours of labour, that he was not even in the apartment much of the time—had left an indelible scar. Yet here he was, protective and anxious, his only thought for her well-being. She supposed, as she lay quietly in the half-dark room, that she loved him after all.

She fell asleep happily . . . and awoke in the early hours in near-panic when her sleepy mind registered that she was no longer swollen with the child. After a moment she heard the baby wail briefly in the nursery and subside: the nurse would have heard her. Reassured, Salka was beginning to sink back into sleep when she found that the smell of the roses beside her bed had brought back with unwelcome clarity the hotel garden at Altausee, and the revelation of Leon's infidelity.

They called the child Charlotte. Salka was uncertain at first but tried it experimentally. As the baby grew, it seemed to suit her more. She was a feminine little thing with soft tendrils of brown hair and eyes which were turning each day more speckled and brown, until eventually they were Leon's eyes, deep and intense, so that Salka was disturbed sometimes, taken unawares by the adult gaze in the child's face. The name was shortened until the baby was Lotte—"Much more Viennese," said Leon with satisfaction—and Lotte she remained.

Leon was utterly charmed with her. In his estimation she was perfect— peaceful and pretty, swaddled in little lacy things and unquestionably his. His open adoration of her won Salka and she was convinced that at last there was something tangible between them that would never change. She would hold Lotte and cuddle her, and in the warmed nursery let her lie on the hearthrug, crowing and kicking, curling pink toes and trampling chubby legs, to the horror of the nurse, a prim woman who wore white stockings and heavily-starched aprons. Salka would let Lotte swarm all over her, finding her tiny pleasures in her mother's arms, until she fell into a sleep of rosy repletion, mouth open, like the healthy little animal she was.

When Lotte was walking confidently and using her first hesitant words ("*Entchen*" was the earliest Salka heard, shouted triumphantly at a solemn family of ducklings on the lake near the Döbling house during the child's first summer there), Sandor diffidently suggested to the parents that they employ an English nurse so that the child would be bilingual.

"And if I may suggest it," he added, "perhaps you would consider taking formal instruction also?" He waited for Salka's answer. When she protested, he observed mildly, "You've already told me you learned

193

Russian from books and your father, and picked up German very quickly in Hamburg. It would be a shame to waste your facility."

"But I have no use for English. Have I?" She appealed to Leon, who said, surprising her, "I think Papa would appreciate your learning it, for his own ends."

She turned to him with raised eyebrows. "Yes?"

Sandor spread his hands deprecatingly. "We should have told you before, my dear, but it has only just been settled. We are planning to take Salamans to London—to Lombard Street, to be more precise. We are going into partnership there with Nathan Hartsilver, not a long-established bank, but one with growing interests in Austria."

"An account in London is a necessity for big merchants now, as well as being the pride of wealthy private citizens on the Continent." Leon smiled. "But enough of all this boring talk."

Ignoring him Salka said thoughtfully, "It seems to me an excellent move. Britain has the most stable of all governments. There are no wars within its borders and it has been exposed to no serious revolutionary movements. I believe that is why Consols are the safest of all securities."

Sandor said warmly, "Absolutely, my dear. The name of a London banker has a charmed value. No real panic has overtaken the City since 1866."

"That was the Overend and Gurney collapse, wasn't it?" Salka smiled innocently at Leon, who exchanged a stunned look with his father. Boring talk indeed! In the past, she had listened to the conversations of father and son, never volunteering a remark even when she could have done so, conscious always of the disapprobation with which her father and, later, Jacob had viewed her interjections. But if they were suggesting she might now be useful . . . She said, carefully, "So if I learn English, I could translate documents for you. Is that the idea?"

"If you would care to. But once we are established, there will be personal contacts to be maintained. I am too old to learn another language, and Leon is much occupied with work. But you have the time, so if you also had the inclination . . ." Sandor paused for a moment, then added, persuasively, "then you would be invaluable as an interpreter."

Salka gave him a brilliant smile, and rose.

"Frau Wertheimstein was telling me yesterday that her cousin has just engaged an English governess. I'll ask her for the address of the English woman who arranged the posting."

Leon looked up from his card game. "I wasn't aware you knew the Wertheimstein family."

She allowed herself a touch of malice.

"If you were here more during these lovely summer months you'd know they've taken a nearby villa. Bertha has a child the same age as Lotte and we've become quite friendly."

Sandor said with evident relief, "That's all settled, then," and Salka, on her way to the door, caught a disquieting note in his voice. She paused.

"There's something else, isn't there? It's not just that it will be useful for me to have English. It's more important than that."

Again, Sandor and Leon exchanged a look. Leon said smoothly, "Surely it must be time to dine, Salka?"

"We're waiting for Friedrich, as you well know."

Sandor seized the diversion.

"We'll talk when he gets here, shall we, my dear?"

They had finished the meal and were drinking Cognac before Salka managed to steer the conversation back to the point where Leon had so expertly evaded her question. This time, she phrased it differently. She spoke quietly, to Sandor, "I have a feeling there's another reason, isn't there, why you are opening in London? Not just that it's good commercially—something else."

She became conscious that Leon and Friedrich were listening. Sandor started to deny any other motives but Friedrich interrupted in his unaccented voice, "I think, Papa, that you should tell her the truth. There's no virtue in ignorance in this matter."

The three men looked at each other and Salka made an impatient movement.

"Oh it doesn't matter . . ."

"It does. It does matter." Friedrich turned to the others. "Will you tell her, or shall I?"

Leon said, with a sigh, "It's nothing really. A window was broken at the apartment, that's all, and the police say there's been some trouble with groups of youths roaming the city."

Salka was alarmed now.

"I don't understand. Was someone trying to break in to steal?"

Leon and Friedrich glanced at each other again and Friedrich said, with a forced laugh, "Nothing so innocent, unfortunately. It seems Lueger's been ranting again. You'd think now he was Mayor he'd have enough to do with administering the city, but he's too fond of exploiting people's grievances. The papers reported his speech—did you see it?—blethering about how Jews sow dissension between peoples for their own profit, and how only when they're conquered will the national disputes cease."

Sandor added, soberly, "He believes private capital should be in the hands of the community. He offers me his hand in public, he accepts my gifts to the city, then he incites his rabble against me."

Salka thought for a moment.

195

"You're afraid things will get worse—that's why you're opening in London."

Sandor laced his fingers together.

"It seems prudent, no? I don't want to run from such a man but . . ." The unfinished sentence sent a shiver of apprehension through her.

Seeing the expression on her face Friedrich said, soothingly, "It won't come to anything, of course. But it's as well to be careful." He crossed the room to the piano. "Did you see I brought the arrangement of the Debussy you wanted?" He seated himself at the instrument and started, very lightly, to play part of *L'Après-midi d'un Faune*. Salka stood beside him, turning the pages and trying to hear the music above the anxious voices in her head.

When Lotte was three years old, Salka had her dressed in apricot crêpe de Chine, and Bette put matching ribbon in the hair she had laboriously straightened with papers. Salka herself wore ruched silk and a straw-hat banded with black velvet to match the ribbon round her throat. As she gazed into the shiny eye of the lens beneath the photographer's hood, she reflected that there had been no photographs taken at their wedding: this was the first time she and Leon had posed together. She had sent photographs to her parents, of course, and to Adele, but always individual portraits, as though they were still very much separate people. But now she wanted tangible proof that they were a family and this picture would provide it.

It took a long time to group themselves according to the photographer's satisfaction. He would adjust the folds of her dress, move Leon's arm slightly and then disappear again beneath his cloth hood to stare at the upside-down tableau on the frosted glass. The camera was of polished wood; the lens extension of green cloth in accordion folds. It stood on a wooden tripod almost as tall as its operator and so excited Lotte that she attempted to scramble towards it, upsetting the careful composition of the photographer and eliciting cross clucks from his draped form.

Finally he was satisfied, when Leon stood behind Salka, patriarchal and glossy, his tie secured by a gold pin, one hand firmly grasping the edge of his jacket. The photographer carefully unwrapped a large greenish-yellow plate from its black paper, slotted it into its holder and pulled out the sheet of frosted glass to make way for it. Then he removed the black cork from the lens and counted, slowly, one . . . two . . . three . . . before replacing the cork.

Salka was conscious of the warm weight of the child on her knee and Leon's other hand laid possessively upon her shoulder. Looking at the pictures, as she was to do many times, she found these sensations never lost their sharpness for her. Years later she would still be taken aback by

196

the restlessness in Leon's face, in his stiff stance, and the look in her own eyes. She had felt as contented that day as she had in a year: she seemed to have reached some kind of plateau in her relationship with Leon. Yet the camera revealed a curious, haunted melancholy she had not felt.

Whenever she held it in her hand, long after that September day in 1901, she would be conscious of the time before and after it was taken. That likeness of the three of them (the quality of the print blurred with the passage of time, as though the edges had been burnt away) became for her infinitely more than the image of herself with her family. It implied what had happened before it was taken, and what was to come afterwards.

Chapter 18

In the autumn of 1904, when she was twenty-six years old, Salka found that she was again with child. For the first few weeks she could not quite accept the evidence. After Lotte's birth she had believed the old wives' tale that while she was feeding one child herself she would not conceive another. Bette had been shocked when Salka insisted on continuing after the first two weeks: no society lady, she claimed, fed her own babies. That was the duty of wet nurses, plump women from the country districts—unmarried mothers quite often—who lived in, boarded out their own infants nearby and fed both children themselves.

After Lotte was weaned, Salka made no attempt to avoid conception, but nothing happened. It did not worry her. She was busy with her charitable work for the Jewish immigrants who crowded into the city from Eastern Europe, with running her household and with lessons. Louise Chambers had been with them over four years now, and had fully lived up to the high references with which she had arrived. The daughter of a Northamptonshire clergyman, she was a pleasant-looking girl, somewhat dumpy, with a wholehearted smile that transformed her face and made people forget the ordinary brown hair and the scrubbed complexion. She had a fund of poems Lotte loved to recite, such as Lear's *Laughable Lyrics*, and Salka would join them in Lotte's room at bedtime to listen to *Alice in Wonderland*.

Louise had been teaching Salka French grammar and conversation: to her surprise, she found she had absorbed a good deal during those slow afternoons listening to Adele recite interminable verbs in the stuffy Hamburg rooms. She suspected that Louise's French accent was a little eccentric, but that seemed a small price to pay, for the girl was a natural teacher.

Now, it seemed, there would be another baby, and Salka almost resented it: an intruder upon her relationship with Lotte. She acknowledged that this was due to a great degree to her ambivalent attitude towards Leon: it took her aback, that so positive a result could have come from her uncertain feelings. Leon's, when she told him the news, were clearly equally confused and in the seconds before he smiled and kissed her, and assumed the slightly self-satisfied air of *der Vater*, a shadow of concern crossed his face.

She thought about that look for a long time, wondering what it had meant. In the seven years she had known him, Leon had become more of a philanderer. In contrast, Friedrich, immersed in his chemistry, seemed ever less concerned with any kind of social life. He was certainly very different from his brother: puritanical where the younger man was prurient, self-deprecating where the other was so aggressively self-centred. Odd how with time the characteristics of each man became more exaggerated.

Friedrich spent a good deal of time with Lotte, enjoying her breathless chatter and childish confidences. Salka had once said impulsively, seeing her whisper to him, "Friedrich, you should have babies of your own. It's such a waste for you to be a mere uncle."

He looked grave.

"Too late for me now, I fear."

"Nonsense. Vienna must be swarming with young women who'd be delighted to marry you. I'll find one for you myself, if you like."

Immediately she had spoken, she could have bitten her tongue. His face darkened with regret and he left soon afterwards, brushing aside her stumbling apologies. She was afraid she had offended him, but he never mentioned the incident again and she had more sense than to refer to it even indirectly, although she puzzled over it a good deal. It was not that he was indifferent to women. Sandor had told her how devoted he had been to his fiancée, and how distraught at her death. Salka privately thought that the elder son, who was ten years old when his mother died, had been more disturbed than anyone had realised. And then to lose his prospective wife also must have seemed a horrible twist of fate.

Friedrich was, like Leon, a romantic, but of a very different kind. His emotions found spiritual rather than physical release. As a youth he had spent long hours reading translations of medieval English ballads, and the concept of courtly love, avowed but never consummated, always appealed to him. He liked few German writers and infinitely preferred the English poets, with their innocence and the women of unassailable purity they evoked. He had tried his contemporaries, like Felix Dörmann, and turned in disgust from neurotic lovers, sated and exhausted, back to Lovelace and Keats.

He expected women to be passive creatures, sweet and docile as his fiancée had been. She, poor girl, had been rendered even more perfect by her death, and the ideal woman for him was chaste, pale and quiet. When he had first met his brother's tense Russian bride, she had been quiet enough, though the considering look she had given him from those strange golden eyes had been disconcerting. Almost against his will he had become increasingly fond of her. At first he had been drawn by the way she had come alive that chilly afternoon on the great wheel in Praterstern, flattered that she had so clearly enjoyed his company. Later, he had

199

become conscious of her strength—something he did not expect to find in a woman.

He surprised himself by the frank way he could speak with her. She knew more about him, he sometimes thought, than anyone else alive. He sensed that she cared about his happiness and he had not been offended, as she had feared, by her absurd and impulsive offer to find him a wife. He had, rather, been touched by her concern, but he preferred to let the matter rest rather than point out that after her any other woman would seem to him insipid and dull.

Salka had brought a warmth into his life that had been lacking, he supposed, since his mother had died. More and more over the years of her marriage to his brother, Friedrich found he was making excuses to call at the Praterstrasse apartment, ostensibly to see his father, or Lotte, but in reality it was Salka who drew him there. He made a habit of finding odd, enchanting gifts for the child, which he knew would delight her mother also, for the private pleasure of seeing those golden eyes gleam. He took a wooden monkey which climbed up and down a stick and a brightly-coloured clockwork cat of tin; another time it was a row of ivory elephants linked trunk to tail, the smallest no bigger than Lotte's finger-nail, the largest holding a ball of crystal.

On the afternoon when he produced a wooden treasure-chest which played part of the *Sugar Plum Fairy*, Leon also brought a present for Lotte. He arrived looking particularly benevolent and gave her the long box he held. The adults watched as she fumbled with the tissue paper and brought out a doll. Even at five years old she sensed this was no ordinary toy. With reverential fingers she examined the body of cream kid and the cotton legs with stockings of knitted white silk. She touched the cheeks of matt bisque and the fringe of hair. She tipped it forwards and back and the sleeping eyes opened softly.

Salka was quite overcome. "I've never seen anything so beautiful. Its eyes! And the hair!"

"Armand Marseilles made it." Leon turned to Lotte. "Her name's FloraDora. There's other's just like her, all called FloraDora. But this one belongs just to you."

"When I was little, my dolls were made of wood. I could never have imagined one like this." Salka smoothed the pale silk dress with its spider-fine embroidery. She glanced across to Friedrich and saw with sudden compassion the withdrawn look he wore. There was no enmity there, just the resignation of a man accustomed to playing the minor role: once more Leon had unthinkingly eclipsed him. Moving unobtrusively, she picked up the wooden chest he had just given Lotte from the chair where it had been discarded.

Leon was talking seriously to Lotte, treating her as though she were an

200

adult. "You'll take great care of her, won't you? She needs to be loved, you know, and if you're careful, she'll stay with you until you're an old, old lady."

Lotte stared at him, thumb in mouth, her eyes as round and dark and long-lashed as FloraDora's. She nodded solemnly. Leon laughed and turned away, while Salka helped Lotte lay the doll in the box. And all that day, the doll's face was before her eyes, its velvety gaze human and patient.

As though to stop herself thinking, Salka spent the autumn in frenzied activity. It was the best season in Vienna, still mild enough for *Ständerlin*, as the Viennese called their "little standing talks", when she met acquaintances in the fashionable pavement-cafés of the Ringstrasse. The Prater trees dropped their rusty leaves and furriers' windows were suddenly enticing again. In Leopoldstadt the mobile coffee-stall did a roaring trade all day, the proprietors busy filling their little glasses from the polished brass taps, and the fat old women who sat in the courtyard gates were constantly replenishing the hot bread-rings they sold from great baskets at their feet.

Salka and Leon went to the Burgtheater to see the mime Adolph von Sonnenthal and to the Vienna Court Opera where Mahler was conducting. (Sandor refused to go with them, on the grounds that Mahler had converted to Catholicism in order to obtain the post.) He did, however, accompany his daughter-in-law to hear Hugo von Hofmannsthal reading his work. To look at Hofmannsthal was a disappointment: a plumpish, unpoetic man wtih a dark moustache and thick-lensed spectacles; but Salka listened with awe to the unexpectedly beautiful voice. The blank verse was masterly, a web of questions and description bound together by a majestic final line. *I am my ancestors.* Beside her, Sandor was utterly still. *I am my ancestors and my descendants. I am the future and the past.* She knew how deeply that must touch him, how it mirrored his tower of Salaman. Now she thought of it, she remembered that Hofmannsthal was of Jewish and Italian descent. The same obsessions clearly dominated him: she could hear it in every line.

With a slight start, she realised she was scarcely listening to the poet. Her mind was on Leon. Like her husband, Hofmannsthal had the typical Viennese mentality, cynical, soft and half-despairing. Only Leon had not always been like that. When they married she had found him fierce and male. But perhaps that had been due more to her inexperience than his personality. Or had he changed? She detected in him now something more decadent, more corrupt, and with a quiver of recognition she heard Hofmannsthal linking bloom and decay, heard his mournful imagery of death as music, of life as a dream only. Fascinated and repelled, she saw

201

again in her mind that studio where she had searched in vain for Leon, smelled again the cloying scent of opium.

When they got home that night she sat lost in her thoughts, the sewing she had intended to do idle in her hands.

Sandor was reading the *Neue Freie Presse* across the room and glancing at her occasionally. He laid the paper aside and asked, "What is that you are sewing?"

She glanced down in her lap as though she had no idea what he was talking about.

"This? I'm not really . . . it's a sort of crochet work, I think." She held it up so that he could see the twisted threads of unbleached linen she was lacing together to make one long strand. "You start at the centre and make circular cloths. My mother used to do it."

"Mine also. I've not seen it done for years—and then only in Germany, by Russian immigrants. Never here."

He brooded for a moment, fingering the silver spectacle-case on the table beside him. When he spoke it was abruptly, as though he surprised himself.

"If you could be ready early tomorrow, perhaps you would like to accompany me to Hoher Markt."

"To the bank?" He hid a smile at her response: the invitation had proved as effective as he had hoped.

Salka knew only approximately where the bank was, and on the way there Sandor enjoyed explaining to her that Hoher Markt had been the trade centre of Vienna during the Middle Ages, lined with merchants' and guild houses. "I should add that the courthouse and the pillory were also situated here, and executions were carried out in the centre of the square, which casts an interesting light on medieval trading morals, *nein?*"

The Mercedes drew to a halt in front of the ornate façade of No. 6, with its bay windows and beyond, the ancient inner-court brightened by tubs of geraniums, where young men in sober suits spoke earnestly together, and hurried about their business when they saw Herr Salaman arriving. He paused under the gilded sign which hung proudly in its wrought-iron frame above the door: SALAMAN UND SOHN. PRIVAT-BANK, over a twisting lizard wreathed in flames.

Salka said, "But what's that?"

Sandor looked puzzled.

"You've never seen it before? It's a salamander, a mythical creature which had the power to endure fire without harm. When the last of my partners died it seemed an inspiring image to adopt, and it suits the name. '*Der guter Name ist das eigentliches Kleinod.*' A good name is the true

202

jewel. Do you know Shakespeare?" Sandor smiled with proprietorial satisfaction and opened the door of his domain.

He guided her through two long rooms, their wooden floors highly polished, in each of which ten men were busy working. Some stood at tilted desks which supported massive ledgers; others pored over columns of figures. They stopped politely as the banker approached, and bowed to Salka. Sandor ushered her before him into an office at the far end of the second room.

It was smaller, heavily panelled in dark wood, with ceiling-high mahogany bookcases reached by a circular library-ladder. The windows were screened with brown blinds. Sandor lifted one, remarking, "Too much light weakens the eyes when working," and switched on the brass desk-lamp, its frosted-glass shade like a white inverted tulip.

By its light, Salka investigated the room while Sandor attended to the letters that awaited him in a dark-green morocco folder. She examined the waist-high globe on its wooden stand, the piles of shipping reports and the long lists of share prices impaled on spikes so they hung trailing to the carpet. On one wall hung a framed list of Austrian banks, rather like the document she remembered from Jacob Radin's stuffy little office in Hamburg: Creditanstalt, Anglo-Austrian Bank, Wiener Wechslerbank, Wiener Maklerbank, Wiener Bankverein. The date on the document, she saw with interest, was 1873. Sandor looked up and saw her studying the document.

He said, "That is a list of banks in Vienna the year we opened here. During the previous six years sixty-three new banks were established here, as well as sixty-six in the provinces. When the *Krach* came, that May, it was a terrible time."

Salka sighed.

"What did they do, those poor people?"

"Some of them did not wait to see." Sandor shrugged. "The consequences were far-reaching and long-lasting. It was as if an epidemic gripped people—an epidemic of suicides. Many took their own lives, not only in Stock Exchange circles. And do you know, that was over thirty years ago. It was 1900 before the number of stocks and shares quoted on the Vienna Stock Exchange again reached the figures of 1873."

"Tell me, would you, why you came to Vienna? You said, when we talked that night, it was because after the *Krach* you foresaw opportunities if you had the nerve to take them. Was that the only reason?"

Sandor smiled, and got up. He raised one of the brown blinds, and looked out on to the busy, Baroque street below his window.

"I'd never seen this city, you know, before I made the decision to bring the bank here: Strauss und Strauss, as it was then, and not even a *privatbank*, in the sense it is now. Walter and Joseph operated what was virtually a foreign-exchange shop. When they began in Darmstadt that type of commerce was essential, for there were so many different principalities within the country, each coining its own currency: ducats, gulden and thalers had to be exchanged in order to move from place to place and cross frontiers. Carrying gold was one of the first things I did for Joseph Strauss. Then they discovered that their accumulated capital permitted them to enter the world of debt financing, which was highly profitable, since it didn't entail prolonged commitment of capital. Money turned over and yielded iinterest quickly."

Salka said, "I remember reading in one of Jacob Radin's books that the classic eighteenth-century tradition for bankers was to be money-changers at the outset, then gradually expand to include tradesman's activities— stocking up a combination of goods to sell later at a higher price."

"Like Mayer Amschel with his warehouses in Frankfurt. Banking then was a trade. Only now can it be called a profession. Well, we will never rival the Rothschild's fortunes—but nor have we ever soiled our hands with blood money."

"Whatever do you mean by that?"

"Mayer Amschel's first steps to becoming a banker included involvement with the Landgrave of Hesse, a debauched aristocrat who made a great deal of money by hiring out his subjects as mercenaries—soldiers— to any country that wanted them: mainly England. The governments involved paid Prince Wilhelm a lump sum, a supplementary amount for each soldier wounded, and then a considerably greater one for a man's death. Very profitable for all concerned—except, of course, for the subjects of Hesse." Sandor grinned at Salka's expression. "You look remarkably prudish. Business, as they say, is business. One tries not to become tainted, but it's often not possible to be both entirely ethical and successful, unfortunately. When I came to Vienna, I benefited from the misfortunes of others, and yet at the time that did not seem to me to be reprehensible. Though now, I do confess to some shame at my opportunism."

Sandor tipped back on his buttoned leather chair and fiddled meditatively with a silver seal on his desk, which was used for stamping wax seals on official documents. Salka saw that the design on its base was of the twisting salamander.

"Did you know that until the middle of the century, a Jew had to obtain special authorisation to visit Vienna, and was forced to pay a special tax in order to do so? Such practices were discontinued before my day, but it was a long time before I found a way through the complex structure of salon society. I don't believe I would ever have done so without my wife. Jews are still not allowed to own property here: did you

204

know that, I wonder? We merely rent these offices and the house in Döbling was Anna's: she left it to the boys. It is not mine."

She had not known. "That's iniquitous."

"No." Sandor corrected her mildly. "Merely inconvenient, given the fact that real estate would consolidate what we have achieved here. But I can no more change the system than I can overcome the feelings that brought it about. Do you realise that when I first came to this city—indeed, until very recently—I had never heard the word 'anti-Semitism'? It simply did not exist. The term then was '*Judenfresser*'. Jew devourer."

Salka shuddered.

"That doesn't mean it wasn't an emotion," Sandor went on. "But it was not important either socially or politically. Once the feeling was given a name, it was as though that legitimised it. Now"—he made a rueful gesture, palms upwards and spread—"it is acknowledged among the best circles."

"But is it worth all that? To be here, in Vienna?"

Sandor leant across the wide desk and patted her hand. "Is it worth it, my girl? Is it worth it? I *am* Vienna, I and people like me. I have been here for thirty years; I have put down my roots and built my life. I have walked into alleyways down which Beethoven walked, and stood in the palace where Maria Theresa listened to young Mozart. I have seen Strauss, a man possessed, conducting at the Sperl amusement-palace in Leopoldstadt, violin in hand. I have sat at pavement cafés in the Ringstrasse and talked with Klimt and Kafka."

He drew a deep breath. "My wife was an aristocrat, born to the old Vienna, and because it was hers by right she accepted casually what to me has never ceased to be an excitement, a pleasure. Vienna is not just a city—but by now, you know that—it is a state of mind, of many minds. It is brilliant ideas, sharp intellect and sharper tongues. I sometimes feel everything stems from here. Not just music and literature, theatre and poetry, but science, medicine, surgery . . . and in all of this, Salka, no one has contributed more than the Jews: the bankers—the Ephrussi, the Schreys and Todescos; composers such as Schönberg and Mahler; men of the theatre—the producer Max Reinhardt, and the actors Egon Friell and von Sonnenthal. Jewish lawyers set the tone in politics while industrialists—von Königswarter, for example—expanded the city's technical horizons. And most of all, the writers: Molár, Schnitzler, Karl Kraus, the greatest satirist of modern German literature, Peter Altenberg with his brilliant word-sketches." Sandor paused.

"All of these men share my background, or one very similar. Often born in other countries, but drawn here, to Vienna, nourished by it, inspired by it and yet, like myself, finding it hostile. Vienna *is* its Jews, Salka. How ironic that it should not like them."

Sandor and Salka left the Hoher Markt in the Mercedes. Sandor sat beside her in the luxurious gloom of the curtained vehicle which smelled richly of leather and polish, a gloved hand on the walnut arm-rest, and told her how their bank had helped Daimler finance these new motors.

When they reached Leopoldstadt the nature of the streets changed. They were less wide, not so prosperous, lacking the lavish shop-fronts of Kärntnerstrasse and the sophisticated pedestrians of the Ringstrasse. Most vehicles here were still horse-drawn, though occasionally the thin tyres of the Mercedes caught in the tramlines set in the cobbled road and the driver had to wrench the wheel to free them.

When they were almost home the driver suddenly braked sharply. Sandor leaned forward and picked up the speaking tube.

"Was istes?"

"These fools, sir, excuse me, will get themselves killed if they step out into the road like that."

Salka drew aside the curtain and saw, beside the bonnet, two men and a boy of perhaps nine. One of the men was stooped and white-bearded, the other younger and painfully thin in the shapeless black gabardine coat that fell to his feet. The boy was dressed exactly as the adults, and beneath the wide-brimmed black hat of the religious Jew Salka saw the long, unshorn ear-ringlets. Unabashed, the child stared back at her, eyes wide with interest in the pretty lady and the gleaming vehicle.

"Galician Jews," Sandor said quietly. "The city is full of them at the moment. And Rumanians too, have you noticed? Mass migration started there last year. Most of them want to reach America."

Salka had not thought for years of the wary voyager Jacob Radin had entertained to dinner that long-ago *Shabbes* night, with his worn shoes and his desperate anxiety. She fumbled for her purse.

"Stop a minute. Let me give them something." She had five gulden with her. Sandor opened his own wallet and added five more notes. When she held the money out to the younger man he made a dignified gesture of refusal.

"Please," Salka said in Yiddish, "please take it." The man shook his head, but she saw his comprehension. She turned swiftly and caught the child's hand, pressing the money into it and stepping back into the motor so hurriedly that before the man realised what she had done they were driving off.

They were quiet until the motor drew up in the Praterstrasse before the stately apartment-building, windows gleaming in the evening light and sumptuous interiors half-visible between heavy drapes. Sandor, lost in a reverie, did not seem to notice where they were, so that Salka had to say, "We're here. We're home," before he looked up at her standing on the pavement and said, in painful self-realisation, "Do you know, I have not come so far as I had thought?"

206

Chapter 19

Come my beloved to meet the bride.
Let us welcome the presence of the Sabbath
Come in peace and come in joy . . .
Come O Bride! Come, O Bride!

Salka thought for a moment she was dreaming. She had not heard that song since the Hamburg days. *Lekhah Dodi*, the tune to welcome in the Sabbath. The bride of the week was awaited with yearning, met and welcomed. When the last verse of the song was finished, the entire congregation of the synagogue would turn from the Ark to the entrance, and bow to the bride who was about to enter. And just as the departure of a bride occasions sadness, so the end of the Sabbath brought regret.

She opened the door of the dining-room and saw it was Sandor, singing in that vibrating voice, brazen as a brass gong, inherited from his father, Ozer, who had been *chazzen* of the Pinsk community. When he saw her, Sandor gestured for her to enter. He looked both pleased and self-conscious. Before him the table was set for the evening meal, with tall silver candlesticks she had not seen before, a heavy silver goblet beside a bottle of wine and a loaf of plaited bread, the *challah*.

He said, oddly shy, "I thought it was time to begin again, for Lotte's sake. I did not do this for my boys, and I have regretted that. A child should know where it belongs."

When the service began, Salka lit the candles, symbol of the divine in man.

Blessed are You, Lord our God, King of the Universe, who has sanctified us with His commandments, and commanded us to light the Shabbat candles.

The Hebrew words came to her easily, and she opened her eyes and smiled at Leon standing opposite. He seemed a little taken aback when Sandor gestured towards the silver *Kiddush* cup, and obediently filled it from the bottle of wine. More hesitantly than Salka, he recited the benedictions for wine and bread, evidently relieved when he had finished.

At the end of the meal Sandor said, "I should like to do this every week," and to Salka's surprise Leon agreed.

After that, it gradually became part of their lives to observe the domestic ritual and soon Friedrich began to join them for it. One Friday,

207

after Lotte had gone to bed and the adults were lingering over the remnants of the meal, Salka and Friedrich were talking about the new German chancellor, Prince von Bülow, and eating nuts when Leon said angrily to his father, "He's a friend of mine and I believe him! If he says he'll repay us within another two months, he'll do so."

Friedrich and Salka exchanged glances as Sandor remonstrated. "I don't trust him. He'll say one thing and do another. To tell you business is going well, to show you a balance sheet, means nothing. He can lie, and so can columns of figures. You put a lot of money into his business, and in my view he has all the acumen of a sheep."

Leon shrugged. "If he says things are going well now, then I for one accept his word."

Sandor, clearly angry, left the room and Leon stared moodily into the dregs of his glass. Salka asked tentatively, "Were you talking about Herr Landesmann? His factory makes locomotive parts, but he needed capital for new machine-tools?"

Leon gave an irritable nod of assent. "Why do you ask?"

She answered slowly, reluctant to condemn the man. "It may not come to anything, but I went to Bleichröder the other day to get my fur jacket out of storage. Frau Landesmann was there but she didn't see me, she was in such a state. She was arguing about a stole Bleichröder had made for her. It was beautiful—ocelot, obviously very expensive. She kept saying it was badly made, and that the skins were not perfectly matched."

Leon looked bored. "Well, so he'd made a poor garment."

"No, Bleichröder wouldn't do that, he's too much of a craftsman. In the end he stopped arguing. He just apologised and took back the stole, and she swept out of the shop."

By now Leon was getting ready to leave the table. "So what's the point of the story?"

"When she'd gone, Bleichröder turned to his assistant and said something, and they both laughed. It was obvious to everyone in the shop that it was a wonderful wrap—there wasn't a thing wrong with it. But Frau Landesmann couldn't afford it and didn't want to say so."

Leon said peevishly, "So the woman's a fool. I never thought much of her."

"*No!*" Salka was impatient now. "Don't you see it means your father is right. There are obviously big money problems at Landesmann's. She must have ordered the ocelot months ago, when you first lent the money, but things haven't gone as they hoped and she can't pay."

"I'm sure this isn't relevant to David's business matters."

"Of course it is." She felt helpless, forced to admit that what Sandor always said of Leon was true: he lacked the instinctive touch of a true banker for knowing which investments were sound. Because of his background on his mother's side—the haughty disdain of the aristocratic von Saars for the world of commerce—he did not allow himself to be totally absorbed by his business, but remained always detached.

Friedrich asked mildly, "What will you do?" and Leon said shortly, "Nothing."

"But you heard what Salka said. Even to me—and I know nothing about it—there would seem to be grounds for extreme caution."

Leon said, with childlike rudeness, "But you know nothing about it, do you?" and Friedrich went red.

Salka waited, but for two weeks Leon did not act. Then, unexpectedly, Salaman und Sohn withdrew funds from the Landesmann factories and days later she heard they had gone bankrupt with debts which would be revealed as many thousands of gulden. Only then did Sandor tell her that it was he who had put a stop to Landesmann's borrowing. "Thanks to you," he had added.

"I didn't think Leon had told you."

"Leon told me nothing," Sandor sounded grim. "Friedrich finally decided the information was too important to allow Leon to ignore it."

"The last thing I want is to cause bad feeling for Leon. That's why I didn't go direct to you after I saw Frau Landesmann at Bleichröder's."

"I appreciate your wifely concern. But I'd be most grateful if you would speak out next time you notice something. As it is, we only saved our money by a hair's breadth." He paused, then added abruptly, "I'd like you to come to Hoher Markt more regularly—three or four times a week."

Salka, who had been pouring coffee, almost dropped her cup in surprise.

"But . . . why?"

"I think you would enjoy it. You could get to know what goes on there, and I see you're interested." He did not add the true reason: that Salka, inexperienced though she was, showed promise of proving more adept than her husband at evaluating the potential of clients.

So Salka attended the bank regularly throughout her second pregnancy. She came to comprehend that Sandor's patience was an important part of his success as a merchant banker. She would sit at a side desk in the heavily-shaded room, listening to the information that streamed into the office through couriers, from telegraph messages and—more rarely— through the recently installed telephone, which Sandor treated with meticulous care, adjusting his expression before speaking into the mouthpiece.

Salka observed Sandor's practice, during negotiations, of listening intently and speaking rarely; success in the business world, he claimed, "is never a matter of luck. It is based on sound knowledge and mature reflection."

The more she learned of financial history, the more she appreciated that Sandor, starting out with so little and building for himself a financial empire, was also an adventurer. She realised that he possessed initiative and courage, and, above all else, a taste for risk.

During those months, Sandor poured out all he knew of the banking world, and she absorbed the information eagerly. He explained how the private banks were large purchasers on foreign stock-exchanges, principally because their financial connections abroad were excellent. She learned of the many areas in which he himself had invested: thanks to his contacts with Darmstadt, he had money in a considerable number of German ventures in Turkey, for instance, such as the Baghdad and Anatolian railways in Asiatic Turkey, the Oriental railways in European Turkey, the Port Company at Haida-Pasha and the Tramway Company at Constantinople.

She became familiar with all the names of the private banks who had conducted foreign financing long before the corporate institutions were created—Mendelssohn, Warburg, Speyer, Schröder, Oppenheim—and Sandor told her that however influential they had been in the past, their days of importance were numbered.

"Private banks will gradually become subordinate to the Great Banks, like the Darmstädter Bank who work with Rothschild, and the Österreichische Credit-Anstalt für Handel und Gewerbe, one of the largest Austrian banks. Some of the private banks will be bought up, and the rest cannot undertake business of the first magnitude by themselves."

"What about Salaman und Sohn? Will we be swallowed up?"

He rubbed a pencil absently between his fingers.

"I hope not. I'm content to remain small and independent. Anxious to do so, in fact. It suits me, to operate as we do, and I should like to know that the name continues after me."

"With Leon?"

Sandor did not answer.

In May 1905 Salka was delivered of another child, a boy. This second childbed was shorter and less arduous, as she had heard it would be. The arrival of a son brought back the words of the rabbi of Polotsk: *You have it in you to be the cornerstone of a great family*.

She lay in bed, the white-draped cot Adele had sent for Lotte once more beside her. The baby inside this time had a very small, rounded head, oddly flat at the back, the result of the "moulding" of its soft skull-bone during delivery: Doktor Schindler assured her it would disappear within the first day or two.

The last seven hours were a confusion of images: the mackintosh sheet on the bed sticky and slippery beneath her; the scissors to cut the umbilical cord in a pan of boiling water; the heat of the room and the sweat running down her back. When the first birth-pangs came, she found she remembered exactly that inimitable flow and ebb of pain. *Oh yes, that's how it is.* She was not frightened this time by the involuntary actions of her body, seemingly held by a giant hand which clenched and then released, clenched and released. She went with it and, as if in reward, the child was born early, the head crowning in a rush of pure sensation that was both pain and unspeakable pleasure, so that she cried out, the same wordless, entreating sound she had uttered at the moment of the child's conception.

Salka lay on her side, one hand beneath her cheek, looking at her son. She was filled with wonder at the transformation from womb to world, at the perfection of the long lashes and the tight little fists. *Man comes into the world with hands closed, and leaves it with them open.* She could almost hear Dora's voice. Poor Dora. She had died more than a year ago now, and though Salka had mourned, she knew she had already accepted her mother's death long before. It was her father she felt for, the more so since his letters had become so odd and disjointed. She had talked to Sandor about the possibility of bringing Jonas to Vienna, but he was beyond the journey now. Salka had been the child of their middle years, and Jonas had been many years older than his wife: Salka believed he must be around seventy, though she was never certain.

How they would have loved this tiny boy. She had seen peace come over Sandor's face as he peered into the crib, and he had given her a look of such feeling that tears had come into her eyes, for she knew how passionately he wanted the name of Salaman carried on and this baby was his surety.

But it was Leon's reaction that had amazed her. He had been at home when she had felt that first intimation of the birth and given a sudden violent shudder of apprehension. That had been at five o'clock yesterday afternoon. Before ten, it was over. Leon had not come near her during the intervening hours, but he came in as soon as the last signs of the delivery had been cleared away. Perhaps because he was more familiar with small babies now—perhaps because of its sex, she didn't know—he took the swaddled little figure with real emotion. When Sandor, summoned by Doktor Schindler, came in also, Leon held out the baby to show him.

"Here," he said, "is my son. My *Kaddish*."

Salka and Sandor looked at him, stunned. 'My *Kaddish*' was a phrase they had never thought to hear from Leon, a phrase common among

Orthodox Jews. *My* Kaddish, *the son and heir who will see me to the grave and say over me the last prayer, to help the departed soul find peace.*

They chose the name Emil, and planned to have the circumcision ceremony on the eighth day, as was customary. But the rabbi, when he came to the apartment, counselled waiting another week because the baby seemed very small. It was the first time anyone had said that to her, and Salka questioned the nurse anxiously. The woman brushed aside her fears. He was taking all the milk Salka could give him, she herself could see how he was filling out. . . In another seven days, the rabbi pronounced himself satisfied and the ceremony was performed. Friedrich held the child at Leon's behest: he did not think he could face the sight of that quick double-edged silver knife on his son's flesh.

When the *brith* was over, there was a reception. The long rooms were crowded, and Salka's legs trembled with the effort of standing and the effects of the early and unseasonal heat. It was mid-June, but already the leaves were yellowing on the Prater trees, and even in the apartment she could smell the summer stink of the city, of gutters and drains and decay. As soon as Emil had recovered from the circumcision, she promised herself, they would go to the house in Döbling.

The following evening, Louise Chambers knocked late on Salka's door. She looked anxious: her curly brown hair had evidently been hastily smoothed and she stammered slightly, as she had done when she first came to them.

"Has something happened?" Salka was holding Emil against her shoulder, patting his back while he made contented burping sounds and dribbled milk into the folds of her neck, his eyes wide and wise as a little owl. Louise smiled at him briefly.

"I'm not sure, Frau Salaman, but Lotte seems to have a nosebleed and I'm finding it hard to stop. She's feverish, also, and she hasn't been to sleep. I wonder—would you look at her, please?"

Between them, the two women settled Lotte for the night and next day she seemed to have recovered, though for a week she showed signs of lassitude. When she started to complain of a headache, Salka called Doktor Schindler. He examined the child carefully, pressing her abdomen and looking at her tongue. He wanted to know if she was constipated and whether she had a temperature in the evenings. Salka and Louise answered carefully, and Doktor Schindler looked grave. When he murmured the words "enteric fever" Salka thought that it must be something slight. A fever would soon pass.

"I don't say my diagnosis is correct, mind you," the doctor went on. "But it seems possible. We know it to be in the city already, and unfortunately it attacks the well-to-do as frequently as the poor. And as you know, it's most common among the young."

212

Salka said, "I'll take her to the country, to Döbling. I'm sure she'll recover there."

"I don't really advise moving her at the moment, Frau Salaman."

"But you say it's only a fever . . ."

"It's enteric fever, I believe, yes. But I don't want to mislead you. It has another name. Typhoid."

Within ten days, consciousness of the contagion swept the city. The fever hospitals were full and the newspapers speculated daily as to the possible causes: insanitary drainage, contaminated milk, the eating of oysters infected by sewage. All the Salaman staff lived in, and Friedrich helped them organise the disinfecting and cleansing of food and the apartment, so that apart from Lotte, they escaped unscathed.

The child continued to ail for another week. All normal activities in the household ceased. Sandor and Leon conducted much of the banking business from the apartment rather than risk the epidemic in the city. Salka's first concern was of course the children, particularly Emil. She kept his cot in her room and woke constantly in the night to look at him, but he continued to thrive, though she had to admit he was still a small baby.

By the end of the third week, Lotte's symptoms had increased in intensity. Her tongue was dry and brown, her pulse rapid and feeble. She was so emaciated her fragile bones felt sharp beneath the skin, and the red curls clung to her head in damp tendrils. Salka, Bette and Louise Chambers took it in turns to stay with her day and night. She complained constantly that her tummy hurt her and Doktor Schindler, explained to Salka that the spleen was soft and enlarged.

Salka made sure that the most elaborate health precautions were taken. Sheets and towels from the sick-room were disinfected, and anyone who touched Lotte washed their hands after leaving the room.

It was, the doctor continually assured them, the very mildest of attacks, and the best treatment was a powder of ipecacuanha and morphine for the fever, and boric lotion in tepid water to wash the child's mouth. Salka used ointment she made herself from oil of almonds, white wax and rose-water to soothe Lotte's dry lips and tongue.

When the fever became dangerously high, it would take two of them to administer a wet pack. Salka hated this almost as much as Lotte, who screamed and sobbed as they stripped her and wrapped her tightly in a cold wet sheet, pushing it between her legs and between each arm and her chest, so that skin did not touch skin. While she struggled and writhed, the sheet painfully cold on her flushed flesh, they tucked it round her neck and folded it beneath her feet, then wrapped her tightly in a blanket so that she was held firmly. A smaller wet towel was wound round her

213

head, and then they would sit beside the helpless little girl for the long minutes it took to cool her.

Salka would sing to her in Yiddish a lullaby out of her own childhood: *Faygeleh*—Little bird. Dora used to call her that, in another country.

> *Sleep my birdie,*
> *Close your eyes.*
> *Sleep with joy,*
> *You know tomorrow.*
> *Sleep with health, my child.*

Such food as the child could take was carefully checked: barley water and simple soups, meat jellies and boiled bread and milk. She took very little and kept less down, until finally she refused even the limewater mixed with milk that she had been reluctantly swallowing. They made her toast water, to give her at least some nourishment, putting three slices of toast in a large jug and pouring over them a quart of boiling water. This was allowed to cool, sweetened with sugar and then flavoured with lemon.

Salka had been attempting unsuccessfully to get Lotte to drink this infusion in the early hours of a Tuesday morning. It was somewhere around three o'clock and, although the heat persisted even at night, Salka was tired enough to feel cold. She was sitting close to the bed, the bowl of water for sponging Lotte's face and arms beside her. The child had finally become drowsy and fallen into a troubled sleep, and in the dimly lit room Salka could feel her head droop and nod.

Suddenly she was awake. Lotte's head was rolling wildly from side to side on the pillow, and she was saying, over and over again, "Don't do it. Don't do it," though Salka had to strain to make out the mumbled words. She put her hand on the child's hot forehead and made soothing murmurs. To her horror, she felt the little body tense and jerk in uncontrollable tremors beneath her hand, the spasms twisting Lotte's limbs so that she looked as stiff and inhuman as the marionettes in the Praterstern she so loved.

Salka gasped. The doctor had warned her of such nervous disturbances. She quickly pulled back the thin sheet that covered the child and unbuttoned her nightdress. She poured fresh water and started to cover her body with cool wet cloths. She was reluctant to open the window because of unhealthy night vapours, but she found the big woven-palm fan Leon had brought in and used it over the bed. After what seemed a very long time, the child grew cooler and the twitching ceased, but for the next hour she kept renewing the cloths and fanning.

When at last it was light, Salka took Lotte's temperature. It was lower than it had been the previous morning. When Doktor Schindler made his call, he nodded in satisfaction.

"The child has been unwell now for twenty-five days, is that right? If her temperature continues to descend morning and evening, then this is the lysis." Seeing Salka's puzzlement, he added, "A gradual subsidence of the symptoms will hopefully occur. Her pulse will become stronger; the tongue will be seen to be clean. But it will all take time and we must be on guard, for relapses are apt to occur."

It was not long before Salka was able to take the children—with Lotte swathed in blankets upon Leon's knee—to Döbling. It was the end of July, and the avenues of plane trees were heavy and still with heat. They put Lotte to bed in her cool white bedroom, and in these different surroundings Salka saw clearly the bruised eyelids and the wasted body.

As she improved, they moved her into the garden, to a swing-seat in the shade. At first the light hurt her eyes, despite the sun-hats she wore, but each day brought an improvement. Her hair, cut so short at the onset of her illness to keep her cool, began to curl again and, despite the shady hats, freckles appeared on her nose. The weeks of inactivity had had a deleterious effect upon childish muscles and she could stand for only short periods. But she was obstinate and determined: soon she would not stay in the swing-seat but wandered round the garden, picking flowers and stopping frequently to rest. Salka would sit and push Emil's perambulator to keep him asleep, recovering herself from the efforts of the past two months. She would watch Lotte as she moved from place to place and think how this illness had changed her from a pudgy baby to a lean little girl.

Leon came down for a week, to rest. He was under a lot of strain, Salka knew, for Sandor had recently been delegating more responsibility. At the same time, the older man was reluctant to relinquish his hold over Salaman und Sohn and would question Leon about his decisions. She also understood—as Leon did not—that Sandor's anxiety over his family during the typhoid epidemic found its outlet in worry about the bank. Many times during those horrible days he had sat at Lotte's bedside: many times Salka had woken at night and gone into the child's room to find her holding her grandfather's finger for safety as she slept.

Leon, who hated illness, did not spend much time near Lotte, but had developed the habit of breaking off from his work to peep at Emil, as if to reassure himself that all was well. Even after the typhoid outbreak had subsided, and the Salamans had returned to the bank, Leon had checked several times each day on his son's health—they had just had a telephone installed in the apartment.

The last two months had taken their toll of Leon, as, Salka felt, they had of her: he seemed quieter, more restrained, the wildness she had

215

always sensed in him somehow quenched. The shock of Lotte's illness and fears for the new-born baby had united them in a protective anxiety that transcended their own immediate difficulties.

Seeing Leon one evening go upstairs to look in on Emil, she thought that the baby had touched him as no one else could have done.

Later that night Leon came to her bed. The room was dark and she was almost asleep. He got in quietly, drawing the covers aside. She stirred. "Is it late?"

"No. Barely twelve o'clock."

She stretched and shifted her weight, giving a groan as she felt the almost permanent backache she had experienced since the birth. Leon murmured, "Is it your back? I'll rub it for you," and she felt his hands kneading away the discomfort, warming her, rousing her, so that the blood sang in her ears.

Before she slept, she had read a new book of poems by Rainer Maria Rilke. *In my arms forests sleep . . . and all the darkness of my nature is the darkness that is in violins.* She had marvelled at the word-magic—*the darkness that is in violins*—and now she felt that deep darkness rising in her own body in response to Leon's sensuous stroking. As always in bed with him, words ceased to be of any importance. The language which mattered here was of rise and fall, thrust and withdrawal, and to interrupt was unthinkable. Half-asleep, she was compelled for her own salvation to answer Leon's demands, to respond to his movements with movements of her own, so that the music became faster and faster, more and more intense . . .

And then she could not hear it any more.

A week later Leon returned to the city. He planned to spend three days in Hamburg on business, returning to Döbling for the weekend with Friedrich. Pleased at the prospect of seeing her brother-in-law for the first time since the typhoid epidemic had started, Salka planned menus and busied herself in the kitchen making geranium creams and café sherbets. She had made up all the sleep lost during Lotte's illness and Emil's first weeks. Her hair and skin were glossy with health and her body had regained its lissom, supple lines. She had enjoyed the fashionable curves that had been so briefly hers during pregnancy and immediately after the birth: she had looked crossly into the glass as she dressed that morning, seeing her stomach flat again, her thighs once more lean now their covering of fat had gone, her waist small. The only sign of her recent pregnancy was the butterfly pigmentation that had appeared around her eyes with the first of the April sunshine, so distinctive and exotic that, despite her condition, men had stared after her in the streets.

It was after three by the time she finished in the kitchen, and she wiped her hands and hung up her apron with a satisfied yawn. Louise had the afternoon off, and Bette had said she would take the children for a walk when their afternoon nap was over: they must have gone without her noticing, she had been so busy. She thought she would wash her face and then lie down for an hour: Doktor Schindler told her that if she would insist on feeding the baby herself, she must get plenty of rest.

She paused for a moment in the hallway to pick up one of Lotte's toys, a round platter her parents had sent from Russia on which half a dozen carved hens pecked busily for corn, their actions driven by their own weight. They moved as she picked up the platter and she watched, charmed by the childish simplicity of the article and the soft wooden peck-peck of their beaks.

Around her the house was empty and utterly quiet, so that even that slight sound was loud. Sunlight slanted on to the polished parquet and she could see the faint flowery dust beneath the vases of irises. A curtain lifted in a small breeze, and dropped. The silence caused her a faint unease. It was such a long time since she had been totally alone, it seemed almost unnatural: no children; no nurses.

She walked upstairs, her bare feet soundless on the carpet, and paused at the landing window. The drone of pollen-heavy bees was reassuring, and she could hear a child's voice. Lotte. There she was, far up the avenue with Bette, her chatter carried on the still air. Salka looked again, but no, Bette was not pushing the baby carriage. Perhaps Emil was in the garden, then. She hurried down the stairs and out into the garden, not knowing why she should feel anxious. The carriage wasn't in its accustomed place in the shade beside the box hedge . . . nor under the porch. Then she saw it outside the kitchen door. The covers were drawn up and fastened against cats, but Emil was not inside.

He must be upstairs. She was sweating as she pushed the kitchen door open and raced once more up the stairs. Outside Emil's door she stood, hand on the knob, hesitant. She told herself she didn't want to disturb the sleeping baby, but that was not the real truth. She was afraid. The silent walls, suddenly and inexplicably hostile, pressed in on her. She opened the door.

Emil's cot was on the far side of the small white room, near the dormer window. This was open, and the cretonne curtains were drawn against the sunlight. Salka paused in the doorway, her eyes on the neatly covered little figure, his downy head dark against the lace trim of the cot. There he was, after all. So why did the house still feel so empty, as though she were alone in it?

She forced herself to walk the few paces to the window, and drew back the curtains, her eyes on the baby. He was sleeping, his breathing so light as to be undetectable. Often, when Lotte was small, she used to put her

217

face close to feel the faint breath fan her cheek, to reassure herself that the child hadn't forgotten, in sleep, how to breathe.

Emil was sleeping too long, surely. He was lying on his side, his hands beside his head, fingers open and relaxed. Usually he slept with them curled into tight little fists, pugnacious even in sleep. With a swift movement she pounced on the cot, drew back the covers and turned Emil over. One cheek was pale, the other blotchy where he had been lying. As she lifted him, one hand on his back, the other on his chest, wetness came out of his mouth in a little gush. He often did that, bringing back undigested milk. Then she saw that his mouth was twisted, the upper lip raised in a half-smile, one eye closed. His face was somehow distorted. Different.

She knew then that her ridiculous, stupid, irrational fears of the last few minutes were realised. Emil was dead.

She wouldn't let herself believe it, though. She picked him up and held him tightly, his head lolling soft against her neck. The wetness ran down her dress like tears. He felt heavy, so heavy, all his little weight sagging limp. She fought down panic. There was no telephone. She must get him to a doctor. The road. Any vehicle would do.

Somehow Salka got down the stairs and out of the house. She was still barefoot and the hot gravel hurt her feet—but what did it matter? She ran awkwardly with her tragic burden towards the gate, although she knew very well all efforts would prove useless. Her baby was dead.

The most terrible thing that could happen to any woman had happened to her.

Chapter 20

They found her on the dusty road into the village.

It was Emma von Ephrussi of the nearby palatial villa who saw her. The older woman, being driven home from a luncheon in Vienna, did not at first recognise her neighbour in the distraught, barefoot girl with tears streaming down her face and her hair dishevelled, clutching a tiny baby to her breast. Always kindly, the wife of the eminent banker stopped to ask if anything was wrong, and was appalled to find it was Salka in such a state.

Between them, she and her chauffeur got Salka into the motor, where she sat hugging Emil's body, telling in a hoarse voice of the painfully slow minutes it had taken her to find Emil and realise what had happened.

"It took me so long," she kept saying, "so long to find him. If I'd been quicker, if I hadn't been in the kitchen—making *sweets*, why was I making sweets?—if I'd gone to him sooner, he might have lived. It's my fault, it's all my fault." She put her head down on to the baby's body in her lap and wept, deep racking tears that shook her shoulders and made the older woman cry in sympathy as she held Salka's arm in both her hands.

"We'll get him to the doctor in Döbling, my dear, in just a moment now. I'm sure he'll know what to do."

Salka whispered, "It's no good. No good. I knew before I even touched him." She pulled back the shawl in which Emil was wrapped and silently showed Frau von Ephrussi how colour had drained from his skin. Every feature was perfect. He was unmarked, flawless. How, then, could his tiny fingernails be turning blue, his feet feel like ice inside their woolly bootees?

Salka put her face to his neck and drew a deep breath, searching for the warm smell of him that had given her such pleasure, the scent of milk and powder, clean cotton and fresh skin, but all she got was a sad little odour of regret.

The doctor, when the chauffeur found him, was a young man, newly qualified and pompous in his high white collar and narrow spectacles. But he handled Emil with competent concern, taking him from Salka and putting him on the table in his surgery. He pulled up the child's long dress to expose his chest, and bent close to listen for his heart. Then he held a wisp of cotton-wool to the nose and open lips, and Salka, standing watching with Emma von Ephrussi's arm supportive round her waist, saw that no breath stirred it.

"There could be an obstruction in his windpipe." The doctor was speaking half to himself.

"I don't think so." Salka felt cruel hope rising. "He takes only milk; I feed him myself."

"Still, let's see." As he spoke, he prised open Emil's mouth, flashing a light down his throat. "There doesn't seem to be anything. How long ago did you find him like this?"

Salka looked around her. "I don't . . . I can't . . . it feels like a long time."

Emma von Ephrussi spoke.

"The journey here took about eight minutes. I don't know how long she was walking, but she had come about a quarter of a mile from the house."

"Mmmm."

He turned the baby over but not before Salka noticed that Emil's mouth remained open, like a fledgeling waiting for food. Pressing with his thumbs just below the shoulder-blades, the doctor began exerting a light pressure on Emil's back. He continued for long minutes, stopping occasionally to listen for a heartbeat. He tried pulling Emil's arms above his head with rhythmic movements, but that brought no response either. Lifting the baby's hand, the doctor inspected the fingernails, then with his own nail pressed sharply on one of them. He looked again at the nail and said, without emotion, "No change."

Emma von Ephrussi exclaimed, desperately, "There must be *something* we can do."

The doctor glanced up at her, then bent back to the child before him. He carefully laid him on his back. When he used his fingers to open Emil's eyes, Salka could see that they looked sunken and glazed. With a sudden swift movement the doctor clenched his fist and gave the baby a single sharp blow on the chest. Salka made a sound and reached out, but Emma held her back. The doctor waited a moment then put the ball of his hand over Emil's breastbone, covered it with the other hand and pressed down sharply and quickly, over and over again. He stopped and felt Emil's neck for the pulse.

Salka had not taken her eyes off him all this time. Now she watched him straighten slowly and hope was extinguished. He brushed the back of his hand over his eyes and gave a sigh. He picked up the shawl, very tenderly wrapped the baby in it and handed him back to Salka.

"I am so very sorry, *meine Frau*. So very sorry."

Salka received the body of her child. She held him in the motor and as Emma von Ephrussi and the chauffeur helped her into her house. She no longer felt anything. The sun did not warm her; the tears that streamed ceaselessly down her face did not make her wet. She did not taste the brandy they forced between her lips ("Come along now dear, you must, for the shock,") nor experience any sensation when they bathed her feet, exclaiming over the filthy cuts and bits of gravel embedded under the skin. She did not feel tired when night fell and they lit the lamps, and she knew neither hunger nor thirst.

It made no difference to her what they did, or what they said. She saw their faces: Louise Chambers, shocked and tearful; Bette clearly on the verge of collapse. She heard the endless reiterations of what had happened, how Bette had peeped in, seen Emil peacefully asleep and decided not to waken him. She listened when Emma von Ephrussi told her she had telephoned Leon and Sandor, and that they would be here soon. Docile, she let herself be led upstairs.

But not for one moment did she let go of Emil. When Emma tried gently to take him from her Salka stiffened, and let out a deep groan so like a growl that the older woman stopped short. Salka held him as he grew cold and then, after three hours, stiff. She held on to Emil because she knew that once she surrendered him he would be lost to her for ever, and that was more than she could bear.

She could not relinquish him. While she cradled him he was hers still. For whole long minutes she could convince herself that in a little while he would open his eyes and nuzzle his face against the side of her breast, as he always did when he was hungry. She would feel her flood of milk as she thought this, and the front of her dress grew damp until she pressed her arm hard against her nipples to stop the flow. By evening her breasts ached with milk for Emil, and even though she knew it was another woman to whom this dreadful thing had happened, she felt that discomfort.

Dry-eyed now, Salka sat in her bedroom staring unseeing at the wall, the body of her baby clasped tightly in her arms, refusing to believe the unbelievable, unable to face her unendurable loss. He could not have been taken from her: he had been hers too briefly. Only weeks. *Fourteen weeks*. Poor little boy. Poor little Emil.

Disjointed, feverish, her thoughts twisted and jumped. Over and over and over again she relived those minutes—had they only been minutes?— between her unconscious awareness that something was terribly wrong and the confirmation of it, as if by so doing she could change the course of events. She saw herself entering Emil's room, picking him up, saw him open his eyes and blink at her, alert and responsive. Yes, that's how it had been. The other was a nightmare, of no account. She looked down at Emil lying in her lap, smiled at him, and sang to his still and dreaming face. *Sleep with joy, you know tomorrow*.

She was, for those hours, out of her mind.

221

She opened her eyes some time during the long night to see Sandor sitting opposite her, his hand over his face. She said, conversationally, "I didn't hear you come in. I've just been waiting for Emil to wake so I can feed him."

Sandor took his hand from his face and looked at her without speaking. She chattered on: "Have you had the papers you were expecting from London yet? I'm very proficient in English now, Louise says, and I don't think we'll need to use a professional translator this time. It'll be quicker . . ."

"Salka. Stop it."

She looked offended.

"Whatever do you mean? Oh, of course, I'm talking too much, and I should be concentrating on silly little Emil here, who won't wake up." She looked fondly down at the baby's bundled shape and patted him. "Not long now, and he'll say hallo to Grandpapa, won't he, darling?"

Sandor knelt stiffly on the ground in front of her so that she exclaimed, surprised, "Whatever are you doing? You'll spoil your lovely suit."

"Never mind. Salka. I want you to let me hold Emil. Just for a moment."

"Oh, no." She stiffened and leaned away from him. "Oh, no. I can't do that. You see"—her voice was very cool, very reasonable: she felt proud of herself—"you see, he'll be frightened if he wakes and sees you holding him. He's been asleep for such a long time, since before lunch. I don't know what's come over him."

"Nevertheless, I only want to hold him for a moment. Please, Salka, I'll be most careful."

She shook her head vehemently, and Sandor saw the light of crazy cunning in her beautiful golden eyes.

"They won't let me give him to anyone else, you see. It's too dangerous for him."

Sandor said quietly, "I see. Of course. Well, at least let me help you lie on the bed with him, for a little rest. Emma thinks that would do you good, don't you Emma?"

Emma von Ephrussi, who Salka now saw was seated by the door, stood up.

"I do think it's a sensible idea, really I do. You won't have any milk for him, you know, if you don't rest."

Salka frowned, seeing the sense of this, and conceded reluctantly, "I suppose so. All right. Just for a few minutes. Till it's time for his feed."

"Now," said Sandor, when they had settled her under a rug of English wool, "we'll let Emma go home, and I'll sit with you just for a while." He touched Salka's hand, seeing with pain how she clutched Emil's body so tightly that the veins stood out. She was tense and wary, but gradually he felt her relaxing, despite herself, in the warmth. He had never thought to see her like this, her pale dress stained and crumpled, her feet clumsily bound in strips of sheet spotted with blood. Her black hair stood out wildly, full of electricity, like the hair of a madwoman, and she smelled of sweat and something else, something that twitched his nostrils unpleasantly. She smelled of fear.

Salka surfaced slowly, forcing her way through the web of dreams which hung around her, sad and hopeless. She still had her baby firmly in her arms.

She opened her eyes, and saw that what she held was a cushion from the morning-room wrapped in Emil's shawl.

Across the room, Sandor slept hunched in an armchair, his face old and defeated, its lines and furrows deepened by sorrow. He must have taken Emil from her as she slept. Poor Sandor, what a dreadful task.

Bette tiptoed in, her face blotched from crying, bringing hot chocolate and later, when she saw that Salka was herself again, she fetched Lotte in to kiss her mother. Salka had to force herself not to hug her too tightly, when all she wanted to do was clutch the slender limbs and the bouncy curls and hold her safe. But Lotte, as all small children do, sensed Salka's misery and struggled to get away from her, frightened by grief, although she did not understand the cause.

The mournful day trailed on. People—neighbours, the young doctor from the previous day—called at the house to pay their respects. Bette had lowered all the blinds, so the rooms were dim and vague. This suited Salka whose head ached from the scent of the flowers the unwelcome visitors had brought.

Salka was lying on her bed when Leon came home. A great lassitude had seized her—she was too weary to think or to move, caught in a skein of sorrow from which she would never be free. She heard Leon's tread on the stairs, slower than his normal brisk step, and when he opened the door she was shocked, even through the veil of her suffering, by the look on his face.

He was ashen, so that his dark eyes burned in his head and he seemed somehow to have shrunk inside his clothes: his jacket hung carelessly on him, his trousers were creased. He was unkempt, his hair untidy, his beard rough. He stood staring at her.

"How did it happen, my God, how did it happen?"

She told him again, as she had told the doctor and Sandor, and she realised that he could not absorb it any more than she had been able to. He sank into a chair, his hands dangling between his knees, head bent. Then she saw that tears were dripping on to his hands and the floor, slow,

223

painful, male tears. She got out of bed and knelt beside him. Putting her arms about his shoulders, she tried to summon words of comfort.

She asked, "Have you seen him?"

Leon blew his nose. "Just now. He looks . . . empty. As though there were nothing there at all."

Salka said, her voice so low Leon could hardly hear, "It's my fault. I was in the kitchen, I didn't go to him soon enough. If I'd been quicker, then perhaps . . ."

"If we think like that, we shall surely go out of our minds."

Doktor Schindler arrived later, to examine Emil's body and satisfy himself that the child had not died through a condition he had failed to diagnose. He was an old man now, Salka noticed through her grief, sitting hunched in his chair.

He said, painfully, "I can find no obvious cause of death. He did not asphyxiate, nor are there any signs of infection, or we would conclude he had contracted typhoid fever." He turned to Salka and asked, his voice gentle, "Did you or the nurse notice whether he seemed feverish these last few days?"

Salka shook her head. "Neither of us can recall anything untoward. He wasn't restless or crying—nothing to make us think . . ." She drew a shuddering breath and stopped.

Doktor Schindler waited for a moment, then observed, "In a very young child, some internal defect incurred during delivery may be responsible, but I myself was present throughout the birth and saw no sign of distress."

"Then *what?*" Leon spoke out of a deep exhaustion.

Doktor Schindler passed a weary hand across his face.

"During the first few months of life, any small irritation may result in convulsions which lead to death. It could be the onset of teething, or even indigestion."

"So little a thing can kill?" It was the first time Sandor had spoken.

Doktor Schindler nodded. "I have talked to the young doctor in Döbling who examined Emil. We are agreed that there is no other possible cause. He said also that your presence of mind in getting to him so quickly was commendable."

He addressed this last remark to Salka, who made a choking sound and hurried from the room, Leon following behind.

When they were calmer, they talked about Emil.

It was an obsession: how beautiful he was, the way he hiccuped against Salka's shoulder like a sleepy little owl, his lustrous dark hair. It hurt them to say these things, but words were all they had of him. He had left almost nothing of himself behind for them. He had been too small for even the simplest toys, too young for a teething ring, a rattle. Just his

224

clothes, that shawl, and the cot-sheet bearing the faint yellowish marks where he had dribbled in his sleep. For a long time Salka would not have it washed, but kept it folded in the drawer of her night-table, the only tangible proof that Emil had existed.

The other physical evidence of her baby had long since vanished. Before he left, Doktor Schindler had advised her to bind her breasts tightly for a few days. She had looked at him blankly.

"The milk," he had said, patiently. "You must stop it now."

She winced at the recollection of the intense discomfort and the emotional anguish of obeying him, made worse by her irrational fear that Emil would somehow be restored to her, and that she would not be able to feed him. She knew that was impossible but still the fantasy persisted: she would open the nursery door one day and find him asleep, or she would hear his cry from the garden and hurry to pick him up.

Salka did, in fact, hear him cry often, when it was quiet. Emil had had a characteristic voice, plaintive, and it returned to her unexpectedly. She would stop what she was doing in order to go to him before recognising that she was hearing him only with her heart.

She learnt slowly and painfully that she would go through the rest of her life scarred by her son's death. In time, she supposed, she would recover: there would be a day—it seemed impossible, but everyone assured her it would be so—when she would wake and not wonder in that moment before full awareness returned why she was so unhappy, why her throat ached and she felt so abandoned.

What hurt her most, the thought that faced her bleakly in the slow nights when she couldn't sleep for the empty aching to hold him again, was that he had had nothing. She saw him like a traveller to an unknown land, without luggage or papers. An adult would have much to remember: memories, people, experience . . . a life. But Emil had not begun: he had been untouched, unmarked. How could he exist, if there was another existence, when his only knowledge had been faces and people's hands, the sight of his own moving fingers which so entranced him, the sensation of hunger and of being fed?

As she thought this, she felt madness welling inside her again, struggling for domination. It lured her with the promise of forgetfulness; seductively her mind whispered that this way lay oblivion from sorrow. That one night, she knew, she had given it free rein in her extremity, had felt herself slipping into delirium as fathomless as the waters of the Altaussee, which even in summer had lain with scarcely a ripple, cold in the sun.

She could not give way because others needed her. Leon's grief, it sometimes seemed, was more powerful than her own. He had loved Emil as he had never loved anyone before, fiercely, protectively, obsessively. He had loved him for his innocence and his frailty. He saw the child as part of himself and had been determined that this boy would be different, would not be fingered by corruption as he now felt himself to be. In the baby's wondering eyes, in his soft murmurings, Leon found a new and unimagined joy. He had always adored Lotte but she was a girl, a little woman, and Leon, much as he wanted them around him, could never wholly trust a woman. Emil made him aware for the first time how Sandor felt about the tower of Salaman. And Emil's death had brought the first real intimation of his own mortality.

Whenever she looked at Leon, the words "dust and ashes" came into Salka's mind. He seemed to have grown older overnight, his hair more liberally speckled with grey, his intense dark gaze now brooding and morose, as though the melancholy he had always carried was now activated. There was a hopelessness about him: despair was etched sharply into his face and his every action. He held himself differently: the swaggering, erect carriage was gone. He was not a tall man and now he seemed diminished, his vigour vitiated by his grief. He spent a good deal of time in his father's company, although the two men talked little. Salka would see them pacing up the road in the evening light, hands clasped behind their backs, heads bent, not speaking but communicating nonetheless.

Sandor's own black bitterness was hidden from his family. He endured it alone, not wishing to intrude it upon them. He began, as he had after Anna's death, to spend long hours at the bank and found to his relief that work still gave him solace.

After a time, he persuaded Leon to accompany him, and although the younger man did not lose himself in the bustle of the dark Hoher Markt offices, he did gradually begin to regain his equilibrium. But something had gone out of him that Salka was never to see again: the careless, assured arrogance of a man who had never been hurt by anyone had vanished.

As the months crept slowly by, taking them further and further from that terrible day, Salka was increasingly aware that her relationship with Leon had entered yet another phase. Immediately after Emil's death—though she never used those words to herself—they had been drawn together by their desolation. After a while Leon had retreated again. It was as though he could not sustain an emotional bond for any length of time but had to shy away from prolonged commitment.

She watched this happen with pain but did nothing to halt it. Possibly a move from her, an appeal, would have brought him close again. But she checked any impulse to act, mindful of his behaviour so soon after she had discovered her love for him, unable to risk the demonstrative affection she had given beside the Altaussee.

Incompatibility was established between them now, unpromising as winter.

# Chapter 21

Friedrich Salaman found it hard to come to terms with Emil's death. The grief of Leon and Salka, so much starker than anything he had ever seen before, alienated and embarrassed him. Having himself neither children nor the desire for them, he could only hazard their misery.

He had been nearly ten years old at the time of his mother's death— quite old enough to suffer deeply. Years later, when his fiancée had died, he had shut himself away for a week after the funeral. He had emerged from his room as quiet and self-contained as ever and had scarcely mentioned her name again. It was his way of dealing with bereavement, but it successfully hid from his family just how stricken he was. The loss of Emil and all the sad trappings of his passing—the poignant words of prayer for his brief life, the painfully small coffin—struck in Friedrich a chord of sorrow that he seemed always to have heard, just beneath the surface of consciousness, since he was a boy. He could not bring himself to go to the Praterstrasse apartment for weeks at a time, and such visits as he managed were hurried and uncommunicative.

When the first anniversary of Emil's death came round, it was time to observe the ceremony of the *Yahrzeit*. Year's time. The preceding evening Leon lit a memorial candle in the synagogue in Seitenstettengasse and Salka lit one at home. These burned softly from sunset to sunset and the two of them recited the *Kaddish*, the mourners' prayer. Salka fasted for twenty-four hours: she would give herself up to thoughts of her lost baby, and then try to put the past where it belonged. Leaving the synagogue in the late afternoon she stumbled as she came down the stairs from the gallery where the women sat together. Friedrich was the first at her side. She gave him a grateful look and leaned on his arm for the moment it took to recover herself.

Friedrich straightened his shoulders, feeling suddenly taller. He had missed his sister-in-law these long months, missed her interest, the sudden warmth of her golden glance. Half a dozen times a day he had thought of something he wanted to say to her and had even gone to the apartment for the express purpose of talking to her. But always he had held back at the last minute, too full of compassion for her predicament to be able to hold a light conversation.

'Dear Friedrich,' thought Salka as they returned to the apartment. She had rightly divined that his absence had been a form of self-defence and determined that from now on she would attempt to hide her unhappiness. As a result, Friedrich no longer found it a threat to his peace of mind and they resumed their old companionship. He sought her advice on choosing his suits, invited her to attend a particularly interesting lecture with him and took her and Lotte out for the sweet pastries which were the one indulgence he permitted himself.

While Friedrich was relieved to see that Leon also had apparently worked through the worst of his sorrow, he disapproved more heartily than ever of his younger brother's behaviour where women were concerned. He had innocently supposed that now Leon's philanderings would cease altogether, and was appalled to discover quite accidentally—at the home of a bachelor acquaintance—that this was far from the case.

In the September of 1905, Friedrich sent Salka a note: *I am constrained to purchase a new piano. I will be at Ehrber by 3 p.m. tomorrow. If you were able to join me, I should value your opinion.*

The establishment of the piano manufacturers occupied the far end of Mühlgasse, the name repeated endlessly in gilt across the frontage of glass. A deferential salesman clicked his heels and led Salka through to where, at the far end of the second of the vast interconnecting rooms, she saw Friedrich. His pearl-grey Homburg and cane by his side, his head resting on a propped arm, he fingered the keys and listened to the echoes of the notes. She watched him affectionately for a moment, so absorbed was he in the music, but he felt her gaze and looked up. He seemed anxious and tired, then he smiled and rose. The salesman stepped forward.

"If you would care to, Sir and Madam, we have a *Musikant* on the premises who would be happy to perform for you on any of these instruments."

Salka looked round at the waiting pianos, rosewood and satinwood gleaming. Friedrich pointed to a small upright, its front embellished with pleated green silk.

"I think I would prefer to try them myself. Does that one have a good tone?"

For an hour he and Salka wandered in the sunny rooms, their whispers sibilant in the silence, taking it in turns to play experimental phrases.

When Friedrich had made his choice, a solid upright patterned with flowers in contrasting wood, he motioned her on to the stool of the instrument directly behind them, so that they sat back to back. While the salesman disappeared to make delivery arrangements, Friedrich idly picked out a melody—Wolf's *Der Gärtner*—and Salka, who had grown to like *lieder*, joined him. It was charming, she thought, and civilised: the measured music, the faint smell of wood and dust, the pleasant sensation of an expensive instrument under her hands. She said idly, "I do love shopping, you know, though I rarely have time these days. I like spending money, especially other people's."

When he answered, it was clear he had not heard her.

"There is something I must tell you," he said, and she could hear the reluctance in his voice. "I don't want to, but I'm afraid if I do not, then others will be only too happy to do so."

The spell of the last hour shattered. She looked down at her hands on the keyboard: square, practical hands—peasant hands.

"I don't want to hear it."

"You must, Salka. Better from me than from someone who might be pleased to see you hurt."

They still sat, back to back on the velvet piano-stools. Neither wanted to look at the other.

"Why should I be hurt?"

She had no need to ask. She knew it would be Leon.

"He's done something unforgiveable this time, and I warned him so often. He's a fool: he doesn't stop to think, ever, he just behaves as he wants, and tells himself it's *männlich*."

Friedrich spoke in a rush, words tumbling out, quite unlike his usual considered speech. Salka sat very straight, her back to him, waiting for what was coming. He told her what in her heart she had already accepted: that Leon had resumed his habitual conduct and taken a mistress. She nodded as Friedrich told her this, relief making her feel light-headed. She had known this ever since the night of the storm—she could live with this. And then she realised that Friedrich was saying something else. ". . . won't consider alternatives . . . inevitable consequences . . . unfortunate child."

She swung round on the piano-stool, her voice strident so that the deferential assistant, moving towards them on silent feet, turned and hurried back to his desk.

"A child? You're telling me Leon's mistress is having his child?"

Friedrich nodded reluctantly. She stared at him, seeking confirmation in his face and finding the strained look again. Anger brought her to her feet, anger and jealousy so sharp it made her gasp, opening a brilliant, biting, bitter wound somewhere deep inside.

"We must take this seriously," Friedrich was saying. "Under Austrian law, if Leon acknowledges the child and it is a boy, he will inherit over any claims of Lotte's. I've told him how wretched it will make you, but you know Leon. He just looked at me with those black eyes and said nothing." Friedrich slammed his open palm down on the keys before him, so that a harsh discord echoed through the listening space.

Salka stood some feet away from him, staring out at Mühlgasse which was bright with the harsh electric glare from street lights. She noticed the shop directly opposite her and thought, absurdly, that she must remember some time to buy a new umbrella from Schaller. She heard herself ask, in a hoarse voice that didn't sound like her own, "How far gone is she, the woman?"

Taken aback, Friedrich stammered, "I don't know . . . not long, I think. Perhaps three months."

She started, ridiculously, to laugh; harsh, hysterical laughter that blurred her eyes with tears. 'How ugly I sound,' she thought. 'How ugly.'

Friedrich hovered anxiously around her, quite unable to deal with this outburst, and made ineffectual soothing noises. She caught his arm, for something to hold on to. In a desperate attempt to calm her Friedrich offered, "Anything could happen. Women often lose a child around this time, so perhaps we won't have to face this after all."

She shook her head, vehemently.

"Don't say that, please. Don't say such things. I can't bear it."

"No, of course. I wasn't thinking." He hit his chest with an open palm, an uncharacteristically violent gesture. "I shouldn't have told you such news in a place like this. In public."

Salka blew her nose. Her delicate handkerchief of Brussels lace was already useless. She struggled to keep her voice level. "I'll be all right." The relief on Friedrich's face made her smile despite herself. "I've known about Leon for a very long time. It was just a shock to hear about the baby."

She moved across to the window, willing herself to breathe deeply, and watched people hurrying home. Fine rain polished pavements and roofs, and a group of young women, assistants in one of the shops probably, ran past in a billowing group, laughing and holding their hats, their pale blouses moist and drooping. Tempted by the artificially warm day they had left their coats at home; tomorrow they would wear them, and winter would be here.

Salka sighed. "Does anyone else know?"

"Not yet. But I think I must tell Papa. Leon refuses to do so, and you may be sure some well-meaning friend will inform him if I don't." He stood up. "Let me just sign for this instrument and I'll take you home. No . . ."—he shook his head at her protests—"if I have to speak to him, today's as good a time as any."

In Mühlgasse they waited until a horse-drawn cab appeared, both wishing to prolong the drive home: Salka wanting time to collect herself; Friedrich in order—although he did not admit this even privately—to remain alone in Salka's company, something which happened rarely. He sat beside her in the creaking cab and realised that she was now composed and apparently in control of herself. He could not begin to understand the relationship between her and his brother: no one knew better than he the

230

dark fires in Leon's blood. For a few months he, like Sandor, had hoped Salka had tamed him, and had seen with despair the gradual reversal to his old habits: the late nights, the disreputable associates. Friedrich despised decadence, the more so since Leon so ardently espoused it. On an impulse he reached out and took Salka's hand.

"I'm so sorry. You don't deserve all this."

She stirred, his voice breaking into her reverie.

"It's not your fault Leon is what he is. I don't even think it's mine. He'll never change now, I know that."

"You're right. But angry as I am with him, I still love him."

"That's exactly how I feel." She squeezed his hand so hard it hurt him. "We'll get through this, won't we?" Her voice rasped with the tears she tried not to shed, so that Friedrich, desperate to console her, said with a conviction he did not feel, "Of course. Of course."

Neither of them believed him.

Sandor took the news badly.

Friedrich told him nervously what little he knew, and his father listened without speaking. He went pale, so that his eyes burned more fiercely than ever, and Friedrich saw the pulse beating frantically at his temple. Sandor was holding a glass of Madeira and in his agitation it spilled on to his suit of pale-grey English woollen. He dabbed fastidiously with his handkerchief and when he finished he had assumed a studied calm.

Salka found this more frightening than an outburst, for she felt it was a sheet of ice over the depths of his anger.

Leon did not return home that night until late, and he found Sandor waiting for him. Salka never knew what was said between them, and never asked. For many months afterwards there was constraint between father and son, and they spoke only about the business at the bank. Yet gradually the constraint softened. It was not that Sandor approved his son's behaviour—he was violently opposed to his blatant infidelity—rather that he, like Salka and Friedrich, had reluctantly to concede that he had either to accept Leon or alienate him.

For Salka there were no choices. She thought sometimes that there had never been many in her life. Decisions had been taken for her, arrangements made. She was, after all, a woman. *A woman has long hair and short sense.* Her father had said that to her once, teasing but meaning it, when she was washing her hair. She had been offended by his words but her mother had laughed, seeing no harm in the sentiment. And Leon took the same view. She was his wife: it did not matter what she felt, whether his actions hurt her or not. He had not deserted her, had not left her short of money, or beaten her. Of what, then, could she complain?

The trouble was, she fumed angrily to herself, that to a large degree he was right. She would put up with him. Not from passivity, as he supposed, but because she loved him and could not bring herself to jeopardise the times when they *were* happy together. Even when she knew about the expected child, she did not speak her mind, for what good would it do? She was the one who had most to lose, for she might lose Leon. She did not want that.

One sunny October afternoon Leon came home early from Hoher Markt and suggested he take Lotte to the Volksprater. After a pause he asked, diffidently, "Will you come also?"

Taken aback, she agreed. They walked among the side-shows and clowns. Lotte was enthralled by a tightrope walker, a scrawny little thing of perhaps fourteen, who wavered precariously on the thin wire above their heads, taking two steps backwards for every one she managed forward, her feet in their little leather slippers curving desperately to maintain her balance. Watching her, Salka thought, 'I do that, every day.'

After a while, Leon took Lotte's hand and they wandered across to watch a sallow Italian who was playing a hurdy-gurdy. Salka had seen him there often, over the years, always with a couple of monkeys, sad-faced mangy creatures dressed in bright red jackets, little hats fastened over one ear. They must be different animals each time; their life-span would be short in such an environment. Lotte didn't care that they were probably flea-ridden but found them entrancing, and Leon pretended one was going to bite him. He soon grew bored with them, though, and his expression became moody and slightly sullen. Salka noticed that he was showing signs of age: fine lines on his forehead; dark pouches beneath his eyes which made him look dissipated and fascinating, like an actor waiting in the wings.

She was not the only woman looking at him, Salka observed. A petite creature, blonde and Germanic, had turned away from her companion and was eyeing him. After a moment he became conscious of her gaze and returned it, straightening his shoulders in the old challenging way. Salka knew that hot liquid glance, knew how it mesmerised women. This one was no exception: her lips parted and her chin came up as she posed for him.

Salka felt herself flush with anger, the anger that had not visited her for so long now. Must he behave like this in front of her, in front of his daughter? Must he exert his charm upon every woman who crossed his path? With a great effort she stifled the words that rose to her lips and said, instead, "It's time we went back, don't you think? Lotte has a piano lesson at six."

Leon turned with a faint smile. "You two go back. I'll join you later."

Salka took Lotte home. She went to her room and started to take off

232

her hat. In the glass her face was stiff with unhappiness. She took a step back, so she could see better. She wore a coat and skirt in saxe-blue frieze, with a tucked front and collar and revers of cream linen. Her hair was dressed high and shone with health; her skin was clear. Without vanity, she knew she appeared as desirable as the woman in the park—more so, for the other had been dumpy, with a florid complexion. But that woman had one overriding charm for Leon: she was unknown, unconquered.

The anger that had been kindled that day stayed with her for almost a week. On the fifth day she went to shop in Mariahilferstrasse. She did not normally go there, but a new store had been opened. Gerngros was the largest of its kind in Vienna, and she wanted to get some silk stockings.

The store boasted the new revolving doors of heavy plate glass. Beyond, there was a hallway panelled in dark wood. From floor to ceiling a tall board proclaimed in gilt the numerous departments and the floor number. Ladieswear was on the mezzanine, where smiling salesgirls in white shirtwaists stood at long tables laden with skeins of ribbon, hat-pins and collars. Modern, glass-fronted shelves displayed silk petticoats and bead purses, corsets and chemises.

Salka found the stockings she wanted, purchased a dozen pairs, and waited for her change to be returned in the small brass tube the salesgirl had sent, in its overhead basket, clacking along the wires to the cashier's office. She walked through Dress goods (rolls of damask, gingham, taffeta and madras, sewing patterns and panels of embroidery) and took the elevator to Mens wear. She glanced along the counters at woollen hose, suspenders, detachable collars and cuffs until she found a display of silk scarves. It would be Sandor's birthday the following week—perhaps one would make a suitable gift from Lotte. As she stood there, fingering the materials, she heard a woman's voice near by, light and rather common.

"Oh, I can't decide. I think the white. He's very dark. I'm sure that would suit him best. He'll be here in a minute, anyway."

Salka turned her head. It was the petite woman who had exchanged glances with Leon in the Volksprater five days before. An odd coincidence. Annoying. She thought she had forgotten that incident.

Irritated, she left the scarves and waited for the elevator to the ground floor. It was a cage of wrought iron decorated in gold leaf, with seats of black leather. She stood there as it slowly ascended and the uniformed boy in his short jacket opened the gates. The passengers were two men. One of them was Leon.

She did not want to remember, afterwards, the things she said that morning. Screamed, in fact, in the House Furnishings Department, among

233

the wallpaper and blankets, the hammocks and the forty-two-piece dinner-sets. She had controlled herself for years in the face of Leon's flagrant infidelity. She had not reproached him, or begged him to stop, or pleaded her love for him. If he knew she had been to Saphir's the night of the storm, he had not heard it from her.

And now she didn't want to behave properly any more. It mattered not at all that she was the wife of a prosperous banker, with a child and a position in society to protect. All she thought of was that pretty, vacant face, the overelaborate blonde curls, and the high voice of the woman who waited upstairs for Leon.

Salka heard her own voice, hoarse with emotion and appallingly loud, saying words she couldn't believe she was uttering, calling Leon names she must have learnt in some other life, cursing as bitterly as any squabbling market-trader in Polotsk. Standing right there, surrounded by beds and blankets, the fury that had festered for so long found release in a savagery that horrified her. She didn't cry—she was far beyond that—but she poured out all the hate she felt, all the hurt of loneliness and the experience of rejection.

And all around her, the sales staff politely ignored them. Unmoved, they sold sheets and pillowcases, towels and eiderdowns. A few glanced curiously towards them, a couple of the younger women giggled nervously, but mostly they were left completely alone.

Someone cleared his throat behind them. It was a salesman, holding a glass of water for her. She drew a shuddering breath. "Thank you."

"I'll call a cab for you, Madam, if you wish?"

"No. That won't be necessary."

Leon had been quiet throughout. He had not once raised his voice, or remonstrated. He had just taken everything she said as though he knew how richly he deserved it. Salka said now, weary, "Go on. Go to her."

"Let her wait. She's not important."

"Are any of them?" She could have laughed.

"No." She could hardly hear him. "Of course not."

There was a long silence.

"I'm going home." She put the glass of water down and rubbed her forehead with a childish gesture. Her head hurt. She started to walk away, and halted. Over her shoulder she said, "They weren't important to me, either, all these little friends of yours. All these years and have I ever said a word about them? And don't think I wasn't aware of them. I put up with them and I'd have gone on doing so. But a baby." She was whispering now. "A baby."

"So Friedrich told you. I suppose he felt he had to." Leon shrugged. "It's not of my choosing, that. It was all over between us before I knew of her condition."

"But she's having the child."

Leon sounded defiant. "I told her it would make no difference to my feelings for her. I urged her to get rid of it"—Salka winced—"but she refused. She said it was hers and she wanted it. She says she's going to her mother in the Tyrol and it'll be born there. So you see," he put a conciliatory hand on her arm, "poor Friedrich doesn't understand these things. I've no doubt he blew it up out of all proportion in the telling."

Salka pulled away from him. Her voice was terse with hostility. "He understands what it is to have decent feelings. Which is more than can be said for you."

She turned towards the stairs: she couldn't face that elevator again. Leon followed her. The stairs were empty and endless. Down and down they went, clutching the polished handrail, their feet echoing on the stone. Leon was talking, talking.

". . . overexcited just at the moment. When you're calmer, you'll see how silly it is to get upset over nothing. It doesn't make any difference to our marriage. Do I treat you badly? Have I ever denied you anything? Salka?"

She shook off his hand on her back but he persisted.

"It's just the way I am. They don't mean anything, any of them. I always come home, don't I? Home to you and Lotte. Surely that proves you matter to me. I didn't have to marry you, after all. I refused Adele for you. What more can I do?"

They were at the bottom of the steps, and Leon pushed open the outer door. They walked along Mariahilferstrasse, not quite together, not quite apart, Leon slightly behind her hurrying figure. He was still talking, calmly, rationally, reasoning with her. And she had imagined him to be chastened by her outburst. God, what a fool she was. For the first time, she told herself she would leave him. Enough was enough.

She stopped suddenly, so that he almost ran into her.

"And what about the child?" she demanded. "This baby that is to be born. Does that mean nothing either? Is that to be forgotten when you tire of it?"

They were on the street corner. It was almost lunch-time and the road was packed: trolley-buses, horse-drawn drays, motors and bicycles were everywhere. Businessmen in formal suits, women in fox-furs, nursemaids with children, liveried messengers, all eddied on the pavements. And in the midst of the bustle and noise, the sounds of klaxons and shouts, Salka stared at her husband and saw on his face a look that was smug, self-satisfied and arrogant. He saw the baby as a proof of his prowess, that was all. He would be more of a man because of it. The child itself would not, perhaps, matter to him.

But it would matter to *her*. Without speaking she continued walking

235

home, not caring how long it took. When the child was born, it wouldn't be hers, but the child of some unknown woman. Only it would be Leon's baby also, and Lotte's half brother. She recalled something Jacob had muttered that first evening in Hamburg about the ties of blood binding them all.

I am the future and the past. I am my ancestors and my descendants. . . .

Where did those words, that idea, come from, beating in her head so that it hurt? *I am the future and the past.* Was it Sandor and his tower of Salaman? Some forgotten fragment of a poem? Long ago, Jacob had told her she looked exactly like Sossel, his grandmother and her own great-grandmother. Lotte's narrow hands were Anna von Saar's, and her eyes were from Leon. This other, strange baby yet to be born would also carry irrefutable proof of its paternity: those eyes, perhaps, that hair? That baby, too, would resemble men and women it had never known.

Sometimes she used to notice that Emil, tiny as he was, had reminded her of Jonas when he turned his head slightly as though amused by his own joke. She had caught the likeness and, later, she would have told Emil about his grandfather, and all his life he would have kept that characteristic little gesture that had come from the old man in Russia. *I am my ancestors and my descendants.*

But Leon's by-blow, what would he be told? Who would recognise in his crumpled face the features of the family, see in his small movements the habits of another? Isolated, unacknowledged, how would he know of his forebears: the merchant and his tower of Salaman beyond the Pale; the haughty von Saars on their ancient Austrian estates?

Salka found she was crying—sobbing for an unborn baby carried by her husband's paramour. Eventually she got home, Leon somewhere in her wake, and went to her room to lie down. 'You utter fool,' she told herself, furious at her weakness, and tried to stem the tears with the backs of her hands. Then Leon was in the room, roused as always by the sight of her grief. She found it incomprehensible, that this more than anything should excite him. He pulled her hands from her eyes, watching in fascination the tears that gathered and fell without any contraction of her face. He started to kiss her wet cheeks, asking softly why she was crying. She shook her head, seeking to evade his eyes and his caressing hands. He had brought this sorrow, and so many others. She hated him, surely. Leon had married her against her wishes, had neglected her and sought love elsewhere, careless of her feelings. She was not central to his life, though he was to hers. She was one of many women he had known, while he represented the sum total of her own experience.

But even as she held aloof from him, she knew she would capitulate. The bond which held them together was a living thing, twisted from so many strands over the years that she could never disentangle their lives

236

one from the other. They were of the same stock, the same root. Leon too had felt the shock of recognition when he saw her first, sure confirmation that their angels had each called out the name of the other. They had in common their daughter, and the loss of Emil. Salka remembered how Leon had been gripped by grief. She could never forgive him for fathering a child on another woman, but she was not Jonas Radin's daughter for nothing. The practical common-sense she had inherited told her that Leon was a young man and in a perverse way she was almost relieved at this evidence of his recovery.

He murmured indistinguishable words, his lips against her hair, and his tenderness moved her as it never failed to do—his tenderness and his sudden flashes of sweetness, the generosity he always displayed towards her, the devoted love he gave their daughter. From him had come all that was important: her child, her situation, her self.

He touched her like a bridegroom and she did not care that he was unfaithful. She had just told herself and him that their physical relationship was over—she had screamed it: they even knew in the House Furnishings Department at Gerngros—but words were no protection against Leon.

She could not resist him now, she never could resist him. He was in her blood and in her arms, and their love-making brought them both a measure of peace.

Chapter 22

Salka strove to keep up appearances: for the servants, for Sandor and the bank, and above all for Lotte. The people amongst whom they moved were worldly and quick to catch the subtlest nuance, and she was determined not to betray how much Leon's actions had upset her. She went out with him a good deal and entertained.

Emma von Ephrussi, of the eminent banking family, asked her to help organise the raising of funds to assist the growing tide of Jewish refugees from Russia which had begun again in 1905. She became increasingly involved with their plight, and would spend evenings in the boarding-houses where they were temporarily based, trying to help them solve their numerous problems. Many of them had been the prey of sharpers, forced to hand over even their pathetic bundles of possessions—a little money, a tin cup, a coffee-pot—in exchange for the chance to slink over the Austrian border. Fleeced and exhausted, the women would cradle their children for warmth and listen wonderingly as Salka assured their menfolk, in Yiddish, *"In Kanade vet ir ferdinen gelt."* In Canada you will earn a living. Sandor frequently accompanied her, dispensing money and sympathy to his *Landsleit*, his fellow countrymen. But Leon, although he approved of her work, refused to involve himself.

Emma von Ephrussi was an imperious woman accustomed to command. She liked Salka increasingly for the practical work she did, her cool silences, and the amusement she had to turn away to hide when the committee ladies, having discussed at length the provision of kosher meals and suitable clothing for the refugees, permitted themselves the luxury of gossip.

Salka, for her part, sensed that between the two of them now was a bond nothing would shake. Emma's kindness that dreadful day in Döbling, the way she had stayed at the house for much of the night, the pain she still shared with Salka when the younger woman needed to talk about Emil, all made her more than a friend. The younger woman became a frequent visitor at the Palais Ephrussi, a vast and ornate building with its five storeys and rows of carved caryatids opposite the Votive Church. (The Ephrussi originated in Greece and Russia, Sandor explained, adding dryly that it was presumably the Greek connection which inspired the grandiose architectural style of their home.)

Salka was sophisticated enough by now to be comfortable with Emma, but even so she was still awed by the Palais Ephrussi: endless corridors lined with busts of eminent, expired Ephrussi; vast public rooms filled with paintings and parquet; Meissen characters by Kaendler; damascene vases and salvers; tortoiseshell, ivory and brass inlaid buhl furniture. She frequently thought that Emma must surely dress to echo her background. She was a big woman, with an impressive prow of a bosom of which she was justly proud, wearing satin meteor and corded silk, and low necklines edged with finest lace or embroidered lawn. Her features were overlarge— firm nose, fleshy lips and heavy chin—but her eyes were a calm grey beneath level black brows, and her voice was soft and deep.

She was a woman of cultivation and taste and she enjoyed playing mentor to the young Russian. She introduced her to the intellectual elite of Vienna at her Tuesday salons, where journalist Felix Salten would arrive with the doctor-dramatist Arthur Schnitzler, discussing the latter's newly-produced play, and the plump young Ferenc Molnár would sit at Emma's feet describing his newest light comedy. At the Palais Ephrussi Salka met the Zionist Martin Buber and another time Max Reinhardt from the *Theater in der Josefstadt*. Frequently, Emma von Ephrussi would invite all the Salamans, but Leon did not care for such occasions and Sandor would go only if Salka assured him that some of his banker friends would be there: a member of the Todesco family, perhaps, or von Schey-Koromla. Friedrich, though Emma extended her invitations to him also, rarely made an appearance.

Emma, who missed nothing, noted the strain on Salka's face when she thought she was unobserved, heard rumours about Leon and made the correct deduction. One afternoon when the young Russian woman looked particularly bleak, Emma asked quietly, "Why do you put up with him? You have a choice, you know. You could leave him. No one would censure you."

Salka avoided her eyes, fearful that if she gave voice to such a possibility if would somehow set in motion events which, once initiated, would irrevocably change all their lives. Emma's marriage was a good one, she knew. Karl was an admirable husband, intelligent, energetic and affectionate. He was also bald, reached only to his wife's shoulder and appeared to be as wide as he was high. Salka did not believe that Emma von Ephrussi felt for Karl the complex and compelling emotions that Leon roused in her. So she excused herself, kissed Emma goodbye and all the way home brooded over their situation.

She and Leon never discussed his other life. It was between them, dangerous as an open knife, and both shrank from referring to it although it affected their every thought. It lay beneath each day, hidden, disquieting, and unsettling.

She found Leon's intrigues abhorrent, but she had only to look around

239

at their acquaintances to see men behaving as he did. She knew several wives, women admittedly older than herself, whose husbands were reputed to enjoy the company of little dancers or milliners. This was gossip which came through the servants or from Bette. The women themselves seemed not to know. Now, wiser, Salka saw that they were indeed aware of the situation but accepted it because they had no alternative: men were as they were.

A double standard was tolerated by everyone involved. It was perfectly acceptable for a married man to seek the favours of other women. But for a married woman to be so much as seen in the company of another man would be reprehensible, even if her husband had already strayed.

Just once, Salka started to speak to the wife of a lawyer she knew as a card-playing associate of Leon's, who, Bette whispered, had been seen with Leon at Rademacher's Revue. Salka had asked, hesitantly, how she was able to continue so equably with her daily life. Frau Kosterman had understood immediately what Salka meant. She had put a hand on her arm. "I wait for the times when Otto comes home to me," she said, "because I know he will return. He stays away only when passion is his master. I try to remember that."

Salka had nodded. There had been a couple in Polotsk whose squabbling was notorious. Her mother had professed to be scandalised, but her father had laughed. *Between husband and wife only God should judge.*

She saw, as though a dark stage had suddenly been illumined for her by a flash of brilliant but artificial light, that she was bound to a man who was growing daily more foreign to her. Once Leon had seemed so dominating, so strong and demanding: the hunter, the possessor. Now she saw him differently: a degenerate man engaged in an eternal quest for new sensations.

Salka felt, intuitively, that in this, as in so much else, Leon Salaman exactly mirrored the city of his birth. Voluptuous Vienna, imbibing its moods from the many nations surrounding it—Italian, Slav, French— cynical and world-weary, the city of suicides: decadent, corrupt, *lebensmatt.*

Salka acknowledged that at last she had the measure of Leon, and it was a bitter revelation. It hurt her pride and it hurt her heart, for she found that even this did not affect her love for him. She did not understand what possessed him, but she knew it was beyond him to control.

Emma von Ephrussi, so sensible and capable, would never understand.

Salka did not allow herself to contemplate leaving Leon even for a short time. And then two events occurred which changed her mind.

After Emil's death, it was Lotte who exhibited all the violent emotions which her elders subdued. Little Lotte, barely eight years old, could not understand what had happened to her brother. Kindly adults told her euphemistically that he had 'gone away for a little while'. Bette, the country girl, told her that he had gone to play in beautiful green fields. Confused and bewildered, the child understood that he was lost, and began frantically to search for him. She would become panic-stricken as she opened cupboards and peered behind bushes, calling all the time "Emil, Emil," in her high voice, so that Salka, appalled, clapped her hands over her ears and ran to her room to collapse on the bed.

She would pull herself together and go to Lotte and hold her on her knee, trying to explain in words the child could absorb what had happened, but Lotte was too small and the tragedy too big for comprehension. The little girl, buffeted by adult unhappiness, could only see that her mother had failed to keep the baby safe: that he had somehow slipped from her grasp and disappeared. She would burst into tears of rage, hitting out at Salka in her fury, unable to put into words the feelings that were beyond her to express: that it was her own fault, also, because she had not always been good. "Eat up your dinner," Cook would tell her, "or else something nasty will happen!"

In time the outbursts became less frequent and they all thought Lotte had forgotten the baby brother she had known so briefly. Then one day when the little girl was playing in the Döbling garden, sitting quietly beneath the table where Bette and the gardener's wife were talking unawares, she learned that it was only Emil's body which had been buried. An hour later Salka found her in her parents' bedroom tumbling the contents of drawers upon the floor, trampling through petticoats and linen sachets in her desperate search. Surprised by such wanton naughtiness, Salka questioned her, and between hiccups of emotion Lotte admitted she was looking for the baby's arms and legs.

Salka took the sobbing little figure on her lap, rocking and soothing, humming the tune to which she always resorted for comfort: *Sleep my birdie, close your eyes. Sleep with joy, you know tomorrow.* "Poor little *faygeleh*," she whispered in Yiddish. "Poor little bird." Gradually the sobs subsided and Lotte relaxed against her. Five minutes later she was asleep.

When she told Leon, he suggested more outdoor activities for Lotte: he would teach her to ride himself, he declared. The following weekend he called his wife and daughter into the garden to find, waiting on the gravel drive, a short man with the bowed legs of a jockey beside a sturdy grey pony. Lotte's eyes widened in disbelief, then she caught Leon's hand with a squeak of delight.

They would walk together, Lotte on the grey's back, Leon holding the leading rein, up and down the tree-lined road for hours at a time. Salka wondered at his tireless patience: for Lotte, she reflected, Leon displayed depths of kindness no one else could tap.

When the family returned to Vienna, the pony was stabled in a riding school in the Praterstern and throughout the winter father and daughter would spend their Sunday mornings there. It was reassuringly ordinary and domestic, so that Salka was lulled into a sense of false security. It was not until the evening of just such a Sunday that she glimpsed again the abyss on the edge of which she lived.

She was sitting hidden deep in an armchair with Lotte beside her, both engrossed in the gaily-coloured pieces of jigsaw spread on a low table. The door opened behind them and before either could speak, Salka heard Sandor say in a strained voice, "There are no tears like those of a *mamzer*."

He spoke in Yiddish—an extraordinary lapse for him. And then the meaning of the phrase penetrated. A *mamzer*. A bastard. It had happened, then. She gave a little sigh and Lotte glanced up. She was getting on for nine years old now, impulsive, affectionate and alert—but very much Leon's daughter, the dark eyes burning against her pale skin. She mustn't hear this. Salka jumped to her feet and turned to Sandor, a finger on her lips. Lotte wouldn't understand but no hint of this must reach her.

Somehow, Salka finished the jigsaw and got Lotte off to bed. When she returned to the big salon Friedrich and Sandor were standing by the window staring out over the yellow lights of Praterstrasse, sunk in silence. When they heard Salka both turned and Friedrich asked, solicitous as ever, "Can I get you anything?"

"No. Thank you."

There was a pause. Then he asked, very quietly, "Do you want to know . . . ?"

"Nothing. I want to hear nothing about it!" She had to force herself not to shout. She said a hurried good-night and rushed towards the door. But her eyes were so full of tears she stumbled over a small table holding a silver dish of nuts which flew in all directions. She bent to retrieve some, to hide her face, and Friedrich knelt beside her to gather up the rest. Not meaning to, unable to halt the question, she whispered, "Is it . . . ?"

"A boy."

The knowledge added another dimension to her pain. She locked her bedroom door that night. A futile gesture, since she did not think Leon would be home until late, but the small vengefulness of turning the key helped. The following day she telegraphed the gardener and his wife who looked after the Döbling house, and took Lotte and Louise there. For hours she sat in Emil's room, or roamed the wet roads and windy garden in her English waterproof, her skirt hem muddy and full of leaves. Her mind was in turmoil, but when she caught sight of herself in a glass she looked tranquil.

After a week she went back to the Praterstrasse apartment. She only returned then because the following day was her birthday, and she could not bear to disappoint Lotte by not celebrating the occasion as they had always done in the past, by going to Demel on Kohlmarkt, famous as the court patissier for its extravagantly rich pastries.

Leon was relieved to see them back. He sat opposite Salka as they dined that night and was struck more forcibly than ever by her sombre beauty and the sense of darkness she imparted. It was not merely her colouring, the night-dark hair and those level brows, but an aura of stillness about her more tangible than he remembered. It put him on his mettle, excited him, but if she was aware of it she made no response. Leon smiled at her, flattered her, and found he could not look into her eyes: they were too deep for him, too fathomless.

When she went to her room that night, there was a jeweller's box on her night-table. She sat on the bed, remembering the little box of sweetmeats topped with velvet violets Leon had left beside her bed in Baden-Baden. She did not touch this one until much later, when she had put on her nightdress. From blue velvet an orchid glowed, an art nouveau fantasy wrought in gold on a supple neck-band. Hairfine stamens shivered at her breath and a lustrous baroque pearl lay in their midst. It was delicate and disturbing, the flower of a fevered mind. She could see at once why it appealed to Leon and why she found it both compelling and hateful: overpowering as the odour of opium she had choked upon in Saphir's.

Leon had never given her jewellery before, knowing she was indifferent to it and only ever wore the gold bracelet from Paul and Adele. But tomorrow was her birthday, and he wanted to show her that she was still important to him.

She touched the orchid with the tip of a finger. It was flawless, a collector's piece. She thought of that other woman, lying somewhere with a newborn son in her arms. *A woman may have pearls round her neck though she has stones on her heart.*

Salka sat for a long time, staring into the distance. She had to get away from Leon, from his dominance, his possessiveness. These last months she had behaved like a child, refusing to see what was going on, as if by so doing she could stop herself from being hurt by it. But Leon's second son was born now, and she couldn't bear to remain here.

She would go to the only person who could understand. She would go to Adele.

Very carefully, Salka shut the blue morocco box.

Chapter 23

The Paris home of Adele and Paul Sauvel was in Passy, in the Rue Franklin. Unimposing by Viennese standards, it was nevertheless roomy and comfortable. Many-paned windows stretched the height of each room, hung with heavy velvet curtains. There was a flower-filled garden which at one corner overlooked the Boulevard Delessert, so they could sit amongst the greenery and watch the passersby below them.

Salka hardly recognised Paul Sauvel. He still had the same quiff of floppy brown hair, but the diffidence had gone from his manner. He had matured with marriage and fatherhood, and the hesitant air had been replaced by assurance. He had filled out, no doubt due to Adele's housekeeping, and acquired a comfortable little paunch.

Adele, too, was altered. She admitted, laughing, that she had put on weight with each of her three children that had never disappeared, and her elegant Parisian dresses disclosed a soft white throat and flattered her rounded face. She wore her hair in a sleek coil at the back of her head, and her dimpled hands carried many rings beside her diamond wedding and eternity band. She looked what she was, a contented woman, and when she embraced Salka at the door of her house, she smelled warmly of vanilla.

The two women clung together without speaking for a long time, and when they pulled away both had tears in their eyes. Adele drew Salka inside.

"Let me see you. And this is Lotte . . ." she bent to the child, saying something softly to her. Salka caught the words ". . . specially for you. I know you're nearly nine, but you might like to play with the dolls' house, also."

She spoke in German, and glanced up at Salka. "The children all speak German, and it'll do them good to have Lotte to talk to. Me, also—I have so much to tell you!" She smiled up at Salka, who saw in her eyes the concern her cousin was not voicing. She knew how she looked: in the train from Vienna she had tidied herself ready for arrival and had been appalled by the reflection of her drab, sallow skin, and hollow eyes. Beside Adele's ripe prettiness, she felt as she had done all those years ago in Hamburg, when she used to watch the *Friseuse* style the other girl's hair, and saw in the glass her own dark features and black hair, like someone from another world.

For the first two weeks, Salka and Lotte were both quiet and serious: Salka struggling with her own dilemma, Lotte aware that something dramatic had happened, caught up in adult emotions which she sensed but could not define. Then one day Salka went into the nursery and found Lotte playing with nine-month old Hortense, who was just learning to walk. Lotte was holding her pudgy hands while the baby crowed delightedly at her own prowess.

Behind her Adele said, "Lotte would not look at Hortense at all at first. As though it was too painful to see another baby." The two women watched the elder girl's animated face.

"She hasn't laughed like this for a long time."

"Why don't you stay with the children for a while?"

"I . . . couldn't." Salka took a step backward. She had been avoiding the younger children, particularly Hortense. At home, she had found she could cope with each day only as long as she did not permit herself thoughts of Emil. Sometimes she even forgot for a while, chatted and smiled as though she were like anyone else. But with only the slightest touch—a word, glimpsing a pregnant woman—the hurt would throb again and her hard-won control evaporate. And the sight of Hortense, appealing and lovable as her own son should have been—as Leon's son would be, in the near future—was the turning knife.

Adele gave her a penetrating look, but said nothing. A day later, sitting in the garden with Hortense on her lap, she watched Salka standing by the gate listlessly looking across the Boulevard Delessert. Suddenly decisive, Adele got up, carried the baby across to Salka and pushed the child unceremoniously into her arms.

"Here," she said, "will you hold her for a minute? I must have a word in the kitchen." Without looking back she hurried inside.

Salka stood holding the baby away from her, head slightly averted, as though the child were a dangerous animal. Her palms were slippery with anxiety and her only thought was to get away. Hortense, too young to sense anything amiss, gurgled and chortled to herself. She kicked out wildly with her soft kid shoes, trying to get down to the grass, and Salka instinctively tightened her grip. Hortense, the demonstrative pet of a large family, thought it was a hug and hugged back, her fat little arms tight around Salka's neck, her damp cheeks and soft hair pressed against her face. For a moment Salka thought something in her head would burst—and then she was crying, clutching the baby as though she would never let her go, releasing all the pent-up grief of the last year.

When at last she was able to stop, attempting to dry her eyes on the full sleeves of her dress, and sniffing, a man's voice said, "Take this, Madame. Your need is greater than mine," and a large white linen handkerchief was pushed into her hand.

She mopped her eyes gratefully, and saw that the man who had spoken was her neighbour from the far side of the hedge. He watched her sympathetically.

"Better now?"

She nodded. "You're very kind. I'll have this washed and return it to you."

He waved a dismissive hand. "It's of no consequence, I assure you. I'm only sorry you needed it."

Salka, recovering her equilibrium, noted with surprise how easily she understood him. His diction was perfect: he made French sound more beautiful than she would have thought possible, and she looked at him with sudden interest. He was at least sixty, of rather less than average height, with a high forehead and prominant cheekbones. His hair was grey, his eyes bright under bushy brows, and he wore a heavy walrus moustache. Under her scrutiny he smiled, and immediately his face was younger, roguish. He made a small bow.

"Georges Clemenceau, Madame, *à votre service*."

They exchanged a few words. Salka told him she was visiting from Vienna, and Monsieur Clemenceau exclaimed, animatedly, "Aha! Do you know, perhaps, my great friend Moritz Szeps?"

"The director of the *Neuer Wiener Tageblatt*? Indeed. He is a friend of my father-in-law." She thought for a moment. "A Monsieur Georges Clemenceau writes articles for the *Neue Freie Presse* quite often. Is that . . .?"

His bushy eyebrows shot up. "I had not supposed my Viennese readers to be so charming. I can't believe you have the time or the inclination to read the outpourings of an old fogey like myself. I have written several million words and yet I find writing difficult: like Dr Johnson, I believe no man but a blockhead ever wrote, except for money."

Despite herself, Salka laughed out loud. "Indeed Monsieur Clemenceau, you are mistaken. I have read your opinions on divorce, the guillotine, soup kitchens and singing mice."

"Ah, the singing mice. They really do, you know. I have heard them often, at home in the Vendée." He smiled down at Hortense. "Have you ever heard mice sing, little one? They have sweet high voices, like this . . ." He gave a series of high squeaks, and Hortense widened her eyes in amazement and continued to suck her thumb.

Salka told Adele and Paul about her encounter with their neighbour.

"He's a wonderful man," Paul said warmly. "Do you remember *l'affaire Dreyfus*?"

"Of course. He was the Jewish officer sent to Devil's Island."

"Accused of spying for Germany." Paul nodded. "But did you know that Clemenceau was instrumental in getting poor Alfred pardoned?"

"You helped also, Paul," Adele interrupted. She turned to Salka. "Dreyfus has a brother, Mathieu, whom Paul has known for many years. Paul introduced him to Georges, who was then chief editorial writer for *L'Aurore*, one of our best daily papers. He wrote time after time demanding a re-trial. Then Emile Zola sent in an article. It appeared across all six columns of the front page and sold more than 300,000 issues."

"Of course," Salka said. "It was called *J'accuse*."

"That's right. And it was Clemenceau who gave it that title. It brought Zola into the dock but it opened the way to a second court-martial for Dreyfus."

"But wasn't he found guilty again?"

Adele sighed. "Yes. With what they called 'extenuating circumstances'. Georges wrote that the extenuating circumstances were not for the accused but for the judges."

"Anyway," said Paul, "in the end, Dreyfus was pardoned by President Loubet, though we're still waiting for him to be reinstated in the army. The whole episode is *exécrable*. It has had a deleterious effect on relations between the army and the nation, as well as bringing out racial conflict in France between Jews and anti-Semites."

Salka observed, "We are growing increasingly aware of such feelings in Vienna also, and we needed no Dreyfus to activate them."

Adele said, sadly, "My sister had an unpleasant experience, You know Rosa married a year ago? Well, her husband is a teacher, like Papa used to be. He applied for a new post in Hamburg, and when his application form came back, the authorities had stamped it *German of Jewish faith*. Papa is furious. You know how German he considers himself to be, and Dirk's parents were themselves Hamburg-born. And worse, he didn't get the position, which he was well qualified for."

There was silence round the table. Then Salka asked, changing the subject, "Does he still write for *L'Aurore*, your Monsieur Clemenceau?"

"Since early last year he's been running a small paper of his own, a weekly gazette called 'Le Bloc'. He used to write all the articles himself. Next door"—Paul jerked his head—"he's got a great horseshoe-shaped desk in his study where he starts work at an unholy hour. But he's stopped it for the moment: he's just been appointed Senator for the Var."

Adele laughed. "Be careful, Salka. He's obviously fascinating you. He has a reputation for enjoying friendships with young women who are greatly his junior."

"It's not just gossip either," added Paul. "They say he has a *belle amie* for every night of the week. Famous actresses are reputed to be his mistresses . . ."

"Rose Caron," interjected Adele, "the opera singer. And Suzanne

247

Reichenberg of the Comédie-Française. And he's seen amongst the ballet-girls of the Opera."

Salka remained in the house in the Rue Franklin for many months. Every time she spoke of going, Adele implored her to stay, "Just a few weeks more," and Paul seconded her.

"It has been so long since Adele saw you," he would say, "and your presence makes her so happy. Please stay." Salka watched Lotte's face grow brighter and more relaxed, saw the child expanding in the love of the Sauvel family, putting behind her the grey days of Vienna. Salka envied the child's ability to live for the moment, and did all she could to hide her own despondent thoughts.

She succeeded with Lotte, but not Adele. The German woman was too perceptive to be taken in by the bland façade her relative presented, but too kindly to attempt to breach it. Until the morning when she watched her guest open a letter, glance at it and then hurry to her room, to emerge two hours later with her olive skin blotched by emotion.

"I was about to take Hortense for a walk. Come with us."

Salka started to refuse but Adele said firmly, "I think you should. I want to talk to you," and she accepted with docility the jacket and hat Adele held out to her with the same gesture she used for her children.

They walked together down the wide and empty streets in fitful sunshine, stepping carefully to avoid puddles, and speaking of inconsequentialities. As they waited for a heavy dray drawn by four straining horses to pass before they crossed the boulevard, Adele asked, not looking at Salka, "Why don't you tell me?" The sympathy in her voice was so real, and the need to unburden herself so great, that Salka started, haltingly, to describe the state of her marriage. Once she had started, it seemed she could not stop, but poured out the experiences of the last years. Adele, listening, recognised parts of the story from discreet references Salka had made in her letters, but she had never imagined the whole to be so far beyond the bounds of decency.

When Salka, finally, had finished—they were by now a long way from the Boulevard Delessert—Adele could only say, "It's inconceivable."

Salka said, wryly, "It's also very close to the things you and I imagined all those years ago when we tried to understand why Leon broke off your engagement. D'you remember? We felt sure he must have had a relationship with another woman."

"But . . . he wasn't married then. And you say he did everything in his power to make you love him, and then carried on as he always had." She looked at Salka, suddenly sharp. "And did you let him know how you felt? Or did you hide it?"

"If I had been able to keep that hidden," Salka spoke in a low voice, "then perhaps Leon would have been faithful. He only began again with those women when he was quite sure of me."

Adele pushed the perambulator in reflective silence for a while. Hortense slept, soft mouth closed firmly on her thumb.

"You must leave him." Adele's face was white with distress. "It's not my place to interfere, but this situation is intolerable for you. And you can't bring Lotte up in such an atmosphere. As she gets older she'll become aware of what's going on. Worse, someone will enlighten her."

Salka said slowly, "You mean leave him for good. Not like this, staying away for a long visit. You want me to cut myself off from him. Lead a separate life."

"There is the possibility of divorce."

Adele had linked arms with Salka, and now she felt the Russian woman stiffen and draw slightly away from her. She went on, "We'll do everything we can to help. Paul knows a lot of lawyers. Perhaps you could take some advice here and then when you go back to Vienna, you'll have an idea how to set about things." She glanced at her companion, whose face betrayed nothing. Her voice changed and a note of exasperation came into it. "*Salka*. Things can't be allowed to go on as you've described them. My father and mother would be horrified to think the marriage they . . . they . . ." She faltered. Salka gave a grim little smile and supplied the end of the sentence for her.

". . . they propelled me into, that's what you were going to say." A picture of Jacob and Magda Radin as she had last seen them flashed into her mind, both of them half-awed by the Salamans' splendid apartment, embarrassed by her illness—she had been in bed, still feverish after the wedding—and anxious to be gone, their duty towards her discharged for good.

"I don't really think," she observed, "that your parents will do much, do you? After all these years. The truth is, Adele." She slid her arm back into her friend's. "The truth is, if I leave Leon, I leave my whole life: Sandor, the bank, Friedrich. Apart from you, they are all the family I have. I couldn't go back to Russia now at any price, not to that meagre existence after what I've known in Vienna. And I wouldn't want to drag Lotte from everything familiar." She stood still, so that she and Adele were face to face. "So what would I do?"

"Gain your self-respect." Adele's voice was crisp. "You'd find a way to manage. You always have. To throw away your life on a man like Leon is madness."

Salka stared at her. "I can't believe this, from you of all people. You, with a husband you worship and a house full of children, you're telling me to give up what I have?"

Adele's hand went to her bosom and she pressed her heart as though to halt its rapid beating. She was trembling with agitation: she and Salka had never before exchanged so much as a cross word, and here they were quarrelling.

She said, trying to keep her voice level, "I have no experience of Vienna, but in Germany the situation of women has not improved since my childhood. You live amongst a family only of men. You are used to being treated as my father treated us when we were young—as if we had no minds of our own. I don't mean your father-in-law, but certainly Leon's attitude to you is demeaning. I don't understand why you can't see that."

"France is surely little different," Salka retorted. "You may have more social liberation here, yet your Senate will have nothing to do with votes for women. It's still at the cave-woman stage."

"Maybe so. But you have a right to what you want, as well as Leon. God knows I carry no banners for these so-called suffragettes. Still, I find your attitude very old-fashioned, Salka." She stopped abruptly. "I'm sorry, I've said too much. And I don't want us to argue."

Salka shook her head. "No. You're right. I haven't changed my attitudes at all, really, in these years since Hamburg. All my ideas are theoretical—I don't apply them to myself, or my life. I used to think I had no choices—nor had I, in those years. I had to leave my parents, I was sent to Hamburg, and your people insisted I married Leon when he asked for me. And I've gone on believing there were no choices." She put out a hand to Adele. "D'you remember talking about love, when we were girls? You said you could not learn to love just anyone . . ."

"And you convinced me there was an angel who called your husband's name forty days before your birth!"

They both smiled at the recollection and then Salka said, thoughtfully, "The trouble is, Adele, the trouble is, that idea is engrained so deep in me that I can't shake free of it, however hard I try." She dropped Adele's hand. She could not say, in the public street, in brittle daylight, the words that rose to her lips: we are not two people, Leon and I, but one, of the same flesh. He is my double, my mirror image, the reflected face for which I looked.

Just as Salka had learned Vienna six years before, now she learned Paris: the great tree-lined walks of the Luxembourg, the tended lawns of the Parc Monceau on the Boulevard de Courcelles, the low, broad walls of the Seine's Left Bank where workmen ate their lunch in the sun. She discovered the flower market at the Madeleine and drank iced tea in the Boulevard Haussmann. Together with Paul and Adele she spent a Sunday afternoon at the Palais du Châtelet when Colonne conducted the *Damnation of Faust*.

Adele and Paul gave a series of small dinner parties for Salka to meet their friends. Twice, Georges Clemenceau was invited, dapper in tailcoat and white tie, a cigar in his mouth, a gardenia in his buttonhole, smelling faintly of cologne. The second time, he was seated next to her, and she noticed that the skin was grey beneath his eyes.

She remembered how kind he had been that day in the garden and said, impulsively, but keeping her voice low, "You look tired. Are you in good health?"

He made a grimace. "I thought I had effected the perfect disguise." He gestured towards his formal suit. "But not effective enough to deceive a woman's eyes, eh? I had a bout of ill-health following influenza, and though I'm now in full convalescence, my strength is coming back only very slowly."

Salka made a sympathetic sound and he added, with a wry smile, "Do you know, for a time I thought I was dead. Every part of me seemed to be giving up. I felt a bitter distaste for everything, my will-power was plunging into the darkness."

Salka stared at him. "I've felt that. Exactly that."

"When your son died." He nodded. "Adele spoke of it. But now I am at the helm again, at any rate for a few years more. And you?"

Salka was saved from the need to reply by the arrival of the next course, *Poulet Soubise*, chicken which Adele's cook had been marinating in a thick onion sauce for forty-eight hours.

Adele, sitting opposite the statesman, smiled at him and called, "In your honour, Georges."

He raised his glass to her and said to Salka, "Did you know this is a Vendean dish, named after the Prince de Soubise, a seventeenth-century marshal from my province." He tasted it, chewed vigorously for a moment, and then said, in a stage-whisper, "I like the sauce better than the marshal."

Salka giggled and Clemenceau looked at her thoughtfully. She was a pretty sight. She wore a black velvet dress which clung to her rounded hips and emphasised the cloudy dark hair. She put no artificial colour on her face, which was faintly golden from the summer. He had always had a taste for showy women—actresses, *chanteuses*—but this young Russian wore no jewellery except for a gold neckband set with a strange orchid in which glimmered a great baroque pearl. Below it, her admirable neck and shoulders were bare, gleaming against the dense material of her dress. He leant forward, deferential and courtly, and on his other side Madame Sauvel, Paul's soignée mother, gave Salka an unmistakeable wink.

"Let me take you out somewhere tomorrow, if you're free." Seeing her hesitation, he added persuasively. "Let me show you my newspaper. Do, to please an old man."

* * *

251

Georges Clemenceau took Salka with him to the offices of *L'Aurore,* where he was due to correct the proofs of the daily article he had written at his desk that morning at dawn, following his usual practice.

"This voyage to the Rue Montmartre," he told Salka as they set off, "is my only exercise many days. I'm sixty-one, and I have my senatorial duties as well. *A mon âge, c'est probablement le dernier coup de feu.*"

The May streets were hot, and the offices when they reached them stifling, the atmosphere compounded of cheroots and printer's ink.

Salka waited in the writers' room, watching the staff of busy young men working at their long tables and listening to political theorising on the far side of the wooden partition.

"The Radical Socialist party is undoubtedly the great French national party of the early twentieth century," someone said heatedly.

There was a babble of dissent then another voice hissed urgently, "Look out! Here comes the Tiger!"

Salka heard a step on the stair and a moment later Clemenceau came in, holding long sheets of paper which fluttered almost to the floor. He settled himself at a table, donned a green eyeshade and started to work.

At one point he looked up and said to Salka, "I'm sorry my dear, it's going to take rather longer than I had thought. Do you mind staying? You could telephone if you wish."

She started to say she would go home, then changed her mind and made the call. Adele said with satisfaction, "Splendid. Stay as long as you want. We'll see you later."

By the time Clemenceau had finished, it was gone seven, and Salka had tried her French on several newspapers—*La Libre Parole, La Petite République*—and listened to a discussion on whether King Edward VII's visit to Paris would prove effective in improving Anglo-French relations.

"Delcassé's foreign policy is inept." This from a pale, slight young man who looked Jewish. "He wants France to support British policy in Egypt, in return for British support of French policy in Morocco. But nothing is mentioned of Anglo-French military co-operation in Europe."

Clemenceau looked up at this. "Ah," he said, wryly, "the shrimp has no ideas, but he would defend them to the death."

"Shame!" said the man who had called Clemenceau 'the Tiger'. Salka had been introduced to him as Emile Buré. He, too, was young, with a keen, experienced face. "Mandel knows every relevant fact and date about the Third Republic. His articles are competent and well-balanced." He grinned down at Salka. "Georges takes untoward satisfaction in wounding comments. He doesn't believe them himself, but they're so witty he can't resist making them."

Certainly Mandel didn't appear to be ruffled by the criticism. He shrugged and wound paper into his typewriter, glancing up at the clock. "I'm starving. Who's turn is it tonight?"

Buré groaned, "Mine," and took himself off, to return ten minutes later with two large bottles of cider and several packets of white paper, which he placed on a table. He poured a glass for Salka and offered her one of the packets.

"Roast chestnuts? We are, as you see, frugal but discerning."

She peeled the nuts with her fingernails and nibbled the hard pale interior. Mandel came and sat next to her. She smiled at him and encouraged he asked, "Did I understand you are Madame Salaman?" She nodded. "Of Vienna? then you must be some relation of Sandor Salaman, a banker there."

Taken aback by his perspicacity Salka said, "My father-in-law. But how did you . . ."

"Mandel is my mother's maiden name. I use it because it sounds more suitable for a left-wing journalist than my own." Salka raised her eyebrows. "I was born Georges Rothschild, and the financial world is as familiar to me as my own hand. I find it fascinating but less enthralling than politics."

She smiled at his certainty. For such a young man—she doubted he was more than twenty—he had a great deal of assurance.

"Is this your first employment?"

"I wrote some articles for *Le Siècle* and Georges brought me here with him when he was appointed editor-in-chief."

Clemenceau had finished correcting his proofs and wandered over to them, glass in hand. Salka noticed, as she had at the dinner party, that he drank only water.

"You two look very earnest."

"We are comparing notes on our financial backgrounds." Mandel turned to him. "You didn't tell me this lady was one of the banking Salamans."

"Oh, I forgot your expertise in this field also. My young friend Pierrot," he said to Salka, "would know everything if he knew how to write."

"I'm learning, Maître, I'm learning. And now, if you'll excuse me," he bowed to Salka, "I have work to do. I shall hope to meet you again."

When he had gone, Clemenceau reached over and helped himself to a chestnut out of Salka's packet. He chewed it ruminatively.

"I should like to meet your father-in-law," he observed. "I have long held the theory that the world today belongs to the bourgeois dynasties. They are a nobility. Apart from the force of arms, the greatest power is in that of wealth, which includes all other powers. The richest are the strongest. That is the brutal fact."

Salka reflected. She supposed the Salamans were exactly that: a bourgeois dynasty. The name certainly fitted Sandor's tower of Salaman.

"But surely," she said, "a politician has far more impact on his country than the richest man?"

Clemenceau ran a hand over his moustache, smoothing it, and she saw a flash of the vanity she was accustomed to in Leon. He smiled at her, and his eyes were warm.

"That, if I say so, is a remark of staggering naivety. You do not really believe that. The politician who has no need of financing in order to bring about policies he desires is rare indeed. I am not talking about lining one's own pockets with millions of francs: my own daughter married without a dowry. But one must always be a realist. And I tell you, wealth is power."

Later they walked home against an acid wind, speaking idly of Adele ("She is an astonishing creature, your cousin," Clemenceau observed, "obsessed with these ravishing little creatures she produces.") and Hamburg, which he did not know. He asked about her memories of Russia and listened with an interest which flattered her. It had been a long time since a man had sought her favour like this. And such a man: Paul had told her that he was expected to take ministerial office soon. "And one day," Paul had added, "I believe he will be asked to form his own government. France has not many men of his calibre."

The Tiger. It suited him, that nickname. She was aware of the strength of will in that indomitable face.

"My dear Madame Salaman," he was saying now, as he steered her round á puddle, "to look at you, one is not remotely surprised by the change in your fortunes. Your husband must love you a great deal, to give you the extraordinary jewel you wore last night. I assume it was from him?"

He gave her a roguish look and she glanced at him from under her eyelashes, enjoying the mild flirtation. And then the meaning of his words came home to her and she paused for a moment beneath a many-branched gas-light which illumined her face so her companion could see the expression that passed over it like a brief shadow on water.

He paused for a moment, then took her arm protectively. "I am an old man, my dear," he said with a sigh, "and I talk too much. But I can tell you that life is a very fine spectacle, only we are badly placed for seeing it. And we do not understand what we see," he added half beneath his breath.

Salka, aware of his comprehension, said in a flat voice, "It was a birthday gift from my husband. You're right—he gave it because he loves me . . ." She swallowed hard and her listener was aware of the effort her candour cost her ". . . and because he does not love me enough. When I left Vienna, I was running from him. I didn't mean to bring his orchid with me, but I found the box tucked among my things. Lotte thought she'd seen her father closing the trunk, so perhaps . . . Anyway, Adele was so anxious for me to make a good impression that I gave in to her pleading and wore it."

A fine, slanting rain had begun to fall. Georges Clemenceau opened a capacious umbrella and they strolled on, scarcely noticing their damp clothes, both deep in their thoughts and yet enjoying the companionship.

After a while Salka began, tentatively, "Might I now ask you a personal question?" He pressed her arm in reassurance. "Adele thinks I should leave Leon. Divorce him." The words tumbled out in her anxiety. "And I thought perhaps you could tell me . . . you've been through that, haven't you? Please don't think I'm prying, I only want to know if it's very hard to arrange."

He took so long to answer she felt sure he was offended, but then he observed heavily, "It did me little credit, that. I was very upset at the time, and I insisted that my wife leave for America. Our divorce was pronounced the day her boat docked in New York. It's hard in tranquillity to recall old emotions, but I hope I would not behave that way now."

Salka asked, "They say it was your wife . . ."

"Yes. I went my own way during our married life. But I admit I'm an old-fashioned man. When she decided that what was sauce for the gander was sauce for the goose also, I was infuriated. A double standard of morality seemed to me perfectly acceptable, with different rules for men and women."

Salka smiled in the darkness and he could hear the amusement in her voice. "And have you changed?"

"But certainly! A life as long as mine allows one to alter opinions, no? My wife was an American, and women there are more advanced than here in France, where so many are convent-educated. All the same, I am myself now very much in favour of social liberation. But you were asking me about the past, and in those days divorce was neither acceptable nor agreeable. And I don't imagine *that* has changed."

He dropped the humorous tone and added, seriously, "Is it absolutely necessary for you to take such a step? I presume it is your husband who is unfaithful?" He felt rather than saw her nod of assent. "Well, you asked for my advice, and for what it's worth I give it: divorce will hurt you far more than him. In France a divorced woman, however good her grounds, is looked upon with suspicion. Even a comfortable liaison is considered more respectable. I imagine Viennese Jewish society to be equally close and conventional. You will surely be seen to damage its fabric, however justified you may be."

She said, childishly disconsolate, "But you both tell me different things, you and Adele."

"What else do you expect? She is a woman with high ideals married to a good man. Their love is plain to see, like the admiration and respect they have for each other. But I—" he tightened his hold on her elbow as they waited for a flock of sheep to pass on their way to distant fields, curly rumps bobbing, hooves pattering on the hard road "—I am an elderly cynic who knows too much. Adele wants you to be happy. My concern is to protect you in a harsh world."

He bent forward and peered at her averted face beneath the wide-brimmed hat.

"Smile," he advised her. "These things have a way of solving themselves. When you get home, everything might be different. And if you burst into tears again, as I fear you are about to do, I must tell you that I do not have a spare handkerchief on my person."

She started to giggle, as he had intended, and presently they arrived at the Rue Franklin amiably discussing Zola. While they climbed the steps of the Sauvels' house, Clemenceau was thoughtful and as they stood waiting for the bell to be answered he observed, rather sadly, "You know, I believe that love is difficult. But marriage is more or less unworkable."

Chapter 24

In the October of 1907, Salka and Lotte travelled back to Vienna. The Mercedes was waiting at the station to drive them past golden domes and dirty alleyways, palaces and grubby white houses so tall they blocked sunlight from the street. Salka breathed deeply. The city smelt of creosote and coffee. She knew she was home.

When she saw Leon, she felt she had been right to stay away so long. All the furious anger had gone out of him; he had lost the tormented air which had become habitual. On the surface at least he was calm. And the surface, for the moment, was all he let her see.

He had greeted Lotte with outstretched arms and held her for a long moment, savouring the feel of her curls against his cheek, her round arms encircling his neck. Over her head he looked at Salka. *Have you come back to me?* She closed her eyes just for a second against the emotion which tightened fine as wire round her chest.

They kissed with guarded formality, each shielded against the impact of the other. Like adversaries momentarily on common ground, they exchanged civilities and pleasantries about Paris, the family, the journey, and all the time, flowing beneath the wary words, they sensed the current of mutual longing.

Neither acknowledged it. Leon was unaccountably nervous of the assured and competent woman who stripped off pale suede gloves whilst telling the staff where to distribute the luggage in that voice he had almost forgotten (slightly hoarse and throaty, his little peasant). Only she did not look like a peasant. By Viennese standards she was too thin, without an ounce of spare flesh, her body supple and straight in the discreet travelling costume of English flannel, her hair dressed low and sleek.

For her part Salka discovered that she was reluctant to voice the decision she had reached on the Austrian-bound train: to lead a separate life from her husband. A year's separation and independence had allowed her to believe she could achieve this. But when she saw him again, saw that crisp hair and intent, assessing eyes, then her fingers remembered the feel of his skin, and she longed to touch him as she had once yearned to touch the bronze boy in the Belvedere gardens.

She was surprised and shocked by the impact Leon's physical presence had upon her, sapping her determination, undermining her will. She contrived for almost two weeks never to be alone with him, and kept the door between their bedrooms locked. He made no reference to this but she knew that soon she must tell him of her decision. Only that would bring about change, which she hated. She valued certainty, continuity, and the thought of an undefined future frightened her.

One afternoon Friedrich arrived unannounced at the apartment. He had brought Salka golden chrysanthemums chosen—though he did not of course tell her this—because they were the same colour as her eyes. He watched her with gratification as she arranged them in a long bowl while he talked of the university and a lecture he was to give on the properties of advanced medicines obtained from artificial rather than natural sources. It had been a long time since she heard him speak with enthusiasm of his work. Since his own research into a simple pain-killer which could be made widely available had been pre-empted by the discovery of the new drug aspirin, he had refused to discuss his own projects with anyone outside his laboratory.

Now she said, happy for him, "We must all come to hear you."

He gave her an odd look. "It may be your last chance."

"Whatever do you mean by that?"

He got up and wandered round the room, cracking his fingerjoints in a way that made her wince.

"Hasn't Papa told you? He wants me to go back into the bank."

Salka was taken aback. "Good heavens. What on earth for? I thought all that had been settled years ago."

"So did I, by God, so did I!" She had never heard him so vehement. "But I can't claim to be achieving any startling results, can I? And Papa is growing older, he needs more support . . ."

Salka interrupted him. "He's got Leon. I don't understand why he requires your help too."

Friedrich made the horrid cracking noise again. "Leon's not a lot of use at the moment." He was mumbling, clearly discomfited, avoiding her eyes.

"Why not? They haven't had another argument, have they?"

Friedrich said hastily, "No. No, nothing like that. It's just that . . . he's a bit preoccupied at the moment. He doesn't put in the time it needs and you know how deeply Papa cares about the bank. He sees Leon more and more as a dilettante, and fears for the future. If I went back, he says, he could be sure everything will be carried on as he wishes."

"And he wants you to give up your own work—all you've gained— when he knows the life doesn't suit you. You must refuse, Friedrich."

"Easy enough to say." He ran his fingers through his soft hair in a gesture that was Sandor's. "I find it hard to stand my ground against him. He's a very forceful man," he added, with reluctant admiration.

"I know." She thought for a moment. "Let me talk to Leon. Perhaps we should find out why he's spending the time he should be in the office elsewhere. Although," she made a wry grimace, "I don't believe I want to learn the answer to that."

Clearly embarrassed, for he was not accustomed to asking personal questions, Friedrich said awkwardly, "You haven't talked much with Leon since you got back?"

She answered shortly, "No."

"I don't want to intrude again where I have no rights. Only I owe you an apology—both of you. I shouldn't have spoken to you of Leon's child—it wasn't my place to inform on him."

Salka's look was opaque and unreadable. "You did what you thought best."

He stared miserably at the carpet. "No. I might have known you'd think that. But it isn't true. I was angry with Leon, I wanted to hurt him. I didn't give him a chance to tell you himself." He moved clumsily, so that a small table behind him tumbled unheeded. He could not bring himself to tell her the truth. *I thought perhaps you would turn to me.* Instead he said, "But you went away. I wrote you many letters, you know." And in a lower voice, "Only I did not post them."

Absentmindedly Salka picked a dry leaf from one of the bronze flowers. Her affection for her brother-in-law and her intuition allowed her to hear the words he did not say.

Before he went, she gave him the inkwell she had found in a Paris antique shop (a square of heavy cut-glass), and her promise that she would try to intercede for him with Sandor, and watched his face light up with pleasure and gratitude. He was her senior by thirteen years, but at that moment his blue eyes were as trustful as a small boy's.

It proved harder than she had imagined to plead Friedrich's case with Sandor: he had evidently shut his mind to his elder son's personal desires and happiness, as he had subordinated his own all those years ago to his work. The bank must come first, the tower of Salaman. Listening to him, Salka realised with a pang that Sandor—although she was sure he was unaware of this—was still suffering from the effects of Emil's death. With the birth of a grandson, she knew he had believed his tower to be inviolable. Now with Leon apparently disinterested, he was looking to Friedrich to accomplish his dreams. Friedrich, the dry and gentle man for whom fulfilment was concentrated in his neat laboratory among test tubes and mysterious crystals. It was not neat columns of figures which held Friedrich rapt as they did Sandor, but the incomprehensible symbols of the chemist.

Salka perceived she would have to find some other way to resolve Friedrich's dilemma. Sandor had survived so much, strong and whole as he was, precisely because he was able to close his eyes to everything but

259

his goal. She watched him now, pacing the room as he excitedly outlined his plans for investing in a factory to produce roller bearings ("They're going to bring about a minor revolution in industry"), watched his eyes gleam with enthusiasm, his square and beautiful hands etching empires in the air.

He paused for a moment and grinned, catching the expression of amused tenderness on her face. "I know," he said, "you think I'm jumping the gun again. But in a couple of years we'll show 'em."

She shook her head. "I was thinking no such thing. You take risks, but you're proved right so often they become certainties."

Sandor looked oddly shy at her praise. "It's good to have you back," he said. "We must go over the financial situation in Paris before I go to Berlin next week. And that reminds me . . ." He riffled through the papers on his desk until he found a telegraph which he dropped on to her lap. "Would you and Leon do the honours for me? I've just received this from Nathan Hartsilver in London. Young relative of his, fellow called Asher Raphael, is due in Vienna soon on his wedding tour. I'd planned to invite them to dinner and then a visit to a theatre with the two of you. Apparently their itinerary has been changed. According to this—" he touched the yellow paper of the telegraph "—they'll be here at the end of the week, just when I'm in Berlin. I want to be hospitable for Nathan's sake and—" he peered at her over the top of his spectacles "—it's a perfect opportunity to practise your English. So would you arrange something? A concert, perhaps? Some sort of outing?"

"Of course," she said, pleased. "I'd enjoy it. Where do I reach them?"

"They're staying at the Sacher, I believe."

Salka had flowers sent to the Raphaels' suite and telephoned a day later. When she was put through, the wife answered warily, a very young voice with an odd accent—she was from Manchester, in the North of England, Salka later discovered. Salka herself felt nervous, since this was the first time she had attempted her English on anyone but Louise Chambers. She need not have worried.

Mrs Raphael said, in evident relief, "Oh, I can understand you perfectly. I've been struggling to speak Yiddish with my husband's relatives. It will be so nice to talk to you."

"My father-in-law is away on business, I'm afraid. But we thought perhaps you and your husband might like to see something of our city."

She picked them up at the hotel in Philharmonikerstrasse, just behind the Opera. The Mercedes waited for her as she went into the reception hall, passing the oil paintings, sculptures and objets d'art decorating the hallways and rooms. A couple were sitting on a love-seat beneath a bust of Mozart, gazing into each other's eyes. Salka saw them with a little pang. How young they were, how happy. In the moment before they became conscious of her presence, she took in Asher Raphael's slender, solemn good looks, the heavily carved turquoise ring on his little finger. And the wife—Sadie, a pretty name—looked charming. She was swathed in a full-length coat of clear grey fur worked diagonally, and carried a matching muff. A grey velvet hat showed off her coppery coils of hair, the clear line of her jaw and wide eyes of a changeable grey-green, inquiring as a cat's. Salka liked her immediately, and more so when she had made herself known to them and Mrs Raphael took her hand impulsively.

"So it was you who sent the flowers to our room: what a lovely thing to do."

They smiled warmly at each other. Salka explained that Leon would join them later in the day, and added, "If you haven't seen it, I thought I might take you first to the Vienna City Museum?" She paused, questioningly.

The couple exchanged a look then Asher said, a trifle shyly, "Would it be possible, d'you think, for us to skate?"

Salka laughed. "What a marvellous idea. I haven't done that for years." She turned to Sadie. "Can you skate?"

The girl shook her head. "No. But it doesn't matter. He'll teach me." She gave her husband an adoring look. It was an odd little trick of hers, Salka noticed, always to speak of Asher as 'He' with a capital letter, as though the word could refer only to one person. 'He' was clearly the centre of this nineteen-year-old girl's world, Salka thought as she crossed the foyer to telephone Leon. She suddenly felt very old.

She took them to the indoor rink, *der Eispalast*. She had been there before, with Lotte. They secured a table looking down on to the rink, and ordered hot chocolate. The air was cold from the scarred ice below them, and the harsh overhead lights hid the faces of the skaters, making their eyes dark holes, their skin white, and shadowed the women beneath their hats. Absorbed, they watched the figures whirling and waltzing together, bent by the rush of their movement, their skates flashing metallic and emitting the thin screeching sound of diamonds drawn down glass.

Sadie said excitedly, "Oh, I must try!"

"I'll get us some skates."

"Do you want me to hire them for you?" Salka asked him.

"No, thank you. My German is quite good, my father was born in Vienna. Do you know Raphael's? The confectioners on the Josefstädterstrasse, just beyond the Piaristengasse?"

"Of course I do—their pastries are wonderful. Lotte and I go there for tea sometimes on Sundays."

Salka watched them on the ice for a time: the young man holding his wife's hands and supporting her as she clutched him nervously, her face pink with the effort of keeping her balance. When Leon joined her, after about twenty minutes, he was already holding a glass of schnapps. She glanced round and started to speak, then paused. Everyone in the arena looked pallid from the reflection of the ice, but Leon was drawn and grey-skinned.

She said, "What's the matter? Have you caught a cold?"

He shook his head and sat down. "*Nein*" He rubbed a hand wearily across his eyes. "I have a headache." He was bent forward and she noticed with a slight shock that his hair seemed thin and lustreless. Surely he couldn't be losing it already? She waited a moment.

"I thought I'd skate. Will you?"

"I don't feel like it. I'll watch." As she was getting up he added, "What are they like, the Raphaels?"

"I like them. Very wrapped up in each other. I'll see you in half an hour."

On the ice, she forgot her anxiety over Leon, forgot everything but the pure pleasure of gliding, feet together and balanced, weaving her way between the other skaters, feeling the cold strike up from the ice and listening to the rasp of the blades roughening the surface. When she was finally breathless, she went to lean on the barrier, arms crossed. Leon walked down the steps and stood beside her, both of them watching Asher Raphael tenderly unlacing his wife's boots. Salka turned to Leon but he forestalled her.

"There's something I have to say. I want to tell you now, quickly. Before my brother takes it upon himself to inform you."

She turned to confront him, the question in her eyes. He did not meet them, but looked over her head.

"I'm ill, Salka. I've known for quite a time, but I've now been to Doktor Schindler." His voice was so low she had to strain to hear him. "He says I am suffering from consumption."

"*What?*" She couldn't have heard him right. "But consumption is . . ."

He finished the sentence for her. "Tuberculosis."

She held on to the barrier tightly, searching his face. It was impossible. He had been overtired lately, that was all. Why, she had never even heard him cough. She opened her mouth to protest, and then realised this wasn't true. She *had* heard him cough. At night, often, even before she went to Paris, a short, dry little sound that would waken her briefly. And in the morning she would have forgotten.

A man's voice broke into her panic. Asher Raphael was saying.

". . . delightful afternoon, but Sadie's very tired . . . we'll walk back to the hotel, if that's all right, to get some air."

Distracted, she turned to the couple, forced herself to behave correctly. "You haven't met my husband . . ." She made the introductions and saw

Leon's brief smile. "I'll telephone you soon, she promised Sadie, "and we'll go shopping."

She said other things, though she didn't know what, and then they were gone. Left alone, she and Leon stood silent, he on one side of the barrier, she still on the ice. A youth in a light grey outfit skidded to a halt near them, panting. Salka found the steps off the ice and sat on the nearest seat to undo her skates with hands that trembled. Leon took the seat next to her.

She asked fearfully, "How long have you been ill?"

(*How long have you been ill and no one has noticed? How long have you been ill and not told me?*)

"I don't know. A considerable time, I think. I supposed it was neurasthenia—tried to cure it with pepto-iron. I knew I was listless, but after Emil . . . I felt so awful anyway, I just didn't care."

Salka said, talking quickly, trying to keep the desperation out of her voice, "We'll go away into the country. You can take things very quietly there. Surely that's all you need? To rest and eat good food?"

"It's too late for all that. Too late for tonic wines and kind words."

"But Leon." She was whispering, her voice would go no louder. "You can't have tuberculosis. It's impossible. I thought only people who lived in bad conditions suffered from it. But not you, Leon, not you." She was pleading with him to deny it, but he shut his eyes wearily.

"The Jewish disease. The tailor's disease." He started to laugh, an ugly, bitter sound, and then it made him cough and press a handkerchief to his lips. When he did that she thought, Oh, dear God, he'd been coughing like that for months before I went away. I heard him and I did nothing. I went away, I planned to leave him. If I had been here, perhaps this would not have happened. In a rush of contrition she put her arms round him, felt that rasping cough shake her too.

When the paroxysm had passed, he sat for a moment, hunched with apprehension. Then with a sigh of relief, like a child whose hurt had been kissed better, he buried his face against Salka's shoulder. And for a long time they sat like that, heedless of the cries of skaters below, the elaborately dressed woman with feathers trailing from her hat who seated herself noisily behind them, the yapping of the silly little lap-dog some girl had left tethered to a table.

Salka held her husband close, as if by doing so she could shield him from harm.

Together, they went to consult Doktor Schindler, who sent them in turn to a specialist. Doktor Krauss was an immensely tall, angular man, with wrists that protruded from his white coat and eyes which were surprisingly kindly in his ascetic face. While they were waiting to see him, a woman

263

assistant walked them round the large and ugly villa, where patients sat in bed or muffled in wheelchairs. Salka noticed with a painful start a child, a boy of no more than twelve, seated in a conservatory, a meal of coffee, graham bread and honey untouched on the table before him.

After he had examined Leon, Doktor Krauss washed his hands meticulously and then seated himself at his desk. Leon was still dressing in the examination room, and the doctor studied his notes and then asked, "If I may, a few questions before your husband joins us?" His voice was oddly light, she noticed, for so tall a frame. She waited patiently while he tapped his teeth with a pencil.

"Predisposing conditions in this illness are identified as psychological, biological and environmental. Your husband has not, I imagine, a sedentary nature? I would not suppose he undertakes over-strenuous physical labour, either. However, if I suggest to you that he over-exerts his intellectual capacities, would you agree?"

Salka said doubtfully, "He works very hard at the bank, certainly, but he's not under any strain there that I know of. And his father works with him: he isn't carrying responsibility alone."

Doktor Krauss fingered the papers reflectively. "If not overwork of the brain, then I am forced to conclude that he may be suffering from some sort of anxiety of mind." When he saw Salka's hesitant reaction to this he added, slowly, "It is just possible, you see, that unknown to him or his family, your husband suffered from early tuberculosis at some time in childhood and then recovered. The disease can apparently disappear for years. But when there is some business reverse or family trouble, then it reappears. When that happens, the patient may succumb rapidly."

Salka made a great effort to control her voice. "In that case, Herr Doktor Krauss, I should tell you that we lost our baby son two years ago. It happened very suddenly, and Leon was in a terrible state for a long time." She paused, then went on, not quite meeting his eyes. "And perhaps you should also know that my husband leads a very—" she swallowed painfully—"a very irregular life."

He nodded without speaking as Leon came back into the room, pulling together the lapels of his jacket. He was pale, and when he sat down beside Salka she held out her hand and found that his palms were damp. The doctor took off his spectacles and moved across to the window.

"Consumption," he said conversationally, "has been recognised as a disease from the earliest times: Hippocrates knew it, and a Baghdad physician well before the birth of Christ. But little more than twenty years ago, the German bacteriologist Robert Koch identified the tubercle bacillus. Now, its nature is no longer a mystery to us."

Leon cleared his throat. "Is there a cure?"

The doctor crossed the room and perched on the edge of his desk.

"The search for a vaccine has so far yielded nothing. So orthodox medicine will not offer you one, no." He paused for dramatic effect. "But *I* do." He leaned forward, and fixed his gaze on Leon. "If you will trust me, then between us we will defeat this illness."

Leon said, bitterly, "In that case, I do not believe I have the luxury of refusing your kind offer."

The doctor made no sign that he had heard, but continued unruffled. "At my clinics we use nature therapy to counteract predisposing conditions and promote spontaneous recovery. Fresh air, exercise, and above all removal from the sources of worry and fatigue. These are the important factors. I have no faith in specifics and local applications. If you will place yourself entirely in my hands, if you will undertake to give up all control over your own actions for a time, and adopt numerous little precautions to facilitate your recovery, then I can work wonders."

"Can you cure me?" Leon's head was up: he was looking at Doktor Krauss with a mixture of pleading and hostility.

The older man hesitated for a moment, then replied smoothly, "I always tell my patients I can do nothing unless they help themselves. You are suffering from fibro-caseous tuberculosis and it is confined to the lungs. Because you have great powers of resistance, there is an attempt at nature's cure, and although the illness itself may last for years, it is quite possible to arrest its progress if every precaution is taken."

Salka said, "Herr Doktor Krauss, we will do whatever you say. Won't we?" She appealed to Leon. He looked down at his hands which were clenched on his knees.

"Very well," he said.

"Splendid," Doktor Krauss spoke briskly. "Now the first thing I want you to do is get away from the dreadful weather we have here. The winter will do you much harm."

"Where should we go?" Salka asked full of relief at the prospect of positive action.

"You must go to the Mediterranean of course, which offers two main therapeutic advantages. It is comparatively mild at this time of year, so you may be assured of frequent exercise in the open air as well as congenial surroundings: both your physical and mental well-being will duly benefit."

"And the second advantage?" Even Leon was looking more alert.

"It offers a wide range of climates. Climatotherapists like myself pay meticulous attention to the effects of different atmospheres on the nervous and digestive systems. A low pulse, a lymphatic temperament, sluggish or atonic dyspepsia would indicate a disease of debility and indicate a tonic climate: Nice, perhaps or Naples. But in your case, Herr Salaman—" he consulted his notes again—"your high pulse and the nervous nature of

265

your dyspepsia are associated with feverish affections and indicate a sedative therapy to counteract the implications of inflammation and fever. So Rome or Pisa would be suitable, or possibly Venice." He closed Leon's file and stood up. "Take a day or two think it over, and then we'll talk again."

Leon seemed unable to make a decision and in the end Salka settled on Venice.

"We don't want to broadcast Leon's illness," declared Sandor, "and I had an old friend in Venice with whom I did business over the years. He died recently and his son has taken over: it would be most useful if you would go and see him for me. Such a visit would perfectly explain your going there. And to combine it with a much-needed rest is merely sensible: no one will so much as comment."

When Doktor Krauss gave Leon his list of 'numerous little precautions' to be observed, they amounted to a rubric of regulations which were to govern every move he—and to some degree Salka—could make. He was advised what to take with him, and the composition of his underwear, outer garments and footwear were detailed. He had to travel at specific times, to avoid the chills of dawn and the evening mists, and occupy a west-facing room which must at all times be well-ventilated. His diet was planned for him: he must eat good quality food, and more than that taken in health, despite the lack of exertion. He had to have a great deal of fat—butter, cream, cod-liver oil—and drink a large amount of milk. Rigid adherence to regular meal-times was essential. Doktor Krauss told them the times and nature of suitable excursions, and prescribed rest-times. Evening pursuits were suggested—card games, listening to music, conversation. No drinking, gambling or evening promenades.

Leon contemplated this neatly written list—it covered seven pages—with alarm, then flung it down.

"D'you realise what this is?" he demanded, white with fury. "It's a near-impossible regimen. Not a moment of my time, not an aspect of my life, will be free from these peremptory constraints. It's unthinkable!"

Salka, who was on her knees packing a cabin trunk, tried to calm him, "It won't be like that once we are there. The rest will do us both good. And it won't hurt us not to go out at night."

She could remember very clearly what Doktor Krauss had said to her as they were leaving, drawing her aside: "*The phthisical constitution is the most difficult of all to control. Consumptive patients are forever committing indiscretions which are perilous to themselves. They frequently become wilful and intractable. Do your best to make him see reason.*"

She repeated Doktor Krauss' last phrase. "You must be reasonable, so that . . ." Under Leon's scornful gaze her voice died away.

"I must be reasonable, must I? To what end? So that I may live a chequered life, trembling with overwrought sensibility? So that our friends may shudder and draw away as I am wheeled past in a bathchair, and whisper to each other that I have the white plague. *But then, you know*, and Leon parodied the drawling, cultivated accents of his peers, *he has hardly lived an exemplary life, has he?*"

Salka listened to him with pity first, and then with a sudden flare of anger. She got to her feet in a swift movement, and her voice was hoarse with temper.

"No one is saying it's your fault. Such a disease is an act of God. And no one has talked of bathchairs, have they?"

He had his head down, his arms crossed defensively over his chest. Her anger evaporated in a moment. She put her hands on his upper arms. "Leon. Don't dry up with self-pity before there's need. You're ill, and it's a terrible illness. But we haven't even had time to attempt the cure yet. Doktor Krauss says that many of his patients recover completely. And you will: I'll make you better."

"My God, Salka, you're talking like a fool! This isn't a little problem at the bank, that you can right with common sense and practicality! Tuberculosis ravages men, it maims them, it kills them. And you'll make me better!" He pulled the knot of his neck-tie to loosen it, and she could see him sweating with the effort of shouting. She caught his hands.

"Don't Leon. Don't. All I want is a chance to try. I don't relish the thought of living according to that horrible list any more than you do. But I'll do it with you, as much as I can, if it will help. And I'm sure it *will* help, but not at once. Time must pass, and gradually you'll get better. If you do as the doctor says, if you eat well and exercise properly, you're young enough and strong enough to recover."

She was willing him to believe her. With relief she saw hope dawning in his eyes.

"Do you think so? Do you really think so?" He sat down heavily. "Salka. I feel I've never really lived. It can't be over for me yet. It can't."

"Of course it isn't," she said softly. "We'll go to Venice, and you will get well."

He nodded, picking up the discarded list. "I'd better order some of these abominable undervests."

"They're very good vests. The best. They come from Neuburg."

He glanced up at her with a flash of the wry tenderness he used to display in the past.

"So," he asked, "and do the vests of Neuburg always bring tears to your eyes?"

She brushed them away, wondering again at these exhausting, lightning mood changes he now underwent. She knew she must hide the compassion

267

she felt for him, hide any implication that she knew how totally their roles were reversed. For all the years of their marriage, it had been Leon who glittered with assurance, whose confidence had been so tangible that at times she had felt herself almost invisible beside him. At a stroke all that had evaporated.

Leon was the supplicant now.

Chapter 25

For the first two days in Venice Leon stayed in bed. It surprised him as much as Salka, this sudden weakness. The journey had been more arduous than they had expected and though they had been able to walk down the station steps right to the Grand Canal, he had been drained and tired when they finally reached their hotel.

The *Principessa* was where Sandor used to stay as a young man, and lay on a side waterway a little back from the Grand Canal. The ponderous exterior was in a state of genteel dilapidation, with peeling shutters and lower walls shadowed green from the water, but the blinds were new, the brasswork upon the front door sparkled and the landing stage was freshly painted. The loquacious proprietress led them to a bedroom so polished and prinked that even Doktor Krauss would have been hard pressed to find a speck of dust. The decor was ornate, with tasselled curtains and paintings in faded frames showing views of Venice, while the furniture suggested that the hotel had been inhabited in turn by representatives of those victorious armies who briefly seized her: the bed head with its unlikely gilded eagle could have been shipped in by one of Napoleon's generals, while the bulbous Austrian wardrobe might have been brought by a member of Marshal Radetzky's staff during their second occupation.

Leon had still not recovered by the third day, when Luca Manin called upon them. Or, more precisely, upon Salka, since it was she he found staring dreamily out at the tenuous reflections of the water against the walls of the houses opposite.

Luca Manin coughed discreetly. "Signora Salaman?"

She did not turn but said, absently, speaking German, "Oh, thank you. Would you put it on the table, please?"

He smiled to himself and instead said in German, "Would that I could, to please a lady."

She turned and blushed and held out her hand. "I know who you are, Signor Manin. Do forgive me: I wasn't expecting you just yet."

He asked, curiously, "How, then, did you recognise me?" But she could not explain, without sounding rude, how perfectly he fitted her conception of a Venetian banker. Luca Manin was in his fifties, swart and sophisticated. His sober dark suit and white neckties could have belonged to a lawyer, but he would have looked more at home, she privately considered, in the flowing robes and embroidered cap of a Levantine usurer. He listened soberly as she explained that Leon was ill: she found herself telling him more than she had intended.

When she had finished he said, "I imagine you would prefer I did not speak of this to your husband? Nor will I mention it to anyone else. But I am glad you told me: I had wondered at the proposed length of your stay here." He shot her a puzzled glance. "One thing I don't understand. Your father-in-law wrote that there were various business transactions to be undertaken. If your husband is ill, then . . ."

"I am sure he will be quite well enough to do all that is necessary."

Luca Manin started to answer, then changed his mind. Instead, he politely invited her to visit his family one afternoon. Introduced to his sweet-faced, smiling wife and their five children, Salka dutifully chatted and gave out little presents. It was a long time since she had been in a home like this, with its silver Sabbath candlesticks displayed in a place of honour and traditional values as openly evident as the traditional furnishings. Watching the close-knit group, it occurred to Salka how bizarre this conventional Jewish woman would find her own family life in Vienna.

A fortnight later Leon felt so much better that he insisted on arranging a business meeting with Luca Manin. Salka accompanied him to the bank beside the eastern end of the Ponte di Rialto. He walked slowly but his colour was better and he had put on a little weight. She handed him the leather portfolio she had been carrying.

"Shall I come in with you?"

"Certainly not. Off you go and enjoy yourself. I'll only be an hour."

Salka recrossed the queer crooked hump of the Rialto. She had read her Baedeker and knew that the Grand Canal followed an ancient river, the Rivo Alto, from which the bridge, at one time the only one to cross the canal, took its name. What she had not realised until now was that this district was the Venetian equivalent of London's Cheapside or New York's Wall Street. She wandered through the crowds, peering in at luxurious jewellers' shops beneath the arcades, smelling the rich earthy odours emanating from the nearby vegetable market, the Erberia. She was enjoying herself, reassured that Leon was recovering his health, happy to see him once more authoritative and confident. She convinced herself that when they returned to Vienna their lives would flow on uninterrupted, only surely now the new closeness between them would remain.

When she finally reached Luca Manin's office she found Leon huddled in a chair. The Venetian reassured her ("Signora Salaman, your husband became unwell and so we have not really completed our discussions") but as she anxiously took her husband's arm, she caught the banker's eloquent shrug, which said plainer than words, *I'm sorry. But I cannot do business with a sick man.*

270

It took Leon many days to recover from the effort he had made to prepare for and attend that meeting. Luca Manin called at the hotel to inquire after his health and stayed late on one occasion to drink a glass of pale wine with Salka. When he smiled at the heap of guide-books beside her chair she protested.

"I haven't been wasting my time here. I have read, for instance, that your name is that of a Doge of Venice. You must have illustrious forebears."

He looked pleased. "And have you discovered also that I am descended from one Daniele Manin, whose statue stands in the Campo Manin, who was president of the revolutionary republic, defender of Venice against you Austrians?"

Salka shook her head and he went on, "For a full year he held out, but in the end he had to surrender, and spent the remainder of his days teaching Italian in Paris. That was my father's side, of course. My mother's family is also remarkable: she is descended from the Austrian court jeweller. If your husband is well enough, you must both come and meet her. I'll take you there on Sunday, if that suits you."

At the appointed time they made their way to the north-east part of the city, and Luca Manin was waiting for them at the Campo del Ghetto Nuovo, the only large open space in the area. On one side of the square was a high wall, the opposite side was nothing but tall tenement houses, the highest they had seen in Venice, five and six storeys. He led them into a street so narrow it seemed the occupants of the houses on either side must be able to touch hands. Above the windows, suspended across the street on improvised lines, hung bright washing, hopefully anticipating sunlight that could never penetrate to such a depth. Their steps rang sharply on old paving stones, for it was still the time when the inhabitants were busy preparing the evening meal, and the streets were quiet except for the occasional child playing on a doorstep with pieces of wood. They passed a boy of about thirteen, his features stern with concentration, playing on a flute a piercing, poignant little Jewish tune that echoed through the streets to Salka as it had echoed through those of Polotsk in her childhood, but with the addition of notes she did not recall, undertones reminding that in this city the East began, that these stones bridged Occident and Orient.

They stopped outside one of the tall houses, the open door leading to a fusty passageway. Luca Manin paused, his face a mixture of emotions: embarrassment that his mother should still choose to live here in these poor surroundings, and a perverse pride that she retained her independence. He spread his hands in a deprecatory gesture, and led the way inside.

The apartment was on the first floor. Luca let himself in and showed

271

them into an unexpectedly large room overlooking the street. Salka stepped over the threshold and stopped, with a little cry of wonder. The whole room was alive; chirping and cheeping, fluttering and preening, quivering with feathered life. Cages were everywhere, suspended before the closed windows, hanging from the iron balcony beyond them, balanced on tables and chairs, strung on a wire that crossed one end of the room. In all of them were tiny birds, dozens of them, their plumage flaunting bright against the heavily furnished room.

Salka and Leon gazed in utter astonishment at this spectacle, hearing the soft chirruping and whistling, taking in the Oriental carpets that covered the floor, tapestries upon the walls, ornately carved chairs with their embossed velvet seats and antimacassars of worked linen. All the colours—except for the birds—were muted by time, and it took a minute or two before Salka saw, seated in a chair with a wicker hood by the window, a figure in grey silk with a grey crochet shawl about her shoulders.

Behind her, Luca said, "Come and meet Mother," and as they crossed the room the old lady turned to look at them, as though only her son's voice could penetrate the forest of birdsong around her. She too, was grey: grey curls beneath the lace cap on her head, grey eyes in a pale, indoor face. She held out a hand which Salka took reluctantly, afraid it would feel like a claw—she was sure the old lady was herself a bird—but it was warm, the skin soft and dry as tissue paper, its pressure on her own unexpectedly firm, and the voice was not the tremulous quaver she had expected but cultured and authoritative, the Austrian accent overlaid with the softer slurred vowels of Venice.

Amalia Manin gestured to Salka and Leon to sit beside her, and an elderly manservant, discreet and silent, brought in China tea with transparent slices of lemon, and *langues de chat* biscuits. Salka said hardly a word, but listened to the talk and the babble of birds.

When the tea was drunk, Salka glanced at Leon: he was tired again, they must go. Gathering her gloves, thanking the old lady for her hospitality, Salka took her hand to say goodbye and found it held firmly.

"Come back and see me soon," Amalia Manin commanded. "Come alone, if you can. If you would like."

"Yes," said Salka, surprised and oddly flattered by the invitation. "Yes, I will."

It rained for a full week from a low and leaden sky, the air smelling moistly of drains and sodden stones. On the first dry day Leon and Salka boarded a steamer at the fairground of the Riva degli Schiavoni. It was afternoon and very still, the water milky-green as it slapped against the sides of the vessel. The crescent curve of the lagoon was drained of colour, a dazzling desolation of mud-banks and reed-beds and distant islets, of tamarisks and pines.

The man seated beside them, his face wrinkled leather from years of exposure to the salt winds of the Adriatic, pointed to one of the smaller islands. "Isola Tessera," he said and added in explanation, "Fish." They looked at the low houses hung about with greenery and noticed crowded below them the stubby boats of a ramshackle fleet, the furled sails umber, orange, magenta.

It was even colder on the steamer than they had anticipated. Leon turned up his collar and a little later went below. He had passed a disturbed night: he was subject to drenching night sweats particularly in the early hours, and Salka had grown accustomed to helping him change his nightclothes perhaps twice. She was grateful for a few minutes to be alone. They were approaching more land, bleak on the vaporous water, not so much islands as huge rocks of melancholy aspect, the buildings they bore severe and forbidding: a deserted lighthouse on one, the square stub of a fortress on another, a high white building dominated a third.

The old man touched her arm, nodding towards them. "For the sick," he informed her lugubriously. "Isolation hospitals. Lunatic asylums."

She could make out a paved garden, bay trees in tubs on the step, two women in white uniforms, supporting between them a third figure. She turned to the old man.

"What kind of hospitals?" She asked. He rolled his eyes.

"Sanatoria," he said. "For the consumptive. We call those islands *Isole del Dolore*."

She nodded politely and left her seat to get away from him and his mournful information. She had been told there were places here for the incurables, for the consumptives who had come to Venice desperate for health, who had sought a distant country only to find in it a grave. But that happened to other men, other wives. Never to Leon, never to her. *Isole del Dolore*. She shivered, and not from cold.

Salka insisted on accompanying Leon to the second meeting with Manin, and this time he did not even argue. Again, she carried his portfolio for him and he did not notice that she also had another, smaller case.

The meeting was extremely formal, attended by two young men besides Luca Manin. They produced documents detailing potential investments for Salaman und Sohn, showed balance sheets and share certificates, spoke of stability and securities. Luca Manin sat a little to one side, occasionally scribbling something on a morocco pad. When they had finished, he summed up briefly. He was as courteous as ever, but Salka thought that she detected something a little patronising in his manner, as

273

though he had decided he was dealing merely with an invalid and a woman.

"Does that meet with your approval?" he asked Leon politely. "If so, I shall give instructions for the purchase of these investments in your name."

Leon agreed too readily. He had evidently found the concentrated effort of listening too much: he looked irritable and when he spoke his voice had a querulous ring.

"If you recommend them, then presumably you consider them sound. I'd be grateful if you would proceed."

Salka felt her heart sink. He had asked no questions, raised not a single objection. He had allowed himself to be manoeuvred as easily as the elderly women who came to Sandor for advice on investing their fortunes. She waited for a moment until she was sure Luca Manin had nothing more to say, then spoke almost for the first time.

"It must be wonderful to be part of a tradition that is one of the most vital facts of European history. It is true that the banks of the Rialto dominated the international exchange until the sixteenth century?" She made a movement of her head toward the great painted map that hung behind Manin's desk, a copy of the one she had spied on the Rialto colonnade, illustrating the trade routes of long-ago Venetian commerce.

The banker had been putting together his papers, signalling the meeting was at an end. Now he went to the window to point out the site of many a great enterprise, explaining to Salka how the district had been the principal channel of finance between East and West. She listened intently, keeping him talking, waiting until the two young men had taken their leave and left the room. Then she sat down again and, while Luca Manin and Leon watched in amazement, proceeded to open the flat black leather case she had placed beside her chair and draw out a sheaf of papers.

"You will forgive me for taking up a little more of your time," she told the Venetian, "but I think there are one or two possibilities we may have overlooked."

He gave a grunt of surprise. "Signora Salaman, I don't doubt your good intentions, but I would not dream of wearying you with such things."

Salka consciously sat a little straighter in her chair and folded her hands together in a precise, scholarly gesture. Her voice betrayed no impatience.

"Signor Manin. In Vienna I spend a good deal of my time at Salaman und Sohn and I do my part in making day-to-day decisions. You can see that my husband is tired and we would both therefore appreciate your co-operation."

Luca Manin looked at her thoughtfully, stroking an imaginary beard. Leon slumped a little in his chair, relaxing in relief as she lifted the burden of decision from his shoulders.

274

"Now," she went on, consulting the list of proposed investments that had been prepared for their visit, "I see that the emphasis here is on purchasing Italian railway stock."

"Very sound," the banker commented.

"Of course. A great many German banks have been prevailed upon over the years to support the market by being given assurance of preference in railway financing, I believe. As you say, they are sound, but we are a small bank as you know, Signor Manin. We think on our feet." Salka glanced up from her papers and gave him a ravishing smile. "Now I suggest—and I'm sure you will agree—that we would do much better to look at industrial enterprises."

"What had you in mind?" The Venetian accent was very faintly mocking.

Unperturbed, Salka drummed her fingers lightly on the arm of her chair.

"Oh, I don't know. I imagine primarily chemical and electrical equipment—although textiles interest me at the moment."

"That seems eminently practicable," Manin conceded, and spread out his own papers once more.

Salka turned to Leon, "We'll go over these together, shall we?"

Leon's half-smile was an enigmatic refusal. "Why don't I just listen, my dear?"

She paused for a moment. The resignation in his voice hurt her. It was exactly the opposite of the reaction she had been hoping for. And she should have foreseen it. She had wanted Leon to be as assured and argumentative as she remembered, had pushed him into a situation where he would be able to exhibit these qualities. He, too, had hoped for the best and connived with her, spending hours the previous day reading and working. But when it came to the point his physical exhaustion was so great he could not control it and did not even want to. He was a sick man, and knew it. And so did she.

She gave her attention back to Luca Manin, her mind made up. "One further matter, if I may. I've spent a good deal of time these last few days looking into your hydro-electric and marine industries here. With your approval, we'd like to make considerable investment in these areas."

Salka made the promised return visit to Amalia Manin, having first sent a note. The elderly manservant let her in so quickly he must have been waiting behind the front door, and she found herself anticipating that room of birds. It was as she had remembered, the cages and the soft chirruping, the dusty smell of feathers. Amalia sat in exactly the same position as she had the week before. Salka fancied she had not moved in all that time. Perhaps the old lady did not even go to bed, but just tucked

275

her head beneath her arm, like her birds. The thought made her giggle, and though she managed to straighten her mouth the laughter remained in her eyes, so that she greeted the old woman with a vivid smile. Those quiet eyes looked into hers, tranquil and unexpectedly tender.

"You make me think," the old woman said on a sigh, "of what it was to be young. I have been old for so long, you know, so very long, that I have almost forgotten that I ever danced and flirted and made young men miserable." She made a sign to the black-clad servant who disappeared, only to return in a few minutes with more of the delicate China tea. Amalia gestured towards the tray, and Salka obediently poured for them both. In a companionable silence they sipped, their eyes on the birds.

"They love birds, the Venetians." Salka noticed that today the accent was more Austrian. "In the spring they open their shutters to the sun and hang out the cages to take the air, and all the waterways and balconies are filled with their song."

Salka moved to the window. Beyond the brass birdcages she could see that the houses opposite teemed with life: women in headsquares conversed from their windows with their neighbours, babies scrambled in half-hidden rooms, children shrieked and jumped in the dingy alleyways beneath the ever-present lines of washing and narrow-shouldered men in black hurried about their mysterious business.

She could hear the sound of the city beyond, the ring of shoes on stone, cries of market-men, somewhere shrill-voiced women squabbling, and over it all the sound of evening bells carolling from a myriad of church-towers. Above the crooked housetops, beyond the high blank walls of the Ghetto, she knew there was the most ravishing skyline in the world, domed and pinnacled, encrusted with campaniles, but here in these dark confines it was no more than hearsay. She turned back to the old lady.

"Why do you live here?" Her gesture took in the lavish room in its incongruous setting: the dilapidated façade outside the window, the nearby canal green with slime and refuse. "When you could have a home anywhere in this incredible city?"

Amalia shook her head. "No. This is where my husband brought me when we married, and when I leave it will be feet first. It's not a question of money, but sentiment. The Ghetto of Venice was the first ever established, in the sixteenth century, though Jews had come to the city at least two centuries before that." She crumbled a slice of sponge cake between her fingers and pushed it between the bars of the cage beside her to a flurry of tiny finches. "The Ghetto was put up on the site of old ironworks, and the name comes from the Italian 'gettare', to cast in iron. It was cut off entirely from the rest of the city—you've seen the walls, windowless on the outside—and at sunset the gates were locked and

276

Christian guards were posted. Paid, of course," she added drily, "by the Jews."

Salka nodded. "In Russia also they did this."

"Oh, in many ways here it was a good system: we were protected against public violence and although they exploited us to financial advantage, that gave us the chance to become prosperous. At the end of the eighteenth century Napoleon abolished it, but many chose to live here still, my husband's family amongst them. When I came here from Vienna, they were all still alive: his parents, the old uncles and aunts. Now, only I am left here, clinging on like old ivy to familiar stones." She gave a wheezy chuckle.

"How old," Salka asked, encouraged by the old lady's obvious desire to talk, "were you when you left Austria?"

"Nothing but a girl: they married us off young in those days. Seventeen? Eighteen? I daresay the Vienna I remember has changed more than Venice." She put up a hand to smoothe her hair, still concerned with her looks despite her age, which Salka reckoned now must be almost ninety. She added, musingly, "I was a Markbreiter then, a family to be proud of. We lived on Giselastrasse, and went every day as children to that lovely park they called Paradeisgartel." Salka could tell she was seeing it in her mind's eye more clearly than the room around her. "There was a low, white building there with long windows, and before it stood fragile white tables and chairs. We played among the flower beds on lawns so green and smooth . . ." She turned anxiously to Salka. "You must know it? They couldn't have changed my park."

Salka hesitated for a moment. She had often walked down Giselastrasse, and there was no park there, nor had there been, she could guess from the buildings, for fifty years and more. But she could not rob the old lady of her cherished memory.

"Yes," she said, "it's still there."

Amalia gave her a shrewd look, but made no comment. She gestured toward a bureau. "I received a letter today from your father-in-law." She paused meaningfully. "He tells me a great deal."

Salka put down her cup with a hand suddenly unsteady. "About Leon?"

"Among other things. When Anna died, I believe I was the only person he confided in. We have exchanged letters for more than forty years, ever since he first came to Venice. He is broken-hearted over this."

"I know." Salka thought of Sandor, writing grief-stricken letters all those years ago, sitting in Anna's room perhaps, that hidden room full of porcelain and the echoes of love.

"Not," added Amalia surprisingly, "that I needed telling. I knew about your Leon straight away."

Salka was shaken. "But I hoped . . . he's looking so much better."

The old lady snorted. "I'm beyond deceiving, my girl. You think I sit here and rot among my birds and see nothing, eh? I no sooner set my eyes on him than I could tell. I know them, the incurables," she went on. "They are everywhere in Italy. You see them in Rome, propped in carriages or surveying ruins on the arms of their attendants. You hear their short, dry coughing in the churches and galleries of Florence. In Pisa their infirmities pervade social chatter with talk of lungs. Here in Venice they sit in tents to take the air on the Lido. Then they go home to die." She shook her head. "The poor boy. And you with a child to rear."

Salka made an involuntary little sound of distress and Amalia looked at her sharply. "But you knew?" she asked. "You surely knew?"

"Yes." Salka could hardly speak. "Yes. Only I didn't—I wouldn't—let myself believe it. Almost as though it would all go away if I didn't admit it was there."

Amalia laid a compassionate hand upon hers and at that touch, so light, so insubstantial, Salka felt as though her heart was actually moving in her chest from emotion.

These past months, she had faced Leon's illness with enough courage for both of them, but only because she had not allowed herself to contemplate anything but his recovery. She had let herself believe that this disease could be fought and subdued if he and she were sufficiently determined. Until this moment she had not admitted even the possibility of a more desolate outcome.

She sat in that dim grey room, listening to the dry rustle of birds' wings, the incessant hopeful cheeping of caged canaries. She turned a despairing face to Amalia.

"What can I do?" she asked. "What am I to do?" (As that young girl had asked her mother, in another life, another country, *What can a woman do?*)

The old lady's shrewd and experienced gaze swept over her. With an unexpectedly quick gesture she pushed aside the rug that covered her knees, and made an impatient sound.

"Don't the women of Russia take responsibility for their own lives? I can't stand to hear mewling. You have your health and strength and your wits about you. What more do you want?" Then she saw Salka's stricken expression and softened. "I may look like a witch—" she cackled at her own witticism "—but I cannot forecast your future, Salka. All I can tell you is that you can do anything you put your mind to." She reached out a hand and turned Salka's chin to the light. "I can see it in your face." She paused. "You say your Leon will be cured. Well, please God that will be so. But it may take time. Even Sandor cannot remain in his prime for ever, and when he can no longer cope alone, he will seek help. And not from that other son of his, Friedrich. When that day comes, the house of

278

Salaman will depend on you. And you must find the strength to support its weight." She drew her grey shawl around her silk-covered shoulders and Salka felt she must have been lovely once, and proud.

She kissed the indomitable old woman goodbye, and walked through the dismal Ghetto courtyards to find a gondola, hearing an inner voice, that of the rabbi of Polotsk with his hat of the tails of seven sable: *You have it in you to be the cornerstone of a great family.* She saw nothing of that journey past the Labia Palace to their hotel, nothing of all of the shuttered villas, the cluttered churches, the odorous fish market near the Grand Canal with its slithery stalls of sea-creatures, or the secretive houses half-hidden behind crumbling walls. The sounds of the city were only a background to her thoughts: the hoarse bellow of the gondolier as he circumvented a bend, the shouts of the greengrocer at his stall echoing up narrow alleyways.

Leon was asleep when she quietly turned the key in the door of their room, lying on his back, an arm across his eyes. She took off her shoes and lay down beside him, and in his sleep he turned towards her.

She held him, feeling the warmth of him beneath the lawn of his shirt. She thought how easily he tired, and how peevish and irritable he had become: symptoms, she knew, of his illness. She smoothed the thick hair, heavily flecked with silver. An image flickered in her mind so that she groaned aloud; Leon, bent like the remote figure on that isolated island, needing the support of two people even to stand. *Isole del Dolore.* She moved her head to see his face, and found he was not asleep after all, but staring into nothingness, his eyes black with melancholy. He felt her gaze and flung an arm round her, burying his face against her throat in a gesture of such unrestrained anguish that tears welled as fast as she tried to blink them away.

He muttered, seeking the comfort he now so desperately needed, "I'll be all right, won't I? You won't let anything happen to me?"

"No," she murmured, soothing. "No. No."

Many times in the past months she had made just such promises, sure of her own ability to pull him through. For it was inconceivable that his body, familiar as her own, could lose its lustre; impossible that the glossy skin across that broad back should become loose and flaccid, the muscled shoulders waste and slacken under the onslaught of disease. .

So she whispered again, "No, no," as she had all those other times. Only now she did so with that dim grey room behind her, that wise and undeceived old woman.

This time, she feared that she lied.

Chapter 26

Leon and Salka returned to Vienna sooner than they had intended. The drifting vapours of Venice seemed to aggravate Leon's cough, and Salka became convinced that if they stayed he would become one more amongst the spectral figures of invalids who haunted the Piazza San Marco.

So she took him back to the sanatorium where Doktor Krauss shook his head and afterwards spoke privately to her. He used vague terms that could have meant anything or nothing: nature's cure, amenable to established lines of treatment, arrest the advancing disease. He prescribed a different diet, a little light exercise, and patience. Not very promising, observed Leon, but he was so relieved to be home he hardly cared.

Sandor listened carefully to Salka's description of their dealings in Venice with Luca Manin, and noted the way in which she said "we asked him" or "we agreed to that."

When she had left them, Leon had glanced at his father and remarked, "You realise, don't you, that I was useless out there? Manin's shrewd, but he and I don't have the relationship you enjoyed with his father. He was co-operative, certainly, but produced nothing startling."

Sandor, looking at the pages of notes Salka had given him, observed, "The investments he proposes here seem to me excellent. I hadn't considered the hydro-electric industry—did he suggest that?"

Leon shook his head. "He did not. Nor did he propose that we buy into textiles. All those proposals were put forward by Salka. She won't tell you that herself, because she's anxious to hide from you the full extent of my failure."

Sandor rubbed the heavy agate ring across his chin and he listened, anxiously scanning his son's face, noting his increased emaciation, the dark rings under his eyes and the pallor beneath the olive skin. He said sympathetically, "I'm sure you're underestimating the part you played. Anyway, you went to Venice primarily for your health."

Leon grimaced. "Well. It would appear I failed in that direction also." He got slowly to his feet. "Papa, Salka was remarkable in Manin's office. If I hadn't been there and heard her myself, I'd not have believed it. She knew exactly what she was talking about and didn't let him get away with a thing." He started for the door. "I tell you, when it comes to business, Salka is worth Friedrich and me put together."

Sandor watched Leon go, reflecting that even a few months ago he would not have dreamt he would ever hear Leon—so competitive, so aggressive, so sure of his own superiority—speak of his wife's banking skills without any trace of chagrin. He recognised that it was a measure of his son's decline. As the unwelcome realisation came to him, he reacted with the only antidote he had ever discovered to personal unhappiness. He reached for Salka's file and set off for his bank.

Ever since returning from Paris, Salka had been writing to Georges Clemenceau. When his first letter arrived she had been taken aback: why would such a man waste his time corresponding with her? She had sent a brief note in reply, imagining that would be the last of it. But undeterred, the Senator continued. Often two letters a week would arrive, and Salka found herself anticipating them with pleasure. He wrote as he talked, with a witty and wounding pen, maliciously commenting on personalities and politics to the extent that she once wrote back: *I feel you should not waste your words on me. I am so small an audience and you have a larger stage.*

He replied at once: *Nonsense. I write to you at night, when I would sooner think of a pretty woman than of my work.* He described for her the way in which, at sixty-five, he had finally been placed in charge of a government department.

Ferdinand Sarrien is, as you know, now prime minister. He speaks little in the corridors of the Palais-Bourbon and not at all in the debating chamber, and is therefore known as the Sphinx. I call him the Sphinx with calf's head, but keep that to yourself. However, I am bound to be more civil in the future. I have just returned from a reception at his house in the Rue de l'Observatoire. Glasses of anisette and orangeade were being offered to the guests, and he asked me most genially what I would have? I replied 'The interior!' And so it is to be. It is the hot seat, of course: a general strike has already been called for the first of May, and the post promises to be onerous.

A little later, he told her in mock despair that the ministry was a desert when he got there at nine o'clock. *When I made my first tour of the ministry to see my staff at work, we found two rooms empty and the occupant of the third asleep. Don't wake him, I said, he'll go away. I now have a pile of notices upon my desk: "Gentlemen are requested not to leave the office before they arrive." Since all other sanctions have failed to make them mend their ways, I'll see what can be done by ridicule.*

In exchange, Salka described for Clemenceau a party she had attended at the Ephrussi Palace, where she had met a writer whose work she had long appreciated, Lou Andreas-Salomé. *Such a lion-hunter. She told me she insists all her relationships remain purely intellectual, and that when the poor Professor Andreas got into bed with her, she throttled him until he gave up. Her own husband! It is said she has been loved by Rilke and Paul Ree and Nietzsche, and now there is gossip of an involvement with Freud . . .*

Another time, Salka detailed for him the financial situation in Vienna in view of the impending alliance between Germany, Austria and Italy. In return, Clemenceau told her to ensure that Sandor had no money tied up in ventures in Casablanca: a fortnight later, the French fleet bombarded the town following anti-foreign outbreaks there.

As time went on and Clemenceau's power increased, it became a source of amusement to Sandor that Salamans' French interests were safeguarded by no less than the country's Prime Minister. ("Your elderly admirer," he would tell Salka, "is a first-rate source.") She laughed at the description, thinking of her old friend with his rolling gait, his skin yellow against the expensive square-tailed coat of black broad-cloth. All the same, she was feminine enough to be secretly flattered that so eminent a man should apparently enjoy her letters, and made sure that they were as informative and accurate as his own.

Her year's absence in Paris and her months in Venice had heightened her perceptions of Vienna. There was tension in the capital, an edginess, undercurrents she had not previously sensed. People seemed to be living on their nerves, and talk among the literary groups in the coffee houses became more intense than ever. She described it for Georges Clemenceau. *There is an excitement here that feeds upon itself, unhealthy and unhappy. Eyes glitter too brightly, emotions are too volatile. Voices are too shrill and the music is too loud.*

The hysteria was not confined to pleasurable pursuits. At the bank, Sandor was besieged by men with grandiose money-making schemes to put before him. He would discuss them with Friedrich who, hesitant and lacking assurance in this unwanted role, gradually developed the habit of taking his problems to Salka. She never failed him. At first, she had talked over bank matters with Leon, but as his health faded she relied increasingly on a mixture of intuition and information garnered from the most unlikely sources.

Unintentionally she found herself so placed that she knew a great deal about the Viennese business world. An afternoon spent at one of Emma von Ephrussi's soirées, a chance encounter at an art exhibition, a casual remark passed at one of her "refugee meetings", as Leon called her charity work, all added up to a mosaic of surprising accuracy. Then there was the "below stairs" gossip that reached her through Bette and Louise: who had been on a drinking-bout, or was in deep financial water, or had been forced to sell some property. These facts were not discussed with malice but only curiosity and Salka heard them without comment. She did not repeat them—that would have been beneath her—but she did not forget them. And not infrequently she was able, perhaps many months later, to recall something unremarkable at the time which in the light of a new event assumed importance.

So when Friedrich reported that Arnold Kohn was seeking to borrow a substantial sum of money, she remarked, "Surely we lent Herr Kohn a large amount last year."

Friedrich agreed. "Papa says his repayments are always on time and exact to the penny. This further advance is to purchase another establishment: it seems that present demand for over-ornate copies of good furniture is insatiable."

Salka frowned. "I don't know," she said slowly. "Something worries me." And she proceeded to tell Friedrich enough to make him run his fingers through his fine brown hair in anxiety and ask her to go into the bank with him to talk to Sandor, who had already determined to agree the loan. Salka started off hesitantly.

"It's probably only idle chatter, but a month ago I went to Gisele Spitzer's. She was telling me about the Kohns, who are some sort of distant cousins on the wife's side. Anyway, she was saying they'd been having terrible arguments lately. Apparently the wife turned up in tears one morning because Herr Kohn had just given notice to two of the maids: he said they couldn't afford to keep enough staff to run Schönbrunn."

"A reasonable observation," Sandor remarked, clearly bored with this domestic trivia.

Salka persisted. "Not really. That's just the point. Gisele says they live quite modestly. Only he has a weakness for the card-tables. Apparently whenever he loses a spectacular amount, he makes reductions in the household. She's got ten children, his wife, there's a lot to do." She flipped through the pages about Herr Kohn's account. "It all looks aboveboard here, doesn't it? But heavy gambling . . ."

Sandor looked at her over his eyeglasses. "You are saying?"

"If Herr Kohn had a large influx of capital, I wonder if it will be used as he claims."

"So you're against our advancing the money?"

"Well, I might be wrong. Is there a way we could secure it? He's obviously a good businessman, we don't want to hold him back."

Sandor frowned, rubbing the agate on his finger reflectively. "Friedrich. What do you think? It's not the amount which concerns me here, but I've never liked these small operations. I wouldn't care to be taken for a fool by Kohn."

Friedrich, always perplexed by decisions, glanced helplessly at Salka.

"I . . . don't know what to say. I shouldn't want to spoil his chances but . . . in view of this . . ."

Sandor caught Salka's eye. "I'm very glad to have your advice." He beckoned his clerk, who was working at a distant desk and now hurried over, pad in hand. "We'll tell Kohn to go ahead and purchase the property and we'll settle with the vendor direct on his behalf. We've done it before. Now . . ." he pulled out his wrist watch. "It's just gone twelve. I'm lunching with Friedrich today. Will you join us?"

Sandor usually went to Fräuenhüber on Kärntnerstrasse for his midday meal, which was always the same: soup, fish and a white wine. At the end of the second course, Friedrich winked at Salka, and they both ordered lavish pastries which they proceeded to eat with relish, while Sandor stirred his black coffee and watched them wistfully.

"If I ate like that, my boy, I'd be the size of my father in a week. But you take after your mother, not me."

Salka noticed Friedrich's eyes flicker, as they always did when Anna was mentioned, with embarrassment and sadness.

He said quickly, to change the subject, "We had another incident at the university today. In the laboratory this time."

Sandor was immediately concerned. "What happened?"

"I didn't catch the beginning of it: I was teaching next door. But it was deliberate provocation, there's no doubt about that. Lang again, as usual." He turned to Salka, "Did I tell you, there's one student I have who is absolutely brilliant, far and away the best in the year. Jewish. Unfortunately for him, there's a couple of trouble-makers who resent him, and keep taunting him. He's easy to taunt, too. because he's studious and boring—doesn't drink, doesn't roister round the dance-parlours with the rest of them."

"What does this Lang do?"

Friedrich winced visibly. "Nothing much. He simply recites the Weidhofen manifesto in a very quiet voice. There are maybe five other Jews in that class, and at first they took no notice, which was much the best way. But they're young, you can't expect them to take that kind of thing lying down. This time, there was only a scuffle—we broke it up pretty fast. But another time, away from any jurisdiction, it might have most unpleasant consequences."

Salka was puzzled. "Reciting a manifesto doesn't sound very offensive."

Sandor said with a sigh, "The Weidhofen Manifesto was issued in the 1880's. It declared that since a Jew was ethically subhuman, it was impossible to insult him. A Jew could not therefore demand satisfaction for any suffered insult. It was brought out by the German Austrian student body to try and stop the large number of their members who were being killed or injured by Jews."

"What used to happen," added Friedrich, "was that many Jewish

284

students became expert and dangerous fencers in order to protect themselves against provocation and attack. The decree was intended to make such duels impossible. It's no longer official. But still, as you can imagine, extremely distasteful."

"It's a sign of the times," Sandor volunteered. "Trouble is building in Europe. Even the ostriches in our diplomatic circles acknowledge it. And when the share-prices fall, anti-Semitism rises."

Salka laid down her fork. She had lost her appetite for the flaky pastry before her.

"Are you saying," she asked, "that it's getting worse here? Georges Clemenceau wrote the other day that there was considerable anti-Semitism in France. Even now, so long after the second court-martial, Frenchmen remain *Dreyfusard* and *anti-Dreyfusard*."

Sandor swallowed the last of his coffee and gathered up his gloves and cane. "It appears to be gathering momentum, yes." He saw the anxiety on her face and took her arm. "Don't worry. It can't touch us."

Salka walked with Sandor and Friedrich towards the doors of Frauenhüber, past glass cabinets lined with liqueur bottles, long counters topped with black marble. A woman sat at a softly lit banquette, her back turned to them, dark hair bound in a bun on top of her head. She looked for a moment—until she turned and Salka saw her face—like that girl from Polotsk, what was her name?

Rosje Feldman. And she had died because she was a Jew in Russia.

Salka thought of the Salaman bank, of the money and position of her husband's family. She thought of Leon's aristocratic relatives. Of course, nothing could touch her now. She was not Russian any longer, but Viennese.

Lotte's most treasured possession was the Armand Marseilles doll Leon had given her when she was small. For a while the child had only been allowed to play with FloraDora on special occasions or when she was ill, and now she treated her like a miniature goddess: she was never allowed to touch the floor but sat on her own small carved chair. A white pinafore was carefully sewn to keep her clothes immaculate and FloraDora was never found, like Lotte's other dolls, untidy and forgotten.

Long after Lotte had abandoned other toys, FloraDora was still adored and always accompanied the girl on her walks in the Prater with Louise Chambers. One afternoon Salka returned early to the apartment to prepare for an evening engagement and found the child and her governess had not yet returned. She was in the middle of changing, her hair loose over her slip, when she heard them. And then, added to the voices in the hallway, was the sound of Lotte's convulsive sobbing.

Salka ran along the corridor. "Whatever's happened? Are you hurt?"

285

In the hallway, Louise Chambers knelt with her arms round Lotte, who stood stiff and straight, her face white with shock. Although she was still sobbing, she shed no tears, just made dry, harsh little sounds that shook her whole body. In her hand was FloraDora, the delicate silk dress ripped and muddy, the head lolling on the torn neck. One of her eyes was shut, the other staring in a wild wink.

"Oh, poor FloraDora! Did you drop her?" Salka put her hand on her daughter's shoulder and only then did she realise that the girl did not seem to know where she was. Quietly she asked Louise Chambers, "Should I call Doktor Schindler?"

"I don't think so. We had a terrible fright, but we're not hurt. Let's get her coat off, and then if you cuddle her for a while, I think that's all she needs."

Later, when Lotte had recovered and was sitting, still without speaking, while the cook chattered to her as she prepared the evening meal, Louise Chambers told Salka what had happened.

They had been walking in Praterstern, she said, making an effort to keep her voice steady, and were passing one of the garden restaurants, when a group of youths passed them, some on bicycles, others running behind. Among them she recognised the boy who delivered groceries to the kitchen entrance of the apartment. A nice boy, Louise had said, he had greeted them both civilly.

She had thought no more of the encounter until they turned to walk home. It was later than she had realised, and although not yet dark, the park lamps were alight. She and Lotte had walked briskly through the dusk, 'talking about the Lake District, would you believe,' and then, quiet as bats, the youths on their bicycles had swooped from behind, surrounding them. No one had said anything. Louise felt Lotte's hand damp with sweat in her own.

"They just stood in front of us, astride those bicycles, and looked at us. In the end I couldn't keep quiet and I said, very sharply, *What do you want? Let us past.* Then one of them laughed and I tell you, Frau Salaman, even though he was only young, I don't think I've ever been so frightened. He laughed and turned his head and spat and then he called me a name."

"A name? What name?"

Louise Chambers said, reluctantly, "He called me a Jew-lover."

"The grocery boy must have said who you were. I'll call the police now and . . ."

"It won't do any good, Frau Salaman, and I don't think the grocery boy meant mischief. It was the others."

Salka watched the distraught young woman, and felt her anger rising.

"Go on," she said.

286

"Well, then they all started saying it—shouting it, over and over. *Jew-lover. Jew-lover.* Lotte put her hands over her ears and started to shake. They were weaving about on their bicycles, coming up close to us and then wheeling away. They didn't hurt us, though." She stopped, making a visible effort to control herself. "Then they saw someone coming and took off, but as they passed one of them grabbed the doll from Lotte's hand and they started throwing it to each other and catching it." She brushed away a tear. "That was worse than the shouting: almost as if it was Lotte they were treating like that."

Salka's heart was pounding so that she had to press her fingertips to her temples to still the ugly images that rose out of memory to confront her. She whispered, "But you got the doll back."

"It was two gentlemen on the path. They started to run when they heard the shouting. They brought us home, and the doll was on the ground in front of the door. The grocery boy must have brought it back. I told you, I'm sure it wasn't his idea."

She looked round Salka's room, at the alabaster lamps shaded with pleated silk, the discreet luxury of the taupe carpets. On one of the grey walls she noticed the shimmering colours of the Klimt painting that Salka had been unable to resist buying, the woman in the golden robe, her arms outstretched, her face impassive, reminding her of a Russian icon. On her lap, Salka held FloraDora. Louise suddenly burst out, "I can't believe it. Sitting here. I can't believe all that happened just a few minutes' walk away." She was in evident distress. "Frau Salaman, no one's ever said anything like that to me before."

Salka put her hand on the younger woman's. "Louise, don't you see, it wasn't directed at you, but at *us*."

"My father always taught me it was wicked to hate anyone. But if you'd seen the faces of those boys . . . they were little more than children really, but they were ugly with hate. I never thought I'd be frightened by a bunch of fifteen-year-old lads."

"Anyone would have been frightened. You were very brave, keeping calm as you did. It doesn't matter about FloraDora, we can have her mended. You got Lotte and yourself home safely, and that's what matters."

That evening, Louise told Sandor and Leon about the incident. The two men listened in silence. Leon was standing by the fireplace, one hand on the marble overmantel, the other holding FloraDora. When the governess had finished and excused herself for the evening, saying she would go early to bed, Leon still did not move. Only when she had left the room did he slam the flat of his hand against the wall in a gesture so violent that Salka gasped, "No! Don't!"

"I'd do it to those young bastards if I could get my hands on them," he

287

said grimly, and then the coughing started, so that he had to turn away from them, a hunched figure struggling alone. When he had recovered himself he looked down at the doll he held, soiled and broken. "We should force the boy Louise recognised to tell us who his friends are." He paused for breath. "The police certainly won't."

Sandor held up an admonitory hand. "I knew when we reported it they would do nothing. This isn't something for the authorities to deal with." He caught Salka's eye and in the glance they exchanged was a terrible anxiety. For each of them, the incident in the Praterstern had brought back ugly recollections from childhood. In Salka's case it went back twenty years, Sandor it took back more than fifty, as though time and history were compressed. They knew from experience—as Leon never could—that one did not turn to authority in cases like this, since all too often authority was the source and instigator of such actions and not the proscriber.

Government agents had inspired the pogroms in Russia such as the one Salka remembered, that caused the death of Rosje Feldman. It was the police who had clubbed indiscriminately the heads of the men, women and children Sandor had seen muffled in bandages. The army had taken those little boys from Vyatka to their deaths, Sandor's ten-year-old cousin amongst them. No. You did not go to the authorities.

Sandor said heavily, "I have watched Vienna reach the zenith of its splendour—and its power. As the capital of a vast empire it has also been one of the greatest financial centres in the world. Its favourable geographical location, its economic unity, the long evolution have made it a vital element in the political and economic life of Europe. But all that is over now. The once Holy Roman Empire is under the erratic rule of a frail, aged man. I can smell its decay; it is crumbling away. And incidents like this, and the ones among Friedrich's students, are all part of the collapse."

"What do you think will happen?" Salka asked, subdued.

"I hesitate to believe it, but there will be war in Europe before long. We have had forty years of peace, and now I sense an impending conflict, as though there are violent emotions which must be released." He got up and crossed the room, drawing back the curtains to gaze down through the gilded balcony railings at the sweep of Praterstrasse beneath the windows. "The British have been worried for a long time about the rapid growth of the German Navy. But the British Naval Attaché in Berlin was refused permission to visit any of the dockyards."

Salka nodded. "I had a letter from Georges last week. Although there is much talk in France of invasion by Germany, no one seriously believes it possible: they think the British Fleet would destroy the German Fleet in case of need. But he himself says that for France the danger of invasion is very real."

Sandor let the curtain drop. "There is a meeting tomorrow between certain members of the Stock Exchange and officials of the Finance Department. We are to discuss French-Austrian banking connections. As you know, in the past they have been excellent. Up until the end of the century, Paris was a large purchaser of Austrian government securities, and in fact the largest single purchaser of Hungarian government securities. Banking houses worked intimately together, and the French retained an interest in the Austrian Länderbank."

Salka nodded. "I take it you are asked to the meeting because of your London connections?"

"Precisely. An incursion into Lombard Street secures an invitation to the Bohemian Imperial Chancellery. Through me, they hope to keep themselves informed of reaction in London." He pulled out his heavy gold watch. "Ten o'clock. I must get some rest before tomorrow's meeting."

At the doorway he halted, and added, "There's to be a reception afterwards. I'd like you both to accompany me."

Late the following afternoon it became obvious that Leon could not attend the reception. Doktor Krauss had taken Salka aside on their last visit and warned her that he feared the disease was advancing: if Leon lost any more weight and became weaker, he would have to move into the sanatorium. Salka had nodded and now, alerted, saw how his temperature, invariably below normal during the early part of the day, soared hectically as evening approached.

Fetching him a cool drink Salka decided she would not go out that night. When she told him, Leon became agitated and she watched in alarm as he held his side.

"You must go," he insisted, his voice rasped by illness. "Friedrich's away, and anyway it's you Papa wants to accompany him. Don't let him down, Salka."

"All right," she murmured, "I'll go then. Only don't get upset, please don't get upset."

She left him in bed, the blankets pushed aside from heat.

As she was leaving he said, "You're not wearing your necklace."

Salka, who was pulling on her gloves, bent her head lower so he should not read her face.

"No."

"I'd like you to wear it."

"Leon, I really don't care for jewellery, you know that." She held out

289

her wrist with the gold and turquoise bangle from Adele and Paul so many years before. "I only ever wear this."

"Nonetheless," he said obstinately, "just for once, would you put on the necklace? I think Papa would like you to make an impression."

She started to argue and then changed her mind. She had thanked Leon for the gift, but neither of them had referred to it since. Now she slid her arms out of the sealskin jacket in order to fasten the jewel in place.

The dress she wore was panne velvet, the neckline cut low and straight, uncompromising and unrelieved, the colour a silvery sage green emphasised by the gleam of the material. She could not have chosen a better foil for the gold neckband with its strange orchid in which glimmered the pearl. She held it round her throat, half-reluctant. In the glass she could see Leon lying in bed, his head averted, his hands lying idle. Going to waste. She fastened the clasp. On an impulse she re-did her hair, which was gathered softly round her face, pulling it back to a tight knot on top of her head. She stared at herself. She rarely bothered to do more than glance into a mirror these days. Her appearance had ceased to interest her. But she could see that the jewel did something she couldn't quite define: made her, by comparison with its baroque beauty, austere.

It was five o'clock when the Mercedes drew up at the elaborate façade of the Böhmische Hofkanzlei in the Wipplingerstrasse. She and Sandor joined the guests who thronged the classical staircase as they waited to be presented to Monsieur Crozier, the French Ambassador to Vienna. He turned out to be a small man, with a head too large for his body, as though in another minute he would have been a dwarf. As the line grew shorter, Salka watched him greet those before her, bowing ceremoniously over the hands of the women, exchanging a word with the men: his German was excellent, she noticed. When she reached the head of the line he was talking to the massive, bearded man beside him, whom she recognised as the city's mayor Karl Lueger. Monsieur Crozier turned to her and she found herself smiling at him: he had blue eyes of such warmth and intelligence that they redeemed his ugly body. He spoke courteously to Sandor, but it was to her that he inclined as he did so. He asked her how she was, and she answered in French. They spoke for a moment of Paris and then the mayor cleared his throat meaningfully behind them.

During the course of the evening, as she moved about among the chattering groups, she was conscious that Monsieur Crozier was watching her. Below the painted ceiling hung chandeliers big as mill-wheels, lit for the occasion with candles which made the rooms unbearably hot: at one point she excused herself and went into one of the window embrasures. After a moment she saw the French Ambassador move away from the group surrounding him. Embarrassed, she looked in the other direction and saw Sandor and Emma von Ephrussi standing together, obviously aware of what was going on.

Then she heard Monsieur Crozier say, "I hope you will allow me to join you?" Without waiting for a reply he settled himself on the seat beside her. "I have had a long day. My Austrian colleagues are over-hospitable. They thwarted my attempts to be abstemious at dinner and their wines have gone to my head."

Salka said, demurely, "After a day of talks with finance ministers and members of the Bourse, you deserve some leisure."

"Oh, I haven't finished working yet," he replied. She looked at him, her eyebrows lifted but he ignored the query and went on, changing the subject abruptly, "I have not met anyone else in Austria who wears the jewels of Georges Fouquet." He gestured toward the orchid at her throat. "He would be flattered to see you tonight."

Salka inclined her head. "Thank you." They talked idly for a few minutes of Paris: Monsieur Crozier was an old friend of Georges Mandel, but she could tell that the Frenchman's mind was elsewhere. He looked as though he were under considerable strain, the skin round his eyes twitching nervously.

After a pause he said, abruptly, "Have you heard the news of the crisis?"

She shook her head. It was common knowledge that Austria was seeking to annex Bosnia and Herzegovina, but she had not heard any confirmation. Now Monsieur Crozier gave it.

"Russia has agreed, and the decree has been drawn up." He stared moodily into his glass. "It could shatter all my hopes, Madame Salaman. The financial relations of France and the Monarchy are important to me. I have fostered them for years."

Puzzled, Salka asked, "But why should that affect finances?"

"Continental alliances are becoming fixed. My country feels that Austrian policy is subordinated to German, and any tension between Austria and Russia intensifies this." His blue eyes were angry. "Hungary seeks to borrow money from the French government. We and the Russians know that it will be used to strengthen military forces and fortifications in the newly annexed provinces."

"Then the money must not be lent."

"Alas, Madame. It is not so easy. Hungary is desperate for financial aid, and without our help she will be forced to turn to Germany. Such a loan would strengthen the bond between the Dual Monarchy and Germany . . ."

". . . and," finished Salka, "Germany is preparing for war. Isn't there a new naval bill to provide funds for more battleships?"

The look Monsieur Crozier gave her was first startled, then appreciative.

291

"It would seem, Madame, that you know about a good deal more than jewels. Germany *is* arming herself and I am convinced the antagonism in Europe will end in war." He drained his glass and set it down on the marble table beside him with a heavy hand. "And yet no one, Madame, wishes to hear what I am saying."

The level of sound in the glittering hall was increasing and Monsieur Crozier stared moodily at the broad back of Karl Lueger and the officials from the Finance Ministry who were conferring busily. "If France refuses Hungary the loan, these gentlemen will seek to borrow from Germany. And such co-operation will be seen by international politicians as proof of the bond between them. You appreciate the implications."

Salka sat a little straighter and unconsciously folded her hands with the same precise, scholarly gesture she had used when forced to assert herself with Luca Manin.

She said, choosing her words carefully, "Have you considered the possibility of a loan being arranged for Hungary through a syndicate of Austrian banks?" She was watching the room as she spoke, outwardly casual, and as she waited for him to consider his answer she became aware that people were glancing toward them. It made her smile to herself; from the looks on their faces they clearly believed that she and the French Ambassador were involved in amatory conversation. Well, let them think what they liked.

At her shoulder, Monsieur Crozier laughed. "I had forgotten for a moment that I am speaking to the wife and the daughter-in-law of bankers. Are you giving me advice, Madame Salaman?"

She caught his bantering tone. "I would not presume to do such a thing, Excellency. But—" her voice became more serious "—if a private loan could be engineered, your government need not be involved, and Hungary would not then require German aid."

"Or at any rate," he finished the thought for her, "not yet."

It suddenly became imperative to Salka that she convince this man of her ability to organise the loan he so desperately needed. She had no doubt she could do it. But would he believe her? She moved very slightly, consciously flirtatious, so that the Frenchman could not fail to notice the dusky scent of the chypre perfume she wore. Even as she did so she mocked herself for resorting to such obvious wiles. It was alien to her to use her looks to achieve what she wanted, but she sensed that this time she needed every asset she had. A man, after all, would have used other methods to further his aims. Sandor or Leon in this conversation would have referred to common masculine interests, trodden ground not open to her in order to establish a relationship.

The French Ambassador's expression was thoughtful.

"It is only a single factor, of course. But if it could be achieved, it might help avert a war in Europe. But I don't know . . ." He rubbed the figured satin of his waistcoat reflectively between finger and thumb. "You do appreciate, Madame Salaman, that no hint of this must reach Germany until such a syndicate is a reality? It will take time to contrive and any hint of what is going on will precipitate a German offer of funds for Hungary. If this is to be arranged through civilian channels, then intrigue must attend the discussions." He lowered his voice. "You appreciate that I cannot myself become involved. My official position . . ."

"I would undertake the planning, Excellency. And I assure you that the utmost discretion will be observed."

"I know your family's bank, of course. Are you in a position to bring in the necessary funds?"

"I am quite certain that my father-in-law will tap every resource he can." She was safe in saying that: she thought how passionately Sandor cared for his adopted country, and how anxious he was about its future. *I can smell decay; it is crumbling away.* "I have only to approach the von Ephrussi family and they will also wish to help. Once they are involved, others will follow. The Schey-Koromla bank, for example. And Kuranda's." She considered for a moment. "Then if further funds are needed, we would invite Max Goldberger and Julius Stametz to co-operate."

She could tell the Ambassador was impressed but all he said was, "And will they do so?"

She said steadily, "It will be a straightforward business proposition. They will see a return on their capital as in any enterprise. As you know better than I, Excellency . . ." she paused and smiled at him ". . . bankers infinitely prefer peace and prosperity to war."

Still he gave no confirmation. She drew a deep breath and stood up. The night air from the half-open window was cool on her shoulders, the street lamps along Wipplingerstrasse revealed the dark shapes of motors and carriages waiting patiently below.

She said, her voice so husky that the Frenchman had to lean forward to hear her, "It never occurred to me until now that in making Vienna my home I have incurred a debt. I owe much to this city. My comfortable existence, my security." She thrust aside Friedrich's warning words about his students over the Weidhofen Manifesto, and the choked voice of Louise Chambers: *they called me Jew-lover.*

Salka turned to the French Ambassador and her eyes were gold with reflected light.

"If there is even the faintest possibility that this loan might help avert a war, Excellency, then I give you my word that the Salaman bank will arrange it." She opened the beaded evening bag that hung on her wrist and handed him an engraved card. "Could I prevail upon you to visit the bank very soon—tomorrow, perhaps? I should like you to meet my father-in-law and my husband. And we would be free to discuss practicalities such as figures and timing."

Monsieur Crozier took the card and slipped it into his waistcoat pocket. Then he stood up and offered her his arm. "Shall we say three o'clock? And now, if we do not leave this secluded spot, everyone in the room will be convinced that we are planning a very different liaison from the one you have proposed."

Six weeks later, a gilt-edged calling card was sent in to Salka announcing a visitor for whom she spent a good three minutes putting up her hair with extra care.

Monsieur Crozier was waiting for her in the small salon. Salka gave him a delighted smile.

"I am so very pleased to see you, Excellency. Do sit down."

"I only have a moment, Madame. I am returning later today to Paris. But before I go, I wanted to give you my thanks for handling the negotiations so ably." As he spoke, she saw how worn he looked, the skin beneath his eyes pouched and lined, his shoulders even more bent than she remembered.

Salka answered, meaning it, "I was pleased to render the service. As you know. Will you remain long in Paris?"

He lifted an expressive shoulder.

"Who can say. I have put all my efforts into reconciling Austria-Hungary and the French-Russian allies, and I confess to you that I am a thorn in the side of the diplomatic service for my pains." A wry smile wrinkled the tired blue eyes. "It has already been suggested to me that my exceptional interest in the financial relations of France and the Monarchy would fit me for the post of director in a bank."

"Are you serious?"

He sighed. "No one wants to believe that war in Europe is a possibility if we are not very careful. My diplomatic career would be a very small casualty compared to what I fear will come about."

Salka asked slowly, "So you really believe it will be war? Despite our efforts?"

"I don't want to upset you, Madame, after all you have done. I am convinced that in raising the Hungarian loan privately we have made an important contribution to the cause of peace. Perhaps we have even secured enough time for the various factions to comprehend the folly of their behaviour." He picked up his gloves and cane. "I could wish sometimes that I were more of an optimist." He raised her hand to his lips. "Thank you again, Madame, for the service you rendered to your country, and to mine."

Chapter 27

It was proving to be a hard winter. Each morning the pavements had to be cleared of snow and in the apartment every doorway wore a heavy velvet curtain against draughts. Leon was not there now. In November, Salka had accompanied him to his appointment with Doktor Krauss. She had tried not to see, as they drove to the sanatorium in Dornbach, his increasing emaciation. It appeared to her that everything they had tried—Venice, tonics and various substances to strengthen him, bitters to stimulate his appetite, the endless cod-liver oil—had achieved little change. And Doktor Krauss, after he had examined Leon, was evidently of the same opinion.

Salka had sat very close beside her husband as they waited for the consultant to finish making his notes. Leon appeared calm, but when she groped for his hand she found it moist with apprehension. Doktor Krauss tapped his teeth with his pen and she felt Leon's irritation at the nervous habit. She had wished he would stop, but when he did so it was to lay down his pen with a gesture which told them both more plainly than words that he was discouraged.

He had not said as much, of course. He had spoken in rational tones of efficient treatment and collapse therapy, and Leon's hand had tightened on hers. He had used words that confused them both and then he had added, "The key to the cure is heavy sacrifice."

Leon had stood up. Salka saw with sadness that he looked small beside the tall doctor, somehow shrunk into himself.

"If you will excuse us, Herr Doktor Krauss, I'd like to go home now."

Salka had risen also, and then noticed with alarm that the doctor was shaking his head.

"Herr Salaman, please be seated." His tone had brooked no argument. They sat. "How old," he had asked, "is your daughter?"

Salka had felt suddenly very cold. "Charlotte is eleven. Why do you ask?"

The doctor had apparently ignored her question. "The biological circumstances predisposing towards consumption," he had said meditatively, "are related to age, heredity and physique. We know that people under the age of twenty are most at risk and that a family history of consumption is prejudicial. If your daughter is susceptible—and we don't

295

of course know this—we must prevent her from coming into contact with the infecting agent, by which I mean the tubercle bacillus."

Leon had given him a hostile stare. "I don't understand."

"Either, Herr Salaman, you must not live at home, or your daughter should be sent away. The two of you must under no circumstances live in close contact. The risks are too great."

Leon had raged against his illness, raged against Doktor Krauss, raged against Salka.

"Don't you see," he had stormed, "are you too stupid to see? His form of medicine puts my self-discipline on trial rather than his skill. I must enter his sanatorium, forswear family ties, professional duties and social position: everything must be forfeit. And if I fail—if I eat my meal half an hour late or wear the wrong kind of shoe-leather—then my death becomes my own fault, not his."

Salka bent her head under the storm of his words. She feared he was right: she could still hear Doktor Krauss warning her in his cool voice that "consumptive patients are forever committing indiscretions which are perilous to themselves and in the last degree exasperating to their doctors."

She had looked across the drive to where Leon was waiting in the Mercedes, and said nervously, "But Herr Doktor Krauss, Leon is a difficult man. He does not behave in a reasonable way. He never has: I don't believe he will do so now. But it isn't because he's consumptive—he has never been any different."

The doctor had stared at her impassively. "Then he jeopardises his chances of recovery," was all he would say. Salka had been left with the terrible certainty that Leon's cynicism was well-founded, and that after all the man was anxious to hide his own impotence.

Leon's fury had eventually given way to his illness. He could not risk Lotte's health and although he and Salka never discussed it, neither of them wanted her to see the paraphernalia of sickness: thermometers, medicines, sputum pots. He had gone one cold afternoon, and the most painful moment had been when Lotte had tried to kiss him goodbye and he had held her at arm's length, frightened now of his power to hurt. Salka had stepped forward.

"As soon as you're a little better we'll bring you home, darling," she had told him, her voice bright with hope she did not feel.

"Yes," Leon had answered. But the resignation on his face belied the word.

So Leon was now in the sanatorium. The room he occupied was exactly like all the others, the bare white walls decorated with nothing but a set of rules, his days punctuated by brief walks, light meals, the routine of being weighed and examined. Like all invalids he quickly became dependent upon the approbation of those who nursed him. ("I've put on weight this week," he would tell Salka proudly when she visited him or, "My liver is in a much better state . . .")

As his condition worsened, they applied an increasing number of potential remedies. He inhaled creosote on respirators and formalin was evaporated over a flame to ease his breathing. When he coughed, they quietened it with morphine, hydrocyanic acid and heroin. Even on the coolest days he spent hours in the garden, lying wrapped in his fur coat on a day bed in an open-air shelter protected on three sides from the weather.

What seemed most cruel to Salka was his irrational and unshakeable belief that he was getting better. At first, she had thought a member of the staff had given him cause for the state of wild elation in which she had found him one afternoon. Flushed and almost incoherent with excitement, he had told her how at last he was responding to treatment, and was sure to be out within two months. Only when she went in search of the sister in charge to ascertain when he might be released had she understood that his elation was due to a curious mental state peculiar to consumption in which the sufferer was buoyed up by the recurring belief that he was improving and would soon be completely recovered.

Salka listened and drew a deep breath. "You mean, he isn't any better?"

The sister answered carefully, "I wouldn't say that, Frau Salaman. He's doing very well. All things considered. But it'll be a while yet before he can go anywhere."

"I see. Thank you, Sister."

Salka stood in the doorway of the sanatorium, watching the figure of Leon lying muffled in scarves against a spiky hedge. When she thought she could make her voice sufficiently light she went out to him.

"Well?" he asked eagerly, "What did she say?"

Salka leaned down and kissed his cheek. "Oh, you know these nurses. They never give a firm answer. They'll have to look at your file and check your charts. But the important thing is that you feel so well. That really means you're progressing."

Even that did not deter him. All afternoon he made grandiose plans and when she left him he was urging her to make arrangements for them to visit London in the near future. She listened and smiled and agreed, and then she had walked slowly back to the house with him, his arm across her shoulders for support. Only when she left him and turned away did her face betray her feelings.

Filled with misgivings, she sat for a long time in a cane chair on the verandah, careless of the growing darkness and the icy night air. She only stirred when a nurse, closing the curtains, started at her white face in the shadows. Then she walked along the side of the villa toward the driveway. The nurse had still not drawn all the curtains and in the dining-room, quite unexpectedly, Salka glimpsed Leon. For a moment he looked exactly as he had that day at the Freudenau so that she experienced the familiar little lurch of the heart for the compact body, the thick dark hair.

Leon must have felt her gaze, for he broke off his conversation with the elderly man who shared his table. He rose and walked slowly towards the French window and then she saw the stoop of those wide shoulders, the way his suit hung loosely on limbs grown thin. She put her hand against the glass and he copied her gesture. For a long moment they looked at each other. He said something—she couldn't read his lips. The glass, cold against her palm, separated them.

It seemed to her that for the first time in their marriage, she was distanced from Leon. Their lives had often been discordant but always dependent one upon the other, balanced like the weights in her glass-fronted bedroom clock. And now that was no longer true. Time and circumstance, like the cool glass, had come between them.

As Leon deteriorated, Salka and Charlotte drew closer. The girl was less than pretty, her movements awkward and graceless as any ten-year-old. But against creamy skin Leon's eyes burned in her face, so that Salka never looked at her without a qualm: had this affectionate, apparently docile child also inherited her father's promiscuous nature?

There was no hint of it in her behaviour or appearance. Under Louise Chambers' influence, Lotte was happy and receptive. The tumble of brown curls was kept out of her eyes with narrow black velvet ribbon, her body was still a child's beneath the starch and buttons. She would beg her mother to tell her about Polotsk, and listen absorbed to stories of Jonas and Dora and the life of a remote Russian town. She had been too young at the time of Dora's death for the event to have made any impression, but Jonas had died only eighteen months before, and Salka's sorrow had reverberated around the girl. For her sake, Salka had tried to muffle her mourning. It was not easy. She had been prepared for Dora's death, and the long illness which preceded it made it almost welcome as a release. But Jonas went suddenly, surrounded by his books, an expression of the utmost surprise on his face and an unfinished letter to her before him. They sent it to her anyway, and by a quirk of fate it arrived before the telegraph informing her of his death, so that she knew without opening the official yellow envelope, informed by the sudden slurring and slipping of the familiar spiky handwriting, the broken-off sentence which said, poignantly, *I long to see you again, my little* . . .

Those were curious hours for Salka, sitting in her sumptuous room where the Klimt glimmered on the wall, conjuring up for Lotte that girl of barely seventeen, with a river of black hair and ugly flat Russian boots, who had crouched on her suitcase on the cold train to Hamburg, listening to the haunting songs of emigré Poles mourning their country.

Watching her daughter, she reflected that there was very little of her in Lotte. That hair came from Sandor's mother Riva, the cool and slender hands recalled Anna von Saar. But her thoughtful silences, her unchildlike composure—they were from Salka. And what in the mother had been forced upon her by uncertainty and strangeness—defence against a hostile environment—became in the daughter evidence of her sheltered and privileged position.

Deep as the understanding was between them, there were two matters they never discussed. One was the death of Emil. Salka would have spoken of it, painful though the subject still was, but it was Lotte whose face closed like a flower before rain whenever she felt her mother come near to it. She had never spoken of the baby's loss. After those frantic months when she had searched in vain for Emil, she had locked him away somewhere deep inside her, beyond words and beyond consolation.

The other topic never raised between them was Lotte's half-brother. Her father's illegitimate child. This time it was Salka who would not be drawn, who found any pretext to hurry from the room when it seemed as though Lotte might say a word, ask a question, *find out*. So she shut her mind and her eyes, and chose not to see what anyone might have told her: that Lotte had always known.

When Leon had been at the Dornbach sanatorium for over a month, he asked Salka to find some papers he had left in the righthand pigeonhole of his writing desk. She found it surprisingly neat, emptied of its usual debris of dossiers and bills: Leon, so immaculate in his person, seemed not to see clothes dropped on the floor or slung across his wooden valet. Books, newspapers and documents all lay discarded in his wake. He had clearly made an effort to be tidy, she decided as she removed the papers he wanted—addresses, it turned out, and unanswered letters. She fumbled through a drawer searching for an envelope large enough to take them, her mind already on a meeting to be held at the bank that afternoon with the directors of a manufacturing company in which Salaman und Sohn proposed to purchase a number of shares. A single sheet of paper slipped to the floor and she bent to retrieve it. And stopped, arrested by the words in Leon's distinctive dark blue scrawl:

I, Leon David Salaman, being of sound mind, do hereby append this codicil to my last will and testament . . . Her eyes flickered over the rest of the legal jargon and came to:

. . . do desire that my son Joseph, of my union with Anni Hauptmann now residing at Fillgradergasse 14 be acknowledged by my family . . .

Salka straightened up slowly. She felt as though she had been hit between the eyes. *My son Joseph.* Still holding the paper, she groped for a chair and sat down with the heaviness of a much older woman. *My son Joseph.* Oh God, how that hurt. She clenched her fists, the paper crumpling in her grasp. Anni Hauptmann's son was alive. But hers, *her* little son . . . She closed her eyes against the image of Emil's silky hair, his minute, grasping fingers.

After a while she rose, attempted to smoothe the document and put it back on the pile where she had found it. She gathered up the papers Leon wanted and took them to her own room, where she put them in an envelope, added an already written letter to him, and addressed it. Then she washed her face and rang for the Mercedes.

As she was driven to the Hoher Markt she was able to think more calmly, and to her surprise, now that she was over the shock, she felt relief. For a long time it had seemed to her a dereliction of duty that Leon, knowing the nature of his disease, had still not amended his will to make proper provision for this child. She knew that he saw the boy regularly though till now she had not known where he went. (Fillgradergasse 14. She was conscious of it, vaguely. Somewhere near the Opera.) She had meant, before he left, to suggest that he should take steps to ensure that the child would be provided for, but at the last minute had shied away from broaching the subject. In the days before he went away, Leon's muted sadness had been so distressing she could not bring herself to raise the matter.

But it had not, it seemed, been necessary. Leon had done this himself and done it, judging from the date at the top of the paper, in the first few months of his illness, before they went to Venice. Long before she had accepted the implications of his disease, he must have known what faced him.

The Mercedes drove along Kärntnerstrasse, past women in lavishly feathered hats hurrying to appointments. Salka stared past them, struggling to reconcile this revelation of Leon's nature with the man she had supposed she knew so well.

It was as if she had formed a picture of him which had not changed since the beginning of their relationship. The arrogant, predatory man who had accosted her at the Freudenau; the perverse sensualist who had found his pleasure in the loss of her innocence; who had gained satisfaction in seeing his bride in the same haunts—taken her in the same bed— where he had pursued other, more tarnished and practised quarry.

Driving through Vienna, she acknowledged once again how closely Leon mirrored the city of his birth. Cynical, sentimental, concupiscent,

300

revelling in dissolute days and debauched nights. And at the same time promising and provocative, witty and wanton both, enticing as a lover but ultimately faithless.

Only this new discovery wasn't the act of a heartless man but of a caring one. Many men fathered bastards and gave no more thought to them than if they had been unwanted puppies: just the other day there had been talk among her friends about the unmarried antique dealer Jacob Dürer, who had abandoned his pregnant mistress, refusing to acknowledge her although she begged him publicly to take her back.

The motor was halted as a frightened horse panicked beside a trolley-bus, and an idling group of Prussian yagers in steel-grey uniforms crossed the road in front of Salka, their broad-brimmed beaver hats looped at the side with an eagle feather, grooved rifles slung over their shoulders. A couple of them peered into the Mercedes at the preoccupied woman in the fur turban but she did not notice, locked into her thoughts. One of them, younger than the rest and cheerful, tapped on her window. She directed at him—*through* him, he felt afterwards—an abstracted gaze from eyes that were the same colour as his bronze buttons, so that he was left, as the motor drew away, staring after her, much to the amusement of his companions.

Salka was painfully recalling incidents that had shown her a different Leon. Not the man who had stayed away from home during the hours of her first confinement, but the father who had peeped into Emil's nursery a dozen times a day while typhoid raged. Not the arrogant figure of the music-room in Baden-Baden, but the dishevelled man wracked with sobs for his dead child.

She had identified Leon in a role, and allowed him to play no other. He was a philanderer, and carnal. What he wanted he took, for his youth and his strength and his need allowed it. She had known that, and accepted it, but she had chosen not to acknowledge the other side of that difficult personality: the constant need for reassurance, sexual and emotional; the depths of despair to which he had sunk after Emil's death. Not long afterwards she had gone to Paris with Lotte, depriving him for almost a year of the child he loved and needed to have near him. (She chided herself harshly for that, almost failing to recall that she had gone because of the birth of Leon's second son. It did not matter in the face of all that had happened since.)

It seemed to her that if Leon had faults, hers were as great. If his were sins of commission, hers were of omission. She had acted as though her fidelity was an overriding virtue, when in truth she had never been tempted to behave otherwise. And once her pride had been hurt, once Leon had turned to other women knowing how much she loved him, she had struggled to hide her feelings. It had become a matter of principle

301

that he should not know how his philandering affected her. (She gave an involuntary shudder, remembering the jealousy she had endured, the tightening of her heart as he rose after a meal, remarking casually that he would probably be late home . . .)

Sitting huddled in the motor, staring blindly at the weather-reddened neck of the driver above his uniform, Salka wondered how she could have been such a fool. If she had let Leon see the price she was paying, everything might have been different. *If only*, she could hear her mother's voice, *if only* are the saddest words in any language.

She had told him only once how bitter she found the taste of his rejection, that morning in Gerngros among the linens and draperies, but by the time she did so Leon's infidelity was so established, so accepted between them, that he had been unable to comprehend the depth of her pain. And afterwards—she blushed at the recollection—afterwards he had taken her to bed where she responded to his ardour as she always had. Even when she was furious with him, she told herself angrily, she had been unable or unwilling to deprive herself of that pleasure.

So, instead, she had allowed herself to forget their mutual delight and the craving they aroused in each other. She had retained memories of Leon's duplicity and obliterated his desire for her; she had remembered the terrible tempers which sometimes possessed him, when in a rage he would hold himself very still and then suddenly make a gesture of such force that even across a room she had to brace herself against it. And she had pushed aside the many moments of tenderness between them. *Kleine Russin. My little Russian.*

The way his face looked now haunted her: the eyes that used to shine dark and brilliant were sunken, the glittering self-assurance gone. The new lines around that enigmatic mouth were etched by endurance, and suffering, not time, had hollowed his cheeks.

Salka leaned her forehead against the window. Only a week before, the pane of glass between them had seemed an insuperable barrier, so that she had thought they were separate people.

How little she had known, to believe the bonds of eleven years could be severed at will. What held her and Leon together was not of their choosing. Stronger than love, more urgent than desire, more tenacious than need, the strands which linked them reached back further than she could remember, to the time forty days before her birth when the angel had called out Leon's name and sealed their destinies.

Chapter 28

In the Spring of 1909 Nathan Hartsilver went to Marienbad to take the waters for his rheumatism and after the cure he and his wife spent several days in Vienna. It was the first time Salka had met Sandor's London partner, and she was charmed by the genial, puckish man with his old-fashioned frock-coat and the wing collars she remembered Jacob Radin wearing in Hamburg. He had a number of affectations that in another man would have seemed mannered: he wore his thinning hair slightly too long and pulled forward in a number of carefully positioned curls, and it was only after something he said about the former Prime Minister's novel, *The Wondrous Tale of Alroy*, that Salka realised he modelled himself upon Benjamin Disraeli. If he did, she reflected with some amusement, he had chosen the wrong wife in Florence. She was, she told Salka proudly, a Da Costa, an old Spanish-Portuguese family which arrived in England in 1808, and she held her spare frame with aristocratic dignity, providing the perfect foil for her exuberant little husband.

Florence had strict ideas about the role of women, and when she heard that Salka was to attend the board meeting at the bank later in the week, she stared at her with some hostility and asked pointedly whether the suffragette movement had any credence in Austria. She was somewhat mollified when Salka explained that on the contrary there was not even any attempt as yet to initiate a property act for the benefit of married women. As an afterthought, she added that women had, however, just been admitted to German universities, to which information Florence made the acerbic response that she was sure they were no better than they ought to be.

The board meeting which was one of the principal reasons for Nathan Hartsilver's visit to Vienna was held in the Hoher Markt offices. Sandor presided with his English partner at the opposite end of the highly polished table. Friedrich had come from the university, his mind clearly still on some laboratory problem, and Salka sat opposite Leon's empty chair. The sky was overcast and began presently to rain, so that the low room became prematurely dark. A clerk came in to adjust the lights which hung low over their heads. Looking down the table, Salka could see illumined faces and hands, papers with columns of figures, the flash of a gold pen and the hidden glint of an eyeglass on a chain.

The talk, deferring to Sandor and Nathan Hartsilver, was of proposed investment through London in the Grand Trunk Railway of Canada. The Salaman bank already had considerable commitment in the Electrical Development Company of Ontario, but Hartsilver was anxious for them to pull out, since the government proposed to take over power development activities.

"I don't like to get involved in politics," declared Hartsilver. "Makes for complications."

Sandor and Salka glanced at each other and Sandor remarked gently, "Political tension has dramatic effects on financial movement. One ignores it at one's peril."

"For instance," Hartsilver went on as though he had not heard, "My wife tells me that your daughter-in-law was instrumental in arranging the Hungarian loan." He fixed Salka with a chilly eye. "It was no business of ours."

Sandor started to speak and then checked himself.

"Perhaps you, my dear," he said down the table to her, "would like to answer that criticism."

Salka nodded, appreciating the fact that Sandor thought her perfectly capable of defending her own decision.

"It was a sound business proposition," she said quietly. "As was evidenced by the readiness with which the consortium was formed. And as for getting involved politically, it seemed imperative to do anything we could to avert hostilities between the factions in Europe. The French Ambassador believes we helped to avert war, at least for a time."

Nathan Hartsilver was not mollified. "I must say I don't like to hear a woman speaking of war."

Sandor's head went up. "For God's sake, man, this isn't a drawing-room." He ran his hands through his hair in a gesture that revealed his pent-up feelings. "How can we convince you that we have grounds for concern? After forty years of peace no one remembers the horror of war." He looked across at Salka and she silently shook her head. There was no way they could communicate their fear to this affluent English Jew. He moved in a world that was so comfortable, so hedged about with money and security, that he could not smell, as they did, the threat that now hung over Europe, acrid as smoke.

The following day, Salka arrived at the Praterstrasse early from the bank in order to accompany Nathan and Florence Hartsilver to a gallery where they wished to purchase several paintings.

"Do please come with us," Florence had suggested. "It would be such a help if you could translate for us." They took her to the Niernstein gallery in Am Lugeck and only when they got inside did Salka realise that she had met the owner, Max Niernstein, at one of Emma von Ephrussi's soirées.

304

When it was time to discuss payment, he charged them less than the amount he had quoted on their previous visit adding, with a small bow towards Salka, "When dealing with friends one always makes certain small adjustments."

Nathan and Florence were delighted with their purchases, a small painting by Derain, and another by Vlaminck. Salka observed with carefully concealed amusement that the incident had apparently obliterated any hostility the English couple felt. Back at the apartment, they were busy examining the pictures and congratulating themselves when a maid hurried in and whispered urgently to Salka, "Please to come at once."

With barely an apology Salka hurried after her.

"What is it?" She scarcely waited until they were out of the Hartsilver's hearing. The girl's eyes were starting from her head with shock.

"It's the master."

Salka gave a little groan. "Has the sanatorium . . .?"

"Oh, not Herr Leon. It's the older gentleman. He's been hurt."

In Sandor's study, Salka found his valet bending over a chair, an ominously stained white cloth in his hand. He stood aside when he heard her step and she saw the crumpled figure half-lying on the deep leather seat, the closed eyes and the bloody gash on one temple.

"Sandor! What happened?"

At her voice, Sandor opened his eyes and struggled to sit up, pulling his dignity around him, not wanting her to see him in such a state. She noticed that the white cloth smeared with blood was the silk scarf Lotte had given him: he had obviously attempted to staunch his wound with it. His skin was the colour of ashes.

Without waiting for his answer she took the scarf from the man and said, "Telephone immediately for Doktor Schindler."

Kneeling at Sandor's side she added, "Don't move. Just rest." She put her hand on his and felt beneath her palm the cool surface of the agate ring. His skin was cold to her touch, and he was breathing heavily. Too heavily? She knew how dangerous a blow on the temple could be and her father-in-law was no longer young.

"Bring blankets," she told the maid who hovered tearfully in the background. They wrapped them round Sandor, who was still wearing his cashmere overcoat, but he started to shiver. Salka had to fight down panic as she watched him. To see Sandor, so strong and capable, huddled like a wounded animal, his hand quivering beneath hers, was frightening.

It was an hour before the doctor had finished stitching and dressing the broken skin, and longer still before Sandor was in a fit state to describe what had happened. He had been walking home from Hoher Markt, as was his custom. He had scarcely passed the Wedding Fountain there

305

when he had heard shouts and turned to see what was causing the disturbance. He stopped talking at this point and winced at the pain of his head.

Salka said, gently, "Then what happened? You must tell us."

"What's to tell? An old man walks home alone in the darkness like a *meshuggah* and a bunch of hooligans attacks him. They knock him to the ground and scream a few things, then grab his wallet and run off." He shut his eyes. "Thieves in the night."

Salka absorbed this. From across the room, Friedrich asked, "Was no one around to help?"

Sandor looked at his son with infinite sadness.

"Oh yes, there were plenty of people nearby. It wasn't late—not five o'clock. There were young men, a couple of messenger boys." He paused, and when he went on his voice was bitter. "They stood and watched. Someone . . . laughed."

Salka was appalled. "Did no one do *anything*?"

"I believe in the end someone found a policeman. He helped me up and saw me to a cab which was civil of him, considering."

"Considering?"

"I have no doubt he sympathised as much as the rest of the onlookers did with the hooligans."

Friedrich spoke. "You said they were shouting."

"The usual things."

Friedrich and Salka exchanged a glance of comprehension. Sandor lay back against the heaped pillows with a groan of pain. His head was swathed in bandages to hold the gauze pad in place and she was sharply reminded of the nightmare he had once described enduring from the age of seven: a courtyard filled with people, each with a white bandage round his head where he had been clubbed. *Phantoms of the ghetto*, he had said then.

Now the nightmare was on its way here also. She could see it in his eyes.

Sandor was confined to his bed for a week, and it was a sign of how severely he had been hurt that he did not object. On the third day Rabbi Jacobs visited him, and the two men talked for over an hour.

When the rabbi had gone Sandor said to his daughter-in-law, "There is something we have to do for Leon."

When he told her what it was, her mouth went dry and she was suddenly aware of the overwhelming heat of the room.

Twenty-four hours later Rabbi Jacobs returned. He came before dusk, in time for the evening prayers, bringing with him men to make up the *minyan*, the ten male Jews required for religious service. In the study they

306

quietly donned the *tallis* and the *tefillin*—prayer-shawls and phylacteries—and followed the rabbi into Sandor's room. He beckoned to Salka, and holding Lotte's hand she went in and they listened to the low voices rapidly murmuring in Hebrew. She caught Friedrich's eye and they smiled briefly at each other: she sensed his discomfiture with the unfamiliar scene. He alone stood still and stiff. All the other men unconsciously rocked themselves gently forward and back as they prayed.

Then the rabbi spread his arms in a gesture of the utmost compassion, and Salka heard his next words as long ago she had heard the marriage service, surging and fading like the sea outside a cave.

By permission of the supreme King of kings, with the consent of the Omnipresent, blessed be He, with the approbation of the heavenly tribunal we change, alter and supersede the name of this sick person, whose name heretofore was Leon. From this day forward his name shall be no more Leon but Chaim, meaning, Life. And by the name of Chaim shall he be known, mentioned, called, spoken of and named.

Salka felt Lotte's hand clench in her own and she slipped an arm round the girl's shoulder to hold her close. The prayer continued, beseeching and entreating:

May the supreme King of kings annul all severe and evil decrees against him: may He heal his wounds and pains; pardon all his sins, forgive all his errors and lengthen his span of life . . . heal him with a perfect cure and restore his health.

Lotte muttered in a desolate little voice, "I'm frightened. Will Papa be all right?" and buried her face against her mother. Who could not tell her, it is superstition only, a desperate attempt to repudiate the decree of death which that superior judge has signed against him. Salka, who had grown up in an atmosphere steeped in omen and prophecy, heard the Cabalistic invocation and longed to put her trust in it, as Jews had done since the Middle Ages.

In response to Lotte, she whispered soothing words she had used to her in babyhood (*Faygeleh*, little bird), hoping against hope that the child was young enough to mistake compassion for confirmation. Across the room, Friedrich was listening to the rabbi with an intent and anxious expression. But Sandor, propped on pillows, held his *tallis* before his eyes as though unable to look truth in the face.

On the Tuesday afternoon Sandor was still unwell, his headache worse than ever after the effort he had made for Leon. He had asked for papers to be sent from the bank and this she had refused to allow. Later, she relented sufficiently to compromise: she would let him know exactly what was being done but he must not attempt to read himself. This Sandor was content to accept. He had grown increasingly dependent on Salka during the last weeks. Friedrich's indecisiveness, his lack of understanding and, above all, his timidity in a world where nerve and courage were vital, had all conspired to make Sandor reluctantly concede that Friedrich simply would not do. He had always trusted Salka's judgement but had bowed to the convention that women stayed behind the scenes. For someone of their class to take her place publicly in any business was unthinkable and Sandor would not have contemplated it even a few months ago. He had watched in amazement as the shy girl from Polotsk displayed qualities he had previous only suspected. Her encyclopaedic knowledge of the banking systems of other countries—particularly France and England—may have come from books, but it was impeccable. Her ability to cut through unnecessary detail and above all her manner with his staff—authoritative but never dictatorial—impressed him.

That day, helpless and tired, he had to admit that he should not have waited so long to give her the place in the Salaman bank she so richly deserved. He was about to tell her that Friedrich should go back to his laboratories—a mere formality, since with Salka's increased involvement he already slipped away for much of the week—and ask if she was prepared to accept openly the role she already filled, when Nathan and Florence Hartsilver were announced.

The English couple were dressed for travelling. Nathan's suit of green loden had evidently been purchased in Vienna and Salka and Sandor avoided each other's eyes for fear they would burst out laughing at the incongruous figure he cut in the knee-length trousers and thick Alpine stockings. But there was nothing lighthearted about his expression. Both he and Florence wore sombre frowns. After a few minutes Sandor inquired what was wrong. Nathan made a dismissive gesture but Florence exclaimed, forgetting herself and speaking so fast that Salka had to interpret for Sandor.

"This horrible country. I can't wait to get home." And then she started to cry. Nathan put his arm round her and explained that the previous evening they had dined with friends in a restaurant on Liliengasse near St Stephen's. *Fledermaus*, some name like that. The meal had been excellent and afterwards there had been an entertainment.

"You know the sort of thing," Nathan said, embarrassed. "A little coarse for the ladies but nothing to which one could object. There were a series of sketches. We naturally found them hard to follow but we got the gist of them. The last was the most distasteful. It featured an old man, the caricature of a Jew . . ." he glanced across at Salka, ". . . Greased down hair and a black moustache. A fur coat." She nodded, realising what was coming. "And then the other actors started insulting him, throwing food and shouting jibes."

"The audience loved it," put in Florence. "We couldn't believe it. To

308

see elegant people behaving in that way. We were with Heinrich and Sophie Koch, and of course they were as offended as we were. So we all started to leave. And then . . ." her eyes filled with tears again ". . . the audience started laughing at *us*, and shouting things, and banging on the tables . . ." She dissolved into helpless sobs.

Nathan laid a hand on Sandor's arm. "We didn't know," he said soberly, "we didn't realise what you were talking about. We really thought when you hurt your head it was an accident—a mistake. We see now that the situation here is as you say. Florence won't stay here another day and I agree with her. We are going back to London. And, my dear friend, we beg you to do the same."

Sandor gave a faint smile. "It's not so simple. This is our home, our city. Our lives are here."

Salka listened and thought of the time he had told her *I am Vienna, I and men like me*. Images crowded in: FloraDora with her broken body, Louise Chambers' shocked face, Lotte's clenched hands. And behind them were other images. Hopeless figures with their heads wrapped in white bandages. Little boys huddled in ragged ranks wearing soldiers' greatcoats. And the pretty face of Rosje Feldman, who had died when she was eighteen because she was a Jew.

Beside her, Florence made an impatient sound. "Now it is you who refuses to see what is before your eyes." She dabbed her own with a bit of lace. "There is no question of choice. For God's sake, get out of Austria before it's too late."

Sandor said soothingly, "We are already making considerably more investment in England than we did even a year ago. Soon, perhaps, we will be in a position to make a decision . . . don't you agree, my dear?"

Salka did not reply. Respect for Sandor would not allow her to oppose him before others. Only when the English couple had said their farewells and left, Nathan leading his wife from the room, did Sandor ask her, "What do you think?"

She chose her words carefully, "You've said often that you are Viennese now, that this is your adopted city. You love it, and I see why. You married into it, you did your part in building up its commerce and trade."

Sandor nodded, his face suddenly relaxed and young with the remembrance of his early days. She went on, more sure of herself now.

"I love it too, but not as you do. I married into it also, and that brought me a life I could never have dreamt of." She made a wide sweeping movement of her arm that took in the room, the bank, the status she had been given with the name of Salaman. She took a deep breath. "But we aren't Viennese, you and I. Nor Russian, not any more. I don't believe we have roots anywhere. You've been with me often enough to visit the refugees on their way to the New World. I've heard you telling them about the fresh lives they must make for themselves." She paused and asked lightly, "Are we any different?"

Sandor lowered his head in a stubborn movement. He brushed his hands through his thick head of hair as he always did when he thought deeply. Only this time his fingers encountered the bandage he still wore as a result of the attack outside the bank. She saw his fingers slide across the soft pad on his temple and stop, pressing on the wound he had received from an unknown assailant. Unknown, but undoubtedly a fellow countryman.

Salka watched all this with commiseration. She said, "We have done everything we could for this city. It is over for us here."

And added, after a moment, "We should leave very soon."

When Doktor Krauss told Salka it was time for Leon to come home, she understood what he was really saying. She arranged for the Döbling house to be opened and aired and Louise took Lotte there to stay.

Once those two were gone, the Praterstrasse apartment became too quiet. She bustled about, preparing Leon's room, giving orders for the windows and curtains to be washed, rugs to be taken up. There must be no dust, no danger. She took down pictures in carved frames and put away his books in glass-fronted cupboards.

They brought him home from the sanatorium on a stretcher. She was waiting at the street door for them to bring him up. She had not seen him for a week and she had a smile ready on her lips for him.

She thought, just for a second, that they had brought the wrong man. This could not be Leon—he was old, old, his eyes sunken and his mouth pale and dry. She looked at him before he knew she was there and wanted to groan with pity at the way disease had mutilated his beauty and brought him to this.

When he saw her he made the huge effort to sit up and compose his features to be alert and cheerful, so that the nurse had to restrain him, but not before Salka had heard the insistent cough that could no longer be quieted. They took him to his room and put him to bed and after two weeks Salka could not remember a time when she had not been exhausted with the effort of tending him, talking to him, pretending for him that in another few days, in another week, he would be able to get up.

At night she would lie on her bed and hear in the next room, through the door he could not bear to have closed, the light sound as Leon turned the pages of the book he was trying to read. It was almost the only thing he could do unaided and she experienced his humiliation as sharply as if it were her own. She would never be accustomed to the way he looked at her now. All the assurance was gone, the assessing, challenging glances, the arrogant masculine pride that had marked him out from other men.

310

He was humble, and she could not bear to see it, diffident and uncertain, dependent now on her goodwill as long ago she had been on his.

It was hard to recall that she had once wished he would be hers alone, had yearned for him to renounce his promiscuous ways. Well, she had her wish, granted by a derisive fate, for the man who lay next door was only a travesty of the Leon she loved.

And because she loved him, she would not let him see what it cost her to smile at him, and bathe his fevered skin, how it hurt to spoon food into the mouth which had been demanding and possessive. She loved him, and she hid what was happening as best she could.

But the day came when he awoke as though he had been rejuvenated, full of nervous energy, disjointed words and a wild excitement that suffused his cheeks with hectic colour and made the nurse shake her head as she went out to telephone the doctor. Leon held Salka's hand tightly in his and talked of what they would do together now he was recovering.

"We'll travel," he promised her. "You always wanted to visit your parents. We'll go to Polotsk, and show off the children." He chuckled. "What will they make of Emil, eh?"

Salka got up, her face working. Sandor had come in silently and heard Leon's words. He led her outside and for the first time in all the years she had known him gathered her into his arms so that she stood, her cheek pressed against his stiff shirt-front, and shook with fear.

Sandor knew there was nothing to be said. He offered only his caring presence and deep concern, and when she was calmer he told her, "Get some rest. I'll stay with him."

She went gratefully—not to her own room, which was too near, but to Lotte's. She lay on the narrow bed among dolls and girlish cushions and was astonished, on waking, to find she had slept. The angle of the light told her it was early evening and after a while she rang for coffee. It came with a scribbled note from Sandor: *The doctor says, not long.*

She bathed hurriedly and went to her own room wrapped in one of Lotte's dressing-gowns. She was so thin from anxiety that it went round her easily though it was much too short. She smiled briefly at her ridiculous reflection and then looked more carefully at herself. Leaning towards the glass, she fingered the drawn skin at the corners of her eyes, frowned at the unkempt hair. On an impulse she pulled her dress of sage green velvet from a wardrobe and hurriedly put it on, brushed her hair and pinned it rapidly high on her head. She must make herself beautiful for Leon, who so loved pretty women.

When she reached the bedside he seemed to be asleep. Sandor was there, reading by the light of a single lamp. They spoke briefly of the doctor's visit and then she said, "I feel much better, thanks to you. I'll stay now, while you have something to eat."

311

She moved round the room, putting on more lamps. She wasn't sure why she did this, only that the dark seemed hostile. Still Leon slept his drugged sleep. The nurse went about her business, the sounds of the apartment reassuring in the distance.

She closed her eyes, just for a moment, and heard with a start Leon's voice—his real voice, the amused, caressing, intimate tones that always stirred her.

"You must be going to meet a lover, to look so wonderful. My little peasant."

She opened her eyes, touched the folds of her velvet skirt. "It's for you. Only for you."

He coughed and when he spoke again it was with the rasp of his illness. "You've . . . forgotten the necklace."

Obediently she went into her room and found the velvet box. The supple gold band was cool round her throat and the strange orchid shivered with her breath. *A woman may have pearls round her neck though she have stones on her heart.* When she returned to him, he seemed to be asleep again. Beneath the blankets his body appeared flat and insubstantial, his hands lying on the sheet were those of an invalid, white and unused.

She lay down on the bed beside him and pulled his head gently so that it rested in the hollow between her ear and shoulder, the warm place he had so often sought. She thought, I'm doing this for the last time. If she did not look at him, it was almost as though nothing had changed.

The nurse came in just then and demanded sharply, "Frau Salaman, whatever are you thinking of?"

Salka asked quietly, "Will it make any difference? Now?" The woman's face softened, and she went away.

Salka could not tell how long she lay with Leon that night, holding him defiantly, protecting him. He needed only her now and she forgot any misery she had endured because of him. That didn't matter. Nothing mattered but to ease his laboured breathing as he held on, hour by hour, struggling against shadows she could sense crowding the room beyond the lamps she had so carefully lit.

Some time during the slow night Sandor and the nurse were there and then reluctantly she surrendered her burden and instead sat at the foot of the bed.

Once, Leon spoke. "Is it dark?"

Salka glanced toward the many gleaming lights.

"No," she said tenderly. "It isn't dark at all."

He did not say anything else for a long while: she could see the muscles working as he struggled for words.

"Then I have gone blind."

312

He turned his face to the wall. When she tried to take his hand she felt it twitch as though he wished to escape. Instead she held his cold feet to warm them. He began to gasp, rhythmic, pounding breaths that filled the room, on and on until she couldn't bear it.

And then, quite suddenly, there were no more. The nurse hurried forward and put her ear to his chest: she nodded. He was alive, but Salka understood that this abrupt and terrible stillness had taken him away from her.

Under her hands she could feel faint tremors running through his body, the only sign that he was fighting. She concentrated on him so that she was unaware of what went on around them. She vaguely heard Sandor, and the rabbi's deep speech, and somewhere nearby Friedrich's heart-broken voice. She wanted to say, you're all too late, it's over, only his tired body won't let go.

When Doktor Schindler stood beside her and the room was briefly empty, Salka caught his arm and pleaded with him to give Leon something—anything—to bring an end, to make him die more quickly, to stop his trapped tremors that she felt in every nerve.

But the stooped old physician, who had seen many men and women in extremity, shook his head and said beneath his breath, "Now then, Frau Salaman. Now then," and the waiting went on.

Leon died, in the end, without a sound. She was alone with him, and she only realised what had happened because his feet, which she still held, grew colder and colder. She did not, at that moment, feel regret or anguish—nothing but relief that he was freed, stunned bewilderment that a man in whom life had burned so fiercely should relinquish it as easily as a little animal.

Salka did not call to the nurse. She continued to cradle Leon's feet until Sandor came in and saw what had happened and uttered the words of faith over his son. She would not let go until the night was over and the ritual candles lit at his head and feet. Only when the men came to wash his body and lay him gently on the floor in the old way would she consent to leave him.

The next days were nothing to do with her or Leon. She endured them mechanically: the ritual and the prayers ("Our death is in Your hand"), the journey with the plain wooden coffin through the streets (stopping seven times on the way for the seven times that the word *hevel*—utter futility—occurs in the Book of Ecclesiastes) to the old Jewish cemetery in Seilegasse, where beneath spidery trees tablets of stone stood haphazard, some leaning one against the other, as if for consolation in the unkempt grass.

Salka discovered that although Leon was dead, although he lay so quietly beneath the lichened stones, he had not left her. He was in the dark pools of Lotte's eyes, in the smoky scent of his cologne that clung to the cushions of a bedroom chair (so that at night she would sit on the floor in the dark, resting her cheek against them). She saw a pale reflection of him sometimes when she talked with Friedrich, or caught in Sandor the shape of Leon's head, in the hair that grew the same way, thick and lustrous and low on the nape, warm and wiry to her touch.

Leon was there for her in ways she could never have anticipated: in a note that fell from a book unread since before his illness, in scribbled comments on files at the bank, in sleep when his muscular body covered hers. She would waken with her hands pressed to her breasts, quivering as though he had scarcely withdrawn from her, taken by a dream.

They did not sadden her, these sudden flashes of recollection. Just the opposite. They lit her days like little candles, warming and reassuring, proof that Leon was hers, possessed absolutely, faithful at last.

Salka did not delude herself. It would not continue, this curious period of acceptance, but vanish and leave her widowed and bereaved, forced— for she was a realist, like her father—to remember that she was a young woman, barely thirty-one. There would be other relationships for her, perhaps even another marriage. She always cut such thoughts short: it was too soon to permit them, they were a betrayal.

For the moment she was content to do no more than exist, and know that her love was stronger even than death.

Chapter 29

Magnified and praised be the living God; He exists, but His existence is not limited by time. He is One and His unity is unlike all others; it is incomprehensible and endless. He has no bodily form, He is incorporeal and we can compare nought unto Him in His holiness. He existed before all creation; He was the first but had no beginning . . .

Salka let the words of the prayer roll over her, the mysterious litany of medieval Castile. She was in Bevis Marks, the ancient synagogue founded in London for Spanish and Portuguese Jews. She came here often, together with Lotte and Sandor. As she thought his name she searched for him, sitting among the men in the long wooden pews that sprayed out from the towering Ark of the Law, its green marble pillars gleaming with reflected light. There he was, head and shoulders above the rest, the heavy linen *tallis* reaching to his feet.

. . . The dead will God, in His great loving-kindness, quicken, blessed be His glorious name for evermore. These are the Thirteen Principles of our faith, they are the foundation of faith in God and of His law . . .

The scene below her shimmered in the gleam of the multitude of thick candles which illumined the synagogue, placed in solid brass holders before the Ark, suspended in low, many-branched candelabra, held in sconces which flared just below the Women's Gallery where she sat. The service was over, the congregation rose, and the women around her overflowed their seats with their fashionable hats and furs, exchanging kisses and salutations, filling the air with a veil of perfume that mingled with the smell of candle-wax and oil.

Salka took Lotte's arm and together they walked down the staircase, through the heavy wooden door into the court outside. It had rained while they were in the synagogue and the uneven paving stones which extended the whole length of Bury Street gleamed with a damp sheen. They were in a village in the heart of the City of London, a Jewish village with its mikvah, the ritual bath, the butcher's shop and the houses of the synagogue dignitaries, the rabbi, the cantor and the beadle.

As they waited for Sandor to emerge, Salka smoothed her skirt absentmindedly. She was still in mourning, a summer dress of dark violet in corded silk, with white lace revers and the skirt gathered to one side. Her hat was French and wide-brimmed, trimmed with ostrich feathers, and beneath it the black hair was as dense as ever in its tight knot: she was far too idiosyncratic in appearance ever to be truly fashionable. And she was no one's idea of a widow. Grief had only deepened the touching dark shadows above her eyes, carved delicate hollows in her cheeks, and intensified the brooding Russian silences she had always experienced.

"My dear, you're all coming to me for luncheon. Nathan's in Paris, but a little gossip won't hurt Sandor." Florence Hartsilver hurried across and embraced Salka and Charlotte warmly, then stood back to consider the girl. "Lotte, don't you look the young lady today?"

Lotte, who liked Florence, gave her a reproving look. She was sixteen and considered herself beyond such childish compliments. The four years she had spent in London with Salka and Sandor had given her a poise her mother found enviable and an impeccable accent which made her grandfather shake his head with pride.

He joined the women now, kissing them on both cheeks in the Viennese way, elegant and formal as ever in his black and white. They were standing talking quietly, reluctant to break up the pleasant Sabbath atmosphere, when a middle-aged man cleared his throat behind them.

"Mr Salaman, sir, excuse me but . . ."

Salka was surprised to see John Burnham, a pleasant fellow employed by the Salaman-Hartsilver bank. What on earth was he doing at the synagogue on a Saturday morning? Sandor, evidently of the same opinion, looked mildly irritated.

"Yes, Mr Burnham. What can I do for you?"

The senior clerk, clearly embarrassed by the number of onlookers, drew him to one side. They conferred for a few minutes, then Sandor nodded slowly. He looked across the heads of the still-gossiping congregation to Salka and evidently told Burnham to wait.

When her father-in-law rejoined her, she asked, "Why did they want you? Is something wrong?"

Sandor steered her out of Florence Hartsilver's hearing. He said, speaking quickly, "They've received a telephone call from Vienna. From Friedrich. He's heard that Austrian troops are mobilising on the Russian frontier. War could be declared at any time."

Salka frowned. "That might mean fighting begins throughout Europe. Will Friedrich . . .?"

Sandor nodded. "He's coming to London as soon as he can get on a train."

"It's all happened sooner than we thought."

"And we need to act immediately. We may have no more than twenty-four hours to withdraw our assets before hostilities open."

"Then we must make our move now. Will you get in touch with Nathan?"

He shook his head. "Not until we've decided what's to be done."

Salka smiled at his phrase. "It's your decision, surely."

Sandor grunted but did not reply. Behind him, John Burnham waited with urgency in every line of his body. Still, Sandor did not respond.

After a while Salka murmured, "You must tell him what to do."

Sandor nodded absently, his face shadowed by thought. Then he lifted his head and smiled at her, every inch the energetic, vital man he had been in Vienna. And there, before all those interested spectators, he took Salka's hand and raised it to his lips.

"No, my dear," he said quietly. "He is not waiting for my answer, but for yours."

Salka stared at him, her extraordinary eyes gleaming like bronze metal. There was no question but that Sandor meant what he said. For months now he had been hinting that the time had come for him to step down. He needed a chance to rest, he claimed, he was an old man. Neither of them believed this, yet the truth was that the loss of Leon had affected him deeply. He had adored his wayward second son, seeing in him a constant reminder of his beloved Anna. He had built up his bank to be Leon's inheritance and his death—and Emil's before it—had laid his hopes waste. Still he had struggled to carry on. It was he who had engineered their move to London, but only after Salka insisted upon it. And now, despite his vigour, he was tired. A lifetime of hard work had left scant opportunity for leisure, and he had just bought a country house with land which had aroused in him a hitherto unsuspected passion for gardening.

Salka looked across the oasis of greenery round the *schul* to the narrow iron gates in the high wall and the promise of another life beyond.

And far more clearly than the grey streets and gilded signs of the City and its banks, she saw a young Russian girl, angry and hurt at being called *Ostjude*, heard the echo of her own pleading, *But what can a woman do?* She was quite unconscious of children's voices from the open windows of the Jewish school behind her where boys piped their Talmudic portion. The voice to which she listened came to her faintly out of memory: *You have it in you to be the cornerstone of a great family.*

Salka straightened her shoulders in unconscious imitation of the old woman in Venice who had warned her she must one day find the strength to carry the weight of the tower of Salaman. Beside her, Sandor took a step back, so that she was left facing John Burnham by herself.

She took a deep breath and nodded to him. The clerk hurried forward and she began to issue swift instructions . . .

* * *

317

When he had gone back to the City and all the congregation had finally drifted away, Salka remained in the shadow of the synagogue.

She stood alone in that secluded court in the heart of London and felt on her hair, in blessing, the fine hands of the rabbi of Polotsk with his hat of seven sable.